The
Window
and the
Mirror

Henry Thomas

The Window and the Mirror

Book One

Oesteria and the War of Goblinkind Series

RARE BIRD
LOS ANGELES, CALIF.

THIS IS A GENUINE RARE BIRD BOOK

Rare Bird Books
6044 North Figueroa Street
Los Angeles, California 90042
rarebirdbooks.com

Copyright © 2023 by Henry Thomas

FIRST TRADE PAPERBACK EDITION

A Rare Bird Book | Rare Bird Books
Subsidiary Rights Department,
6044 North Figueroa Street
Los Angeles, California 90042

Set in Minion
Printed in the United States

10 9 8 7 6 5 4 3 2 1

HARDCOVER ISBN: 9781644280102
PAPERBACK ISBN: 9781644283295

Publisher's Cataloging-in-Publication Data
Names: Thomas, Henry Jackson, author.
Title: The Window and the Mirror: Book One :
Oesteria and the War of Goblinkind / Henry Thomas.
Series: Oesteria and the War of Goblinkind.
Description: First Hardcover Edition | A Genuine Rare Bird Book | New York, NY;
Los Angeles, CA: Rare Bird Books, 2019.
Identifiers: ISBN 9781644280102
Subjects: LCSH Goblins—Fiction. | Magic—Fiction. | Good and evil—Fiction. |
Imaginary wars and battles—Fiction. | Fantasy fiction. | BISAC FICTION / Fantasy
/ Dark Fantasy
Classification: LCC PS3620.H62795 W56 2019| DDC 813.6—dc23

For Hazel, Evelyn, and Henry

Prologue

Kingsbridge. Oesteria. Mid-Fall.

IT WAS NEAR DAWN when the flaming barrel interrupted his sleep, crashing through the shingled roof of the inn and exploding through a beam that pinned the Innkeeper to his hearth. The man in the cloak levered the cracked beam as the family hurriedly dragged the Innkeeper to safety. The family kept thanking the man as he walked out the door.

"Don't go to the Upper Ward," he found himself saying. "As soon as he can move, you should clear out of this town."

"Where will we go?"

"Anywhere. Just don't be here when the soldiers come."

Her eyes registered that she knew what happened when the soldiers came. "How will we get out of the city?"

"The river or the Low Gate is your best chance."

She smiled at him for a moment, and it almost seemed to him that this were some grand game that they were all playing—that as the dawn broke all the pieces on the board would reset for the next game. But he knew war and he knew that did not happen, and he knew that he may have already lost the precious advantage of surprise in his attempt to escape the besieged town.

"Farewell, lady." He inclined his head toward her and stepped back out onto the street. He cursed to himself as he looked up at the lightening sky. He was hoping for darkness, at least until he was through the attackers' picket lines and had cleared the town walls. If it were too risky, he could always try to swim the river. He could take his place among the other corpses that would soon be bobbing along the surface and float out of the town and no one would pay him any mind. Not his first choice, but it would do.

If I get a choice, he thought.

His chances were dwindling rapidly. A gang of youths armed with rods and makeshift weapons came careening around a corner ahead of him, most of them making for the bridges, but a few troublemakers stopped to loot an already-looted storefront and throw stones at him. He rounded a corner and listened to them whoop and holler by him, beating their sticks and stones against their beleaguered town's walls.

He silently switched back and forth down one small winding alley then the next until he had eluded the mob and edged closer toward the unknown danger of what lay beyond the wall. By the time he reckoned he was within a few hundred strides of the Low Gate, he had been walking undisturbed for a time. In the east was the dusky glow of sunrise through the smoke and glare from fires spreading well into all parts of the Lower Ward. The townsfolk had fled this part of the city, it seemed. The building tops blazed all around him as he picked his way toward the Low Gate of the town wall. There would be the gatehouse, either abandoned or overrun. If he found it abandoned, as he hoped to, he could use it to scout a way out of the enemy's lines, maybe to the baggage train of the attacker's army. There he could lose himself in the sea of camp followers that trailed after every army.

The whores and the knaves look out for one another, he thought. They'd never give me over to the Lord Fieldmaster, or whatever his rank was called in whatever bloody army it is out there; except he was neither a whore nor a knave. Faulty logic, he chided himself. He stooped beneath an overhanging beam of a half-collapsed house. In a few days, he would disappear again.

And no one will ever miss me, he mused. If I can make it to the gatehouse, and if it isn't crawling with combatants; otherwise I might be swimming for it, he thought, grimacing at the chill of the morning. He had half risen beyond the low timber beam when the rumbling of cart wheels and the sharp sounds of an ironshod team clattering over the stones reached his ears. He dropped into a low crouch and backed himself under the shadow of the ramshackle wattle and daub house that had checked his progress.

Whoever it was, he thought, they were coming fast. He sat there and laughed ruefully for a moment. What a morning this had turned out to be. And what a mess, what a bloody mess— and for no good reason. This town was valuable, he would not argue that, but it was a fool move to take it. Whoever did this would have legions of spears on them from the larger garrisons downriver and upriver and be trapped in a matter of days and driven to the coast. Off the cliffs and into the sea or on the point of a spear, death waited for them. He could count offhand three times in recent memory when similar fates had befallen some jumped-up bandit or petty warlord, but never at a town like Kingsbridge. It was small and hard to defend, but it was of strategic value.

He had been traveling quite a bit these last few months and had neither seen sign nor heard word of any large army on the march, and he would have seen or heard something if this force outside the walls was more than a couple hundred strong. Hell, everyone would know. Although there was a tinge of unrest at any given time, threats were dealt with in short order. You could not hide a large force; they ate up the countryside like a plague of insects with their foraging. Then there was the inevitability of crime within the camp, and the crimes committed by the soldiers against the country folk who sought to protect their livestock or their daughters, even their sons, and the ropes and the hanged men and the butchery. The basest of men were sometimes conscripted into soldiery, and their basest passions seemed to blaze brighter as they moved further away from wherever it was they called home. Every dog is free when no master holds his leash, and men were difficult animals to control when they thought they had no one to answer to for their actions. How many soldiers had he hanged on his marches? How many deserters and miscreants had met their deaths by his decree? One hundred and nine, he remembered. One hundred and nine men he had ordered killed. So few, considering the size of his forces, yet he remembered every one, at least by number. Hard decisions had to be made and he had made them without remorse. Such was the life of a man of power, who held a command and many lives in the balance. But if that man was who he had been, then he was but a shadow of that man now. He was little more than a fugitive.

He squinted into the smoky haze and thought he saw a flitter of movement, but then it was gone. There would have been grievances and word would have traveled ahead faster than any army could have. There was something afoot here that he could not grasp, he thought, as he huddled in the waning shadows. He craned his neck as the horses grew louder and the large rolling cart came around the corner and into view. It skidded a bit as it made the turn, and the metal rims of the wheels struck sparks on the cobblestones. It was a jailer's cart, tall and square with iron furniture girding its jostling bulk all the way around in several riveted bands that gave the cart a striped look in the half light. The driver cracked his whip and urged the team on in a shrill voice dripping with fear. The road made a low dip and rose again, climbing past where he was concealed and turning as it spilled its way through the Lower Ward and toward the river. He could now see there was another figure atop the wagon, a furtive-looking youth lying on the roof and pointing a crossbow behind him as the wagon bounced over the stones and began to make its way uphill. The exhausted horses slowed and were straining at the traces as the immense weight of the cart came to bear down on them, and the whip's crack and the fear in the driver's voice was making them panicked. The lead horses reared and threw their heads, slinging lather and snot to dapple the stones and buildings around them. The driver cursed as they slowed. The younger man with the crossbow was screaming for the driver to whip the horses up the hill, but it was no use. The team was done and the two men had chosen poorly if they had chosen the jailer's cart for speed.

It was the perfect spot for an ambush, he realized. And then he saw them coming and heard the men screaming for mercy as six riders made to ride them down. The two men had both leapt down from the stalled cart, the driver drawing his long knife and motioning the crossbowman toward the cluster of unburned buildings, but the younger man was panicked and attempting to cut a horse free from its traces with his belt knife. He shook himself free from the fleeing driver and had managed to get the horse halfway out of the harness when the riders were almost upon him. The youth was waving his hands and screaming at them to stop, but decided at the last moment to retrieve his crossbow, and with a loud plunking sound he shot his quarrel and managed to hit one of his attackers before he was cut down in a red wash and a scream.

The driver was making straight for his hiding place, he realized, but his chances of making it were almost too slim to calculate with any certainty, he thought, as he watched two of the riders peel away and move to cut the driver off.

He cursed himself for sitting there and watching, but he was unarmed and unsure of the events that led to this scene he had witnessed. He reminded himself that he was trying to escape this town first and foremost, and that this business was none of his own. Yet he found his hand closing around a fist-sized stone with a particularly pleasing heftiness to it, and his feet moving him to a clearer position where he might be able to launch an attack. Or at least slow the lead rider for a beat— enough to buy the ill-fated teamster a moment or two to make for cover.

Why do I care to endanger myself recklessly while un-armed? The thought was on his mind even as the stone he'd heaved sailed through the air in its perfect arc, seeming to hang there for a moment before smashing into the side of the lead horse's head and sending it flailing and screaming as it lost its balance and fell, dumping its rider headlong onto the cobbles with a sickening crack. He had been aiming for the rider, but the result was much better than he had hoped for. The driver had stopped and wheeled at the sound of approaching hooves and had raised his long knife over his head in a guard and taken a shaking stand. He could see that the man's hosen were soaked in fresh piss and could hear sobbed oaths choking from his mouth in that shrill voice, but craven or not, he was standing his guard and he was going to face down his attackers. For that the man had let the stone fly, he realized.

The driver didn't have time to notice his good fortune, however, as the second rider was already on him. The steel flashed and sparked in the dim dawn as the driver met the rider's attack and drove it away, but the force of the charge turned him and spilled him onto the street. Now the rider was turning for another pass, his mount skidding to a halt, rearing and wheeling on its hind quarters in a well executed display of horsemanship; he had turned and started back toward his quarry before the driver had managed to regain his feet. It was then that the rider seemed to notice that his comrade had been taken out by an unknown third party in the fight, and judging by the way he had handled his mount, the rider was experienced enough to be wary before he started his second charge. His helmeted head took in the collapsed house for a moment.

The man stepped clear of the rubble and hiked his cloak up over his shoulder so that it would be clear of his legs and arms. He knew that he had been spotted by the rider and the fight was on him now. The other four riders had dismounted; two of them seemed to be attempting to force open the gate of the jailer's cart while the third tended to their wounded comrade, who appeared to have taken a quarrel through the guts. At the moment they were all three looking elsewhere, but he knew only a few blinks would pass before they took notice. The driver cast a furtive look at him.

"Stand away!" the driver warned, brandishing the broad-bladed weapon he held.

The cloaked man's eyes never left the rider. "I stand with you," was all that he said. The driver just looked confused and then scared again.

He could see the rider surging forward, and he ran toward the sprawling horse that was attempting to stand itself on the street, his eyes resting for a moment on the fallen rider with his head twisted back at an unnatural angle, his fixed lifeless eyes unblinking. The horse had managed to get up, and stood unsteadily with its legs splayed out, snorting and throwing its head. He put his hand out toward it, but it reared and bolted away before he could grab hold of the bridle. That would have been sweet, he thought, but he wouldn't place much trust in a mount that had just had its bell rung. You could have simply ridden away though, you great bloody fool. Now it was too late, he knew, but it had been too late from the moment he had picked up the rock, and he knew that too. Nothing to be done for it now, he thought. The sword lay a few yards away where the rider had dropped it and in two running strides he had gathered it up and was sprinting toward the cart. It seemed the most unlikely thing to do, so he simply did it. He could hear the shrill voice of the driver calling to him—calling him back, calling for his help, and cursing. It was hard making decisions when lives hung in the balance, but he had always been able to make them without remorse, and now was just one more of those times. He turned in time to see the driver taking cover in his own former hiding place, and the rider wheeling and slumping in his saddle.

Well, he thought, the craven driver has some skill with the blade it seems. Which was quite good now that he thought about it because the odds of him living out the rest of this horrid morning had greatly increased with the removal of one mounted man intent on laying his skull open. Unfortunately, there were three more just a few strides ahead of him—in varying degrees of alarm at his approach—who most assuredly would try to kill him. He met the first of them at a run and took the man's blade from him as he dealt him a blow to the base of the skull with the flat of his sword, sending him face-first to the ground.

The rider who had been nursing his comrade managed to stand and half draw his blade when the man struck him hard in the mouth with the pommel and sent him sprawling backward and falling over his gut-shot fellow. The last rider near the jailer's cart had just managed to find his stirrup as the man sent one of his captured swords spinning through the air toward him and his mount, causing the animal to rear and spill its rider onto his back onto the street. The fallen man cursed and rolled to his feet while drawing his sword. The rider leapt out and attempted to take the man by surprise with a quick thrust, but the thrust was turned with a blow that took the rider's hands, his severed fingers hitting the street just a moment before the sharp sound of his sword clattered through the morning. The upstroke came before either sound, and the hilt of the man's sword took the rider full in the face, smashing his nose into a bloody mess and leaving him writhing and moaning on the cold stones before he stilled. The man held the sword out in front of him. He wheeled around in a circle and took in what he saw.

He understood the battle was over then, and though he felt as if he had lived it forever, it had all transpired in less than a moment. It was always that way, he knew. The battle could be magic and the moments could be manipulated. "Or so the masters say," he muttered to himself. The driver came trotting up on his trophy horse, eyeing him warily but not without a little wonder mixed in his eyes. Maybe he's just embarrassed now that he reeks of piss, he thought, but the driver had another look in his eyes besides that, and that was the dangerous look he had come to know as the dim glimmer of recognition, which, as someone who was a fugitive, he found to be irksome.

"I want to thank you," spoke the driver. His voice was broken, but the shrillness of it was gone.

"Who is in the locker?" the man said, hoping to curtail the driver's inevitable question.

"Some soldier's girl we was bringing here from Torlucksford," the driver wiped his face with a bloodied hand. He looked as though he was going to cry again, then he blurted out, "Some Dawn Tribe girl, and that's what Sim has to die for?"

His accent was from somewhere north of Kingsbridge; it was Rhaelish perhaps. He saw that the driver could barely stand to look in the direction where the crossbow wielding youth's body lay sprawled on the stones.

"Your son?"

"No. Not mine. My own sister's though." The driver started sobbing again. "What am I to say to her? I didn't save him. I ran. I ran away." His face was pale, and he looked poorly. "I got him in on this line of work and everything. He was going to apprentice to a Weaver, you know, and I says, 'Boy don't need to be kept up inside all day, Sister. Let me take him on,' I says." He shook his head ruefully.

"He managed to shoot one of them, you could tell her that."

"Pity that didn't save him." The driver shifted in the saddle and grimaced.

"I saw you tried to help him, he didn't listen. No one can fault you for that."

He let the sword clatter to the ground and unwrapped his cloak from about his shoulders and waist. "You will be all right," he said to the driver by means of farewell.

"I got the bastard. Got the bastard's horse now." The man smiled at him courteously and inclined his head slightly. As he turned, the driver called out to him, "I know who you are. Don't think I don't."

The man stopped and turned. The sword was only a step away. "It's a dangerous path, friend."

The driver swallowed hard, then let out a thin chuckle, "Don't you worry none, your lordship. Your secret's safe with me. See, I got the bastard, his horse and all...but he managed to stick me pretty fair, see?" His left leg was dangling loosely from the stirrup and the blood was streaming off of the saddle and spattering the cobblestones. "So the way I see it, I got nothing to lose." The mounted man picked his way closer to him.

"I knew it was you by the way you moved with that sword. I seen you many times, as a youth. Not every fool knows a master when he sees one, but this fool does." He gave a thin chuckle again. "Like I says, seen you many times. I was your loyal soldier, my lord. I fought with you at Valianador."

Here it comes, he thought.

"Why did you not avenge their deaths?"

The question stopped time for him, as it always did.

"I don't know."

"Pardon, my lord?"

"I've been stripped of all titles, so you don't bloody have to call me that."

The driver just nodded and lowered his head.

"They said the fight went out of you when they was killed, that's what they said. I can believe that. We was all so sad for you, my lord. All your family."

"Best not to speak of it further. I thank you not to."

"There are many of us still who would follow you if you was to raise your banner again. Many of us, my lord."

"Not another word." His eyes flashed and the driver sobbed into his hands, then held them up in a gesture of supplication. "I'm sorry, my lord."

"You're sitting a horse bleeding to death and you're talking to me of rebellion and treason!" He looked around him at the burning town and the dead men and the jailer's cart and threw his hands in the air. He laughed like a madman. I should have gone with them, he thought, I should have avenged them. I shouldn't have run. But he had run, and he had kept running, and now he didn't quite know how to stop.

"Who did this?"

"We don't know. They hit us right afore we got to the low gate."

"What about the siege lines? How'd you get across in the night, and how big is their force?"

"Weren't no siege lines, begging your lordship's pardon. Didn't see no army to speak of neither. We's halfway over the last hill and we sees the bloody town lighting up, and then riders coming after us."

It was making less and less sense to him the more he heard, but he knew that the man was telling him the truth. At least as much of the truth as he knows, he mused.

"Poor Simma. He was only just twenty this summer." With that he slumped from the saddle and would have fallen had the cloaked man not caught him and eased him to the street.

He was silent for a moment but then suddenly opened his eyes and said, "So they made you a commoner now?"

"Yes, I suppose they did."

"If you say so, my lord, but I think it a queer notion." He motioned the man closer to him and reached for his hand.

"Take my knife. It's the closest thing to a sword we commoners can carry." He smiled and closed his eyes. "Us common men, we must look after one another."

"I don't want to take your knife."

"Please, my lord, it would mean so much to me. In honor of my service to you in the past and all."

He could see the man had taken a fatal wound in his thigh. There was a large artery there that would bleed a man out in a short time if opened.

"I thank you for your service," he said to the pale dying man. "I'm sorry...I despise all of this killing."

"I noticed by the way you was hitting them boys, my lord. Like you was drilling." He smiled.

"They'll be stirring soon."

"Don't trouble yourself, my lord. I'm done here. Oh, take my knife, and the key to the lockbox." The driver clawed at a leather thong about his neck, grimacing as he used his failing strength to break the cord, and he pressed it into the man's hands. "Give it to whoever is commanding the garrison here in this cursed place. Rode into a damned hell storm is what happened to us. I'm done. All for a bloody Tribe girl." He was mumbling then, and sobbing and shaking, and in moments he stilled and never moved again.

The man shook his head. What a waste of life, it seemed. All because some man somewhere wants something that he doesn't have, he thought, something that had to do with a Dawn Tribe girl in a rolling cell and an ambitious yet foolhardy attempt on a town of little significance. Things weren't adding up in the mind of the fugitive General Tyl Illithane, but to the cloaked man who now stood belting on a commoner's sword, the only thing that mattered was that he had just missed his chance at a clean escape.

He stared at the key in his hand. He'd had to make hard decisions, and he had made them without remorse. Such was the life of a man of power who held a command and many lives in the balance.

Or even just one, he thought.

One

A month before the attack on Kingsbridge.
Dawn Tribe Territory. Fall.

IT PISSED RAIN. A steady flow fell from the heavens. Here they were, miles from anywhere familiar, doing the Magistry's bidding. One hundred and thirty-two Oestermen serving the High Mage in Dawn Tribe land, no less. Of all the forsaken places in the world, he never dreamed he would find himself here.

Joth shifted his helm a bit so that the raindrops stopped finding their way down the nape of his neck and into his undergarments, his mood as foul as the weather. Here in these vales and mountain passes, in their squalid huts and caves and clandestine shit holes lived the bloody Dawn Tribes. For the last month they'd ridden, walked, hiked, and climbed through this unwelcoming territory, going from one shit-stained settlement to the next, looking for some secret something the bloody mages were after. Each time they entered a territory or left a village, he had felt the eyes of the men watching them from the tree lines. There had been skirmishes, and once what seemed to have been a planned ambush in a mountain pass that claimed the lives of twelve of their number. They hate us, every one of them, Joth knew from the history between his people and the bloody Dawn Tribe. The Oestermen had come long ago and battled with the People of the Dawn Tribe and driven them from the land. Now they were forced to live in the poorest areas with the least arable land here in the mountains, where they scratched out their existences.

Living the way Oestermen haven't lived for a thousand years, Joth mused as he spat angrily at the ground. These people lived like animals. They smelled like animals, they ate like animals, rutted with each other like animals, and their language was foreign and crude. He had seen women in a few of the settlements who would have been beautiful he thought, had they not had their hair all braided and hung with savage jewelry, and if they had worn some decent clothing instead of their garish checked and striped homespun wool. If they hadn't already been soiled from lying with their wild cave men. He had been away too long if he was starting to fancy the savage girls, he reminded himself. I'll be back soon, I'll be back home, and I won't have to bloody look twenty places at once all the time. He thought, I'll be able to sleep sound and not worry about arrows or darts or knives in the night. Just barracks food, full rations, and good Oestern ale in my cup. The thought almost made Joth smile, but a raindrop had dripped onto a sensitive patch of skin near his nose that sent him into a sneezing fit.

"Bloody hell, get hold of yerself," Wat said behind him. "Here comes the mage, be ready boys." It was the usual signal that had come to signify the ritual they had undertaken in countless settlements all through the territory since they had left Oesteria. Sometimes they would make three villages in a day. It was the beginning of the madness bound to ensue should the mage choose anyone from the settlement, and they had better be ready for it.

Then the mage was walking his horse through their ranks. Joth could feel the hairs on the back of his neck stand on end. This mage, Lord Uhlmet, had made him uneasy from the beginning. It was not something he could ever voice to anyone, not even to Wat whom he trusted more than any of the others, but he had lost several friends in the ambush less than a fortnight before and he knew the Lord Uhlmet was to blame. Joth might think ill of the Dawn Tribe and their ways, but Lord Uhlmet had a deep-seated hatred and irreverence for not only their people but their customs and superstitions as well, and he relished in tormenting and humiliating them at every opportunity. In the first village, if you could call it that, the mage had separated the families from their children and then ordered all of the womenfolk to be stripped naked and made to parade about in a circle before the men. Joth didn't fully understand it, but apparently Lord Uhlmet knew something of their tribal beliefs and exploited that knowledge to further shame them.

When the women refused to circle and began to get unruly, he ordered the children brought forth and selecting a fair-haired youth, he drew his dagger and made to slit the boy's throat, upon which a great lamentation went up among them all and they finally complied in order to save the young boy's life.

"They believe fair hair to be an omen of good, especially if it sprouts from a buck," Uhlmet had said as though he were lecturing them all on how to best flush game from a bush. "Tell them that their women wouldn't pass for even the basest whores in any Oestern city." He had looked over the men then, a thin smile on his lips that never made it to his eyes, and then he waited.

The translator had swallowed a few times and only began to speak after Lord Uhlmet raised his eyebrows expectantly. He waited to see if any of them would move or lose their tempers but they just fixed their eyes straight ahead, some of them closing their eyes in shame. The translator relayed the mage's words for another hour as he subjected the People to more shame and humiliation, and when Lord Uhlmet had finally had enough, he ordered the Oestermen to burn the women's discarded clothing and to confiscate any gold or silver jewelry that any of the natives might be wearing. He then selected the three children with the fairest hair, and had them bound together like prisoners and led out of the settlement, leaving the wailing mothers and fathers and their fellow villagers behind as he mounted his horse and rode at the head of the column of men, jerking his prisoners along at an uncomfortable gait. Joth didn't like that too much, watching those kids get dragged along. Wat didn't either, he knew that, but neither of them was going to say a word to Lord Uhlmet or they would most likely end up dangling from a tree in one of these scenic bloody mountain valleys.

"These people are dogs. They will only understand you when you treat them accordingly!" The mage had said it as they left the first village, and he had said it a score of times since with every settlement through which they passed. The three fair children weren't there when they broke camp the next day, and the talk was that Lord Uhlmet had let them go and sent them wandering home. But Joth had his doubts, and in less than two day's time they were attacked in an icy pass and hounded ever since. They had lost at least one sentry every night, and the new orders had been to pair up for any activity outside of formation. Shitting in teams of three was highly recommended after one sentry was found speared to death with his hosen about his ankles. The irony in the dead sentry having been the company's Drillmaster didn't escape

Joth, especially since the man had always ended weapons drills by saying, "Be ever ready for a fight, men." One of the wits had done a rousing impression of the dead man, grasping his ankles and hunkering down, shouting loudly, "Be ever ready for a shite, men!" They had all laughed, but it was Joth and Wat who had to string that lad up on the mage's orders. Now he was getting grave looks at mess, and more than once he heard men stop talking at his approach. The lad had been well-liked by the men.

Morale had dipped since the attack in the pass, but the hanging had dragged it down even lower. Now here they are again, waiting in the pissing rain on the bloody mage's pleasure. Joth stood at attention as he heard the mage's horse pick its way through the ranks behind him, the familiar sound of weapons and men shuffling aside with the whispered calls, "On your left" or "Right behind." Men in formation talked to each other out of habit every time they moved. But the calls sounded half-hearted and worn down to Joth's ears, as though uttered by a company that had only known defeat. If Lord Uhlmet had any sense of command, he'd know it too, he thought, as he was shouldered aside by the man on his left. He missed the man's call. The rain had picked up and its spattering on his helm had drowned out the man's whisper. As Lord Uhlmet rode past him, he felt the tension in the ranks behind him subside and indeed he felt much better just knowing that the mage was where he could see him. Now that he could see the mage, Joth knew that Lord Uhlmet was most displeased by what he saw before him.

The village was larger than any they had come upon before, but the array of its residents was the smallest that Joth had seen. Three old men stood leaning on staves near the timber-framed entrance of the largest hovel, two old women sat on a rug beside the open door, sheltered from the rain by an overhang. They were well adorned with gold, all of them, and their hair was richly dressed and arrayed in thick braids that chimed as they moved, for many of these savages wore bells and trinkets of metal in their hair as a sort of national costume. Pity they don't build their houses to impress, Joth mused, as he took a look about the village at the thatch and timber structures, all of them round and low to the ground. He could smell the animal dung through the downpour and thought if the sun were to ever shine there and dry the place up, that it would only smell worse.

As Lord Uhlmet cleared the first rank, the translator jogged up and adjusted his cloak, which he had been using to cover his balding head. "Ask these old fools why they've not gathered the other villagers," Lord Uhlmet spat at the translator, his eyes never leaving the assembly. The translator did as he was commanded and rolled some savage words off of his tongue and awaited an answer, his eyes swiveling back and forth from the old men and women to the mage like some wild-eyed horse. One of the old women said something and spat just beyond the border of the rug on which she sat. Lord Uhlmet's head snapped toward her, his eyes narrowing. "Archers, feather the bitch if she speaks another word out of turn!" He turned his scowl to his translator, saying, "You can tell them that too, you dullard!"

The thin balding man reddened and bobbed up and down a few times in supplication to the mage, muttering pardons and apologies all the while. Lord Uhlmet shook his boot free from his stirrup and kicked the man forward, attempted to elicit a laugh perhaps, but Joth wasn't about to laugh. I'd be dancing at the end of a rope in bloody Tribe territory. The only sounds were those of the wind and the animals, and the tense moment passed through the men, but no one laughed. It was good that he abstained, because everyone else seemed to have the same idea about humor and Lord Uhlmet since the wit got hanged. Lord Uhlmet was fond of hangings.

As the translator began to address the savages, Joth saw the foremost elder hold his hand out and wave the man into silence. Then, surprising everyone, he spoke directly to Lord Uhlmet in perfect, barely accented Oestersh, stepping forward and leaning on his staff. "Thus is the way of Uhlmet? To threaten old women and murder children in the lands of the People?" His voice was mellifluous and clear, and when he spoke people were listening. "You are not invited to our lands for plunder, Mage, nor are you invited to subject our peoples to cruelties!"

Uhlmet was seething. "You shall address me as lord or I shall have you killed where you stand!"

Then Joth heard laughter, but it wasn't coming from the ranks; it was the old savages. Could they all speak Oestersh? That seemed impossible to him, but here they were, all of them having a laugh at Lord Uhlmet's expense. "Have the Oestern mages mastered death now? You can just call it down on anyone at your whim, O great lord mage?" There was mirth in his voice, but steel in his old gray eyes.

Lord Uhlmet's mouth hung open in disbelief for the blink of an eye. "You shall pay for that with your lives." He turned back to the company of Oestermen standing in formation and lifted his hand. Joth could see the arrogant and cruel grin tugging at the corners of the mage's mouth as he began to speak. "Burn this bloody place to the—"

Suddenly Lord Uhlmet's horse reared and fell over, and chaos ensued.

The men around Joth surged forward and drew their weapons. Uhlmet was screaming as he was dragged into the large roundhouse by the village elders. Suddenly, armed tribesmen rushed from within the house and slammed into the archers before they could draw. He saw the archers trying to get back to the middle ranks but the spearmen were too tightly massed for them to pass through easily and the formation began to break up as rank and file were jostled between the low huts and pig stys in the village center. He could feel a sense of panic as several horns were sounded and he thought it was Wat he heard saying, "Fall back! Fall back to the trees!"

The horns were louder now, and they were not coming from the ranks; they surrounded Joth, and he couldn't quite tell if they were coming from outside or inside the village. He barely had time to raise his sword and avoid running his comrade through as the rank in front of him fell back and crashed into his. The ranks behind him were surging forward now and the whole formation was wheeling right, but Joth never heard the order. He could not hear much at all but rain on his helm and the confusion of the men next to him as he found himself spun around and slipping in the muddy footing of the village sty. It was Wat who lifted him up.

"What's bloody happening, Wat?"

"They're on us, that's what! Stand!" Wat was looking around furtively.

"Where?"

"Stand and move, damn you! I know as much as you!"

There was a flurry of movement in the ranks on Joth's left as the enemy appeared and flung their darts into the massed and broken formation. There were more than two hundred of the bloody javelineers. Joth had never seen so many tribesmen at once. Scores of javelins were bristling in the men of the front ranks and many of them fell in the mud pierced through by a dozen or more. A cry went up all around the village, terrifying the Oestermen.

Joth surged forward to overtake the fallen men of the front ranks when the cavalry hit the company from the rear. Wat was next to him, shouting, "Form ranks, damn you!" But the company was being hit on all sides as more fighting men from the tribes surged out with spears and swords from within the huts of the village. The morale that had been teetering on the brink for a week or more among the Oestermen came crashing down in an all-out panic as knots of men tried to flee for their lives, desperate to get clear of the ambush. It broke in an instant, and Joth found himself running with Wat and a score of others past a low round hut and out of the village center. A dart careened off the helm of the man next to him and sent him sprawling into the mud, but Joth didn't stop running to look back. He and Wat had almost made the treeline. It was very close now that they had gotten clear of the last hovel and broken into a run over a fallow field. A man was crying close behind him, screaming "Horses! Horses!" Only then did Joth whip his head down and under his arm out of habit to allow himself an uninhibited view behind through the ocular in his helm. He was lucky that he did, he realized, as a mounted man sailed past him and he managed to miss getting lanced by a hair's breadth. He was raising his blade to defend himself when the rider's foot sent him down into the wet grass and he lost his wind. He rolled and had his feet in an instant, but he could not get air into his lungs and the strength in his legs was leaving him. He had to kneel for a moment.

I'll die here in the bloody tribe lands, he thought. I'm going to die here.

He looked around and saw Wat speared through the back just a few yards off. He was still crawling for the trees with a foot and a half of broken shaft sticking out of him, his dirty jack brightened with a growing patch of red around his wound. The horses were wheeling back, the tribesmen calling to each other and laughing as they cut down the Oestermen who had fled with him and Wat.

I've got to get to Wat, Joth thought. We can make the trees. I've got to help him.

Forcing himself onto his feet and gulping down air, he broke into as near a run as he could manage and got his arm under Wat, half carrying, half dragging him to the trees. Bloody hell, he was a big man, but Joth was strong. Wat groaned as they hit the edge of the wood, telling Joth to let him go, but Joth kept pulling him and telling him they would make it. "Just a bit farther and we'll lose them, Wat!" he said, dragging the wounded man up the densely wooded hill. He could hear the enemy crashing through the woods behind them, all traces of subtlety and silence gone now, like hounds that were close to the kill with their blood up. The trees and brush here were too dense to ride through, their pursuers would have to dismount, and he knew that would buy them some time.

Joth was beginning to feel the hopelessness of his flight drag his will down to the breaking point, but he steeled himself and told himself that he would keep fighting, that he had to. He reached down almost without thinking and pulled the spear head out of Wat's back, tossing it down the hill behind him as the big man screamed a curse at him.

"You'll move easier now," he said.

"You bloody fool, I need to staunch the bleeding now." Wat's jaw was clenched so tight and his breathing so labored that Joth could barely make out the words. More horns sounded from the village, and the sound of their pursuers subsided for a moment.

They're being called back, Joth knew, a glimmer of hope in a shared look between him and Wat. A nod between them and the wounded man drew a deep breath and pushed himself to his feet unsteadily. Wat was shaky, but they'd make the top of the hill faster this way. The hill was getting steeper now as they climbed and pulled their way through holly stands and knotty oaks, using the trees for handholds and finding footholds in the rocky earth. They were moving quickly, but Wat's jack was wet with blood and it dripped down his sleeve and onto anything he touched as he clambered. His face was ashen and his eyes were wide and staying fixed on things long enough to cause him to stumble.

Wat was fading.

"Just there, Wat. Over this rock and we will rest on the other side for a moment."

Wat looked as if he were going to argue but he just nodded grimly.

It was really more of a rocky seam in the earth that the roots of an ancient oak had cracked and pushed through as it sought its way slowly to the depths of the hillside, through centuries perhaps. Joth did not know how old the tree was, nor did he especially care about it, but he was glad to find that on the other side of the root gnarled rock there was a small outcrop that they could shelter under and, more importantly, he could face someone without being surrounded and ridden down. They'll have to drag us out of here like a badger from its den, he thought. It didn't pay to think past that point, he knew.

Not with Wat's blood all over the hillside.

The horn sounded again from the village. He and Wat settled into the hollow and Joth climbed onto the old oak's roots and peered over the top of the outcrop and down the hillside. About halfway down the hill he could see a young warrior standing there, peering up toward him, scanning the hill for movement. Joth stood stock still, and held his breath.

The warrior was tall for a tribesman, maybe even as tall as Joth. Oestermen were tall. In the fashion of his people, the warrior's dark hair was hung with a few golden ornaments and braided back away from his beardless face. He looked young, but Joth knew in the tribes you were a man after fourteen winters. Wat had told him that.

The youth was holding something, turning it over in his hand. The broken spear, Joth realized. He kept scanning the hill like a hunter waiting for movement, some sight of his quarry. A voice carried up the hill from below. Joth could only watch as the young warrior called back, and though he could not understand the words they spoke, he understood the tone, and it was one of frustration. He wants to finish me and Wat, Joth thought, finish us here and now while the trail is fresh and he could be done with it, this young warrior.

The youth stood staring for a beat longer, then yelled out what Joth could only imagine was some sort of curse to the hillside, and throwing the broken spear down he turned and made his way down the hill toward the village. As he turned Joth sank back down and breathed again deeply. The sky had thundered and raged as they had made their way up the hill, and now it began to rain in earnest, heavy raindrops beating out a rhythm through the branches of the trees, water sheeting off of the rocky outcrop he and Wat sheltered beneath.

They sat without moving for a long time.

"Help me get this off." It was Wat fumbling with his jack lacings.

"Put your hands down, I'll do it."

The jacks they wore were made to stop arrows and turn a sword blow. Made from a score of layered linen canvas with a stag's skin sandwiched somewhere inside and stitched through to form a near impenetrable half-sleeved coat that was then waxed on its outer layer to make it weatherproof, the jack was lighter than coat armor and cheap enough for the poorest soldier to obtain. You could tell how long a man had campaigned by how broken in his jack was. Wat's was as supple a jack as Joth had ever seen, and the filthiest as well. As he worked the laces free he had to wrinkle his nose at the rank smell.

"Sit up a bit, Wat. Let's pull this off you."

The big man groaned as Joth wriggled the coat free. Wat sat there leaning forward, his singlet soaked through with blood and sweat and grime.

The wound wasn't as bad as Joth had imagined it to be. Wat had been pierced under his shoulder blade and he probably had a broken rib or two. The filthy reeking jack had saved Wat's life, but he was still bleeding like a stuck pig and Joth needed a fire and a hot iron to stop that.

"We can't risk a fire this close to them," Wat wheezed.

"You'll bleed to death."

"It's pissing rain out. How could you anyhow?"

"There's some tinder here, look."

"Yer a bloody fool if you think they won't be on us before the rain stops."

"The rain'll hide the smell and the smoke, and we'll put it out quick."

Wat didn't look convinced.

"I'll use your jack to tent it."

Wat sighed and gave the slightest of nods.

"You'll get us both killed, but I don't have the strength to stop you. Bloody fool, Joth." They shared a grim smile, and laughed in spite of themselves.

"Shhh…they'll hear us!" Wat hissed, but this only illicited more laughter. They were safe now, even if their safety was precarious and fleeting and doomed. They had escaped for the moment, and now the elation of being alive had given them a grim hope. It felt good to laugh. Joth could almost forget he wasn't back in the barracks at the garrison. He could almost forget Lord Uhlmet and the hellish mess of the last few weeks' march. The faces of his lost comrades came floating up at him and his mirth slowly died, and he knew Wat was thinking the same. He removed his own jack and covered Wat with it to stop his shivering, for the rain had brought with it a chill and Wat was weak from his wound.

"I'll be quick about this."

He set about making the fire. Everything was so damp that it seemed nigh impossible to accomplish, but Joth kept trying to coax a spark to life within the tinder. The first few died as they fell through the air. Twice he caught a spark in the dry bark nest he had made, but as he tried to breath life into them the sparks faded and lost their fiery glow, failing into black specks within the nest of tinder. When he had almost given up, a hearty strike sent a brilliant spark arcing into the stringy bark and it held there, glowing. Slowly, steadily, he blew into the spark and watched it flare and smoke, gaining strength from his breath and finally bursting into flame. Carefully he added the small twigs he had gathered from under the outcrop, then some larger sticks, and finally a large piece of dried dead wood he had scavenged from the base of the ancient tree.

Once the flames had quickened, Joth made a tent over the fire with the blood soaked jack he had peeled from Wat. He then fanned the smoke with his hands, wafting out into the rainy sky. Wat coughed and cursed. Shivering and wearing his singlet and hosen, Joth removed his helm and used it to try to spread the smoke out a bit, hoping that he had not just alerted their enemies to their whereabouts. He met with mixed results. But by the time he felt the smoke had dissipated enough, his teeth were chattering and his singlet was soaked through, his ash blonde hair a murky brown and plastered to his head. He retreated once again under the outcrop once he had checked the bottom of the hill and found no signs of any watchers.

The flames had grown and consumed the smaller sticks, turning them to glowing coals, burning with a pale blue fire that licked at the larger pieces of wood stacked carefully atop them. Joth had built the fire well, and she would burn for quite a while if they needed her to. He took the half-moon shaped fire striker that he had used to start the blaze and placed it carefully in the coals where the heart of the fire was burning the deepest red and waited for his steel to get hot. Wat cried out as Joth pulled the blood-soaked singlet down to expose the gaping wound. He helped Wat have a drink of water from his cupped hands and then washed out his wound with the rainwater.

"This is going to bloody hurt, Joth."

"Don't cry out." He gave Wat his own belt knife and placed the bone handle between his teeth.

Wat clamped down on the knife, set his jaw and nodded. He was as ready as he could be given the sorry situation they were both in now. Joth gave a grim nod and turned back to the fire.

The steel striker had gone black and the edge was glowing a dull orange where it lay touching the burning coals. Joth levered the smoking metal up with a stick and got the edge of Wat's jack under it, using it like a potholder to protect his hand. The metal sizzled and spat when it touched the wet filthy cloth. It was clumsy at best. He dropped it several times before he managed to fully remove it from the coals, but at last he held it firmly and turned back to Wat.

"Do it," Wat said with the knife in his teeth.

Joth held his eyes for a beat, then nodded grimly.

It was over in an instant. The scream that Wat released died in a whimper, but Joth couldn't tell if anyone would have been able to hear anything over the rain. He would not have believed three days ago that he would be thanking the heavens for spitting on him now, but he was thanking them with all his might. "Don't move, Wat. Let me have a look at you."

There was an angry crescent-shaped mark burned over the wound on Wat's back. He had cauterized it fairly well considering that he wasn't a barber, and only the edges of the wound still bled. If it didn't fester and Wat could rest for a time, he might survive. If they didn't get speared again trying to escape the bloody tribe lands, he thought gloomily. He made a crude bandage out of a piece of wadding he cut from Wat's helmet lining and tied it in place with his scarf, then carefully arranged the bloody singlet so that the entire bandage was secure beneath it. It was not the best, but it was the best he could do for his comrade. "Rest now. I'll put out the fire and have a look down the hill."

Wat grunted and closed his eyes.

After he had smothered their fire with the earth and soaked the smoldering mound with a helmet full of rain, Joth ate a piece of hard tack from his ration sack and chewed on a hard biscuit that left his mouth dry and his jaw sore. The rainwater tasted fair enough, but what he really longed for was a flagon of ale to calm him and warm him up. May as well piss in my hand and wish it were ale, he thought, I'll be lucky to ever see another flagon again. As far as he could reckon, he and Wat were at least a week's march from the Oestern borderlands. Wat would never make it in his state, Joth mused. The circuitous route they had taken with their company under Lord Uhlmet had led them out of their barracks at Castle Immerdale in the east and across the Dalemoors on the Magister's Road for an easy two days' ride west by northwest until they had come to the Borderhills. There they had left the road and turned due west, riding through the low hills for three days before coming to a magnificent vale no one seemed to know the name of, at which point he realized they were in Dawn Tribe territory.

Technically the border was somewhat disputed, but the topography granted a natural border that no one could deny, a deep vale with hills on the Oestern side and mountain walls on the other. The company followed the vale south on horseback for three more days until reaching Rhael's Pass, and they crossed it in a day and a night. Then had come the first settlement, and with it the beginning of their woes. Their horses had all been stolen that night, all save one. Joth still wondered why they had left one bloody horse for Lord Uhlmet. He supposed it was some Dawn Tribe superstition, or perhaps even a joke, if they were capable of such. He realized that he knew less and less about these people as he thought more on them. That they were cunning and more fierce than any soldier had been led to believe had been proven to him now. That he knew for certain.

He and Wat needed horses if they hoped to make it back home. He knew that, too. Black luck, he thought. Black luck is on me now. The rain had let up a bit. Joth raised himself back up among the roots and peered out. It was dusk now and he searched the base of the hill with his eyes in the fading light but saw nothing. Were they waiting for the rain to stop, he wondered? It unnerved him, knowing that the enemy host was so nearby and that he was trapped here on this hill with his wounded friend and no hope of relief from his plight.

Joth was no general, but he knew that he had to get himself and Wat out of there before the enemy came looking for them. For he knew being discovered would mean certain death. If word were to reach the Magistry that there were armed tribesmen openly attacking a survey company, there would be dire consequences for the Dawn Tribes. The savages knew that for certain. If the savages could steal horses, then so could he, Joth thought. I'll wait for them to celebrate their victory, and in the darkness I'll creep down to the village and bring back two horses, then it's Wat and me away from here. As he gazed down at the darkening hillside and listened to the rain stop he knew it was their only way home.

Two

LORD RHAEL UHLMET, MAGE Imperator, was not used to feeling helpless. It was, he realized, one of his deepest fears and his least pleasant way of feeling. It was especially horrible for him to be stripped and tied out like an animal for slaughter, and whipped by children while the elders looked on in laughter. The indignation of being captured by these savage goat herders in the first place was compounded by the slow steady torture being exacted on him since he had been dragged into the roundhouse as his men were ambushed and ultimately defeated. Worthless command, he thought, absolutely worthless. An entire company armed and outfitted, unable to defeat these savage bush men and their simple tactics. He would have words with his subordinates upon his return. He may even word a formal complaint to his higher-ups. He was meant to have experienced soldiers under him, soldiers who obeyed and knew how to handle themselves in a fight, but what he had gotten were a bunch of sniveling ninnies who had balked at every turn. Now I must suffer this indignation at the hands of these primitives, he thought, wincing as a birch switch caught him painfully in the pit of his outstretched arm.

Apart from the pain and indignation, the fact that he could not understand anything that was being said was wearing on his mind, driving him to a state of fuming inner rage that threatened to consume him. They would beat him for a time and then all fall to chattering like a bunch of birds in their savage language. Rhael had always liked to know everything, he was infinitely curious and his vast knowledge often gave him control of every situation he found himself in. He knew how different he was, his mind capable of more than the average highborn man. He could out-think and out-strip lowborn men all day long without even straining himself. These fools having their fun with him now would pay. He would flay all of them alive, starting with their eyelids and faces and draw it out for as long as they could live, forcing them to watch as he did it. Perhaps the strong among them would survive for a week or more. That thought almost made Rhael smile. That one I'll save for last, he thought, casting his eye on the old savage who had addressed him so boorishly at the onset of this debacle. He was still not quite sure how, but the old man had spooked his mount out from under him with a whispered word and before he had even time to reach for his belt they had been on him, stamping and dragging him into their squalid hut.

Had he been able to quaff a bit of the potion that he kept in his silver flagon at his belt then these savages would all be burnt to cinders by now. Lord Rhael Uhlmet knew how to harness magic and bend it to his will, he was one of the few Mage Imperators whom had handled the energy and lived to tell it, and his mind was still sound. No, he thought, better. His mind was made to work magic, his body like a conduit. He was able to afford the finest specimens for his elixirs. His family owned vast interests in the shipping trade, and the shipping trade was built on toads and newts, salamanders and lizards from all over the world. These rare beasts were processed in a very meticulous fashion by his brethren, although a lower form of mage than he, one without the charisma or proper breeding to lead and exert power in the field, but useful in their own right as makers of potions, blenders of this strain or that strain of essence that allowed the more skillful and talented people like himself to harness magical energy and use it to his will.

The Mage Alchemists were useful, for lowborn men, but they lacked the natural confidence and force of spirit that made men great, the natural high-born spirit of someone like Lord Rhael Uhlmet. Men needed the elixir to open their inner portals to the energy, otherwise the door remained hidden to the seeker. Rhael knew where to look, but he needed the elixir to lubricate his mind and allow the energy to enter him before he could access and bend it. This was the price of being a mortal, but Rhael believed he could change that and he never stopped seeking a way around it. That the Magistry believed the answer lay in Dawn Tribe lands, Rhael could not fathom. I should be in Kuilgarthen talking with the Crafters, he thought, not here in this cesspit. Kuilgarthen was the famed trade city where the Goblin Crafters sold their machines and magical devices. Men needed elixir to wield magic, but Goblinkind had developed a way long ago to trap magical energy and store it in machines and devices built to harness the power and focus it to a specific task. Some items were commonplace, such as the spoon he used in the mornings to stir his tea, which had the magical attribute of heating water rapidly; some items were rare and powerful: enchanted weapons and orbs of metal or glass capable of great destruction. To learn the secret that the Crafters used to harness power, the secret that they guarded with great care and jealously, this would be a great and powerful tool. It was one of his deep desires, finding out how the Crafters created the energy to be captured. Great power was what he wanted, but Rhael had submitted to the Council's decision and led the survey company to the Dawn Tribe lands. He had spoken with other mages and they had told him of the savage lands and the custom the natives had of wearing gold and silver, and although he was already quite wealthy, Lord Uhlmet could always find a use for gold. That these other fools never thought of stripping the savages and filling their coffers while on survey seemed quite ridiculous to him. How else was one meant to profit from such an exercise? Interview and survey the fair-haired youths of the Dawn Tribe, count their number and indicate on the map where they were located and what sort of impression he had gotten from them in his interview, those were his orders. What a load of rubbish, mused Rhael. Someone must have bribed the Council to send him off on survey so that they could push about in his research unhindered, probably that lickspittle Norden, rifling through his rooms looking for his potions no doubt. Let him look, he won't be able to make sense of any of it and he'll never find my elixirs, thought Rhael. Norden would be grinning with delight and capering about like a fool if he knew where I was now, Rhael raged. The beating had subsided for a moment, but it was more savage gibberish and laughter. Rather than listen and be frustrated by his lack of understanding, Rhael let his limbs go slack and tried to overcome the pain and exhaustion that burned through to his very core, but the bonds were tied in such a way that when he released the strength in his arms his legs suffered, and when he relaxed his legs his shoulders were torqued in a painful stretch. If he gave up entirely, his breath would only come in gasps. so tight was the pressure on his throat and chest.

At least he wasn't alone, he thought, eyeing the balding head of the incompetent translator as it swiveled round to gaze his way. They had strung the man up by the ankles and beaten him with switches as well, but the women had hit him and only the children had beaten Rhael. Now the sorry-looking man was weeping and sniveling and saying omething over and over again. This was the behavior of the lowborn, to break and turn into weeping wretches who begged for mercy and forgiveness from their tormentors without a thought of honor and revenge, or escape and retribution. "Weak minds and weak wills make the lowborn." Rhael's father had taught him that, and to never give up.

"Shut your maw, you gaping dullard!" Rhael hissed at the translator. The man just kept repeating himself, going so far as to actually ignore Rhael entirely.

Whatever the present situation, the man should have never broken protocol.

Rhael was still his better, and he still held command. When he escaped he would be sure to have the man executed. Let's see how he looks hanging from his neck, he thought, at least he won't be as noisome. He would have smiled then had he been able to through the pain that was spread over him like a blanket, his limbs involuntarily spasming and shaking with strain. He clenched his jaw tight and vowed that he would not cry out or whimper, that he wouldn't give his savage captors the satisfaction of seeing him break. There was more of the savage chattering, it was all he could hear. It seemed to go on and on for such a very long time. It was maddening to him. His breath was coming rapidly now, and he could no longer control his convulsions. He was shocked and appalled by his body's betrayal as a low animalistic moan escaped his throat and tears streamed over his cheeks and pooled in his ears. It took a few moments for Rhael to realize that he was weeping uncontrollably, like a child. He wept and wept, and cried out and forgot everything but what had happened to him and his physical pain and predicament. He forgot that he was highborn, and his arrogance failed and he was simply a man writhing in pain, bound and staked out in a round house in the dirt, and he wanted more than anything else at that moment for his pain to end.

It would not end. It kept coming for him over and over in a relentless rush, an unending infinite torrent that left him weeping and moaning until he was hoarse and dry and croaking. He did not know for how long he wept, nor how long he lay bound and in agony, but he found himself staring through the hole in the center of the ceiling at the night sky when his bonds were slackened. He was unable to move and all of his strength had left him. Rough hands hauled him to his feet, but his legs failed and he went sprawling to the dirt. He managed to turn his head at the last moment and avoid breaking his nose but even that was difficult. He realized then that he had lost control of his bowels at some point and was covered in his own reeking filth.

"Lord Uhlmet," said the man. It was not a question. The man spoke his name like a dire sentence. "In the village of Tregethrin you led away three youths. What became of them?"

He tried to speak but nothing came out. The old man said a word in his savage tongue and a woman approached Rhael and roughly tilted his head back. He tried to struggle until he realized she was pouring water down his throat. He gulped at it greedily, too quickly, and he was sputtering and coughing. She was gone when his eyes cleared.

"What became of the three youths?" the old man repeated.

"I…asked them…questions." Rhael could barely form words.

"What became of them? I have asked you, yet you tell me nothing." The old man fixed him with an unwavering gaze. "Perhaps you wish to return to your place on the floor?"

"No! Please, I will tell you!" Rhael felt as though he were listening to someone else speak. "I asked them questions and released them. I sent them back to their homes."

The man looked at him unblinking. "Why did they never reach their homes, Lord Uhlmet?" Such a fine voice the man had.

"I don't know. I don't know why!" Rhael lied. They were dead. He had attempted to draw out their life energies and store them in a glass orb, an experiment he had hoped to repeat at every village in an effort to create a weapon like those of the Goblinkind, but he needed more subjects to perfect his transference theories. Magics needed to be carefully noted and experiments conducted in controlled situations so that the results would be reliable, otherwise the theory would remain unproven, and the council would never promote him based on an unreliable theory.

The old man was still watching. Waiting.

"I let them go, I've told you." How would they ever know? He was the only person in his tent and he burned the bodies to ash with his energies once the experiment had failed.

The translator was still hanging by his feet repeating himself. Rhael had regained enough of his senses that the man was annoying him again. "Why does he keep saying that over and over again?"

"It is mine to question, Lord Uhlmet." The old man stepped forward. He now stood directly over Rhael. "If I am to believe you, then no harm befell the three children and they were simply questioned and sent home?"

Oh, but this was tedious, he thought. "Yes, that is what I have told you."

The old man held his eyes for a moment as if weighing his words, then nodded. "Then I have no reason to hold you here like this, I suppose. You are free to go."

"I'm free to go?" What was this, some sort of ruse? Rhael tried to stand but he could not. His limbs were useless.

"Yes, of course, Lord Uhlmet. There is the small matter of the blood price, but a great lord such as yourself can surely afford to pay the families of the missing children their due. After all, you were the last person to have charge of them."

Rhael's mind was racing. What was this old fool playing at? He would have to buy his freedom, ransom himself from these savages. The missing children ruse was simply a threat the old man was waving in his face with one hand while the other reached for his purse strings. Rhael composed himself as best his aching body would allow.

"I can pay you what price is best for you, if that is your wish, but I'll need access to my coffers."

The old man snorted derisively. "We have taken the liberty of bringing your coffers to you, my lord."

He motioned with his staff and two men brought forth a bundle they were holding between them on a blanket and lay it down at the old man's feet.

Wrapped up in another blanket that they now unfolded was a mound of gold and silver ornaments like those the primitives wore in their hair.

"Do you recognize these things, my lord?" the man separated a few bits of gold with the end of his staff as he spoke, "This is what a man wears when his first son makes his third spring. This the mark of a mother of five."

"Perhaps these were taken by the soldiers, I had no knowledge of this."

"Really, Uhlmet, you must stop lying to me."

Rhael was feeling ill. It was a growing feeling of worry that had settled in the pit of his bowels.

How could this old fool know anything? I was the only person in the tent that night. I burned the bodies to ash after it failed. I burned them all to ash, he thought.

"I have other gold among my things. I have a spoon of great value."

"A spoon?"

"Yes, a Goblincraft spoon of great worth!"

"He has a spoon of great worth! A spoon!" The old man's voice boomed throughout the roundhouse, the firelight glinting off of his many golden ornaments as he stretched out his arms and spoke to the assembly of savages like a showman. He was laughing as he proclaimed it, but he was the only one. There was no mirth in the eyes of the crowd. They probably couldn't understand him, thought Rhael. Perhaps the savages don't all speak Oestersh. When the old man turned back there was a cold fury in his gray eyes.

"Tell me, Lord Uhlmet, how many spoons does it take to replace the life of a child?"

Uhlmet started to speak.

"Wait! Before you answer, let me be more exacting." He cast his eyes over the crowd and motioned three men and three women forward. "How many spoons does it take to replace the lives of these people's children?"

The six people stared at Rhael with their haunted expressions.

"Can your magic spoon return a father or mother's affection? Can it do these things, my lord?"

Now the old man's voice had lost all its mellifluous charm and carried with it a dangerous and darkening edge that cut and bit deeper and deeper into Rhael as he spoke, seemingly gaining momentum as he drove his questions.

"Perhaps if my lord has a way of dividing the spoon so that each family can have a small piece of it to aid them in their loss? Does that seem fitting to you, you monster? What were you sent here for Uhlmet? Truth will bring you mercy."

Rhael did not respond at once. A sharp crack to the point of his shoulder with the staff and his arm was numb and on fire.

"I was to survey! I was to interview fair-haired youths! Write down the village names and survey the youths!"

To his shock and dismay Rhael was in tears again, but his mind could not fight the pain and keep up with the questioning. He kept blurting things out. "I followed my orders! My men were unruly and wanted the gold and the women, I was merely keeping them in line!"

"You saved us from your men by taking the children?"

"No! I was following orders!"

"And what orders did you give your men the night after Tregethrin?"

"What night do you mean?"

"The village from where you took the children, Tregethrin. What did you tell your men?"

"Yes, I did that. I took them along. I told them to make camp by the river."

"Yes, and you told them to butcher the last of the goats."

How did he know that? "I'm not sure if I did."

"You did. I have it from one of your men."

Rhael paused.

"You made a jest, it seems, a jest about goats and kids. It's what your translator keeps repeating in our tongue. Over and over again, as you say." Rhael's look of shock and incredulity prompted the old man to continue. "You see, Lord Uhlmet, our spies followed you from Tregethrin and watched three fair children enter your tent. They watched all night and waited for you to release them, but no children came out of your tent. Our spies entered your tent in the night and found only you within. Only the Lord Uhlmet saw the new day dawn." He shook his head disdainfully, "Every means you use to try and escape from the truth shall fail you. We know you killed our children. Now you must reap your harvest."

Rhael tried to protest, but the old man held up his hand and waved him to silence.

"We have prepared a place for you, my lord, though it will not be to your liking. At least that is my greatest wish; long may you linger there."

He saw the old man turn and say something to the men who had brought out the gold and silver, and then he was being hauled to his feet and dragged. As he was shoved through the door he caught sight of the translator. They locked eyes. The man smiled grimly at him, upside down and hanging there. Rhael could only think of him hanging the other way as he was dragged off into the cold night.

Three

JOTH HAD FOUND THE picket lines and taken the two best horses he could in a hurry without being spotted. He had made it back to the base of the hill and tied the horses to a small oak before making a mad scramble up to where he had left Wat sleeping. His heart was pounding in his chest. He was unused to trying to move quietly and avoid being seen, and he knew he was not particularly skilled at it. He was out of practice in regards to everything besides drilling and moving in formation. Now that he was alone without his comrades in the rank and file, Joth felt completely vulnerable and defenseless. Somehow he had managed to get away and back again with two horses in tow, and though he was elated, there was a desperate feeling welling up inside him, a feeling of panic now that he had almost reached Wat. What if they've discovered him? He thought, what if they are waiting for me there with Wat? He pushed these thoughts aside as he climbed up the hill, telling himself over and over again to keep calm and get to Wat so that they could both mount up and leave this sorry mess behind them.

Oestern ale in my cup, he thought, Wat and me in the tavern. He pictured the two of them all bandaged up by the tavern wenches, clinking mugs together next to a roaring fire.

The image gave him strength, as silly as it seemed, as he was slipping and clawing his way up the backside of the slope in the wilderness. He found Wat just how he had left him, sleeping on his good side underneath the overhanging rock with his back to the wall. He nudged him gently.

"Wat. I've got two horses for us. You have to come now."

"Right. Help me."

It was slow going. Wat had not had time to regain any strength and twice he stopped because the pain was too great for him to keep moving. It was all that Joth could do to wait, the urgency of their escape captured in the beat of his pounding heart, and his head swiveling around at the slightest noise or hint of movement. Every fiber in his being was telling him to run, to get clear of this place lightning quick. It was hard not to simply bolt down the hill, jump on his stolen horse, be away and clear of the Dawn Tribe, and never look back. Wat wouldn't leave me here, he thought, and I won't let him die out here if I can help it.

The wounded man gathered his strength and made his way to the bottom of the hill with Joth helping and guiding him to where the two horses were tied.

"Bloody Joth, you stole a white horse! We'll be spotted for sure now."

"You are a funny man, Wat. Give us your foot." Joth laced his fingers and bent his knees, making an easy step up for Wat, who swung his leg painfully over the leather saddle, grimacing as he moved his feet around.

"No stirrups. Bloody Dawn Tribe."

That would make for harder riding and slower going on account of Wat's wound, he knew, but faster than walking.

"You'd complain about a sunrise at dawn."

Wat gave him a slight grin.

Joth had mounted his own horse, a bay with a slightly dished face and mismatched eyes that he just then noticed. They had seemed the finest mounts he'd seen when he took them from the picket. Wat caught his expression and raised his eyebrows.

"Go on, we know you picked them out in a hurry."

They began their way eastward through the foothills in the misty early hours before sunrise, moving as swiftly as they could through the wild country with only the moonlight and Wat's wound keeping them from spurring their mounts into a break neck run for the border. They rode north, to clear a great dense wood of ash and cedar as the sky was lightening. The darkness faded, giving way to a dull blue gray in the heavens. They managed a trot across the open ground at the mouth of the narrow vale they had entered, and then they turned eastward again and skirted the forest at the base of the hill that marked its northernmost edge.

They would be easy to track, Joth knew, but they could not afford to sacrifice speed for caution with Wat's condition already hampering their progress. His great hope was that the savages had simply let them go. Don't be a fool, Joth, he thought as he looked behind to check Wat's progress up the slope. He knew that was absurd. The Magistry could never allow a transgression like this to go unpunished, and the leaders of the warband that attacked Lord Uhlmet's company had to know that there would be retaliation once word made it back to Oesteria. On the other hand, sending an army into Tribe lands would be folly as well. The savages simply would refuse to wage war. They would steal horses, ambush and trap, separate their enemies, then melt away into the mountains and forests and let the harsh seasons starve and demoralize their foes until they simply got fed up and left for home. You won't catch me volunteering, Joth mused. Not that they would ask him what he thought about it. Joth was a simple soldier, and he knew they would order him wherever they pleased. Still, knowing that he hoped for a simple garrison post where he could ride out the end of his tour in a relatively quiet manner. He had two years left to serve in his ten-year tour, and this had been quite enough excitement and high adventure under the cursed command of Lord Uhlmet.

Wat winced each time his mount would step or surge forward over broken ground, and every bit of the ground here was rough and ripe for stumbling horses. Joth knew they would have to rest soon, but he was determined to push onward until Wat said something, and he knew that Wat would say nothing until sunset or one of their mounts pulled up lame, so he just kept pushing his mount hard as he dared. He dozed more than once and would have slipped from his saddle if Wat had not called out to him in time.

They were moving eastward through a narrow defile at the top of the valley when the sun broke through the clouds and bathed the entire vale in brilliant hue, sparkling with the new rain.

Joth pulled up and looked behind him, waiting for Wat to catch up. Joth's belly rumbled incessantly and his vision was blurred with fatigue. Joth needed sleep and a hot meal above all else. He remembered the feast days when he had first signed on to military service with the Magistry, tables piled high with meats and cheeses, breads and every condiment one could think of in every house of the town. Joth and the other youths who enlisted were given freedom of the town and treated like lords everywhere they went, given food and gifts and laden with praise. Many a merchant's daughter and serving girl praised the lads in their own ways that week, virtue be damned. It was an historic event for the town and everyone had felt a part of something larger, as though the veil between the world of the simple and that of the Magistry lifted, and both were close and palpable. He had become a soldier of the first army of the Magistry, an elite corps of fighting men assigned to work hand in hand with the Mage Imperators on their most perilous and important tasks. Well he remembered the words of the officer. He had sung such a pretty tune about service in the army. Halfway up a hill in tribe country in the pissing rain on a dish-faced gelding was not in the song he remembered hearing.

His father had died in the winter. Joth had fallen out with the bowyer he was apprenticed to and shamed his family by carrying on with his master's daughter. Dierna with her blonde hair and her pale eyes always watching him, hanging about to wait for him to be done with her father's tasks.

He thought he loved her, but he was just a boy, and he stupidly thought that because he loved her that it would set things right somehow. But it ended in tears and a broken apprentice contract for Joth's father to deal with. He settled the suit with the bowyer and died a fortnight later. Joth joined the army in the spring, his mother and sister collecting his home-wages and living off of them while he earned his barracks-pay and saved whatever he liked for his own fancy.

New boots, a coat in winter, the odd flagon here and there—Joth was not prone to spending his pay on frivolous things like some of the men, preferring instead to make due with what he could and send the rest home to his mother and sister. Besides, he thought grimly, a fancy silver belt and tooled scabbard meant nothing out here. How many of the lads who flaunted their fine purchases in the barracks were dangling from ash trees or lying in hastily dug graves in this cursed country? At first it was guilt that kept him saving his pay, shame keeping him from rewarding himself with anything.

They never said anything to him to suggest it, but he knew his mother and sister blamed him for the death of his father. It had been hard to arrange the apprenticeship, costly for his father, who saw an opportunity for his son to gain a better trade, perhaps a better life than the one he had been given, only to watch it all fail and end in shame. It had been too much for the man, and Joth was left feeling ashamed and brokenhearted by his own actions, feelings that amplified with guilt and grief upon his father's death. He knew he could never make things right, but he had made sure that his mother and sister lived in comfort and ease. For him that was a great consolation.

Sometimes he would think of Dierna, but he told no one of it—not even Wat. He would remember the first day she came to him outside of her father's workshop asking for help with the fish weirs at the river. He was working at the baskets when suddenly her hands were on him, and then they were both falling in the shallows. It was clumsy at best those first few times that she came to him, but they were magic times and they grew bold in their desire for each other; bold and ultimately too careless to keep things secret. He wondered if Dierna was married now and knew she must be. He wondered if some other apprentice boy married her like he had wanted to do all those years ago. He remembered the way her shift clung to her wet form as she climbed onto the riverbank, how he could see every curve of her body…

"Bloody wake up, Joth!" Wat was picking his way past him, scowling through the drizzle. Joth gave his head a quick shake in an effort to clear it. He was exhausted and now the fatigue was settling into his mind and playing tricks on him. Dierna would have to wait there by the river without him.

He swept his gaze back across the way they had come, searching for any sign of pursuers entering the valley but he found nothing. The misty rain hid much from his vision, a double-edged sword that Joth was somewhat more thankful for than not. The rain was hiding them as well. He turned his mount and continued to climb the narrow trail through the pass and out of the vale. Wat was looking miserable, sitting his saddle stiffly and grimacing with pain. They were both soaked through to the bone within an hour of climbing through the pass. Pale and blue-lipped, teeth chattering, they rode their mounts determinedly eastward through the hills and short valleys without rest until the dwindling sunset shone palely through the clouds behind them and darkness began to settle in.

"We had best stop now, Wat. I can't go any farther."

"I was hoping you'd say that hours ago," he wheezed back.

Joth dismounted stiffly east of the hilltop in a stand of birch. He looked behind him and thought he could just make out the pass they had come through that morning in the misty distance. This was a good place to rest. If pursuers came they would see them through the pass a good day's journey ahead of time. Joth knew no one had followed them through the pass yet, but how could he be certain that they would not slip through in the night and take them unawares? He could hardly stay awake as it was, and he knew Wat could not be relied upon to keep watch, and soon they would be unable to see the pass in any case. He wanted to keep going, but a few hours rest was needed for the horses now if they were to make it. He helped ease Wat painfully out of the saddle and propped him against the smooth trunk of a birch tree. Wat mumbled something and fell to sleep immediately. Joth knelt down and held the reins to both horses in his hands and looked back in the misty darkness toward the pass not truly seeing it, yet playing the game in his mind of where it was in the unknowable stillness. In this way he drifted into sleep within minutes of his watch.

Four

WHEN HE WOKE IN the predawn, his panic spooked the horses and sent them both half rearing and tossing their heads. He had not wanted to fall asleep and now he briefly imagined it was midday and feared that if he look down the slope he would see an army on their heels. Cursing and stumbling to the treeline, Joth peered out into the darkness but saw no sign of anyone or anything. He trotted back over to Wat and touched the man's shoulder.

"We overslept."

"Help me up."

Wat's horse was still jittery from getting startled. Through clenched teeth and cursing, the big man settled into his saddle with a sharp intake of breath as the horse danced about nervously.

"Hold still," Wat hissed pulling in his reins and cursing in pain.

When Wat's mount had settled, Joth mounted the dish-faced bay again and they headed down the hillside toward the glow in the east. By mid-morning Joth felt as though he had never slept at all. Twice that morning the two swung north then south to avoid what they took for settlements by the plumes of smoke they saw on the wind. They kept to the edges of the valleys and the highlands and avoided the broad flats. What they sacrificed in speed they made up for in the safety of going unnoticed. At midday Wat had to dismount and relieve himself and they took a short rest and shared some fresh water and the last of their field rations. It was not particularly satisfying, but it did quell the immediate feeling of starvation and kept the sound of Joth's belly at bay as they trudged on. Wat was pale and feverish and starting to slump in his saddle by late afternoon. When he fell and was holding himself up weakly with one arm, Joth turned and helped him, and they were forced to stop their flight while Wat recovered. Just in the treeline Joth propped Wat up as best he could and tended to his dressing. The wound was festering where he had cauterized it, a yellowish mucous forming on the surface. He cleansed it as best he could and redressed the wound with a fresh bandage cut from inside Wat's jack. Joth was amazed at how clean the linen was on the inside of Wat's filthy armor. Sure, he thought, once you cut through the soiled lining it was not so bad, the stitching that kept missiles out also worked against grime. He doubted that the sour smell of stale sweat could ever be washed out, and the thought of it made him wrinkle his nose. The festering was worrying Joth, but there was nothing for it now. How close were they to the border? He wondered. They had made good speed by his reckoning, but he had no idea how quickly the ground they covered on horseback compared to marching men's pace. Lord Uhlmet had certainly whipped them along at a horse's pace from village to village. It had seemed that way to Joth at any rate. He knew that the land to the west of Oesteria all fell away to harborless coasts and beaches, another way by which the tribes were isolated, conducting much of their trade only with their countrymen. There was nothing to the west of here past the settlements. Just the ocean. Perhaps beyond that some islands or another land, but Joth did not know of such things. He sat there on his haunches, looking west and thinking about the tall sailing ships that traded in exotic things from far off lands, ships he had never laid eyes upon. Yet he knew ships sailed upon those same seas beyond the hills and mountains at that very moment. He wondered what life would be like in a distant land, whether the world elsewhere was like Oesteria or more akin to these hills and valleys. He wondered if he would make it away from these hills alive. There were no signs of pursuers.

But a gnawing fear was growing in Joth's mind, and that was the question of whether or not they were even being chased, or if they were running into a trap that was waiting for them at Rhael's pass. His enemy was cunning. They knew the terrain, and perhaps they knew short-cuts through the passes. Perhaps the rain had covered their trail. Perhaps the natives had celebrated their victory well into the next morning and lost a day. They had made good time. Wat had only slowed them up by a few hours today. Still, they were moving much more quickly than Joth had imagined possible when he thought of Wat riding with his cracked ribs and bloody, festering stab wound.

If indeed they had gained a day, he and Wat were in good standing to escape alive, if Wat could stay in the saddle until they made the border. Now Wat was not looking too well. Joth could hear the man's labored wheezing almost a bowshot away. He worsens, Joth thought. Wat had gotten a chill in his bones and needed the warmth of a good fire, but building one was lunacy. Even if they could risk a fire, the last two days of rain had made that nigh impossible. Joth went to the horses and loosened their girths and inspected them. They had been ridden hard but they were sturdy, and he had chosen well that night on the outskirts of the village. He thought about it for a moment, then he slipped their headstalls down over their necks and let them graze at the clover and grasses that were growing on the hillside near the edge of the trees. He found an apple tree growing a short way in from where the horses were grazing and let them gorge themselves on the fallen fruit. The apples were small and hard and bitter, but he gorged himself as well and spent the last hour of daylight climbing and gathering the best specimens he could and threw to the horses those he could not stomach for himself. He longed for a crust of bread. He tied the horses to the apple tree and carried a few of the more select fruit back to Wat.

"Good lad," he wheezed as he weakly accepted it. Wat polished off three more of the withered apples before muttering "bloody awful" and closing his eyes. He roused himself long enough to have a sip of water at Joth's insistence and then he was sleeping like a stone. Joth listened to his wheezing until he could stand it no more, and he moved off to the treeline and took in the fading sunlight as the sun sank low behind the mountains to the west. There was still no sign of pursuit, and it made Joth all the more uneasy. What if they were waiting ahead for them?

He only knew one route out of these cursed valleys and it was Rhael's Pass. It was a famous battle fought there in ancient days between his people and the Dawn Tribes named after the great Oestern general Ulno Rhael. A famed victory for Oestermen, one in which they sealed the borders of their country from the natives and drove them back over the mountains for good. Everyone knew the story, and all Oestern boys pretended to be General Rhael fighting the Dawn Tribe at their play growing up. It was from those stories that Joth knew the geography of the borderland—from the tales and from the survey, and no more.

He had never seen a map or a globe in all his life. The education of his youth dealt directly with things of a more physical and practical nature. All he knew was the way they had come, and by all that he could reckon that was Rhael's Pass and it lay due east of them. One more day's ride and they would make the pass, and to think beyond that was impossible to Joth. He would get Wat to Oesteria, he swore to himself and to the first star he saw in the west as the sunlight fell away and the cold night settled in over the bedraggled pair of refugees. In the night he unfolded the horse blankets and piled them atop himself and Wat, but it did little good. By morning Joth had slept very little and Wat was burning with a fever and could barely sit upon his horse unassisted. As they climbed over the last of a series of low rises a few hours before midday, a broad vale opened before them bordered in the east by a steep impenetrable mountain wall. Joth knew this valley; he remembered it! Across the vale to the south in the distance Joth could see the jagged outcrop and the shadow of the pass.

"There, Wat!" Joth said excitedly, "We've almost made it. Just a bit more."

Wat nodded feebly. His horse was grazing at some scraggly grasses and was stepping through the reins Wat had dropped unknowingly. Joth dismounted quickly and jerked the horse's head up. He gathered the reins to the big man's horse as he remounted his own.

"Can't ride, Joth." Wat wheezed.

"You just hold yourself on that horse, Wat. I'll lead you."

Wat mumbled something incoherently and gripped the saddle with both hands. Joth set off as fast as he could across the valley once they had climbed their way down the western slope, and Wat managed to hang on for a canter over the flats as Joth made for the pass with growing excitement. It was close enough to taste, yet it could all be lost if their enemy swept across the plain and barred their path to Rhael's Pass. He felt too exposed as he crossed the vale, as though a thousand eyes peered from the western slopes, marking his and Wat's progress. They were across the vale and riding under the retreating shadow of the mountain wall as the sun passed its apex, and Joth knew that they would make the pass and be in Oesteria by nightfall.

They had made it! Against the odds he and Wat had escaped from certain death, but now that they were on the path to safety and solace, Joth began to think about the ramifications of this failed survey under Lord Imperator Uhlmet. What it meant specifically to he and Wat once they arrived back at Castle Immerdale as the lone survivors of the ordeal. Joth frowned. They might be taken for deserters. It wouldn't look good, a wound in the back. Wat had been joking, but Joth knew that it was laced with truth. They had been running away when Wat was wounded, routed. The Magistry did not like their soldiers to run away, in fact it hanged them outright for good measure. Wat, of course, would be in no position to explain the events, so it would be put to Joth alone. There would be an inquiry with a jury and the mages would hold him in a cell and question him, and then once he had recovered from his wound, they would question Wat to see if their stories matched, and then it would be decided whether they had acted appropriately. Perhaps they would be rewarded; earn a rank or be marked as distinguished soldiers. Joth looked back at the pale and feverish Wat slumped in his saddle. They could as easily be marked as cowards and hanged just to keep the Magistry's hands clean and to keep news of a defeat from spreading. It had been an ambush, a trap that Uhlmet had led them into in his arrogance. Surely the jury would see that.

Crack troops routed by savages in a pigsty village somewhere west of the mountains—that would be met with disbelief. Joth did not even have a name to tell them for the village where Uhlmet was dragged from his horse. He could not say with certainty that he would even be able to find his way back there, as reckless as their first day's flight had been. If they did believe him, he would be expected to guide the remounted expedition. He would be kept under lock and key and hanged if there was no evidence of the ambush. Then when the expedition returned they would check in on Wat to make sure he had healed enough to climb the gallows and dangle for his share in it. He could imagine the looks on his mother's and sister's faces when the paymaster refused them his home wages.

"There's a dreary outlook," he muttered to himself as he pushed his horse back into a fast stepping pace. He was doing that more and more as his mount tired. The lather was showing on both of their mounts and Wat's white horse was tossing his head obstinately. The one thing Joth could know with any certainty was that he did not want to get caught on this side of Rhael's Pass by nightfall. If he had to, he would kill these horses to get to the other side. His own dish-faced gelding seemed to sense his thoughts and angled his head around to look at him. When he saw the animal's nostrils flare and his head perk up; he marked it on Wat's mount as well. He knew then that their horses had caught scent of something and his worst fears were confirmed when he looked across the vale and saw riders fanning out toward the pass from the western slopes. He saw by the way they sat their horses that they were natives, and he knew they meant to catch them before they made the pass. He and Wat were too far from the western slopes to turn back; it was now or never.

"Hold on, Wat! Hold on for your life!"

The big man barely seemed to acknowledge him but Joth kicked up his mount and the white horse kept pace. They set out for the pass for all that they were worth, and for all that they were worth was not going to be enough. Joth saw it happen almost the way he had imagined it a few hours earlier, with a few dramatic alterations; the underwhelming factor being that there were only five riders and not the sweeping horde that he had envisioned, and the fact that their mounts looked to be as near as tired as Joth and Wat's own. He had near beaten them shortcut or no, but they had a natural advantage by being closer to the mouth of the pass and coming mostly downhill. Now they were closing ground rapidly as Joth felt his hopes dwindle and die. His mount was giving him his all, and Wat was doubled over his white gelding with his arms around his horse's neck holding on with all his might as they ran for the outcrop that marked the mouth of the pass, racing their pursuers with their lives in the balance. Joth heard the cries of the riders behind him, he was screaming too, urging his mount onward over the broken ground. The five riders in pursuit were only a few hundred yards behind them when Joth and Wat made the mouth of the pass.

For a moment Joth felt an overwhelming sense of victory at having won the race, but his hopes crashed as the white gelding stumbled and he felt the reins jerk free from his grip and saw Wat fly off and tumble from the struggling horse as it went down. Wat windmilled past him in a cloud of dust as the horse rolled and screamed in panic. Joth could have kept spurring his horse on. Somehow he knew that and yet he pulled his horse around and reined him in. He was leaping down from the bay's back when he saw the first rider enter the pass. Joth ran as fast as his spent cramped legs would carry him. He moved to draw his sword and realized for the first time since his flight began that he had dropped it when he helped carry Wat up the hill just after they were ridden down. His belt knife would not be of much service but he had nothing else. So he stood over his friend's body in the middle of the narrow pass with a knife in one hand and the largest rock he could find in the other and prepared for his death. At least they won't take us without a fight, he thought, trying to embolden himself.

What he was feeling was not fear but more a feeling of hopelessness and unavoidable mortal doom. He thought of his mother and sister. His father's disappointment. He thought of Dierna at the river. At the very least he felt like he had known what it was like to love once. You are a bloody fool, Joth, he thought with a grimace. Had it not been for Dierna he would be a master bowyer now, working comfortably in his own shop with a few apprentices. Instead, he would die here in between his world and that of his pursuers and no one in Oesteria would ever know about Lord Uhlmet and his ill-fated company. He thought of these things all in an instant as he watched the first two riders dismount and draw their old-fashioned-looking swords. They carried spined round shields in their off hands, and Joth felt hopelessly unarmed in comparison. If he could throw his stone at one of the warriors as he was closing and get him to raise his shield, he might be able to slip in with his knife and take him out. Then what? He thought, I'll be killed by one of the other four before I have a chance to turn around. No, you're going to bloody die, Joth, so just get it over with.

"Let us go! We don't have a fight with you!" he found himself screaming. His heart was pounding in his chest like never before, thoughts were flitting through his head faster than lightning streaks across the sky. The warriors were advancing slowly behind their shields, golden ornaments in their hair tinkling and chiming with their movements. He recognized one of them as the youth who had followed him and Wat halfway up the hill, the young warrior who had thrown down the broken spear. He met his unwavering gaze, blue eyes burning into his own. This one really wants to kill me, he thought. He could see determination mixed with hatred behind the cautious advance. The other three riders had arrived, but they sat their horses a short distance back. A stone's throw away, Joth thought ruefully, and he would have laughed had Wat said it. Joth saw his death in the young warrior's eyes and he was not ready to die yet. He wanted to save Wat and live. He wanted to see his mother and his sister again. His life was ending and he felt as though he had never had a chance to live. The two warriors spread out, one circling right while the other kept ahead. Joth knew he had to act quickly so he threw the stone as hard as he could at the flanking warrior and as he raised his shield he leapt with his knife toward the young warriors' right side. The flanking warrior yelled something in his own tongue and the young warrior grunted and said something as he leapt back and raised his sword. It was then that Joth switched his attention back to the flanking warrior and gave him the strongest kick he could deliver to the middle of his shield and brought the man down. Quick as could be Joth was behind the struggling man, his knife at his throat and his free arm locking up the man's sword arm, wrenching it behind him painfully. The young warrior screamed and charged, but Joth stood his ground and kept himself behind his hostage, and himself between them and Wat.

"Let us go! We just want to go home!" Joth's words echoed through the pass.

The young warrior was seething, but he held back. Joth looked quickly behind him, but Wat just lay there motionless. He was still breathing, Joth could see that. Slowly he dragged his man backward as he retreated before the slowly advancing riders, lessening the distance between him and Wat.

"Please, let us go." He said it evenly but it sounded hollow and pathetic to him. For the first time he let his attention shift to the three riders, taking them in. He saw the old man from the village, the one who had spoken so boldly to Lord Uhlmet. There was another warrior there as well, one whom he did not recognize, and between them a woman, a girl, swaddled in a silvery gray cloak pulled up high to cover her head, hints of gold ornamented red hair peeking through. The man struggled against him for a moment so he wrenched his arm hard until the man complied with the pain. The young warrior started forward again.

The old man said something sharply and the warrior reluctantly halted then screamed in frustration, his eyes never leaving Joth. The old man spoke again. "Put away your knife, Oestman. Let us speak."

Joth threw a quick look to the old man. "He'll kill me if I do."

The old man said another sharp word and the warrior let fall his sword and shield, but he kept still and staring at Joth. "Release him now, Oestman." This time it was the girl who spoke, and the world stopped.

The voice she spoke with was more beautiful and pure than anything he had ever heard before. He could hear mountains and streams, forests and fields of flowers, rivers strongly running, and birds singing, speaking words he understood, the very earth and all its creatures speaking to him and welcoming him. He was a son of the earth and the sky, they said; they were his parents and they all implored him through her voice to listen and to do as she said, and so he let the knife fall and released the man he held. He just wanted to hear her voice again, he just wanted to hear more of it. A word would be like heaven…

Suddenly, Joth realized the two warriors had slammed him to the ground. The shock of his teeth slamming together and the smell of the dirt clashed harshly with the beautiful reverie he had found himself in just a moment before. Joth was confused and unsure of where he was, who he was. He began to weep and he felt as though he would never understand anything again as purely as he had just moments before; he wept at the purity of the moment. The world had returned to him distorted and ugly, as it never had been before. He heard harsh voices and felt rough hands grab him by the hair and haul him to his knees. He blinked dumbly in the daylight and stared up into the faces of his captors. They regarded him as one might regard an animal. They will kill me next, Joth thought as he heard the sound of a blade clearing its scabbard.

"Go on then, make it quick." Joth sat up as tall as he could and waited as the cold blade touched his neck.

"Stand, Oestman." It was the old man speaking again. His sharp eyes cut left and right and Joth felt the blade press against his neck hard, but instead of drawing it over his throat the blade was simply taken away. Joth stood shakily.

He felt at his neck and his hand came away bloody, but it was just a superficial wound. He looked to the warriors behind him and the young one said something harsh and shoved him forward, stumbling.

The girl was looking at him calmly. He wanted her to speak to him.

"What did you do to me?" Joth muttered quizzically, "What do you want from us?"

The old man swung down from his horse spryly. He said something to the other mounted man who nodded and set about gathering the loose horses. "Wat—my friend is sorely wounded, please just let us go home."

"Yes. You will go home but your friend will stay with us."

"Please, let us both go. We are simple soldiers, we want no part of this!"

The old man just gazed at him evenly and made his way toward Wat's prone form. Joth looked behind him again and was buffeted on the head by the young warrior, who spat another harsh word at him. "Enough, my son. This boy is a threat no longer."

The young warrior said something in a respectful tone and inclined his head toward the old man. Whatever had been said, Joth could see that the old man was not pleased with the comment. He looked at the young man for a moment and then he turned his attention to Wat. He addressed Joth as he stood over Wat.

"We have your Lord Uhlmet. He will be staying with us as well. Does this trouble you?"

Joth blinked. "Lord Uhlmet was a bloody fool."

"Is a bloody fool. He's quite alive still."

Joth shrugged. He did not quite understand what he should say.

The old man pointed to the man on horseback who was leading the four loose horses back toward them now. "You very nearly escaped us. You chose your horses well."

Joth nodded. The girl was still staring at him.

"How did you find your way back to the pass?"

"We just kept going east."

"You know these lands? You have been here before?"

"No, never."

The old man seemed impressed somehow. He looked as though he regarded their capture with amusement. Joth was growing more and more confused.

"What are you called?" The old man asked.

"Joth."

"Joth what?"

"Andries. Joth Andries. I am a Line Leader."

"And this man is your Company Commander?"

"Wat. Yes, he was. Is, I suppose."

The old man smiled faintly. "That is why you sacrifice your chance at freedom?"

"He would do the same for me. We're friends."

The man nodded. Joth took it as a signal and looked behind him frantically, but the two warriors hadn't stirred at all. "Don't worry yourself, Joth Andries. Had we meant to kill you, you'd have been dead already."

He motioned Joth over to him. "Help to carry your friend. Let us bring him to some shelter now so that he may live."

"Will he live?"

"That depends upon many things."

The girl was still staring at him evenly. It was unnerving him.

"What did you do to me?" he muttered to her again. They all just watched him.

"You were sleeping, Oestman." She said in a calm voice. "I woke you."

Five

IT WAS LATE EVENING when Joth was brought under guard from a small wattle and daub hut to the large roundhouse in the tiny village. They had carried Wat on a stretcher put together with two spears and the warriors' shields up through the western hills to a settlement next to a raging mountain river. The savages had regarded him with fierce looks upon his arrival a few hours earlier, then at a word from the old man Joth was ushered into a hut lit by numerous small oil lamps and stripped naked by a group of chattering older women who slapped his hands away and hissed at him when he tried to resist them tearing at his jack lacings.

They cackled and howled with laughter at his modesty when they insistently peeled his dirty hosen off. One even went so far as to grab his manhood appraisingly and say something that sent the rest of the old hens into a cacophonous laughing fit that seemed to last for ages as they tumbled him into a wooden washtub and scrubbed him with rough cloths and rubbed his skin with salts scented with oils that gave off a strange perfume. It might have been pleasant had the water been a bit warmer and the women a bit gentler, but Joth came out of the tub feeling abused and violated, albeit cleaner than he had ever been in his life. He asked for his clothes back but he was only hissed at again and made to stand shivering in the corner until his captors came with a thickly napped linen a few ells long and dried him as roughly as they had cleaned him.

Then a linen shirt was pushed over his head, and he was cinched into slightly snug knee-length woolen trousers with a linen belt. Another woman appeared at the door and brought in a woolen tunic that was put on him and his costume was complete, or so Joth had hoped. He felt ridiculous, but the women chattered and looked on approvingly as though they were finally satisfied with him. His shoes were returned to him and his belt, though his belt knife had been removed. The shoes had been cleaned and the leather oiled. They smelled of walnuts now, Joth mused. He smelled like herbs. This is the way they smell, he thought. I smell like one of the bloody Dawn Tribe now. He had thought that the worst of his ordeal was over with until they started painfully combing out his hair and dressing it with more scented oil, as once again his protests and resistance were met with hissing and hand slapping. The combing and the pulling of hair continued until every stroke was met with no discomfort, and then and only then were his tormentors satisfied and he left standing alone in the hut without a word by his attendants. He had waited there for what seemed like forever and nodded off until prodded roughly with the butt of a spear and made to walk to the Roundhouse in front of the two warriors who served as his guards.

When he made it through the door his guards followed him and stood on either side of him, grasped him firmly by the elbows, halting him there. He smelled food and his mouth began to water. Inside, the room was lit by rushlight. A large fire roared on a raised hearth in the center. The smoke escaped through a hole in the roof above. The great conical thatched roof was green on the inside and black near the hole in the center from the constant smoke traveling past. Joth could see stars in the night sky through the smoke. Beautifully carved beams and posts formed the structure that the roof hung upon and the interior was made bright by lime washed wattle and daub walls that filled the spaces in between the posts and formed a smooth circle broken only by the door through which he had come. Seated on woven rugs placed over the packed earth floor before a long low table was the entire population of the village as well as the old man and his company from the pass.

She was there too, sat among his tormentors from before, who chattered and giggled when he appeared. There were earthenware bowls set before them and they drank from short cups of wood and horn. The old man motioned him forward.

"Joth Andries, you look better than the last time we met." There was mirth in his voice. "Come sit and we will speak together for a time."

His guards moved him to a place at the table across from the old man and bid him sit down, which he did. A woman stood from the table and went to the fire where something in a cauldron sat warming. "Your friend is safe and he is being tended to." A short horn cup was set before him and a small bowl full of a dark broth, some mussel shells and vegetables peeking through the surface.

"Where is he?" Joth did not see Wat in the Roundhouse.

"He is safe and well and nearby. Please, eat."

The woman came again and put a basket filled with small round loaves of bread on the table. This was too much for Joth to resist, and so he did as the old man asked him. His hunger was such that he very nearly inhaled his meal, and although the food was flavored strangely to his palate, he found it quite delicious and satisfying. Without asking, another bowl was set before him and he finished it as well, digging out the mussels and bits of crayfish, leaving only shells and some chewy bits of what he guessed were some sort of wild leeks that flavored the broth. The bread was dense and dark and full of seeds and nuts. His horn cup was filled with light crisp mead. Had he not been surrounded by his enemies and dressed in their outlandish garb he might almost feel at home, he thought.

He had not had any alcohol for weeks and the two cups of mead he drank went straight to his head, but his cup was filled every time he drained it. After the third cup he decided that it might be foolish to drink any more until he found out what was going to happen to Wat and himself, and whether or not he might convince the old man to let them both leave together once and for all. When the serving woman came again with the mead he put his hand over the top of the horn cup and shook his head. One of the old hens said something then and the whole table erupted with laughter. Even the girl and the old man laughed, and Joth felt his face redden and his ears burn. It was the young warrior who spoke first and broke the laughter, saying something slowly and insistently that Joth of course did not understand, but he could see the sobering effect of the youth's words on the assembly. The old man smiled and nodded.

"My son is right, even if he is impatient." The old man inclined his head at the boy, and Joth saw the youth's pride melt away for a moment. Somehow he had embarrassed himself or his father by his words, but Joth could only read into it on the surface without a grasp of the language. The old man let the moment hang there, the smile never faded from his lips.

"I am called Traegern," he said to Joth. "I am the Elder of the People. I speak for all."

The entire assembly muttered something in unison, as though they acknowledged his claim. Did they all speak Oestersh? Joth felt more and more confused. The girl kept staring at him.

"The People have long kept to their lands, leaving the Oestmen to their cities, and existing together in peace; or at least as peacefully as the times have allowed." Traegern's voice was rich and easy to listen to, Joth mused; perhaps he had already had too much of the savages' mead.

"We allow the Oestmen to pass into our lands in good faith that they uphold the ancient agreement between our peoples, and honor the treaty of our mutual ancestors."

Joth had no idea what the old man was talking about. Mutual ancestors? He knew of no treaty or agreement, just the famous victory of Ulno Rhael, the man who drove the savages over the mountains. He was growing more perplexed by the moment, but he listened as Traegern continued to speak.

"Now I am an old man, but in my youth the Oestern mages would come to speak with the Elders of the People and they would share knowledge in this way, over a table with gifts of food and laughter. These days are different from those since the Magistry became the power in Oesteria. These are dark days for the People."

He drank from his horn cup and held it out to be filled as he spoke, but even that gesture was not unkind. He commanded but he did so without lording his power.

"At first, the soldiers were few. They came and went without incident. We the People decided it was best not to war with the soldiers, because that would break the words spoken by our ancestors. Now the mages come and demand from us instead of asking. Now they have become greedy for our gold and our knowledge. Now they spill the blood of our children."

Joth felt the room staring at him. The stillness of the place was palpable. "So now we send a message to the High Mage. He must remember the words spoken and honor them, or we shall call down the mountains upon him and his kind."

Joth saw the assembled people nodding and heard them all mutter their agreement, or at least it seemed that was what they were saying. He was still unclear as to what would happen to him and to Wat.

"You want me to be the messenger?" Joth asked tentatively.

Traegern smiled ruefully. "We cannot trust to words alone, Joth Andries. The mages need to be shown. We need to be certain that they will know the truth of things. Only by their knowing the truth can we trust in what they will say." He was looking at the girl now. "My daughter Eilyth will go. You will escort her there and bring her back safely."

Joth just stared at the assembly in disbelief. Eilyth nodded once at him, her red hair chiming with gold. Immediately he heard a disgruntled response from behind him, the voice he recognized as belonging to the young warrior who bore him such a fierce hatred. Traegern shook his head and said a word in response and the young warrior turned and left the assembly, the door of the roundhouse slamming shut behind him.

Joth was flummoxed. "I am just a simple man, I don't think that the High Mage will grant me an audience. I have never even been to Twinton. I only know Immerdale, I was garrisoned there."

It was Eilyth who spoke. "The mage will grant you audience, Joth Andries. This I know."

Traegern looked on and nodded as if he knew it too. "They can not refuse our envoy. You need only escort Eilyth to the High Mage's city and keep her safe. Your Lord Uhlmet and your friend Wat shall be held as assurances." Joth cared not a whim for the safety of Lord Imperator Uhlmet, but he would save Wat's life if he could.

She was staring at him in that unnerving way that she had, as if she were willing him to do her bidding. He felt as though he had to accept even though he felt out of his depth. But Joth was not one to simply give in, however, so he said, "I only ask that I see my commander, my friend, Wat. I need to speak with him before I can say anything one way or the other. I need to know that he is safe."

The old man looked at him intently. "You will do this Oestman. You have no choice in the matter. Your conduct and the well-being of my daughter shall determine whether or not you see your friend again."

Joth knew that he had no room to bargain. Here he was, lost beyond his land's borders and at the mercy of his captors; yet they offered him a way home, a chance at life. He should have been dead by now. He held out his horn cup and allowed it to be filled again, and then drained it in one go. Summoning his resolve he said, "I will conduct the Lady Eilyth to Twinton and seek the High Mage, and I will bring her back safely. On this you have my word, and I shall let no harm befall her. I swear this on my life and the life of my friend, Wat."

A look passed between he and Traegern and Eilyth, and Joth felt as though his words were being weighed. The old man studied him for a beat that seemed to last an eternity. Finally he spoke.

"Very well then, it is settled." Traegern raised his hands and said something in his own tongue and the assembly repeated his words in unison. When the elder lowered his hands more food was brought forth and the villagers all fell to chattering among themselves and eating, seemingly paying him no mind.

Joth tried to eat more, but his mind was reeling and his belly was full. His mead cup was filled twice more, but he left the last cup half full and stood from the rug where he had been kneeling. The room was spinning a bit, Joth thought. The mead had gone straight to his head and the fatigue of being harried for the past few days seemed to hit him like a thunderbolt once he was on his feet again.

The villagers showed no signs of slowing as several of them produced musical instruments and fell to playing among themselves. Here and there a few joined in singing, and soon the atmosphere inside the roundhouse had changed from festive to raucous. Traegern met his eyes.

"You wish to sleep now, Oestman?" he said over the din. At Joth's nod he said something to the man who had escorted him in who grabbed Joth by the elbow and led him back to the wattle and daub hut he had been held in earlier. The man led him to the door but then suddenly Joth was pushed up against the low wall, an elbow at his throat pinning him against the coarse thatch. Joth could barely breathe.

"Harm one hair on her head, Oestman, and I shall end you." The young warrior spoke haltingly, the Oestersh words awkward on his tongue. "One hair…remember."

He held him there a beat longer then shoved him roughly through the door and slammed it behind him. Joth heard them speaking to each other in their strange language outside his door as he picked himself up and got his wind back, rubbing his sore neck. The talking died away, but Joth could feel the presence of the guards outside and he knew that his captors would stand at his door all night and leave nothing to chance. Not that he was planning an escape; he had sworn to bring the strange girl to Twinton, and he was not going to abandon Wat to the savages just to save his own skin. He was confused still. The girl was some sort of witch, she had tricked him into dropping his knife somehow.

No, he thought, she showed me something and it changed me inside. Was that a trick? Magic? He had felt as though he understood everything for the first time in his life, his place in the world, his purpose. Then as quickly as it had been revealed, it was gone and all he was left with was confusion and a longing to know it once again. His throat was still throbbing as he settled down with his back against the wall of the hut and found a blanket to cover himself with hanging from a peg on one of the posts. She must be a witch, he thought again as he closed his eyes and listened to the noises of the night around him. Surely only a witch could have gotten inside his head like that, but as Joth drifted off to sleep he found himself thinking of how sweet the world had seemed when she spoke to him, and how much he wanted to look into her eyes and hear her speak to him again. He wanted to listen forever.

Six

JOTH SPENT THE NEXT week at the village by the river. Apart
from the young warrior the other villagers seemed to have
accepted him as one of their own, going so far as to involve
him in daily chores and welcoming him each night to evening
meals in the Roundhouse. Most of them were friendly toward
him, the biggest barrier being language. He learned that most
of the People understood Oestersh, if not speaking it outright.
Some of them knew it but simply refused to speak it. It was
something that had to do with these ancient oaths and mutual
ancestors that Traegern alluded to that first night when Joth
was brought before the assembly. In the time that Joth spent
with the People his opinion of them had changed. He no
longer regarded them as savages. Before he had thought them
all primitives, but he now looked at them in a different light.
They lived simply, that much was true; but he found himself
appreciating the peace and practicality of the daily lives they
led. They were entirely self-sufficient, living off of the land in a
way that was very close to nature.

In fact, they reveled in the glory of nature, and honored
the natural order of things in every thing they did. What they
took from the land for sustenance, they gave back to it in kind.

They cared for their animals in a nurturing way and they only culled their herds when it was absolutely necessary. Their diet was comprised mostly of field greens and the bounty of their nets and weirs at the river. Life was sacred to them and they celebrated it in their day-to-day dealings with the land. It was foreign and familiar to Joth at the same time. He saw Eilyth only once during that week, in the evening of the third day. Joth noticed that she did not stay in the village with the others, and that the other villagers regarded her with great respect despite her young age. When she would ride down from the hills on her gray mare they would stop their tasks and go to greet her and walk alongside her. Always they would bring her gifts of food and drink and vie for her attention in respectful tones, and she would treat them patiently. She was beautiful and strange, both young and old, and Joth realized that he feared her.

He felt as though she had seen inside his heart and knew every wicked thing he had ever done, every evil thing he had ever thought of. If she were a witch, she was not like the witches in the tales his mother had told him. Her teeth were not filed into points, she carried no hazel wand, her fingers were not dirty and crooked; but Joth was afraid of her because he felt power in her, and her power was mysterious and dangerous to him. It unnerved him even more when she would catch his eyes and regard him with a slight smile as these very thoughts were firing in his head, as if she knew what he thought before he was thinking it. Joth would always look away. It was too much to have her looking into his eyes that way, he felt as though at any moment she could speak one word and he would be dancing to her tune no matter how he resisted. She would use that voice again. I would lose control of myself, he thought. She would be playing me like a harp and I'd be none the wiser for it. That scared him most of all, the thought of her saying a word and making him kill the High Mage without a second thought. Was that Traegern's plan, an elaborate assassination attempt using him as the tool to avenge the People and their suffering at the hands of Uhlmet and the Magistry?

You're a bloody fool, Joth, he thought. That plan made no sense even to him; he was no one special. Why would they send him in to Twinton with the girl if they meant to do that? Surely she could have bewitched him from the start and sent him in alone without ever putting herself at risk. Yet perhaps her power was limited; perhaps she needed to be nearby to exert her control over him, the way players hid beneath the stage and worked their puppets…

He was thinking all of these thoughts as he was helping the villagers haul their nets in, catching the fish that flopped on the banks, depositing them in the great wicker basket in the handcart they used to bring the catch to the Roundhouse. Joth would help clean the fish, and afterward he would transfer all the garbage into another basket that would then be dumped into a large compost heap at the edge of the village. They used the heap to fertilize their planting beds and their fields. Then he would go and wash himself in the hut that housed the washtub and wave off the old hens that would try to offer him help and shriek with laughter at his embarrassment. He was closing his hands around a wiggling brown trout when the hairs on the back of his neck stood on end. He knew that she was there watching him before he turned around. As he stood and saw her, the fish slipped from his grasp and flopped into the river with a splash. Eilyth said something that elicited laughter from the other men and Joth felt his face redden. Then she addressed him.

"We leave on the morrow, Joth Andries. My father has allowed that you see your friend for a time tonight."

Joth nodded.

"They will finish your work. I will take you to him now."

The villagers all bid them farewell as she walked away and Joth followed a few paces behind. As they climbed a low sloping hill along the trail that had been worn by feet and by handcart, she spoke again to him without turning.

"You may walk beside me. You need not fear me."

Joth felt his pulse quicken. He made a muffled reply and hurried his pace. They walked side by side into the village in silence, Eilyth leading him to the one hut he had not been given freedom to visit. She smiled and motioned with her head for him to enter.

"Thank you," he said, and he pushed through the door.

Wat was sitting up on a pile of furs on a low pallet with his back resting against a post at the back of the hut, his torso swathed in bandages. His pallor was still a bit gray, but Joth could see immediately that his comrade was on the mend.

His paranoia broke and gave way to relief at seeing Wat alive, and for the most part, well.

"Joth, it's about bloody time."

"Happy to see you, Wat. They treat you all right?"

"Their women are a bit rough, but I always liked that anyhow."

Joth smiled. He took his friend's hand. "I'm glad you pulled through."

Wat wrinkled his nose. "You reek of fish."

They spoke at length about the events of the days before, about the standoff in the pass and about the quest that Joth had agreed to undertake in exchange for Wat's life. Wat nodded gravely.

"Not that you had much of a say in it, but for what it's worth, I thank you for not just leaving me there."

"Never was a question in my mind."

"Course not, Joth, you're a bloody idiot."

They laughed tersely, briefly.

"I am afraid of her, Wat. I can't get my head around it."

He nodded. "Be wary, but to be honest, Joth, these people have something in them I never saw before."

"You mean about the way they treated us?"

"I mean they have honor. Real honor to them."

He was right. Joth had always been taught that the Dawn Tribe were savages who lacked any sense of honor and who would lie at every turn to press an advantage, but his experience was completely contrary to that. It was confusing him more with each passing day.

"Yes, but what if we are wrong?"

"About being wrong?" Wat raised one eyebrow.

"I don't know, Wat. I don't know what to think."

"Stop thinking, Joth. You're not very bloody good at it anyway."

Wat's humor was good to encounter but it rang hollow in Joth's ears. He nodded. "I don't know how I'm supposed to get an audience with the High Mage. Can't get my head around that one either. I'll probably be locked in a box as soon as we get to Immerdale, then what?"

Wat shook his head once. "Don't go to Immerdale. Go straight to Twinton."

"Seriously? What about the company? Protocol?"

"Glorious Lord Uhlmet already stuck that pig, my lad. You go to Borsford and catch a bloody airship to Twinton and report to the Magistry."

"Airship? How am I supposed to pay for that?"

Wat looked at him long and hard. "You ask the old man for a quill and some parchment for me. Lord bloody Uhlmet is going to pay for it, or at least that's what it'll look like."

Joth spoke with Wat until one of the village women came into the hut and ran him out, chattering away as she did.

Once outside the hut he found that night was falling so he hurried to the washtub and began the daily ritual of bathing he had become accustomed to. The People kept themselves very clean and bathed often, a strange custom by Oestern standards. The Oestermen washed their faces and hands daily, but most common folk only bathed fully perhaps once every season, and rarely in winter. Now that Joth had begun to bathe everyday he looked forward to his evening bath. At first it had seemed an extreme idea to him, unnecessary. The old hens had insisted that he do it, though. After wagging their fingers and scolding him on the second day, Joth had realized that he would know no peace until he had reported to the washtub every evening as the sun fell.

After he had emerged clean and fresh and smelling of herbs he made his way to the roundhouse by the light of a beautifully full, rising moon. As he stopped to gaze up at the shimmering sky and the pale stars that shone above him, he realized that he did not want to leave the village. He had begun to feel at home here; it had warmth and a familiarity that he had grown to love. Bloody fool, Joth, he thought, you've only been here a week, and as a prisoner no less. Still he could not deny that he felt at home there, that he would be a happy man if his life was a routine of fish weirs and compost heaps, washtubs and evening meals. It was simple and it was easy, this kind of life; it was, to Joth, how a life should be. The language was a difficulty; he had learned a few words, but not being able to express himself and or be understood was frustrating. I could learn their tongue over time, I am sure of it, he thought. He was an outsider though, and in many regards he might always be. He had spent his years growing up in Oesteria and he was an Oesterman; nothing would ever change that. But Joth realized for the first time that he was looking through a window into another world that he had never known before. Yet he had discounted it without realizing that its simplicity and its alien qualities held many wondrous treasures, and in appreciating this view as it stood before him then and there beneath the moon, he wondered how many other worlds were out there to explore and enjoy; how many opportunities were there for him to find in the world? It was a little overwhelming for him under the night sky just then, that shrinking feeling that he had. He was suddenly very small and full of wonder at what possibilities existed over all the lands and days and nights of the world. As his belly rumbled he broke from his reverie, his hunger affirming that he was but an animal and subject to all the laws of nature and sustenance, so he made his way to the Roundhouse for what he knew would be his last evening meal in the village. The village by the river would be left behind him in the morning, and he hoped that he might one day see it again, but he had his doubts.

Joth ignored his hunger and took in the night sky for a longer moment, soaking in as much of its peace as he could. He hoped that some of that peace would shadow him in the coming weeks, or at least as far as Twinton.

Seven

IT WAS DAWN WHEN they rode out of the village. Eilyth
said some words and the People repeated them, then she
kissed her father and her brother and mounted her gray mare
swaddled in her silvery cloak. Traegern clasped Joth on the
shoulder once and bid him a safe journey. Joth was given the
horse he had stolen for Wat to ride, and the dish-faced bay
he ponied behind him as a packhorse. The villagers had laden
the horse with bedding and food for their journey as well as
a small bronze cooking pot and a waxed linen tarpaulin that
could be used as a shelter. Joth was given back his helm and
soldier's gear as well, tied up in a bundle on the packsaddle.
The notion of wearing his soldier clothes seemed strange to
him after being accustomed to the comfortable and practical
dress of the People. It was strange that the week he had spent
in the village seemed like a lifetime to him, especially now that
he was leaving it behind.

Many of the villagers embraced him and looked sad to see
him go. Joth found himself moved by their displays of friendship,
especially when one of the old hens bid him a tearful farewell.
The young warrior, Traegern's son and Eilyth's brother, whom
he had learned was called Eilorn, only acknowledged him with

a hard stare and an almost imperceptible nod that said less of "farewell" and more of "watch yourself." But Joth nodded back anyhow and he told Traegern that he would keep his word and conduct his daughter to Twinton as he had said he would: safely. He let Eilorn stare his daggers and mounted his horse. Traegern went to Eilyth and put his hand on her knee and said a word, handing her his staff. She smiled at him kindly and lay it across her lap and set her horse into a traveling pace out of the village, Joth following. When he caught up to her he saw tears on her face and suddenly she seemed very young and frail to him, like his own sister.

"Are you all right, lady?"

She did not look at him. "I do not like farewells."

They rode in silence and made the pass by mid-morning. The sky was overcast, and Eilyth and her mount almost seemed to blend into the horizon except for the red shock of hair and her golden ornaments. She rode easily and spoke to her horse often, sometimes chiding the mare if she took a misstep, petting her neck and soothing her like a child. Joth had never seen anyone treat a horse in such a way, and he suspected that Eilyth spent more time with her horse than she did with people. She called out to him once to point at a flock of birds flying overhead in the same direction as they were going.

"Look! A good sign for us," she said. She seemed very happy to have seen it.

Joth nodded, but he did not trust in such things.

They traveled through the pass and cleared it with a few hours left in the day. The low rolling hills were somehow different on this side, as though the land itself had defined where the border lay between Osteria and the People. Somehow it seemed less wild here, less alive. When he stopped and looked back at Eilyth she seemed to be thinking the same thing, but her face bore a look of concern as she regarded it.

"Is all of your land like this?"

"No, lady," he said. "But there aren't as many mountains as there are in your lands."

"I mean how it feels."

"Lady?"

She smiled resignedly. "The horses are thirsty, let us find a place to water them and stop our travels for the day."

Joth nodded. His thoughts were jumbled and his heart was confused. Ever since she got into my head, he thought, ever since I was bewitched. It was part of his being now, a kind of extra sensory awareness that was just beyond his reach; it was palpable and real, yet elusive. It left him bewildered and feeling small, unsure of whether or not he had a grasp on his own sanity. To make matters worse, Eilyth seemed to know he was confused. She was always regarding him like some wounded animal. He would find her staring at him in that way she had, hairs on the back of his neck standing up, and it was always Joth who looked away first. Somehow he could not bring himself to ask her about it, but he knew that she had the answer to his dilemna.

He kicked his horse up a bit and rode ahead of the strange girl on the gray horse. His uneasiness did not abate, but he felt a little better having her behind him where he was not catching her eyes every five minutes. Joth continued on over the rolling hills for another few miles until they found a small stream where they could water the horses. The sun was sinking low in the sky, and amidst the low hills Joth hobbled the horses and made camp.

Eilyth filled the cook pot with water from the stream and set it on some coals she had separated from the fire and with a small knife she cut some root vegetables and added them to the simmering water. She produced some dried blackish green leaves and added them to the pot as Joth sat down and unrolled his bedding near the small fire.

"This grows in the sea," she answered his unspoken question. "It is very nutritious."

Joth felt like if he nodded any more his head might fall from his neck. He studied the thongs in his shoes instead as though they needed replacing. The People had replaced them a week before. Eilyth sang softly to herself as she stirred the soup and covered the small cooking pot, then got up and went to see to her mare in the fading light. Joth watched her go and cursed under his breath.

He had no idea how he was supposed to get through the journey. The girl was a beauty and pleasant as a summer's day or a fine spring rain, but how she unnerved him. She carried herself with a natural grace born of her station, for she was the equivalent of an Oestern lady at the very least, probably higher born in the eyes of her people; even though Joth had learned that the People held not to titles and pomp like the Oestern people did, her father was greatly revered and respected, and that respect transferred to his children as well. Eilorn, her brother, was young yet held in utmost esteem by the People as a warrior and a leader. Eilorn bore him no love, that much was obvious to Joth, yet Traegern had treated him well, going so far as to compliment him and clasping him on the shoulder like a friend. The more he thought on it, the worse it became for young Joth Andries; he was more confused than he had been that first day with Dierna by the salmon weirs, struggling to come to grips with the aftermath of their spent passions and the consequences he knew would befall him sooner or later, despite his denial of the inevitability of it all. Suddenly and uncharacteristically, Joth buried his head in his hands and began to weep. He wept for the poor lad that he and Wat hanged in the ash grove, for the horrors of battle that he had witnessed. He wept for Dierna and his father and his shame, for his mother and his sister. More than anything else Joth wept for his fear and for his ignorance. He did not know how long he wept, but he could not stop when he became aware of Eilyth standing nearby quietly watching him.

He wiped at his eyes and choked back his sobs, but he could not stop no matter how hard he tried.

"Forgive me, lady." He sounded like a broken-throated boy.

Eilyth spoke to him in soft tones in her own tongue, and Joth felt like she was speaking to him in the same way that she used to soothe her mare when it stumbled. Her words were sweet to his ears, but he was suddenly and superbly aware of the insurmountable barrier of language between them.

"I don't understand," he wept. "I'm sorry but I can't understand!" It was all he could seem to croak out.

Then she was pressing a hot bowl into his hands and stroking his hair, her voice like music. It calmed him, but it was not like the voice she had used in the pass; it was her kindness that pacified him and slowed his grief. She was touching his hair and speaking to him like a mother to a son, and at last his tears stopped and he noticed that the fire was dying and the soup had gone lukewarm in his hands.

She looked at him and smiled, and Joth found himself smiling back at her through his glistening eyes. She put her hands around his and lifted the bowl to his lips and he drank in the broth and thought that it tasted strange, like the oceans he had never laid eyes upon must taste. Eilyth produced some cold flat bread from a leathern bag and handed him a loaf and he hungrily sopped up the rest of the broth. Then she shared with him a skin full of good mead like that he had grown a fondness for in the village. When he took another long pull on the skin of mead Eilyth warned him that it was the last they would taste of her homeland for a time, and Joth handed it back to her feeling admonished. He knew better than to think that mead could wash away his shame. She put more of the wood Joth had gathered earlier on the smoldering coals and then sat beneath the tarpaulin Joth had set up for her to shelter in, cross-legged on her bedding.

"Sleep well, Joth Andries. Let your worries be no more."

With that she closed the flap to her tent and left him to the night sky.

"Thank you, lady," he said softly, as much to the night as to Eilyth.

He listened to her stir in her bedding and settle before he too drifted off to sleep. He awoke in the predawn, dew faced with his breath frosting. The morning was cold and he arose stiff legged and yawning. The fire was a smoldering pile of ash that glowed patchily with red every time the wind tore through the shallow valley between the low hills where they had made camp. Joth walked past the waxed linen tent where Eilyth lay sleeping within and made his way to gather the horses. He carried with him a canvas feed bag with some sweet oats to lure them in, but the hobbled horses had not wandered very far and he caught them quite easily. Their legs and backs were wet with dew and they whinnied to him as he approached. They know me now, he thought. He untied the hobbles and led them back to the camp in time to see Eilyth emerging from the tent wrapping her silvery cloak about her. Joth was surprised to feel unashamed by his outburst the previous evening when their eyes met and she acknowledged him with a kind smile. It seemed to him that somehow he felt lighter in that moment, as though the shedding of his shame through the tears had left him cleansed and refreshed in a way that he had not known for a long while. Eilyth took up her father's staff, regarding him with her stern yet compassionate gaze.

"The night has left you feeling better?"

"Yes, lady." She was still unnerving to him, no matter how hard he tried.

She gave a satisfied nod.

Joth broke the camp and loaded everything back onto the packsaddle while the dish-faced gelding tossed his head impatiently and Eilyth chattered to her horse and fussed with its headstall. The People had packed everything so efficiently that Joth had a difficult time mimicking the job. He thought his arrangement seemed a bit lopsided after the first attempt, so he set about refolding the canvas tarpaulin and cinching it back down again as Eilyth spoke to the pack horse and calmed its jitteriness.

"What's his problem this morning?" Joth asked offhandedly.

"He is a warrior's horse. He does not like this job."

She spoke a few more words to the dish-faced bay and trained his mane to lie uniformly on the right side. The gelding had stopped his head tossing and was now gently nuzzling against her. A warrior's horse, and he had stolen it. How many of the People wished him dead beside her brother, he wondered?

"Does this warrior wish to have his horse back? Does he wish me ill?" Joth asked as the horse regarded him with his one odd pale eye.

"Yes," she said, flashing one of her strange smiles. "You know him, my brother Eilorn."

Many things began to make sense to Joth at that moment.

"Understand also that we are the same, my twin and I."

"Twin?"

"Yes, and a sister besides. There are three of us. Twins, yet different in many ways. I believe in peace, and my brother has chosen the way of war. "

Joth did not know how to respond, so he said nothing. Was this why Traegern had complimented him on his choice of mounts? Perhaps the old man saw the irony in the situation and had chosen to highlight it for that reason. Perhaps he had never meant it as a compliment in the first place and had rather said it to accent his own son's ire. He knew less and less the more he thought on it. She regarded him evenly as he self-consciously gathered the gelding's lead in his hands.

"We take the color of horses as having meaning; the shapes of them, their faces. I don't hate you, Joth Andries."

There she was, reading his thoughts again. He could only nod with what he thought must be a stupid expression on his face. "What of your sister, what path has she chosen?" he finally managed to say.

Eilyth pursed her lips thoughtfully. Joth thought he saw a smile flit across her face. "Her path is her own."

She mounted her gray mare and laid the staff across her lap. She spoke a word to the mare and together they set off toward the east and the rising sun.

Joth stood dumbly for a moment, and then mounted the white gelding and followed, ponying the bay behind him. He muttered a curse to himself under his breath and thought that his fortune had taken a horrid turn as he kicked his mount up and matched pace with Eilyth.

They made their way through the rolling hills over the next few days, camping near the streams that flowed down from the mountains to the west, the mountains that marked the border between their respective lands. After two days, as they sat near a fire and ate the broth that Eilyth prepared every evening with their bread, Joth asked Eilyth what she had meant regarding the colors of horses.

"White is the color of peace. Bay is the color of a war horse, because brown is the color of the earth and it is for the earth that we as a people engage in war."

"When I stole the white horse and the bay horse, what did that mean?"

"That you saved your life, and the life of your friend. You chose wisely, as my father said."

And so the People had thought he was sending them a message of peace because he had stolen a white horse and placed a wounded man on the back of a bay. "Lady," he said, "Eilyth. Listen to me, I didn't choose the colors of those horses because I knew anything. I just picked the best two I could find in a hurry." He passed the wineskin back to her. "I'm not wise."

She said something in her own tongue and laughed to herself. "Silly Joth. Wisdom does not choose sides. It simply is."

He shook his head obstinately. "I'm a simple man. I don't understand this, and I feel like I'm out of my depth here with you."

Eilyth smiled at him. "You are indeed, Oestman."

All he could do was go red and look at his hands. "I mean to say that I don't understand. Anything."

"That is the first step to understanding." She stood and moved to her tent. "I shook you, and now you become awake."

"What of your horse?"

She smiled again and threw open the flap to her tent. "Aila? She is gray, and gray is the color of wisdom."

Joth was left staring at the coals and contemplating her words. She shook him, she said. Yes, she had shaken him, in his heart and soul she had shaken him and his understanding of the world and who he was. It was a long time that he lay thinking before sleep overtook him.

After the fifth day they came upon the Magister's Road. The sky was clouded over and the air was misty cool and their breath and the breath of their horses frosted as they stopped and took in the way before them. It was a touchstone of familiarity for Joth to see the cobbled and raised road, wide and gray, cutting a swath through the green and yellow of the low hills that stretched on for as far as the eye could see. It was broad enough for four wagons to travel abreast upon. After weeks of traveling game trails and dirt tracks through the mountains and hills the road seemed incongruous and unnatural to the landscape, even for Joth.

Eilyth regarded it with wonder. "They made this?" She asked, amazement in her voice.

"Yes, lady."

"How many worked upon this?" She studied it with narrowed eyes.

"I know not. Many, I'll wager."

"It stretches to the cities?"

"Yes, to several of them." Joth wondered what Eilyth would think about the inns and small villages that had grown up around the road as they made their way deeper into Oesteria, what her idea of a city even was.

She shook her head for a long moment and sat her horse. Finally she spoke. "Which direction will we take now?"

"We shall go this way," he said as he pointed. "North by northeast. To Borsford."

He had never been to Borsford, but Wat had told him the way. Wat had written down orders for him as he had said he would, stamped it with his signet ring, and made it look very official, even wording it as though the orders had come from Lord

Uhlmet. On a separate scrap of parchment he had drawn a rough map from the Magister's road to Borsford. Wat had been to both Borsford and Twinton. He used to work as a courier in his youth before he became a soldier. Joth had never seen a city outside of Immerdale or Trieston, where he was raised, but that was hardly a city, more like a hamlet; and Immerdale was just a fortress with a town sprung up around it, nothing like the big cities of the east, like Twinton. Now he was meant to take the girl to the airship harbor and to travel like a lord and seek audience with the High Mage. How fortune had spun her wheel, Joth thought ruefully; hopefully they would not hang him for desertion in Twinton, but perhaps Wat's orders would save his skin.

Eilyth was looking at the stones as if they were somehow animated, as though the road itself might leap into action at any given moment and attack. "The horses won't like it," she said. "Let us ride alongside of it."

Joth nodded. The way he looked at it the horses did not have a say in things, but it was better to listen to the lady and to do as she wished. She had queer notions about horses, but she knew them well. Joth was wise enough to know that much at least.

They rode along beside the Magister's Road for two days and camped near the water that they found there. After the first day Eilyth stopped regarding the road as though it might rear up and grow teeth to bite her, and they ventured onto its cobbled stones for a few miles, their horses stepping cautiously at first before they became used to the sound of their own hooves on the smoothly paved road.

The iron shoes rang out boldly in the quiet stillness, and a great flock of birds took flight from a copse of trees in the distance ahead of them. The People kept their horses shod, at least, Joth had noted. He had grown used to riding now without stirrups, as strange as it had seemed to him at first. He still preferred stirrups, but it was not completely uncomfortable to ride without them once one grew accustomed to it. At first he had relied on using his legs too much and they had become cramped and sore, but after a few days of traveling he had learned to relax and this had made a world of difference.

Eilyth rode along the paved way for a while and then moved off back to the low trail beside the road, saying that her mare was not used to the stones. "I shall teach her a little each day and she will know it better."

"As you like, lady." Joth stayed on the road for a while longer but then moved off when he understood that she had meant that incremental teaching for all of the horses they had brought over from the land of the People.

She smiled at him then and said, "You learn a little each day too, it seems."

Joth felt his face go red when she laughed at her own jest, but then he was laughing too and he realized that Eilyth was only having a go at him. It was hard to fear her when she was lighthearted with him. It was hard for him not to stare at her and regard her with wonder at the same time. She did frighten him, but not because of who she was. He was more afraid of what she was and the mysteries of her powers and his ignorance of them, his ignorance of everything about her that he did not have the power to understand. She made him feel ignorant, brutish, and ugly, because she was the opposite of all of those comparisons he had imposed between her and himself.

Once they had left the border hills, the undulating landscape grew more and more even and flat. They saw no travelers on their journey and Joth felt very much alone and isolated, and he asked Eilyth if she felt the same.

"I never feel alone. Even when I am alone, I'm never alone," she replied.

Joth nodded again for what must have been the thousandth time.

"You nod, Joth, but you don't understand."

Joth sighed heavily. He was becoming weary of feeling like he was being lectured every time he opened his stupid mouth. He could say that the sky were blue and he would catch an earful of the varying shades of blue that the sky could appear to her, all of them different than his own.

"I was only saying that it feels lonely out here, that's all. I was just trying to make some pleasant conversation, I suppose." He did not mean it to sound petulant but it did.

"You grow impatient with me." She smiled. "Everything is alive around you, everything is talking to you. How can you think that you are alone anywhere there is life growing?"

Joth knew that she was right; their horses had personalities like people, he knew that. There were birds and plants and trees and there were the two of them, himself and Eilyth, to share ideas and conversation; but Joth was used to living in a community of people, moving in groups, and working in routines of daily regularity. He was used to seeing the same faces everyday at mess, used to his habits and theirs; it gave him a sense of comfort and security. He was not like Eilyth and her people, as much as he could appreciate them now that he had lived among them. He was an Oesterman, and that was who he was, that was all that he was. He said as much to Eilyth. She only laughed at him and shook her head.

"You are one of the People now—as you always have been, Joth Andries. The 'life' that you speak of is a lie. Your old life is gone."

Joth could only stare as she stepped her horse out ahead of him.

Eight

RHAEL UHLMET WAS ALONE in the dark, naked and cold
and covered in his own filth. His elbows were bloody
and sore, and they were the only things keeping him from
plummeting deeper into the chasm that the dirty savages had
tossed him weeks ago, or what he supposed may have been
weeks ago. He actually had no idea if it were day or night or for
how long he had been suffering in this horrid pit the old cruel
savage had sentenced him to linger. Half crazed, half starved,
he had screamed and screamed until his voice failed him.

Then finally after what seemed to have been seasons passing, a round loaf and a gourd filled with water were lowered
down to him on a string to where he lay straining and bracing
his raw hands and feet against the chasm walls. They had kicked
him head first into the rocky hole after dragging him on his
spent limbs from the Roundhouse. He had bounced against the
rough walls, scrambling for handholds or footholds, any way
to arrest his momentum as he plunged down and down into
the pitch black abyss. The chasm seemed to narrow and twist
in such a way that every sharp edge and jagged outcrop would
find his soft tissue and send him rebounding and hurtling
toward the next hard unyielding surface. His hands were torn

to shreds and his head was throbbing and bleeding. He had spent the longest stint of his time in the chasm wedged into the narrow choking passage upside down, his knees and shins pressing his back against the opposing wall, hanging there like some kind of misbegotten animal. Like an animal he had covered himself with his own urine and feces from his topsy-turvy positioning in a most disgusting manner. The loaves and gourds on strings had come irregularly, and never seemed to be enough to satisfy his needs. His thirst was such that he had even attempted to drink his own urine as it streamed past his chin, but it only made him retch.

When his legs finally went slack and he tumbled further down the shaft, he managed to cover his already filthy, wounded body with whatever vomit had managed to cling to the rough walls of his dark hellish prison. His arms had trembled and shook and at last given out on him. Again he tumbled concussively down through the shaft until at last he bounced and rebounded to a stop in the inky darkness. A low, almost inaudible moan escaped his split lips. One eye blinked unavailingly in the black, the other swollen shut beneath a bleeding goose egg protruding from his once proud brow. Mage Imperator Rhael Lord Uhlmet puked and gagged on the stony floor of the cavern, unable to move except for his broken body's spasms. Wracked with pain, he wept like the broken man that he was; but his weeping was born of pain; compassion never entered into his thoughts. It was as strange to him as the idea of traveling on land might seem to a creature born of the sea. He had no feelings of guilt or shame for his actions, he only cared for his predicament and his insatiable desire for power and knowledge, and above all, revenge. He wanted revenge against the cruel stupid savages who had been so bold as to think that they had any rights whatsoever to challenge the Magistry's own representative, himself, and think that they could punish him for any perceived wrongdoings in such an arrogant and overt manner. Once he found himself outside of this cursed pit and back in Oesteria, in civilization, he would have any survivors of his company's soldiers hanged and mount a new expedition, except this time he would see to it personally that the savages were brought to their knees once and for all. He would end the problem of "sharing the land" through extermination of their kind and culture, and he would see to it personally. So vehement was his hatred that he managed to raise himself up and take a shaking step on his one good leg before his other folded underneath him like a wet reed, broken and useless. He screamed in pain and whimpered there again on the floor, then dragged himself along with his hands and one good knee until he hit a wall.

Rhael began to follow it in the darkness, his hands becoming his eyes as he sought to chart his prison within the vastness of his throbbing head. Such a mind he had, such a powerful brain full of thought and knowledge, and yet it was useless in his present situation; it frustrated and unmanned him to be subjected to such physical pain and mental punishment. A highborn man made to crawl like a worm through the bowels of the earth, this crime far outstripped his own alleged crime of destroying those savage children in an effort to understand magical energies. It was so unfair and ill-conceived. How could they judge him in any light when their lives were so meaningless? He wanted to get his hands around all of their throats at once and throttle them until their eyes bulged out of their heads. He would return at the head of an army, with thirty mages under him all quaffing the finest elixirs and burning holes through the eyes of the self-appointed leaders and elders of these pig folk. He would smell that crisp smell of burning flesh and revel in it. Like the smell of bacon to a hungry man, thought Rhael, that is the way these savages will smell to me as they fry and spasm under my energies; I will fry them all, he vowed.

He pulled himself along for as far as he could but all he felt was an unyielding span of rough cavern wall. His ears had stopped ringing and there was something in the darkness. It was faint, but it sounded like water dripping. At once he began to move toward the sound, his powerful thirst urging him on. He began to fantasize about finding a great pool of water that he could bathe his wounds in, an endless supply of drinking water. Perhaps there would be some creatures inside that he could eat and gain sustenance, replenish his strength and climb his way back up through the chasm and throw his captors back down the way he had come. His split and broken lips cracked a grim smile in the lightless cavern that even the stark yellowy whiteness of his teeth could not reveal. They seek to make this my tomb, Rhael thought, but it is I who shall entomb them before this is over. There will be a great reckoning for the Dawn Tribe, a great reckoning indeed. He willed the thought into a steely hardness and let it seep down into his bones as he crawled his way toward the sound of the phantom spring. As he felt his way with one ragged hand on the floor and the other testing at the craggy wall for what felt like ages, his wall hand gave way and he noticed an empty place, a recession large enough for him to fit his head inside. When he pushed his head cautiously inside he felt cool air and the dripping sound grew louder. A rush of excitement filled him. It was not merely a recessed place he had found; it was a way through the wall and into another cavern, perhaps even a way out of his prison. He scraped and pushed and cried out and shoved himself painfully through the fissure in the stone, bleeding and cursing and panicking as his shoulders became wedged and he was for a long moment stuck there in his blind passage with no way to go forward or back. Feeling his breath coming in ragged gasps, he at last wriggled and inched his way free and through the fissure to the other side where the dripping was louder and the air was cooler. Perhaps it was even moving and flowing through an opening in the walls somewhere. If only he could see something, if only there was light. He began to weep again. Stop it! Stop it! He shouted at himself in his head, you mustn't weep Rhael! He was suddenly a child again before his lord father, crying as he explained himself and his sorry state. Rhael had been thirteen then. His father was the Lord Uhlmet at that time, and Rhael had been run out of the village by his lord father's peasants after he had taken a sword and slain some dogs there. He was only having a bit of fun and his father was the lord of the land, Rhael could do anything he wanted. One of the brazen peasants had even managed to wound him with his staff, and he wept and wept as he showed his father how they had abused him. Then his father had slapped him once across the mouth so hard that his head spun round and he found himself gasping on the cold stones of his lord father's study, shocked into a tearless state.

"Better now that you have silenced your womanly ways." His lord father had said it so calmly.

"Now you shall return to the village and mete out our justice."

He had ridden into the town then with his father's men and hanged every one of the perpetrators, even a few who had nothing to do with it, the ones whom had looked at Rhael in ways that he did not like. He had laughed as the dying boys jerked and danced, some of them getting erections or soiling themselves as they died. Oh, how the womenfolk had wailed then. He wanted to see what happened to a woman when she was hanged, but his father's men did not let him hang the girl. They had said that the Lords Uhlmet were not hangers of women. How his father had beat him upon his return. He had called him a fool and threatened to disown him. Rhael had taken his punishment like a man, and he had not wept once. So fine were his memories of killing the peasants. His father was dead now, perhaps when he made it away from this cursed place then Rhael would change the traditional stance of the Lords Uhlmet on the hanging of women. But the peasants left the land after that incident, they had fled and sought refuge in neighboring fiefdoms even though that was a crime punishable by death.

Peasants were not to leave the land without their lord's permission, for they were inexorably tied to it. As part of his punishment, his lord father had tasked him with rounding up more peasants to work the land and he had found some new ones. There were always lowborn families willing to relocate if one knew where to look and made it sound sweeter than it was; once they were on the land, then of course they would not leave it, dimwits that they were, and it was illegal besides. So Rhael had gone about to his father's vassals and ordered them to give him enough peasants to work the fields of his holdings and they had complied without question, he remembered smugly. The new peasants were just as tiresome as the old ones had been. He never saw the girl again, but he thought about her often; the way she had cried out when he forced himself upon her all those times before the hangings. She had most likely taken up a life as a harlot; that was all she had been good for in any case. Perhaps she was living still in the lands of one of his family's rivals, Lord Tartrim's or Lord Illithane's old holdings. Those were no more, he thought wickedly; at least his lord father had lived to see that day. He calmed himself as an involuntary spasm wracked his body with shuddering pain and he lay convulsing on the cavern floor. When it had passed through him and he lay gasping there in the black he began to hear the sound of the dripping water again. It was indeed louder, closer than it had been. Joy, was it joy that he felt? There was something else now that he heard; a steady roar, a rushing noise met his ears. He began to crawl again with renewed vigor toward the sound of the water as he had done before, one hand on the wall the other on the floor, but this cavern was narrow and he could feel the ceiling as well as both walls as the dripping steadily grew in volume and the roar filled his ears until at last he felt cool water on his face and hands. He drank his fill as he crawled forward licking the wet cavern floor and then suddenly his whole being was submerged in icy water. A brief moment of panic found Rhael floating beneath the surface without a handhold, completely devoid of light and direction, his senses unable to detect anything but the cold and the wet and the black. But then he was breathing air again and moving in the strong current of what he supposed was an underground tributary of some form, a river in the heart of the stone, his hands stretching out and finding the slick bank. It was cold but the cold had numbed his pain and rushed his blood high into his head and cleared it, and now Rhael felt his thoughts racing. His hands could not grip very well in the wet freezing cold and he felt his tenuous grasp slip free of the river's smooth stony bank. He was sputtering and gasping as the powerful current swept him along blindly and violently, rolling him and disorienting him. His feet sought for the bed of the river but it was nowhere to be found and he was struck with the realization that it could be an ell away or fathomless and as long as he was rolling beneath it without air it may as well have been a puddle or an ocean that he was submerged inside, and either way would find him drowned. His head broke free of the surface and he gulped down the air greedily and then he was being sucked down and he had the sensation of falling and yet he was completely under the water, spinning and scraping painfully against the riverbed.

He was being rushed along now in a narrow channel, a tunnel of rock. Rhael could not breathe and the breath that he held in his lungs was expiring, his brain pounding in his head like his heart pounded in his chest. Panicking, he stretched out with his limbs and sought the surface but water surrounded him and he was unsure of any direction except the sinking sensation he had of falling, falling.

Then all at once he slammed into something hard and unyielding and white pain shot through him like a thunderbolt and the air was violently expelled from his lungs by the force of it. He inhaled water and coughed and choked, but there was no air for him, no escape from the pain and no relief from the inevitability of drowning. He clawed like an animal and suddenly broke the surface choking and retching, but his legs were like lead. He began to sink again and he felt himself being pulled again by a current beneath him. More air, he thought, I need more air. He was so panicked that he could not think clearly. The pulling sensation was drawing him along and he could not fight it with his failing strength. Rhael seriously thought about dying for the first time in his life.

He did not believe in anything, certainly not an afterlife. He was the master of his world, the manipulator of everything that he saw. He was a highborn Lord who held dominion over all the creatures of the earth, even his lowborn cousins who were little more than animals themselves. That was his birthright. This was not the death he wanted, in fact, he sought through the energies to circumvent death altogether and without a doubt, given enough time, his vast intellect would grant him the answers he sought. He was destined for great things, not to die escaping his unjust imprisonment, a failure; but the air was burning in his lungs and he was broken and weak and betrayed by his own form, panicking in the darkness unable to sense where the surface was or how he could extract himself from the water that was killing him. He flailed and flailed uselessly, but his strength was gone and he could not match the strength of the current. The darkness was taking him, he could not breathe. He could not breathe. How stupid it was that someone as highborn as himself needed air to survive. Rhael curled into a ball and was swept along in the river under a mile of rock. He was sure he was going to drown now and for a glimmer of a second Rhael's thoughts briefly registered regret; but it was a regret born of longing, longing for greatness.

Regret that his life had not yet measured up to his own high standards of what he so greatly desired beyond all else, his own personal glory, his own name being regarded with awe among his peers for his outstanding achievements beyond the borders of known magical knowledge and experience.

His father had been a powerful lord and he always the lesser son. How he craved air, how he wanted to taste the air in his broken mouth; but he was a lung-burned rag doll tossing in the current without a hope of salvation. Things were growing darker in the darkness and his lungs burst, releasing bubbles that blew past his face as he was hurtled along the underground river, as he spasmed and convulsed with the water entering his nose and lungs, the burning pain in his head and body and the panic of death. He was drowning and he was in a fully inescapable situation, he was dying and helpless to avoid death's certainty. How Lord Uhlmet raged under the mountain at being so commonly dispatched as he gasped and choked and sputtered and struggled to keep his consciousness. The top of his head scraped against the cavernous river passage, and then suddenly he was in the air flying free of the water and puking in the cold. Was he dead? Was this death, he thought? Flying through the air blindly? Coughing and choking and puking, gasping for air, he wondered?

He was falling and sputtering blindly in the darkness, his ears ringing; but he could breathe, he could breathe the air again! It was wonderful to breathe; the pain in his head and body and his lungs was still there but he was alive! He flew and fell and wondered if death was falling forever, choking until he slammed into something that knocked the newfound air out of his ragged lungs and paralyzed him with pain. Then he was falling but this time he was back under the water gagging again, willing himself to make his arms work and struggling in the cold darkness. Then he slammed against the gravelly cave pool floor and more pain shot through him, but he managed to shove and claw his arms against it. He was moving and lifting freely away from the painful ground and floating again, choking and clawing at the water with his spent arms. Until at last he broke the surface and gasped at the cool air, his ears clearing and filled instead with the deafening roar of the subterranean river. He struggled and slapped at the water with his failing strength until at last he felt his body scraping gravel. He slipped and scrambled his way onto a shore of bedrock and lay there gasping and sobbing and writhing in the shooting pain that coursed through his broken body, elated, for he was alive; he had escaped.

Nine

RHAEL WOKE COUGHING AND cold, his entire body
screaming with intense pain. He was half submerged
in the icy, cool water and he scrambled with his hands and
arms and his one good leg up a gravelly ledge of rock and lie
shivering and moaning there on the dry, cold rock. How long
he had slept he did not know, he could not know; for it was still
an impenetrable darkness that he was trapped in, no matter
how free he felt. Yet here it seemed less dark than where he
had been before the underground waterway had swallowed
him and spat him out. Was there in fact light here, Rhael
wondered? He held a hand in front of his face and thought he
could make out the vague shape of his fingers, but he could not
be sure whether or not his mind was playing tricks on him.
He shivered involuntarily as he tried to move, his entire body
riddled with pain. Pain seemed to be the only sensation that he
could feel without doubting himself.

Willing himself to move he pushed with his arms and
wriggled like a worm along the cavern floor, his ragged
right hand following along the edge of the channel that the
underground river had made, the sound of the river filling his
ears and drowning out everything. Rhael knew that all rivers

ran to the seas, besides it was the only path he could follow reliably in the darkness. He moved cautiously, for he did not wish to chance plunging into the cold water again and being spirited along the river's course without a window into his fate, and there were no windows or light to be found down there in the inky blackness. He slithered his way along until the roaring faded away into a dull background noise humming inside his throbbing head. He rested when he could move no more or overcome the spasms of fiery pain. He was resting when he began to hear other noises besides the dull roar of the river and the steady dripping sound. He thought at first it was the chattering of birds and he summoned his last reserve of energy to renew his slithering until something hit his olfactory senses and raised in him an animalistic fear that paralyzed him into a dead-quiet stillness, pressing his body against the cavern floor.

It was the smell of decay, the smell of rotting breath like that of his childhood tutor, Mage Raltet, with his filthy black smile and bloody gums. But this smell of decay was mixed with some other unidentifiable filth that sent a shiver down his spine and froze him with a fear previously unknown to him. Was he just imagining this, he wondered? No, thought Rhael, I can't move; I can't actually move from this position, or I'll be found and that thing with the smell will eat me. He thought how ridiculous this thought sounded to him as it rang out in the last corner of his rational mind. Yet he was immobile and barely breathing as he pondered it. Somewhere in the core of his being he felt an instinctual fear that even his vast incalculable acumen could not deny; for it was the fear prey felt from its predator. Was his mind playing tricks, Rhael asked of himself?

Voices now, chattering like birds, speaking Oestersh; but speaking in a strange and foreign sounding rhythm pitched high like a child's cadence with a gravelly aspirate sound to it, a nightmarish rendering of the familiar that sent Rhael's heart pounding in his chest at an alarmingly fast and frightening beat.

What were they saying, he wondered? He could not quite make out the words, but they were drawing nearer and he still could not move. He worried that his own heartbeat and ragged breathing would give way his position on the cold cavern floor. A scraping noise and a trundling sound like a cart's wheels.

The strange voices were louder now, discernible words met his cringing ears. "I smell it! Do you now, pretty?"

"Yesss, yesss! Near to us, I taste it!"

"Where, oh where's it?"

"Gold like the forest child? Or brown like a nut?"

"I think golden like the sun; I hope, I hope! The masters will pay finely if it is!"

So close now did they sound to Rhael, but he was paralyzed and no matter how he willed himself to flee, he could not.

"Does it feel us now? Does it know fear?"

"Yesss, Yesss. It knows it surely."

No, thought Rhael, please overlook me, please let my limbs work, please let my eyes see a way clear and my legs hale and whole. Please spirit me away and up into the bright world of sun and green; please let me fly from here as swiftly as a deer!

Then came the overpowering stench that caused him immediately to vomit and gag. Over his own convulsions he heard peals of shrieking laughter and mad scrambling and scraping noises, and the fear that had paralyzed him before now caused his very breath to catch in his throat as he choked and sputtered. A small, cold, lifeless hand with unbelievable strength closed its three fingered grip around his neck. A pale-blue light flooded his vision, allowing him to see for the first time in weeks the world around him, a world full of terror with a vaguely reptilian visage regarding him with its cold otherworldly eyes.

"I have it! I have it now! A forest child!" It screamed, the laughter like the shrieking of birds. A forked tongue shot out betwixt the sharply pointed teeth in its stubby snout.

Rhael screamed a voiceless scream as it shook him like a prize, and then the darkness took him and he lost consciousness.

Ten

WON'T BE SERVING YOU bloody savages nothing!"

It was the third time that morning that a Borsford innkeeper had turned them away at the courtyard, and Joth had taken his fill and would take no more.

"I'm a bloody soldier on Magistry business, and you bloody will serve us or I'll have your head!"

Eilyth regarded the innkeep cooly, but Joth could detect the tiniest hint of a smile playing at the corners of her mouth.

The innkeep blustered and started up again as if to protest when Joth cut him off. "Two hot meals, proper breakfast! And get our bloody mounts stabled before I hear another word out of you!"

He had only been back in an Oestern town for two hours and already the glaring rudeness and slanderous attitude toward him and Eilyth because of her hairdressings and their colorful mode of dress was more than Joth could bear. Not only was he angry at being treated like a savage, he found something in it far worse; he was embarrassed for his own people, embarrassed most of all at their treatment of the lady who was under his charge. The innkeep looked as though he had been stricken as Joth spat the vehement Oestern words at him, and he paled and bobbed his head and recoiled slightly when Joth raised his hand to wipe his mouth. The craven man plucked at the reins of the horses, stretching his arm out as far as he could to avoid Joth and the prospect of physical contact between them.

Joth moved out of the way as the man led the horses across the courtyard toward the row of stables opposite the inn. He shook his head.

"I apologize, lady."

"It matters not, Joth. Let us see if your food is more agreeable to me than your people." Joth scowled once more in the direction of the stables as he walked up the broad steps and pulled open the heavy oaken door. Eilyth made her way past him and he glanced up and noticed the sign of the inn for the first time, swaying slightly in the breeze; a rectangular carved rendering of a gilded bolt of cloth bound up by a red cord and blue painted letters spelling out "Cloth of Gold" above it. Probably bloody pricy, thought Joth, as he passed through the doorway and shut the door behind him. But he had his pay and Wat's in his money bag and after the last few weeks of traveling in the inclement weather, he was prepared to sacrifice a bit of thrift for a taste of comfort. All that they had received so far were hard stares and dismissals, but Joth had refused to put his soldier's clothing back on even after Eilyth had suggested that he do so. For some reason it did not sit right with him, and he had told Eilyth as much. She had simply nodded and gone back to riding.

They had ridden past a group of laborers in a field who had all stopped their work to gawk at them, and one of them had even thrown a stone their way as they disappeared over a low rise. It should have come as no surprise to Joth, for he had been under the same spell of hatred and ignorance just a few short weeks before, yet it raised an ire in him that he had a hard time swallowing. He knew better than to rise up to every challenge, so he had kept himself in check on the road when he heard the whispered words or the cruel jibes, ignoring the stones and the rotten vegetables, the spitting and the cursing. When they were turned away at the inns, Joth felt his temperature rise and it bent him well past his own breaking point when he saw that hatred directed at the gray cloak swaddled girl whom he rode beside. In Oesteria an inn was a place of refuge for all travelers. There was a great tradition of hospitality that extended to all ranks of folk, whatever their station in life. An inn was a place where one could come and sit and have food and drink and a fire and respite from the weather and the worries of the day. It should be bloody hospitable anyway, Joth mused, but these Borsford folk had made a piss-poor showing of it thus far. Eilyth had shaken out her cloak and hung it on a peg near the door, and leaned her staff in the corner.

It had rained on them earlier, just after they had broken camp in the early first light of dawn. Joth hung his own damp cloak next to hers and took in the great room of the inn. It was a larger establishment than the previous two they had been refused, and the interior was well furnished, its wooden tables and cabinetry polished to a fine lustrous sheen. Broad glazed windows on the eastern and western walls let in the pale daylight and offered views into the courtyard and the ordered garden behind the inn. A stairway rose up to a wooden balcony that wrapped around the room and offered access to the rooms that could be rented there for travelers or anyone wishing to have some dealings in private away from the bustling noise of the great room. For now it was only Joth and Eilyth who peopled the ground floor and the only hints of activity came by way of rattling plates behind a low bar at the back of the room where the kitchen must have been situated. It smelled of food and of wood smoke, and the vinegar that was used to clean the tables, and the smell was the only thing about it that brought any sense of familiarity or comfort to Joth. He knew at the courtyard that this was a rich man's inn, or at least it was desperately trying to be. Joth preferred smaller establishments without all of the polished wood and rich appointments, a place where a man could go and sit by a roaring fire and put his feet up on a stool without getting a talking to, and a flagon of ale or wine with a cut of meat that came at a reasonable price for folk who worked for their day's wages. The Innkeeper himself was cut out in fine clothes, far too fine to be working in Joth thought, his doublet a soft lilac and his hosen an expensive shade of green. Green was costly, as it had to be dyed twice—once blue, once yellow. He was thinking those hosen would cost him two month's pay. He did not even want to guess at the price of the lilac doublet, which was most likely cut from velvet.

Eilyth took in the room and sat down at a table near the hearth where a fire lay smoldering. Joth settled in across from her, where he could see the door, and tried to shake off the resentment and anger that he had been feeling since they made the outskirts of Borsford. A serving girl bustled from behind the bar carrying two broad platters and a costly Rhaelish jug with animal motifs painted on it in greens and blues. Her eyes nearly popped out of her head when she caught sight of Eilyth's hair and dress, and Joth thought for a moment that she would drop their food on the stone floor, but she somehow managed to regain a semblance of her composure and right the platter that had started dipping downward and deposit it on the table in front of Joth.

"As it please you, sir," she stammered as she set the other plate in front of Eilyth, blatantly regarding her hair ornaments with disdain before adding a muttered "and you as well."

"Leave that jug, if you please." Joth caught her as she started away. Red-faced, she plopped the jug on the table before them and sped back behind the bar and out of the room. Eilyth watched her go with a quizzical expression on her face, then turned her attention to the platter before her and examined its contents curiously.

"Eggs," Joth volunteered.

"Eggs?"

"Yes, chicken eggs. Toasted bread, some marrow bones, sausages and grilled leeks, some turnip mash; this is a proper breakfast."

Eilyth smiled at him and he felt himself smiling back. She was laughing at him, at his enthusiasm, but Joth was past the point of being embarrassed by it any longer. He scooped the marrow from a split bone and spread a hearty layer onto his toast, holding it before him and savoring it before taking a huge bite and then falling against the back of his chair with his eyes closed, the picture of fulfillment and satisfaction. This elicited laughter from Eilyth until they had both nearly fallen out of their chairs after the serving girl made another brief appearance to see what all the commotion was.

"What have they brought us in here?" Joth peered into the Rhaelish jug then brought it to his nose. He had not smelled ale in months, but it was like cresting a hill and seeing one's home again after a long journey away. "Oestern ale, let's hope they make it well here."

He poured the pitcher into two cups that he procured from behind the bar, the serving girl being nowhere in sight, and he and Eilyth talked quietly as they ate their breakfast and drank the ale, which was surprisingly excellent, in Joth's estimation.

But he could not decide if it was truly great brew or if he had just missed and longed for the taste so much that it had improved its quality.

"Do you like it, lady?" he asked.

"It is strange at first, but yes, I do like it. I like the turnip mash more." They laughed again as they finished their breakfast together near the fire and warmth of the hearth and for a moment all was right with Joth Andries' world. He had made it to Borsford safely and relatively easily with the Lady Eilyth, now it was an easy journey by airship to the Oestern city of Twinton. Airships traveled swiftly, more swiftly than a seafaring ship, and much more safely. He had seen an airship before, not closely, but a few times at Immerdale the mages posted there had arrived and left by airship. Slim and graceful with their tubular, bulbous mainsails and large triangular lateral sails, they were said to resemble smaller versions of the tall sailing ships that rode the waves of the sea.

They flew by magic, by Goblincraft engines, and by the wind. The airship captains could operate how high or low the craft flew and the magic made the ship as light as a feather. How any of that was feasible was a mystery to Joth. It had been a childhood dream for him to travel the skies in one, but he never thought it would ever come to fruition. Joth had been born a commoner, and airships were the carriages of the highborn. He would soon know what it was to travel the sky. He would soon see it firsthand; that seemed almost impossible. The serving girl had finally plucked up enough courage to come and collect their platters. She kept glancing at them nervously, almost frantically, as she collected the scullery and organized it into a portable arrangement.

"Can you tell me where I can find the airships?" Joth asked the befuddled girl. "I'll be right back, if it please you, sir." She again beat a hasty retreat toward the kitchen.

"It would please me more if you answered me! I need some directions." He called out after her, but she only glanced at him furtively and put the dirty plates on the bar before scuttling away like the room was on fire.

"Bloody girl can't seem to get hold of herself." Eilyth was still watching the back of the room, her eyes narrowing. "No. Something is wrong, Joth."

"Lady? You're not well?"

"Not with me. Listen. It is quiet. No one works there." She motioned with her chin the way the girl had gone.

Joth listened and heard only silence. His eyes fell on the dirty plates atop the bar. Why not carry those to the kitchen on your way, you mad girl? He wondered. Eilyth was right; there was something wrong, he knew it then too. "I'll take a look out in the courtyard."

He passed around the table and made his way toward the bank of windows that gave view of the courtyard and peered out cautiously from the corner. The gates to the inn had been shut and barred from the inside. There was some activity at the edge of Joth's vision near the stables, but the barred gate told him all he needed to know. They had not been wanted at the inn to begin with, and now someone had decided to keep them from leaving.

"Wait here, lady. I'll go round the back and try a few words with them."

Eilyth looked unconvinced, but inclined her head at him slightly.

Joth moved through the chairs and tables of the great room and went behind the bar as the serving girl had done, finding a narrow half-opened door at the back. Pushing through it, he entered the kitchen and stopped short. There were several men speaking to the cooks and staff out the back of the kitchen, speaking in quiet tones. The men wore uniform livery, and Joth immediately assumed that they were town guardsmen, and they were in deep conversation with the lilac doublet clad innkeeper who was gesticulating and pointing to the inn and the stables and holding his hands out in supplication, and they were all nodding and making sounds of affirmation. It did not take long for Joth to realize that the purple-and-green-clothed man had called the town guard and sold them a story of aggression that warranted their involvement in tossing out the two savage undesirables from the establishment. He made his way back to Eilyth, who was standing and gripping her staff with both hands with her cloak wrapped about her in a way that he had never seen before. She had pulled his cloak down for him and cocked her head toward it as he met her eyes with his.

"Are you looking for a fight?" he asked.

"Never, but I will fight if need be."

"There are a few guardsmen outside, and I'm sure they've been told we're trouble."

"What do we do?" Eilyth was calm, and Joth felt good about that. She had said she was a woman of peace, but the way she stood and her attitude matched that quality of soldier whom Joth had learned to respect. She was ready, and he knew that he could count on her to be with him—whatever his plan may be.

Hopefully there would not be a fight, hopefully they could gather their horses, pay the innkeep, and be on their way. "Just follow my lead, lady."

Eilyth nodded. They walked to the front door and opened it, pale daylight flooding the dark foyer of the inn, and stepped out onto the steps that led down into the courtyard.

Blinking as their eyes adjusted, they were immediately engaged with two guardsmen who lowered spears at them and began shouting, "We've got them!" and "Here in the front!" Joth was beginning to speak as Eilyth spun her staff and took two steps and cracked both guardsmen in the temples and laid them out cold before the stone steps. Joth picked up a spear and drew one of the guardsman's swords from the scabbard at his waist.

"I hadn't really planned for that," he said.

"They threatened us, Joth Andries. Threats must be answered."

"I thought you were a woman of peace?"

Eilyth smiled slightly. "The horses."

They hurried toward the stables as they heard booted feet on the stones from behind the inn. The soldiers had heard their comrades' request for help, and now they would have to deal with them. Joth ran to the gates that lay barred before them.

"Get the horses!" he shouted to Eilyth, pulling at the bar, tossing it down, and kicking open the doors. She ran toward the stables as two gangly guardsmen stepped out with their spears.

"Eilyth!" he cried, seeing her death before him.

She thrust out her staff before her and struck the first guardsman between the eyes, causing him to drop his spear as she stepped lithely past the staggering man, deflecting a spear thrust and clocking the second man with a blow that sent him sprawling. She then turned and dealt the man she had struck between the eyes such a blow to the back of the head that he simply fell over like a piece of timber.

"More come." She said it so simply. Never would Joth have thought such a small, frail-looking girl to possess such skill at arms.

"You are doing well so far!" With the spear butt he whacked the sprawling guardsman solidly, causing him to still.

She smirked at him. Joth heard a shuffle behind him and turned in time to see four more guardsmen of Borsford round the corner of the inn and make their way hastily toward the stables. He hefted the spear and held the sword in his other hand, unsheathed. This was intimidating to fight so many at once. He wished that he were able to speak to them, to tell them that he was on Magistry business, to tell them that he had orders in his saddlebags that would explain everything. But Eilyth had preempted diplomacy with her skillful use of the quarterstaff that her father had given her at the beginning of their journey, and now four town guardsmen from the city of Borsford were laid out cold on the stones of an inn's courtyard because two strangers dressed in the garb of the Dawn Tribe sought to have breakfast. Joth could only shake his head and let his thoughts swim. "We'll have the whole town on us before long!"

Eilyth cocked her head toward the rushing guardsmen. Joth threw his spear at the foremost man and hit him in the face, bringing forth an explosion of blood as the spear glanced off his skull. The man went down and one man screamed and began to run away, but only one of the two who remained gave a second look and both of them drew their swords and circled in on Joth and Eilyth.

The loud cracks she delivered with her staff were like thunder. Joth heard it behind him as the man before him lunged and put a thrust at his face. Joth cut down his blade and turned the thrust, cracking the man in the head and putting him down in a bloody mess.

This was bad, and getting worse. He turned in time to see Eilyth stepping through and delivering a blow to the man that set him to silence. Joth saw the lilac Innkeeper run from the corner of the building and follow the fleeing guardsman toward the kitchen as he turned to Eilyth.

"He'll be shouting like a house on fire!"

She nodded. "Let us fly from here now."

Eilyth led the white horse, her gray mare Aila, and the dish-faced bay gelding with the mismatched eyes that he knew to belong to her brother Eilorn. Eilyth mounted the gray and ponied the white horse behind her. Joth swung onto the back of the bay horse and cut his eyes across the courtyard. There were no more guardsmen to be seen, but a noise drew his attention to the roof as a window in one of the dormers opened and the lilac doublet-wearing Innkeeper appeared with his hunting crossbow. He felt the air whoosh before his face and heard a loud crack as the spent quarrel shattered on the stones behind him.

"Ride, lady! Ride!" He kicked his horse up as the fancily dressed innkeeper worked at reloading his arbalest with a crannequin.

Eilyth whispered a word to Aila and she was galloping out of the inn gates, Joth a horse length behind. The horses clattered on the cobbles once out of the courtyard. Joth's bay slid on the stones for a pace before finding its footing and then they were off like a shot down the street. He looked behind and saw the innkeeper taking aim with his crossbow, so he huddled low over the neck of his horse and screamed for Eilyth to get down, but she did not hear or she chose to ignore him. The bolt shattered and splintered against the stones of the building behind him and he urged his horse onward.

"Take that alleyway!" Joth shouted to Eilyth. Turning there would put a building between them and the inn, preventing them from being shot at by the dandified crossbowman. It was frightening to think of the consequences of being shot through with a quarrel or having one of their horses hit; or worse, if the fool murdered the Lady Eilyth. For what bloody reason had the man decided to fetch down his crossbow in the first place? They cleared the corner and Joth saw the innkeeper leaning out of the window in the second story marking their flight. What would the bloody fool be up to now, Joth wondered. He was a craven, but he had only needed a crossbow to become bold. Once they were out of bowshot, Joth slowed his horse to a trot and told Eilyth to do the same.

"We'll draw too much attention to ourselves running roughshod through the streets," he explained. "I think you were right to begin with."

"Right?"

"About the clothes. I should have put on my Oestern garb, and we should find you a gown to blend in as well."

She nodded. "What now?"

"Now we find the airship harbor and get out of here before those guardsmen raise the alarm." Joth pointed ahead to where a broad street bisected the narrow alley and some people and carts passed. "This way, lady."

With their cloaks on and Eilyth's hair covered for the most part with hers, they could pass for Oestern travelers. They were moving fast enough to attract a little attention, but it registered in his head that it could not be helped under the circumstances. He cradled the bare-bladed arming sword in the crook of his arm and threw his cloak over it to hide its presence.

They checked their horses at the corner then turned out onto the broad cobbled street and into the foot traffic and carts as they climbed the low sloping hill that led to the heart of Borsford. Joth could see the old walls of the fortress that perched up atop the hill and thought that the airship harbor had to be somewhere inside the walls. Where else could it be, he wondered. Was it on the other side of the town? The airships at Immerdale would always set down in the fields outside of the fortress. He frowned. This was a hard place to be in, he hated that events had unfolded in the way that they had. They had done no wrong, they had simply wanted to have a meal and a fire before they continued on.

Perhaps he could have avoided the trouble with a few words, but Eilyth had been too quick with her father's staff. She had taken those boys before Joth could even think twice, and he knew now that they would be dusting each other off and running for more help. It would be a mess once the town guard set out after them in force. Those bastards were probably bored out of their skulls before we showed up and now we've given them a cause for excitement, Joth thought.

He spat onto the cobbles. Joth had never liked town guardsmen. Boring bloody work, and it attracted the worst kind of soldier; in fact, most town guards were men who were either too old or otherwise unfit for active service within the army of the Magistry. Better than conscripts or levies, but not much better, and Joth always got the feeling that most guardsmen felt that they had something to prove. It was always something that seasoned soldiers could pick up on, something one could pick out in new recruits and old boasters alike.

He was looking over his shoulder to see if they were being followed when Eilyth spoke to him.

"Joth, the girl knows where we go."

It dawned on him in an instant, he had asked the girl at the inn about the airships. "We will have to beat them to it, or we are caught for sure."

She nodded grimly.

"It's not lost yet, lady. We have horses and they were all afoot. Let's just keep our pace."

"Do you know where these airships are?"

"No, I'm not certain."

She nodded again, resignedly this time. "We will need to ask someone, then."

Joth started to answer, but Eilyth was faster and turned to a young poorly dressed lad pushing a wheelbarrow on the street beside them and addressed him. "Where do the airships lay, boy?"

The boy blinked in the cool morning sun, squinting up at them. "North past the castle wall. Off the harbor road, lady."

Bloody north, thought Joth. They would need to pass through the entire town to get there.

"There's a good lad, thanks."

As an afterthought he pitched the boy a silver, but as he did so the hilt of the sword he was concealing became visible and he saw the lad's eyes go wide.

The boy dropped the wheelbarrow handles and caught the coin in both hands. "If they ask you, you never saw us. Remember."

The boy looked at the two of them then and took note of Eilyth and their dress, but he just nodded and looked at the silver in his hand. Eilyth's eyes flashed at Joth.

"Let us away."

He nodded and they left the boy staring after them for a pace. He pocketed the coin and made to pick up his barrow again and Joth stopped watching and turned his attention back to Eilyth. She was looking at him nervously. Joth did not like it any more than she did. "That silver will keep his tongue in his mouth."

"You mean he will not betray us?"

"I don't know for sure, but I think he won't." Joth's answer rang weak in his own ears, but he had to hope that the boy would value the coin he had been tossed more than his prejudices, whatever they may be. He met Eilyth's eyes.

"I also think that he won't tell." She broke away from his look at last.

They rode on at a brisk pace, their horses jogging up the street and moving through the pedestrians and handcarts, the wagons and teams. The foot traffic grew more and more dense as they neared the looming walls of Borsford. The half-timbered buildings on either side of the street jumbled closer and closer together and gave Joth the feeling that they were leaning like two drunken men on both sides over the road about to fall in on each other. Street vendors with carts selling hot food hawked their wares at a crossroad. The passersby were not gawking at them at all now, though the occasional carter would furrow his brow at their lack of stirrups, and one lad pointed at Eilyth's hair and commented loudly on the fact that she was not sitting a lady's saddle with both of her legs to one side. Joth ignored it as best he could, but when he looked at Eilyth he could see that she was growing more and more worried by the moment. It was unnerving for her being in the crowded street, he could feel it coming off of her in waves of fear and nervousness. He knew Aila felt it too. The gray mare tossed her head and shied at every creaking cart and shrieking hawker that they passed. It would do no good to give in to fear, it would not serve the situation in any beneficial way, Joth told himself. He tried to think of something he could say, some comforting words, but all that came out was, "What do you think of Oestern cities, lady?"

Eilyth laughed thinly. "I will tell you when this is behind us."

They passed under the wall through the high arch of the gate, murder holes and portcullis and an iron door sandwiched between the walls forming a ten-foot thick corridor, their knees touching in the claustrophobic passage. It was only wide enough to allow one wagon to pass, a defensive measure to ensure only a double rank of fighting men were able to rush through in case the gate were ever breached. There were sally ports on either side of the portcullis to allow the defenders to take care of the divided attackers, or to ambush invaders by hiding men within the walls. Joth had learned these tactics while garrisoned at Immerdale. They had drilled and drilled multiple scenarios as attackers and besieged alike. From the drills Joth took away one thing: it was much easier to defend a fortress than to attack one, but one had to know how and use good tactics, or be overwhelmed. Some of the older soldiers in the force he lived with were veterans of the wars between the rebel lords and the Magistry that had taken place before Joth had memories. They had told the younger men that defenders were often cruelly butchered if the attackers had spent a long siege, and they said the attackers would always break the defense if they kept attacking but the cost of life was high on the attacking side. It seemed that there were always enough men for the purpose; he knew because he was one of them by way of his service to the Magistry, where he was taught to do as he was told. At the least he was not in the garrison of the town guard of Borsford. Same hat, different color, thought Joth. They were all soldiers, servants to their orders. Wat always told him he had a knack for getting into bad situations, and when he first asked him why, Wat had replied, "You joined the First Army of the Magistry, you must be in a dire fix!"

They were made to check their horses to a walk as the crowd was funneled into the choking gatehouse causeway, and they slowed to a stop as a wagon's cargo was checked at the gates. The farmer with the wagon being held for inspection threw his hands into the air in an exasperated gesture and muttered curses as he fished in a pouch for some coins and handed them to the toll man at the gate. Joth heard a snippet of their exchange.

"Just doing our duty, Tyllard."

"You're always doing your duty—that's the problem!" The farmer tied his pouch to his belt and flicked his reins at the team who started the lumbering wagon moving forward again. "And I'm always paying your duties left and right!"

"It's the law," the guardsman said tiredly, raising his eyebrows.

"Why do we stop here?" Eilyth asked.

He wondered if she was overwhelmed with the day's events and all of the sights and sounds; the clamour and chaos of the town making her experience a brief, terse moment of weakness.

"Lady, are you all right?"

"No. I like this place not. This is a place to die."

She was looking at all of the portals, the murder holes and arrow slits.

"We'll be out of here in no time and on our way," Joth reassured her.

"The sooner the better."

They were struggling through the line and queued up for what felt like ages, but slowly they made it closer to the end of the gatehouse tunnel that opened out into the heart of Borsford. The buildings were different here. They were all stone and their roofs were of slate. Fireproof, mused Joth. No thatch would be allowed behind the curtain walls of the town for fear of them being burnt too easily if besieged. It had given rise to a middling class of folk called "slaters" who could afford the expense of slating their roofs, but now it denoted people who could afford to buy houses and operate mercantile businesses within the walls of a city. One had to have a charter to do so. In the old days the lord of the town had to grant it, but now it fell to the Magistry to answer such requests. Part of his duty while garrisoned at Immerdale had been to collect taxes from the slaters every season. Many of them had grown as rich as lords, some even wealthier. Not a one of them had liked to pay their taxes, Joth recalled.

The line began to move forward again. Joth began to feel anxious as he and Eilyth drew closer to the inspectors and the toll man. He wondered if they were looking out for them, if they had already received word somehow. Nothing short of Goblincraft could have given them that, Joth decided. No, they had beaten news of their clash with the town guard at the Cloth of Gold, and no one could have gotten here from there ahead of them. Still, his heart thumped in his chest and his palms were slick with sweat as he passed under the scrutiny of the gate crew. They regarded he and Eilyth briefly, and were on their way to waving them through until the toll man's eyes went wide at Eilyth's gold adorned braid peeking out from the cowl of her silver gray cloak. He stood up from his stool and pointed the quill he was holding straight at Eilyth and opened his mouth, and Joth's heart sank as his mind raced. Eilyth threw a furtive glance at him. Joth gripped the hilt of his sword under the cloak and fought down the panic welling up inside him.

Not here, he thought. This could end badly. There would be crossbows behind those arrow slits and murder holes, and bored men with idle hands itching to squeeze levers and to have a story to tell at the tavern after their watches ended. Maybe they could charge through and surprise the guards. Once they were through the curtain wall they would be safer. Perhaps it had been a mistake to enter the town at all.

Before the quill-pointing toll man could form words, a commotion from behind them in the line stole the attention away from he and Eilyth. A handcart had overturned behind them and spilt its contents onto the pavers. A tall lanky lad was cursing at a boy with an overturned wheelbarrow as he slipped and fell over himself trying to load his cabbages and root vegetables back into the handcart.

The toll man shifted his gaze to the overturned produce and the two guards went to assist the lad with the gathering of his goods, as it had given the already restive queue a completely disordered sense of chaos. Joth caught the lad's eyes for a second and realized the wheelbarrow boy was the same whom he had paid with a silver just a few minutes before. The lad gave Joth a conspiratorial grin and winked at him big as he pleased then went back to nodding apologetically and loading cabbages back onto the handcart of the lanky fellow.

"Let's go," Joth whispered to Eilyth.

They moved forward through the gate and into Borsford proper. They waited until they rounded a corner before urging their horses up into a fast trot along a narrow side street that shot them straight north through the town. They skirted along the western wall of Borsford. When they spied the gate and saw that it was relatively sparsely trafficked, Joth nodded to Eilyth and they made their way outside of the walls again and rode around the outside of the western curtain wall and its gray stones until they came to the north side of the city. They gazed down upon a broad staging plain just east of the narrow causeway ramp that led down from the northern wall gate that had been cleared of all trees and leveled. There, amidst several small cranes and other rope and pulley machinery for the loading and unloading of wares, sat several airships of differing shapes and sizes, hovering magically above the ground where they were tethered and tied off. Brightly hued tubular mainsails and lateral sails in contrasting colors gleaming in the morning sun, animals and other heraldic devices adorning their bowsprits, it was a wonderful spectacle to behold the airships at rest in the Skyharbor of Borsford.

Eilyth made a noise like the sharp intake of breath. There was amazement in her eyes as she pointed to the floating ships. "How do they fly there?"

"Magic, lady. Goblincraft."

She looked at Joth quizzically and then set off down the hill toward the plain where the ships lay tethered. Joth followed. They had made the Skyharbor and were traveling down the broad avenue that was formed between ships and 'docks' of goods for transport and trade when Eilyth stopped her mount and turned her head back to the town, listening.

"Joth," she said sharply, her eyes bearing concern.

He heard it too.

Bells were ringing out.

They had raised the alarm in Borsford.

Eleven

UHLMET FORCED THE PASTY gruel down his throat and grimaced at its foul taste, gagging as the wind shifted and the paralyzing stench of his captors invaded his nostrils and sent an involuntary shiver down his spine. It must have been several days since the monsters had caught him and trundled him away. First, they had bound him painfully with a barbed rope and carted him off in their strange carriage drawn by a team of what seemed to be oversized rats with eerie red glowing eyes and scaly tails. The rats were muzzled with bronze cages that kept their snapping jaws of black razor-like teeth away from their cruel whip-bearing masters, the strange blue-skinned humanoids with reptilian features whose stench paralyzed him at first but now only made him convulse when the wind shifted in the darkness of the inner subterranean world within which he found himself a captive.

They spoke Oestersh, or at least a form of it. Rhael had listened to them chattering incoherently as he was carted along the underground road, the wheels rumbling loudly and the blue light from their strange Goblincraft lanterns bathing the caverns and illuminating the alien world inside the earth, allowing his battered eyes to see. The pain still burned in his body, his bones ached and his head throbbed incessantly, but his captors had given him a drink that they claimed caused the body to heal. It had burned his throat like fire and sent his head spinning the first time the scaly three-fingered hands had forced his mouth open and rammed the bronze funnel down his throat and poured the pale milk like liquid into his mouth, but it had made his pain subside. It also made him sleep soon after he imbibed it. At first Rhael had thought he might be able to open the door and manipulate the energies of his magics to burn the creatures from existence when he had quaffed the bitter potion, but sleep had washed over him almost immediately and he felt himself fall away from where the door lay in his mind, unopened. Initially, he had resisted the attempts made by the strange creatures—the Kuilbolts, as he had learned they were called—but now he welcomed the bitter milk they offered. He had been growing less sleepy after repeated doses, and he was certain that eventually his powerful mind would master the potion. He would soon throw open the door that lay closed, and he would make the beasts writhe in pain while he sizzled them slowly. Then he would eat the foul things, or better yet feed them to the massive rodents. They would fuss over him and stroke him like a prize as they administered the medicine, talking about what a price he would fetch, and proclaiming the joy he would bring to their masters.

"Look at how it regards us! It has depth!" Iztklish was its name. It was taller and broader than the others.

"Depth, yess. Yess." Krilshk was short and bone thin, possessing extraordinary strength. He pitched Rhael's head back and forced his jaws open with his cold hands.

Iztklish inserted the beaten bronze funnel and Krilshk held it in place as they poured the liquid down his throat.

Rhael only resisted a little as he felt the burning liquid fill his body with its discomfiting heat, spasming involuntarily.

"It grows stronger now, see?"

"Yess, it waxes. Its matter heals."

Iztklish pulled the funnel from Rhael's mouth rapidly and hung it from the hook on his pale colored leather belt. He wiped his three-fingered hands down the front of his leather jerkin and its shiny closely knit bronze plates. They all wore those jerkins sewn with plates.

"Across the water, and soon we will bring it before the Masters."

A slithering shrieking noise and Rhael realized that Krilshk was laughing, or something approximating mirth. They are excited to have captured me, Rhael understood, they are happy. They drew close to each other and rapidly shot their snubbed snouts into either side of the other's neck in what Rhael had interpreted as some form of dance of victory or self-satisfied display. Rhael was growing drowsy even now, but he willed himself to cling to consciousness, and he sought to open the door as he concentrated on keeping awake. Let me open it and burn them, let me do this one thing, Rhael thought. But the door remained closed. Iztklish and Krilshk finished their celebration and turned back to the others excitedly. Rhael's vision was starting to swim and blur.

He was accustomed to this feeling and he knew that his time was running short. Soon his consciousness would fade and he would be lost to the realm of sleep. He sought again for the door and was dimly aware of the barbed rope tickling him with pain at his wrists where he was bound. Not the physical world, Rhael thought, I want the metaphysical realm! He grasped at the door but his hands were clumsy and the handle seemed to lose any corporeal substance as he swiped at it.

Had he drifted off for a moment? The world was a fog. He was being carried past the cart by the short reptilian beings. When he glanced down he saw water all around him and a stone dock beneath the feet of his porters. Was it stone or was it the bones of some great beast? Blue the world, blue as blue could be. No, Rhael, stop letting it affect you, he thought! The world was moving now, and Rhael within it. He was on the water in a boat, a hide covered boat with a ragged sail of knitted hair. The shapes of the hides were familiar, strange. He looked over the water and saw the dock where he had been carried and the Kuilbolts with their blue lights and the rat cart. Have they set me out here alone?

Have they set me adrift on this blue sea in the blue world? His thoughts were muddying. Krilshk was there on the pale wooden tiller, gleaming teeth and darting forked tongue. Iztklish pulled him to the mast and retied his bonds. His hands were free for a moment, but he could not will them to life; he could not will them to close around his captor's scrawny neck. Sleep was taking him, and he railed against it like a drowning man flailing at the water. He was too weak, too incredibly weak to struggle. He was dimly aware of Iztklish making a line fast and the sail snapping taut in the strange wind of the underworld, the boat pulling and creaking as the wind caught in the sail and sped them on a course. The Kuilbolts began to make a noise together, a kind of singing he could dimly make out as the darkness closed in on him. He listened to the strange sound as he looked to the prow and realized why the hides that were stitched together to form the hull looked so familiar. They were the tanned hides of men. No sooner had he come to the realization than sleep at last overtook him.

Twelve

I'LL TAKE YOU AND your charge," the captain said. "But the horses'll cost you extra."

"How much bloody extra?" Joth had the reins in his hand. He watched the gaudily dressed airship captain as she pored over his writ.

"Well, so you know, a trio's the limit on horseflesh."

Joth looked over his shoulder and saw Eilyth looking back, up toward the city wall and the northern gatehouse. "My lady captain, we haven't the time to barter and bargain. We will pay, or the Magistry will see you compensated. Let's be aboard and underway." He had used his best approximation at upper-class inflection.

She glanced at the writ once more then narrowed her eyes at him a bit. "All right, all right. Don't work yourself into a fury, my good Linesman Joth Andries, First Army of the Magistry." She read his name and title aloud from the writ, then rolled it up and put it in her belt. "You'll get it back when I get my pay." She turned and started back toward the hovering airship. Its hull brightly painted with animal motifs and heraldic symbols, it bore the famous crests of several cities. Lions and drakes and griffons and swans, cranes and eagles, a great fish, crests of cities to cover the continent. The various arms were quartered in a checkerboard pattern that alternated on the four quarters of the hull. He was about to protest when Eilyth caught his attention, and he followed her gaze to the northern wall to see two squads of town guardsmen marching double time out of the gates.

"Elmund, lower the gangway!" The airship's captain called up to a man in the rigging.

"Aye, lady, my lady." The man growled out and scuttled down the rigging nimbly.

"Just lead your horses on and we'll tie 'em to the mainmast" Joth snapped his head back around and nodded to the silken-clad woman with the plume of feathers in her broad felt hat. "As you say, lady."

Eilyth dismounted and led Aila up the gangway with some coaxing, with the dish-faced bay following him resolutely; but try as he might, the white horse refused the gangway no matter how Joth pushed or pulled. The squads were kicking up a cloud of dust and were drawing ever nearer to the skyharbor as they hurried down the road from the gatehouse. When the white gelding refused the plank for the third time, Joth looked at Eilyth pleadingly, but she was looking at the soldiers' progress as they marched toward them. He tried to throw off the feeling of fear and unrest threatening to overtake him. He breathed deeply and focused on the horse's eye. It was deep and dark and white-rimmed, rolling. There was fear there, but also wonder and curiosity. There was intelligence, and caution and worry, but beneath it all, trust. He knew when he looked at the horse that it trusted him, and he realized in that moment that he trusted it as well. They had been through adventures together, they had relied on each other, and more importantly they had come through for each other.

"Never to worry, my friend," Joth said to the white horse softly and felt he had caught a spark of recognition in its dark eye, then he turned and started up the ramp and the gelding stopped for a moment and splayed out its forelegs, but then it followed him with halting steps up the gangplank. The strange disembodied feeling that came over him as he set foot on the decks of the airship was mirrored in his equine counterpart, which started a bit when he came off the gangplanks. But he followed Joth to the mainmast beneath the brightly painted, bulbous, tubular mainsail that ran beyond the length of the deck. There was a strange look on Lady Eilyth's face when she caught his eyes after he had handed off the horse to one of the four men of the airship's crew that "sailed" with them, and he realized she was looking right at him. He threw a look over his shoulder but the Borsford town soldiers had not made it down off of the road yet, and the cloud of dust was rising a good quarter mile away by his reckoning. No, Eilyth was looking at him as he made his way toward her.

"You spoke to him then," she said appraisingly. "You spoke with your heart."

"My heart?" he said lowly.

"The horse. You spoke to him with your heart and he listened."

She turned away from him and looked to the captain who was barking orders at the four crewmen. Joth was left looking at her.

"Away the lines! Raising off!" The airship captain's voice sounded shrill, but it carried, and her men obeyed her.

Joth heard cries from fore and aft, answering her "Aye, lady, aye!" and two of the crewmen slipped over the sides down the tethering lines from the two ends of the deck and scurried down the ropes, dropping to the ground.

"Ready, all hands!" The captain cried again, and the airship's crewmen that remained went to the fore and aft and looked down on the progress of their fellows below. The ship's captain went to the helm and took a delicate-looking bronze wand from its place at her belt and inserted it into the side of a column of wood and brass that stood there.

"Stand by!" she cried again.

Joth felt the ship lurch ever so slightly, and he realized one of the lines was free as the crewman coiled in the line that served as a tether on the rear of the airship, on its starboard side.

"Aft starboard, line clear!"

"Fore and aft, signal!" the crewman growled from the prow of the ship, it was Elmund that one, Joth noted.

Two cries of "aye, ready!" came from before him and behind him, and then it was the ship's captain at the column saying loudly, "On my mark! One, two, three! Release!"

Joth felt the ship lurch and rock for a moment, and he was filled with a strange sensation in the pit of his bowels as the ship began to slowly rise into the air. He looked to Eilyth and saw fear in her eyes.

"Report!" cried the captain.

"Underway, lady!" came the voices of the crewmen at the ends of the deck. The ship jostled as it rose, and Joth realized that the two crewmen who had untethered the airship were dangling from the tethering lines and climbing them hand over hand to regain their positions on deck. He chanced a look over the side and nearly tasted his hard-won breakfast again. The ground was lurching and he was higher than he had ever been, even higher than the wall at Immerdale, and that was near twenty-five yards. The two crewmen pulling hand over hand and shimmying up the ropes were near to the hull now, but Joth could see the town guard spilling into the Skyharbor and making their way toward the rising airship. Joth could make out the lilac-and-green Innkeeper among their number, brandishing his crossbow.

The airship captain moved the lever to another position. The ship buzzed with energy for a brief moment. Eilyth looked at him nervously.

"All hands, report when ready!"

Joth saw the one crewman helping the other over the webbed rope netting at the aft of the ship.

"All hands ready aft, lady!"

Joth saw the crewman named Elmund in the fore of the ship bend and put his hand out for the crewman struggling up the tether rope when the man slipped and cried out. Elmund fell to the deck and cried out, "Help!"

Joth ran to the man's aid. When he got to the prone crewman, he saw that the man on the tether who was dangling had lost the line now and was only holding on to Elmund's wrist, and Elmund was not able to haul him up.

He lay down and extended his arms and grabbed hold of the man's hand and together he and Elmund hauled the man to his feet on the deck.

"Lucky Dathe," said Elmund to the man whom they had saved.

The man called Dathe was young, maybe of an age with Joth but perhaps even a few years younger. He hadn't seen more than twenty-two summers, Joth thought. Dathe was a bit pale after nearly falling to his death, but he covered it with humor as well as he could.

"It ain't so easy to kill me, Elmund! Why I'm a regular eagle of the skie—" He clutched at the back of his neck as the eyes in his head rolled up and Joth saw blood pouring from his lips and the head of a crossbow bolt shot out of his mouth. He pitched forward into Elmund, who fell onto the deck beneath the man's convulsing body as Dathe went into his death throes, spattering him with blood.

There was screaming, and Joth turned to Eilyth and screamed "Get down!" as he lay down and peered over the side of the rising ship.

One of the guardsmen had knocked the crossbow from the hands of the lever happy innkeeper and was upbraiding him violently and loudly in the Skyharbor below. Elmund had scrambled to his feet, blood covering his colorful silken clothes and tears of rage in his eyes, screaming, "Bloody bastards! They've killed Dathe!"

The crew and the captain let go with a tirade of cursing and woeful cries, raining insults and threats at the rapidly dwindling guardsmen on the ground.

"You!" cried Elmund, pointing at Eilyth and Joth. "You've brought him his death!"

He started toward them and Joth stepped between the man and Eilyth. He held his sword before him.

"Are you threatening me, you bloody dirtworm?" Elmund drew a curved short bladed sword that hung at his belt behind him.

"Stand down, Elmund. Your blood's up and you'll act the fool." It was the captain. Elmund listened and reluctantly sheathed his blade. He shook his head and shouted in rage as he walked away.

It was obvious that the captain had not expected a confrontation with the town guard that would result in the death of one of her crew, and that she wanted to get the situation under her control as soon as possible. She eyed Joth and Eilyth suspiciously. Elmund went back to where Dathe's body lay on the deck.

"Make underway!" she said. "Set sails! We will observe funeral rites once we are clear of this bloody mess."

She shook her head in the direction of Dathe's dead body then turned and pointed to Joth and Eilyth. "You two, get below decks." She motioned to the ladder that was set into the deck at the forecastle.

Joth was about to argue, but Eilyth touched his arm and turned him toward the forecastle and led him below. "Wait, they grieve. We shall speak to them later."

They climbed down the four rungs of the ladder and through a small doorway, and they were immediately below the main deck. Joth had to stoop a bit to avoid scraping his head above. There in the hold was the ship's cargo, bundles of burlap and twine-covered rectangles stacked in an orderly fashion and held in place by rope nets to keep the items from shifting as the airship lurched and twisted in the wind. He was looking at the cargo that packed the hold from end to end when he heard Eilyth call to him.

"Look, Joth. Look at the world now." She was standing near the prow where a porthole was set into the wooden wall of the hull, looking out of it intently with wonder in her eyes.

Joth looked out and his breath caught in his chest. Everything was miniature, the town, the trees, the hills, and the animals and people moving about on the surface of the miniature world seemed to move more slowly. He could make out the Skyharbor and the town wall of Borsford below them, looking like a jumble of bricks and broad rectangular plains, as though a child of gigantic proportions sat down with his building blocks and built a castle on a hill. He could see men and carts and horses like ants winding their way up and down the roads that spiraled out neatly from the center of the town. It had grown colder, and the wind whipped at his hair and face, his breath frosting and his eyes watering. The airship creaked and the sails snapped taut and the ropes groaned as they harnessed the power of the wind and the craft pitched slightly forward, flying. It was a strange feeling, not altogether comfortable. The horses whinnied nervously, and Joth could hear the deckhands calling to each other and the shrill voice of the captain as she ordered them to scurry here and there. He looked behind him out of the porthole and he could see the sails raked and straining under the wind that was pushing them along through the sky. The ship was climbing still, and the white fluffy clouds that Joth had always thought were as solid as the ground were dissolved into a foggy mist as they rose through them, bathing everything in icy dew. He looked out at the blanket of clouds, a sea of white that they floated above peacefully. Joth had never seen anything like it.

"What will become of him?" she asked softly.

"Who? I suppose they will bury him."

"No, the innkeeper. The murderer."

"He'll have to answer to charges. He should be hanged."

"He was trying to kill you, Joth. Trying to kill us, because we are different from him."

Yes, he thought, because he regarded us as savages; because he had been told his entire life that the Dawn Tribe was comprised of the worst element of liars and thieves who would murder your children and slit your throats in the night.

"Yes, lady. It's just ignorance." He meant it to soothe her but it only sounded empty.

"What of the High Mage?"

"Lady?"

"If an innkeeper acts this way, then how will the High Mage receive us?" Joth had no idea how to answer, he did not even know who the High Mage was or what sort of man he might be. He had not thought much past getting Eilyth to Twinton. Now he did not even have his writ and with the death of her crewmember he was not sure if the captain would ever give it back to him.

"I know not, lady. I'll serve to get you there as best I can."

"I know you will. I just question the wisdom of it now."

Joth did not know what to say, so he said nothing. Eilyth was thinking, and she stared out of the porthole at the cloud sea and chewed at her bottom lip pensively for a long time and said nothing. Joth watched her and wanted to say something, but words were hard to find and they all felt empty when he weighed them. At last he took his cloak and wrapped it about her shoulders, over her own. It was bitter cold now, high in the sky as they were, but Joth pretended not to be bothered by it. She started to protest but he wrapped it around her anyway.

"Don't fear, lady."

She smiled at him and he smiled back. Even if he could not know what was going to happen or how the High Mage would receive them, he knew that he would not let anything happen to her. Not because of Wat or his orders or Traegern and his oath, but because of her. It was the only thing Joth could be sure of as the wind blew he and Eilyth across the skies high above Oesteria.

Thirteen

RHAEL SAT IN THE stone cell and listened to the now-familiar sound of the Kuilbolts chattering as they passed the door of his prison. The heavy door was lifted and a brass tin filled with gruel was left for him, then the door was slammed shut again. Rhael waited until their footsteps receded down the hall, the sounds of several more doors lifting and slamming down again letting him know that he was not the only guest of the Kuilbolts here in their dungeons. Slowly he stood, testing his mending leg with his full weight incrementally. It burned and throbbed, causing him to wince and clench his jaw. How it enraged him, waiting for his frail body to mend. His eye was still swollen shut, but the swelling on his forehead had gone away. He limped forward to retrieve his gruel. The gruel was always cold, and nearly flavorless. Sometimes there were bits of meat in it, but Rhael had not a clue as to what type of beast it came from. It tasted of pork, he thought, but everything was said to taste of pork, and that was dullard's talk. He simply ate it as quickly as he could and waited for the bitter sleep milk and hardware to administer it. He was licking the gruel from his fingers and waiting for them against the far wall of his cell when they came for him, Iztklish and Krilshk with their ratskin wine sack filled with the strange milky fluid and their beaten bronze funnel. It was the routine now, the mark by which he measured his time, such as it was.

"Does it wax stronger today?" Iztklish was holding the sack.

"Yess. It waxes. Look at its matter." Krilshk approached Rhael with his strange birdlike gait.

Rhael raised himself on to his knees and put his hands on the floor as he had been instructed when they had brought him to the cell for the first time many feedings ago, the picture of obedience. They had cracked their whips at him until he obeyed, but once he found out that they were giving him more of what he wanted, he complied, and they had praised him. Now when they come their whips stay at their belts, Rhael mused. He was quite pleased with himself for gaining their trust so quickly.

"It knows humility. It respects its masters." Iztklish stated as Krilshk approached and stroked Rhael's head with a cold three-fingered hand.

"What a well-behaved forest child." Krilshk spoke slowly and deliberately and cocked his head at Rhael. He whipped the funnel up from his belt and tilted Rhael's head back as Iztklish approached with the bag and its bone spout. Rhael opened his mouth voluntarily and tried to open his throat as they filled the funnel and let it drain into him.

The burning liquid no longer made him convulse, but he still could not shake the initial pain that set in after he swallowed it down. His eyes teared up and his nose began to drip as Krilshk put the funnel away and they both backed toward the door of the cell. Iztklish wrung the empty bag in his hands as Krilshk scratched at the door with his three-clawed hand, making a high-pitched sound.

"Perhaps it walks in the next feedings?"

"Perhaps it does. Perhaps we harvest it next? We shall see." Iztklish said it as the door was raised and he and Krilshk slunk through the portal. It slammed shut again, but for Rhael it mattered not because the door he was seeking was growing more substantial and real, and once he succeeded in opening it, no prison in the world could contain him. Rhael could feel his limbs begin to sag as the bitter potion took its course within him. He reached out and sought for the door within his mind again. Slowly and methodically Rhael sought for the door and ignored the potions' narcotic effect, willing himself to concentrate on finding and opening it. He was able to do this longer and longer each time after the feedings.

It was hard for Rhael to stay awake and focused after imbibing the milk. His thoughts began to swim, his vision blurred, but he was working toward a goal and that goal was revenge on the filthy, rat-whipping Kuilbolts, then the bloody Dawn Tribe in its entirety. These thoughts would propel him toward the door and allow him glimpses at harnessing energies, but his focus would lapse or his physical state would pull him away and he would lose sight of it once more. It frustrated him beyond everything else about his wretched condition when he would awaken and recollect nothing of the moments before the sleep drug took him. He had to keep his observations in line with his progressions toward unlocking the energies, especially if he were to present it as a new thesis before the council.

Once he was free of this place he would have much to tell the Magistry about his little survey adventure, and for certain they would have an interest in learning that there are rat-whipping, blue-skinned reptilian Oestersh speakers trundling about in carts in the bowels of the earth sailing ships of human skin and hair across cold blue lakes in the dark...he was drifting, drifting, drifting...

Rhael attempted to shake away the sleepiness that the drink had brought on. He had let his mind wander again. It was the drink, he knew, but he had to resist. Focus now, he willed himself to think, seek the door and that is all. It was always so easy with the elixirs, how they sparked his mind and brought everything into sharper clarity; but this milk had the opposite effect, it dulled and slowed him. He felt as though he were under the water again, blind and flailing in the icy cold. He could feel the world shrinking around him and he knew that the potion was seizing control of him, forcing him down into sleep. He redoubled his efforts. Not long now and it will take me, thought Rhael, I must find the door or sleep shall overwhelm me. He fought through the heavy fog that had settled into his mind and pushed onward, inward to the door. He knew it so well, the path. He had traveled it many a time, so familiar it was to him. At last he was there, standing on the precipice of his mind and the realm of energy, energy that he could reach out and use to manipulate this world of sticks and stones, blood and weakness.

Rhael tried to access it but he was met with failure. No, he thought, I haven't time to fail! I must succeed in this, I must destroy my captors and burn them, burn them all to a fiery writhing death of pain and screaming. His world had dimmed. He was losing his consciousness and fading into sleep. No, no, no, Rhael repeated to himself beneath the oppressive weight of sleep that was being lowered onto him, he must not give up on his efforts, he was too close to victory. Overwhelming feelings of frustration and hate coursed through him, and he was screaming at the world and everyone and everything in it. He would see it all burn and wither, and he would watch it all turn to ash, laughing.

His heart raced. Rhael felt a surge of energy pulse through him. A loud cracking sound ripped through the chamber and he was dimly aware of a spider's web of cracks spiraling out from the center of the stone slab that made the door of his prison. He reached out again but the energy was gone and he was falling again, slowly and softly into a sleep that he railed against, but he was satisfied. He had reached it, and he could do it again. He had broken through at last. As he let himself fall into the pull of the bitter sleep milk's power, as his consciousness faded, he imagined Iztklish and Krilshk dancing in fire and screaming. For the first time in many months, Rhael fell to sleep with a smile on his lips.

Fourteen

THE AIRSHIP CAPTAIN HAD assembled them all on deck. The crew had donned their fur coats and hoods. The captain had given both Joth and Eilyth fur cloaks, for it was cold above decks and below. It was late in the afternoon and they had flown all through the morning above the cloud canopy in the cold bright blue sky, flying and sailing the winds eastward. Joth had no idea how far they had come or where they were exactly, but the ship's captain had a device she looked through and navigated the ship by, and from time to time she would move the lever on the post at the helm and the ship would descend through the clouds and she would check their positioning above the land by way of landmarks on the horizon. When they would descend beneath the canopy of clouds, he and Eilyth would stare out of the porthole and study the earth below them, looking intently at the rivers and forests and towns, castles and fields. How everything seemed to move so slowly below them, as though they were barely moving at all, yet Borsford was far behind them now and nowhere to be seen in any direction, and the land had changed from flat plains to rolling hills laced with rivers and streams, and north of them, far in the distance, Joth could see mountains rising out of the earth into the heights. It was something that Eilyth never seemed to tire of, and together they would study the world below them and point out things to each other, traveling around the hold and looking out of the various portholes at the sights. The mood was relaxed below decks with Eilyth, but above on the deck of the airship it was tense and dark. The crew was deeply angered and upset by the death of their fellow, and Joth knew that they blamed him and Eilyth for the accident. Elmund gave him dark looks exclusively, and the others would avert their eyes from him and mutter curses when he made an appearance. It was uncomfortable for Joth, firstly, because he felt as though at any moment he might be swept off the deck and fall to his death as the airship soared up and down in the skies, pitching forward and dipping whenever a gust of wind took the sails, and secondly, because he felt the men's eyes on him whenever he was not looking at them.

Now they all stood on the deck before the tall and slender airship captain in her elaborate feathered hat and her silks, slashed and cut to show the many layers that she wore. He had never seen a woman in hosen before. They all dressed like this, it seemed—man or woman. He had never met an airship's crew before, but they wore outrageous clothing to mark them out. They were commoners, but the nobility allowed them their eccentricities because of the danger involved in their profession, as many airship crewmen were daring and led short lives due to the dangers of sailing the skies, especially in foul weather. Elmund and the other crewmen stood a pace apart from he and Eilyth, standing on the deck free of any handhold as though they were standing on solid ground at their ease. Joth was gripping a handrail and Eilyth held on to his arm firmly.

He did not feel easy on the deck at all, painfully aware of the long open distance below the airship and the real possibility of falling to his death every time the airship caught a rise in the wind or dipped suddenly, and he felt his stomach lurch in an unsettling way. They had wrapped Dathe's body, tied it in burlap, and laid it to rest beside the forecastle. Joth could still see the bloodstain on the deck where the man had taken the quarrel and died just after he and Elmund had saved the man from falling to his death. "We begin preparations to set down for the evening. We stop early today so we can lay our brother Dathe to rest in the earth."

The crew nodded and muttered their agreement. The captain turned to Joth and Eilyth. "Now you can tell us who you are and why the bloody Borsford guard is after you, and you had better tell us the truth. You dress strangely, but so do we, so let's speak plainly here." The captain smirked, but Elmund and the others were staring hard at them both.

"You have my writ. That explains everything." Joth felt Eilyth tighten her grip on his arm.

"It doesn't explain why my man was shot through with a quarrel and killed."

Joth looked to Eilyth. "We were chased out of an inn."

"What did you steal?"

"We are not thieves. We were only after having our breakfast. They refused us because my lady is one of the People."

"The People? What bloody people?"

"She is Dawn Tribe. That's why we are dressed this way."

They just looked and stared at them for a long beat before the crew erupted into spitting and swearing and hands moving toward their hilts.

"Bloody Dawn Tribe? That's what you are?" Elmund roared. "I thought you said they were Magistry!" he said accusingly at the captain.

Joth pushed Eilyth behind him protectively. He had left the sword he had taken from the guardsman below decks. Now he felt naked and vulnerable as the captain and crew fixed their gaze on him and Eilyth, but the captain was looking more contemplative than outraged.

"Stand down!" she said, moving before the three men and holding her arms out. "There'll be no rowdiness, Elmund."

"Aye, lady, aye."

"Nor from you, Galt."

"Aye, lady," grumbled Galt. He was short and dark.

The third man was fair-haired and lean. He had braids in his beard down each side of his mouth and his beard was quite long. It was flapping in the wind like a banneret now, Joth thought. "I won't give you no trouble either, lady," the bearded man offered up.

"The skies love a volunteer, Kipren."

As angry as they were, they broke for a moment and all of them but Elmund had a bit of a laugh together.

"Am I the only fool who sees it?" Elmund roared incredulously. "These two come aboard and Dathe gets murdered, and now we're having a laugh?"

"Easy, man. Stand down."

"Aye lady, but—"

"I'm very interested in your opinion Elmund, but I've given you an order to stand down."

Elmund clenched his jaw and nodded. The captain had diffused the mood, Joth realized. The crewmen were less confrontational now and more curious, all of them, perhaps except for Elmund.

"It is a shame that we lost Dathe. He was a good hand, and a good mate."

"Aye, lady," they all put in.

"We shall put down outside of Grannock within the hour. We can give him our respects there and find an inn to bed down in. There's a good hill for dragging nearby. We've used it before and you know it, so stand by, all hands." She turned away from the men and addressed Joth and Eilyth. "You should have said that there was trouble following you, you could have warned us. To be honest, I knew you were in trouble the moment I saw you, and I don't even know if knowing anything could have prevented one of my crewmen dying anyhow, since you presented me with a writ and by the law I have to give priority to Magistry officers and Magistry correspondence. I went against my gut instinct and I took you aboard to avoid trouble with the law, and then one of my men is killed by the town guard, so you can perhaps sense the frustration I feel."

"It was the Innkeeper," Eilyth said.

"Who?" The captain switched her focus from Joth to Eilyth.

"It was the innkeeper who killed your man, not the town guard."

"Is that true?"

"Yes," Joth offered. "He called the guard down on us while we had our breakfast."

Elmund, Galt, and Kipren were all ears.

"We tried to get to our horses and they made to hold us, so we fought our way out. That's when the bloody fool set out for his arbalest."

"Fought your way out, did you?"

"Yes, the last of the guardsmen and the Innkeeper ran inside the inn." Joth did not like the way she kept on with all of her questions.

The captain nodded. "What inn was it, did you say?"

"The Cloth of Gold."

"Are you lying to me? Because I don't know that inn."

"No, I'm telling you the truth. It's there in Borsford, it's called 'The Cloth of Gold.' The bloody Innkeeper's a fool."

The captain nodded. "You'll tell your superiors about this and you'll see to it that I'm compensated and that justice is served." She leveled a finger at him, "and I'll have it in a writ before I lose sight of you, understand?"

"I understand, but I can't just make you promises."

"I know I'm not allowed to ask what it is you're doing or carrying with you, but you have to tell me if being near you is putting the lives of my crew in jeopardy, right? That's the letter of the law, as they say?"

"I don't know the law, I'm just a soldier."

"Well, I'm telling you that it is, and I'm also telling you that you need to tell me right now if having you aboard runs a risk of more people dying, because if it does then you are on your own once we touch down at Grannock, once I have my writ."

Joth blinked once.

"Understood?"

"Yes, I understand."

"Aye, lady," she said instructively.

"Aye, lady," Joth replied.

"So tell me then, are more people after you? Is the town guard at Grannock looking for you?"

"I've never been to Grannock," Joth said.

"Of course you haven't. You'd know there's no town to guard."

The men laughed at their captain's jest. She had charisma, and her men listened to her.

"You'll stick close to us when we get there, and remember I have your writ, so don't try anything if you want it back someday." Her eyes lingered on Eilyth for a moment, then she turned and barked an order to Elmund and he scurried up the rigging.

They could only hope that the people of Grannock would be more accepting than those of Borsford, or that he could find some clothing for them that attracted less attention. Part of him felt disdain for being forced to conform, Joth realized. He wanted to be accepted as he was, at his word, and he wanted that acceptance for Eilyth. But he knew as well that his people were not easy with accepting the unfamiliar, and he and Eilyth looked like what they regarded as savages. Many of them had never seen nor would ever see in the course of their normal lives a member of the Dawn Tribe, and the prospect of seeing one sent fear through most Oestermen. Savages, they thought them; but Joth knew how wrong they were. Unfortunately, men like the innkeeper in Borsford seem to make up the mindset of the majority. They were quick to judge and take rash action because they believed in the myth of Dawn Tribe savagery. He had thought the same about the People, much to his own shame. It struck Joth as a bit odd that one could dress as outlandishly as the airship's crew did and flit here and there without incident, and he and Eilyth could not even enjoy their breakfast without a chase through town and a man dead. He was thinking about that when he looked at the ship's crew and an idea struck him. He turned to Eilyth as she watched the ship's captain.

"How do you feel about trying on some Oestern garments?"

Fifteen

RHAEL STARED WITH VEHEMENCE behind his placid eyes, but it was satisfaction he felt and a lust for more power coursing through him again. His captors were discussing the shattered cell door and the various possible causes of its present state. Iztklish was insisting that the earth had shifted and Krilshk was blaming it on a fault in the stone itself. Fools, thought Rhael, I broke it with my mind in the same way that I shall soon break you. The power he wielded! The cell door had been a slab of solid granite near to half an ell in thickness and it had shattered like glass at his whim. How he wished that he could push through the door at that very moment and bathe his captors in fire, but the door remained closed without some form of elixir allowing him access. The Kuilbolts fussed and quibbled about the cell door and examined it for a long while; Rhael was not interested in their theories, he just wanted the milk. The tedium of waiting for it was threatening to crack through his façade, but Rhael sat there looking complacent and obedient. He wished that they would stop their inane chattering and administer the medicine; he would grasp again at the door in his mind and fry them to ash. This time he would not allow them to give him the full measure, he would take only enough to lubricate his mind, only enough to break through the barrier between this world and the world of power. Then he could fight off the compulsion to sleep and escape this place in which he found himself incarcerated. His heart raced and his mind danced with glee at the thought of his plan succeeding. He wondered what the Kuilbolt's faces would look like, would they register—surprise or shock? He wondered if he could recognize the sweet moment when shock and surprise would give way to base primal mortal fear, the fear all creatures knew at the moment before their own impending doom. He hoped beyond all else that he would indeed recognize the look.

They were approaching him then. He shivered involuntarily as the fear stench invaded his nostrils, but he composed himself quickly. He had almost gotten over that compulsion completely.

"What a good forest child. Look how it waits even while the door lies shattered."

Krilshk was reaching for the funnel at his belt.

"Yess. It waits. That is good." Iztklish was readying the rat hide wineskin that held the milk.

Krilshk reached down and tilted Rhael's head back and waited for him to open his mouth, holding the bronze funnel at the ready. Rhael could feel the strength in the cold lifeless grip, but Krilshk was holding him lightly because of his compliance. Good, Rhael thought, keep your trust in me for just a moment more.

He held open his mouth and watched as Krilshk's forked tongue darted and he put the funnel into Rhael's mouth. Just a moment more, thought Rhael again.

Iztklish was hoisting the bag up and placing the bone spout into the top of the funnel, and a moment later Rhael tasted the bitter sleep milk begin to pour down his throat. They were looking at the liquid in the funnel, filling the thing to a specific level and measuring out the draught when Rhael seized his moment and threw his head as hard as he could to the side. The bronze funnel went flying, spewing the grayish liquid everywhere in the cell. The Kuilbolts hissed and cursed, and Rhael felt his head being jerked painfully back by his hair.

"What has it done now?" Krilshk screamed. He pushed and let go of Rhael's head, flinging him to the ground. The Kuilbolts were small compared to him, but they were not to be underest-imated for their physical strength, especially not Krilshk. The spilled contents of the funnel and the dripping wineskin ran down the smooth walls and puddled on the floor in several places.

"This forest child is not as good as you believed, Krilshk." Iztklish stepped over Rhael and hauled him to his feet.

Rhael hardly noticed; he was concentrating on finding the door in his mind. He knew the path, he knew it like the back of his hand and the door no longer eluded him. He strode right to it and seized at the handle, but the door was still half formed and non-corporeal. No, thought Rhael, not now! Now you must obey me!

I shall have mine and I shall have it now! How he raged and raged in his own head, struggling and fighting toward the door in his mind even as he was being pushed through the shattered doorway in his cell by Iztklish and Krilshk. He stumbled into a large vaulted tunnel lit by the strange blue lanterns where ladders led up to cells placed higher up on the walls and more Kuilbolts hurried about in teams tending to other prisoners.

"Another hold for it?" Krilshk asked.

"No, we harvest this one now," Iztklish said resolutely.

Rhael felt a slight tingling in his limbs as the diminished dose of the sleep draught began to course through his body, making him feel drowsy and light-headed. He was vaguely aware of a Kuilbolt on a raised platform at the end of the gallery pulling levers at a great contraption, and the high-pitched scratching noises that rang out from within the cells and without as Kuilbolts set about entering and exiting the prisons, some with prisoners in tow and some just feeding or administering medicine. But Rhael's mind was occupied elsewhere, deep within himself. He sought for it ravenously, and he knew that he would not stop until he felt the power coursing through his body once again. There was nothing that he wanted more. Iztklish and Krilshk led him through the long gallery and out through a small dark tunnel where he was forced to crouch down and duck to avoid scraping his head until at last they emerged from the tunnel and entered a gloriously bright and beautiful chamber, almost a palace to Rhael's eyes, situated in the center of a large cavern. On a raised alabaster platform in the center of the chamber there rose a sort of tower with large panels extending high into the ceiling, and there was a radiant golden light emanating from behind the panels and flooding the chamber with a yellow light. The panels were oscillating slightly, gently, as though the structure were somehow alive and breathing. The light in the chamber brightened and faded with the phantom breaths. There was also a noise, a low throbbing hum that vibrated the chamber and caused the hairs on the back of Rhael's neck to stand on end. He was feeling so sleepy and the sound made him wish to close his eyes and drift along…

No! Rhael screamed inside his mind, I must seek the door and open it!

The Kuilbolts were shuffling him toward the base of the strange tower bathed in its golden light within the cavern and Rhael was primally aware that it was a place of mortal doom for himself, but his feet were plodding solidly, one after another toward it as the three-fingered clawed hands guided him.

"The Masters are not here?" Krilshk asked.

"Today is their feastday. We shall harvest this one alone," Iztklish hissed back.

Rhael raged within himself as the sleep draught coursed through his body and his mind surged forward through the portal within the depths of his consciousness and he felt power, raw and real, flowing into him. His captors were pulling him toward the half-opened panel that stretched up straight and smooth to the roof of the cavern, when Rhael began to laugh low and wickedly.

"What does it do, the forest child?" Iztklish sounded annoyed.

"It has mirth, perhaps?" Krilshk offered.

Rhael jerked his arms free of the Kuilbolts and rose to his full height. They hissed in alarm and leapt away from him, hands moving to the pale leather whips they carried at their belts, but Rhael was laughing and feeling power moving through him like a conduit.

The energies were real and deep, limitless in their possibilities and pulsating with power. As they uncoiled their whips and moved to subdue him, Rhael extended his arms and pushed the Kuilbolts against the stone panel and pinned them to it with a phantom force drawn from the power within him. He was looking for the shock in their eyes, but they were so alien that he found reading them impossible. He could not help but relish in the glory of the moment, regardless of that disappointment. He still found it satisfying, to watch them writhe beneath his crushing force as he pinned them and pressed them against the smooth stone panel. He had wanted to burn them but the fire was not coming to him through the weak measure of the sleep milk. "Oh, how I have longed for this moment," Rhael said thickly, the sleep draught slurring his speech slightly through his numbed tongue.

The Kuilbolts squirmed and struggled against his overwhelming energy. Krilshk opened his mouth as if to speak but no sound came forth. Rhael wondered if his energies were trapping them and isolating the air from their lungs or if perhaps this was the way that the Kuilbolts registered shock? Either way, the giddiness welled up inside of Rhael and he shrieked gleefully like a child when he saw the gasping creatures. He was elated, but he felt the power draining him; he felt the energies drawing out his own and he was growing fatigued. No, thought Rhael, I must not slip away now! He gathered himself and pushed harder, attempting to flatten the beasts against the smooth stone panel. They writhed against the magical force that was pressing them, flattening them so that their eyes bulged and their mouths gaped. Rhael pushed again, delighting in the torment he was inflicting when the panel began to give way and pivot on its axis, opening and revealing the center of the chamber and its bright, intense, golden light. The creatures slid off of the smooth stone face and into the center of the chamber as the giant panel gave way and turned completely sideways beneath the force that was being applied to it.

No, Rhael thought again, he wanted to crush them! He was leaping toward the Kuilbolts now, hands outstretched as they slid across the floor, the golden light in the chamber diminishing and sucking back into itself seemingly. The hum grew louder as he leapt closer to the stone panel, it even seemed to pulsate and vibrate with the hum, a breathing, living thing of stone in the heart of the cavern, glowing white and gold.

Rhael stumbled as he landed, his legs going to jelly with the sleep milk in him, his heart racing in his chest, his hands stretching out and extending the strong magical energy that slid the Kuilbolts across the smooth alabaster white floor. The creatures scrambled and struggled to no avail, so strong was the force applied to them. In the center of the chamber stood a low, slender pedestal on which an orb of black glass rested.

The orb is where the light comes from, Rhael realized. It's pulsating and making the hum. Breathing, as it were! He was watching it grow dark when suddenly golden light erupted from its opaque depths and arced out in three lightning bolts of energy that fully struck Iztklish and Krilshk as they writhed there on the floor.

The third bolt arced straight at Rhael. It hit him square in the chest and flung him from the chamber like so much chaff. He landed in a heap near the mouth of the tunnel that led to the prison cells and the bolt retracted back to the orb and the panel slowly closed as the light flashed gold and then died suddenly in pure darkness. The light began to come back slowly. Rhael could barely lift himself from the floor, but he managed to crawl and edge his way toward the chamber and the orb behind the stone panels. When the bolt struck Rhael the power had left him, vanishing behind a wall of pain as he felt something stretch and tear within him, in the very core of his being.

Now he was crawling and stumbling over the smooth white floor to where the panels were slowly opening in unison, the breathing motion ceasing and the glow from the orb low and steady. Rhael looked at the lifeless bodies of his former captors. Iztklish and Krilshk lay tangled in a heap of blue skinned limbs with forked tongues hanging out. Too swiftly did death take you, my pets, Rhael thought ruefully. He had wanted to draw their deaths out for much longer. He pushed past the open stone panel and cautiously made his way toward the glowing orb on its slender pedestal. Rhael proceeded tentatively, unsure whether or not the orb would flare to life and arc an energy bolt straight at him again. His hand held up protectively, guardedly, Rhael made his way toward the pedestal and the glowing glass orb that rested there.

The hum was still there, but only as an undercurrent. Rhael had the impression that the room was resting, that somehow there was an interval of inactivity that allowed him to approach it without incident. He approached on shaking legs, his unsteady hands extending toward the pedestal as he crept closer and closer. The orb was glowing and humming slightly. Tentatively, he reached out to it. His hands closed on it and a flurry of activity and energy flooded his entire being; he sensed three separate entities inside of the glass sphere, and one of them was in some way part of himself. He had the odd sensation of existing both within the orb and without. There was something akin to an electric shock that coursed through him as he felt the consciousness of Iztklish and then Krilshk searching for their bodies and the piece of him that was separated and desperately attempting to rejoin the rest of himself. Rhael trembled and recoiled and the awareness faded from his mind as soon as he broke the physical connection with the orb. He steadied himself and drew a ragged breath. He reached out again and grasped the orb with both hands, the discomfiting and chaotic awareness flooding his mind. He wrestled with the spirits as he lifted the orb from the pedestal and held it before him. The three-fold consciousness inside the orb railed against him.

The energies of the orb were at his command to use as he wished, like the energies that lay behind the door in his mind; yet these energies were at his fingertips and leapt at his command without elixirs or seeking or grasping at elusive handles. A long and high-pitched laugh erupted from Rhael as he lifted the orb above his head and stalked unsteadily from the center of the paneled chamber, the orb glowing an almost purple light.

He looked back at the pedestal and saw another orb appear from somewhere within it. Somewhere within this contraption was the secret of power, Rhael knew, a way of trapping energies and creating objects of wondrous might. At the moment, however, he was quite contented as he reached out into the orb again and pushed the entities inside of it to the center, compressing them and wringing energies from their very essence. He was in the sphere and without it as he felt both power and oppression and red orange flame leapt out and engulfed the dead bodies of the Kuilbolts Iztklish and Krilshk and set them ablaze with a vibrant and searing heat that sent him back shielding his face.

Rhael stood in the middle of the cavern on the edge of the smooth white dais and gazed toward the tunnel that led to the prison cells. Harvesting, they had called it. A grim smile fixed on his face and the purplish orb pulsing in his palm, Rhael made his way to the mouth of the tunnel and wondered how many souls resided in the stone jail from which he had just escaped. He flexed his thoughts and dreamed of power, power that would soon be his.

Sixteen

THE AIRSHIP'S DECK WAS alive with activity as Joth and Eilyth stood near the forecastle and listened to the captain's shrill voice shouting commands to the crewmen. They had reefed the sails and the airship had slowed, seemingly. Now Elmund was at the bowsprit while Kipren and Galt manned the draglines at the stern, all of them answering, "Aye, lady, aye!" when the tall slim lady in the broad feathered hat ordered them about a task from her place at the helm. She was stood near the wooden and brass column, operating the strange bronze lever smoothly and intently.

Joth and Eilyth were wrapped in fur cloaks, clad in their new traveling costumes. A solemn and disgruntled Elmund had escorted them to the crew's quarters after Eilyth had spoken with the captain and Joth had been given access to the late Dathe's crew chest. The man had been of a similar size to Joth, and the strange garments he had pieced together from the man's wardrobe fit relatively well considering. Afterward the tight-lipped Elmund escorted them to the captain's quarters and Joth was made to wait outside on the deck as the captain took over from Elmund and ushered Eilyth into her cabin and shut the door behind her. When they reemerged, Eilyth was swathed in slashed silk from head to toe, and Joth thought that the outfit suited her somehow even with the odd incongruity of her hair ornaments, and she and the slender captain were laughing together. The clothing fit her well.

Joth was still unused to seeing women in hosen, and it was hard not to stare. Perhaps the bodice was a bit too long for her, accounting for the slender and long torso of the elegant ship captain's figure, but the hosen accentuated Eilyth's surprisingly shapely legs, and the bodice pushed forward other aspects of Eilyth's figure that Joth had not realized existed. He found himself getting hot despite the sub-arctic winds blowing in the heights above the cloud canopy that stretched out as far as he could see, seemingly in touching distance below them as they sailed the skies aboard the airship. There she was staring at him and he realized that he had been staring at her since the first time that she had appeared. He felt color flush his cheeks, and he quickly looked away, averting his eyes to the deck.

"What is it?" she asked him simply.

"Nothing. You look very nice, I'm sorry. I mean to apolo—"

"Stop it, Joth. I tease you." She smiled at him. He felt the fool. "You expected me to dress differently?"

"I wasn't expecting that," he said. The captain gave him a wry grin and took her position back at the helm.

Eilyth laughed at him. "You have not seen yourself in a mirror, Joth Andries; your costume is equally provocative."

Joth felt his cheeks burn. "As you say, lady, forgive me."

She had laughed even harder then. The clothing was warm and comfortable, but the way that it sat on his frame felt strange as he moved in it for the first few hours. The clothes were cut to allow a full range of movement, especially at the shoulders and arms, and they fit much differently than anything Joth had ever worn before. He felt a bit ridiculous in the airship crew costume, but the other crewmen looked at them approvingly once they were on deck in the attire.

Kipren winked at them both and said, "Better, much better!"

They had flown through the day and the evening was settling in when it was announced that they were nearing Grannock. They had descended well below the clouds and the crew had worked at the sails and in the rigging as they did so, and now they were watching as the captain and crew prepared to set the airship down.

"Ready, Elmund?" called the captain.

"Aye, lady, aye."

"Away the drags!"

Kipren and Galt dropped large metal grapples over the side then pulled two levers at the stern. Two spools began to play out their lines and wind out.

"Drags away, lady," Galt reported.

The captain waited for a long moment then cried out, "Make fast the draglines!"

"Aye, lady, aye!" Kipren and Galt pushed the levers and the spools slowed to a stop.

"Ready, all hands!" The captain manipulated the bronze lever at the column. The airship began to descend and Joth had a strange panicky feeling in his gut as the ship lurched and fell through the skies. He felt Eilyth's hand tighten on his arm and he knew that she felt it too. The sun was low on the horizon and burning a beautiful crimson shade of orange and the skies were bathed in pink and gray as the landscape below them took on shape and dimension. Trees that had looked like balls of green wool now stretched up and out, their branches and leaves discernible from the deck. Hills stretched up and vales opened out beneath them, and the ground sped past them at an alarming pace. Had they been traveling this swiftly when they were in the heights above the clouds? Surely not, Joth thought, the ground had barely seemed to move at all from up there. Yet here they were, racing faster than Joth had ever traveled before, the world speeding by a mere hundred yards below him.

"Brace for drags!" Elmund cried out from the prow.

The captain nodded toward him and Eilyth.

Joth put his hand on the rail that surrounded the opening in the deck that led to the forecastle hold and kept his other arm around Eilyth. She grabbed the rail with both hands and planted her feet slightly apart on the deck. A few moments later the deck lurched beneath them. Joth nearly lost his footing but managed to only go down to his knees as the deck swam beneath him for a long beat. The drag lines had caught on the earth and were slowing the ship now.

"Nothing like it in the world!" Galt grinned at them. The short, dark man's smile stretched from one jug ear to the next as he dangled from the rigging. The tied-up horses whinnied their disagreement and rolled white eyes at him. Joth had studied the knots well when he had checked the horses earlier, and they had managed to rig them up fairly cleverly, he thought. It was paying off now as the horses skidded and sought purchase on the shifting deck. If one of them panicked and managed to tear free it would be a disaster, Joth mused. The captain looked out to either side.

"How're we dragging?"

"Both lines dragging even!" Kipren hailed back.

"All clear ahead, lush and green!" Elmund called from his place at the prow. "Haul and wind, lads!" the captain ordered, and the men sprang to. "Elmund, take up Dathe's place a-stern." She pointed at Joth. "You take Elmund's place."

He nodded. He had no idea what he was meant to do at the bow, but he knew not to question an order; the First Army of the Magistry had taught him that.

Elmund was eyeing him contemptuously as he passed him on deck. "If you see the ground getting too close too quick then make sure to cry out," he said with a sneer.

"Is that what you stand there for?"

Elmund was ready for a fight, Joth could see it; and part of him wanted one too. He did not like the man's bearing toward him and Eilyth, and he was tired of being the scapegoat for the man's grief at the loss of his comrade. Let him come and fight me, Joth thought. I'm a bloody Linesman of the First Army and I've already beaten the town guard of Borsford today.

Elmund opened his mouth, eyes screwed up with rage and tongue forming a torrent of vehemence, when the captain spoke again.

"Elmund! Haul and wind, mate!"

"Aye, lady, aye!" he spat and walked on to the stern.

Joth watched him go and caught Eilyth looking at him too. He met her eyes and read disapproval there, or perhaps caution. He could not be certain which, but he broke contact and moved to the prow and looked out at the unbelievable spectacle of the world beneath him bathed in the golden light of sunset. Eilyth did not have to approve of everything, he thought. This matter doesn't even concern her; it's about that bastard making such a spectacle and drawing his blade and making threats and then walking about as though he's the bloody cock of the walk and looking at us like we're nothing. Calling him a "bloody dirtworm," whatever the implications of that were meant to be. It did not sit easily with Joth—any of it.

The captain was looking back at the men working on both sides of the airship hauling in the draglines. One man would brace his feet against the ship and then haul at the line while his comrade wound the reel and set the brake, and they were working in unison now hauling the ship down toward where the grapples had made purchase in the earth below. They were chanting something, it was helping them keep rhythm and pace, but Joth was too far away to make out the words for the wind. He looked out ahead of him over the edge of the bow and saw the ground coming closer slowly and steadily as the ship was hauled in by the draglines. The captain looked over the edge once the lines had been reeled in to a certain point and then made one final adjustment with the bronze lever at the column and the ship hummed with a pulse of energy that Joth felt as the deck vibrated and the ship began to fall like a feather, swaying against the draglines that tethered it and sinking down to the surface. "Bowlines!" she commanded.

Galt and Kipren hurried to Joth and hefted anchors over the sides. The anchors were large stones with their centers bored out to allow ropes to be fixed to them, and when they landed the bow dipped as the ship righted itself. The crew left the bowlines there and went back to hauling and winding at the drags. Joth watched as the airship's crew toiled at pulling the ship down toward the earth, winding the reels of the draglines in and applying the brakes to the spools of rope over and over again until finally the airship hovered a few feet above the grassy meadow in the fading light of the day. The captain moved the bronze lever a final time and the ship gently rested down on the ground with a groan. She removed the lever from the column with a twist and deftly hung it from her belt again.

"Lower the gangway, Elmund. Galt, unhitch those horses. Make ready, Kipren. You two, help me with Dathe."

The crew set about their various tasks. Eilyth and Joth helped the captain carry Dathe's body down the gangway and lay it down in the grass near the resting airship. After a few minutes had passed, the crewmen came down the gangway.

They were sweating from their labors at the draglines, and they were all carrying their ditty bags with them. Kipren had a pair of shovels resting on his shoulder. He moved to Joth and handed him one. Galt led the horses down the gangway and passed the leads on to Eilyth, who stood near her gray mare Aila and looked on.

"Let's dig a hole now," Kipren said solemnly to Joth.

He nodded and followed the man as he picked out a suitable resting place for his fallen comrade. As the sun was slipping down behind the rising hills on the horizon they lowered the body of Dathe into the grave they had dug. Elmund and Galt pulled the ropes they had used to lower him free and Kipren coiled them and laid them in the grass. Joth put the shovel into the mound of excavated earth beside the grave and wiped the perspiration from his brow. He stood near Eilyth as she calmly looked on, the horses behind her. The captain undid her chinstrap and removed her hat and cleared her throat.

"Gather 'round, shipmates," she said softly. "We lay the body of our fallen crewman to rest, he who has soared the winds with the eagles now must rest in the dark reaches of the earth. He who has bathed in the sunlight high above the clouds must now know the darkness of the depths. May his spirit soar on high, now and for always!"

"May his spirit soar on high!" the crew repeated.

The captain looked to Elmund and the others. "Words, Elmund?"

Elmund looked as though he was choking back emotion, and he shook his head.

"He was a good lad, and a good hand," Kipren said.

"Aye. Too young to go," Galt muttered.

The captain nodded. "As the captain of the Skyward, I, Ryla Dierns, along with my crew lay the body of our fellow Dathe to rest. May he know peace."

"Aye," they all replied.

They took turns at covering the body with spades full of dirt until at last the grave was covered and in the fading sunlight they set out toward Grannock together in silence. Joth fell back with Eilyth as the ship's crew walked together.

"Lady, shall I take the horses?"

"No, Joth, I am fine. Thank you." She favored him with a smile.

It was dark by the time they made the village. The cobbled road began and ended in a short stretch of a hundred or so yards and strung together the six structures that made up Grannock. The small village was perched atop a low hill and centered about the covered well that stood in the middle of the cobbled path.

The buildings were all made from cut stone and the roofs were thatched, and Joth could see firelight coming from within them all through the windows on the ground and in the upper stories. He smelled food and woodsmoke and heard barking dogs and the more distant sounds of livestock. He began to hear the faint sounds of music as they neared the center of the village, and the noise of people laughing and talking began to grow louder as they walked past the covered well and crossed to a large sprawling building illuminated with torchlight at the end of the cobbled lane. A large wooden sign depicting a peasant with a jug and three yellow haystacks hung from a post over a double door and swayed gently with the cool evening breeze. Joth and Eilyth stood with the horses as Captain Ryla stepped in front of the men and held out her hands, halting them.

"Stay atop your drinking, lads. Don't none of you let your grief cloud your judgment."

"Aye, lady."

"Elmund? Can I count on you?"

"Aye, lady." He rolled his shoulders back and looked her in the eye.

She held his gaze for a long beat. "Cool heads, boys." She turned toward the door then turned back again. "You two wait and I'll fetch the groom."

"You're just gonna leave 'em here on their own with three horses?" Elmund muttered incredulously.

"They ain't going nowhere. I got Shiny's writ, and his word; and Pretty's sticking to Shiny." Captain Ryla gave a wry smile as Galt and Kipren chuckled, and then she turned to the door.

Elmund cast one more narrow-eyed glance their way and then followed his captain and crewmates inside the inn. The volume of the music and the chatter increased for a moment as the doors opened, smells of food baking and wood smoke and ale hit Joth's senses in a wafting wave as the doors shut.

"Leave that with the pack horse." Eilyth motioned with her head at the cloak wrapped sword he held.

"Lady? What if there's trouble wi—"

"No, not here. We will not be needing blades here."

He held her eyes for a long beat then relented and threaded the cloak-shrouded blade through the packsaddle cinching, suspending it. "I hope that you're right."

"I'm always right." She smiled. "It is good to be on the ground again." She gazed up at the night sky, the waxing moon.

"There's always a chance of trouble, lady. I don't know if it's wise to—"

"Tonight is for laughter, Joth Andries. Trust in me when I tell you this, and put your worries away."

Fine for her not to worry, Joth mused, it's me that gets my teeth kicked in when one of the locals gets too much ale down his throat; or worse, Elmund assumes the full character of his attitude and plays his fool hand. He could not argue with the logic of keeping swords out of the equation however, and so he acquiesced and stood waiting with her on the cobbled street. He noticed she had not given up her staff and was about to say something to her about it when the noise and light erupted from the inn's doors as they flew open and a stalwart-looking young lad somewhere in his mid-teenage years toppled out and righted himself before them, shrugging off his laughter.

"I'm Bell, I'm the groom. Just these three then, Master? Hay and oats is extra, should you want them."

Joth passed a silver coin to the lad. "Take good care of them, and we'll settle with you in the morning."

The lad blinked twice in a feeble attempt to cover his astonishment. "Yes, Master, at your pleasure." The stammering boy took the leads to the horses and bowed to them both.

"What is the name of this place?" Joth asked.

"Grannock?" he croaked.

"The inn. What's the name of it?"

"Oh!" he blushed, "I thought you meant the town. It's 'The Merry Haymaker,' Master, but folks 'round here sometimes say 'Grannock Inn' or 'Grannock Tavern' and what-not, if it please you." His eyes lingered on Eilyth and her airship's crew costume a moment too long for Joth's liking, but the boy at last turned and led the horses around the back of the inn to where the stables lay.

"Strange custom, this passing of coin," Eilyth noted curiously.

"It'll keep the horses looked after, that's all I care about."

"Joth Andries, mind your tone with me. You had better get yourself in order now."

He almost began to protest.

"If you do not let yourself be at peace, then Elmund will get the rise out of you that he has been seeking. You shall walk right into his trap. You jeopardize the safety of our envoy, and you dishonor the words you spoke to my father."

And she was right; he deserved it. He had jeopardized their mission, he had been thinking of himself instead of the Lady Eilyth, or Wat, or even his own oath to Tregaern, or his forced-upon oath with Eilyth's brother Eilorn. He felt an even bigger fool as the world came into perspective for him at that moment, and for all that he was and all that he could feel he said to her simply, "I'm very sorry, lady. You are right. It will happen no more."

She nodded to him and walked to the doors of the inn. "Are you coming with me?"

"Yes, of course." He passed her and opened the door for her.

Joth noticed more than a few narrow-eyed glares directed toward him and Eilyth as they entered. Apparently a drunken wit had taken a stab at making fun of the airship crew's fashions and the slim Captain Ryla had said something funnier that set the whole inn to rollicking laughter. But not everyone was laughing, and it was obvious to Joth that the people of this village were wary and distrustful of strangers. For all of that it was a fine inn, Joth noted. The underside of the thatched roof was a vibrant green and the walls were all lime washed a stark white, which made the inn surprisingly bright inside in the lamplight. There were two large fireplaces roaring at either end of the hall, and the tables strewn between were littered with patrons. Four serving girls worked the room shuttling empty flagons back to the bar and bringing bowls and plates laden with food out to the tables. A piper sat on a stool in a corner of the room cradling his instrument and drinking from a tankard, enrapt in conversation with a drunk who was attempting to hum a tune for him, presumably a tune that he wished the piper to play next. A young man kissed a girl by the door and was rewarded with a slap and laughter from the table where his friends all sat spectating.

Some men sat at a table throwing dice, some others were huddled in conversation. One man was crying and singing to himself at the bar. There were a fair few women in the place, Joth thought, more than one usually saw in a village tavern. But most of them were either working at the inn or sitting with their husbands as they grew drunk and talked with their friends. It took Joth a moment to realize that it was the fall harvest, and the village was in the midst of a celebration. Most of these men would be farm hands and laborers, teamsters and drovers working for the season's bounty; and now they would be reaching the end of their labors with the harvest complete or nearly done. They would all be looking to round out their hard work with a little quiet time at the inn and a few flagons. There would most likely be a harvest fair happening soon in the village. There would be animals for the slaughter, masters taking on apprentices, games and contests. Couples would be getting married, girls and boys courting each other with the intent of getting married, crops and goods on sale. My life at one time years ago, Joth mused. He could be sitting at a shaving horse now instead of floating about in airships and running from the town guard but as Eilyth had said to him, his old life was gone; it was no more.

He started toward the captain with Eilyth. "I've settled with the Innkeep and we've hot baths tomorrow and berths for the night, each to their own," Captain Ryla Dierns said by way of greeting.

"Baths? That will be most welcome." Eilyth raised her eyebrows almost imperceptibly. Joth was not sure if that was a personal desire or a wish that extended to present company. He supposed that to Eilyth's nose they were all a bit ripe smelling. They were stood at a bar that had been constructed between two large beams, and the jug-eared Galt was ushering over one of the serving girls, who was balancing a tray of flagons. As they arrived, Kipren smoothed out his long beard and solemnly passed them each a flagon. It was good Oestern ale; Joth could smell the hopped scent as the flagon passed his nose.

"For Dathe," Kipren toasted, raising his mug aloft.

"For Dathe," they all repeated, and drank.

The piper began to play a reeling tune, and the locals began to dance. It was a rollicking scene as they began to clear tables back and mark out a space for the dancing. An argument started between the gamblers and a group of men who were there with their wives and keen on dancing. It was growing heated as he and Eilyth looked on.

"Hit him!" cried Galt, laughing.

"Wind yourself down, fool!" Captain Ryla shot at him, "Don't involve yourself."

He looked down, admonished.

The argument passed without incident, and the gamblers moved their table back away from the area that the others had cleared for dancing, and the villagers were now in full step. They danced as the piper blew out a reel, then a galloping tune that Joth had a hard time keeping time with, and then a country jig to which they all danced a round. Eilyth was watching the dancers with curiosity.

"Do you know how to do that dance?" she asked Joth.

"Not much of a dancer, lady."

She looked back at the dancers and nodded. She looked unspeakably disappointed at his answer.

"I'll give it a try if you would care to dance, lady."

She smiled then and took a drink of her ale before taking his hand in hers and leading him out onto the floor. The mood was lively, and the villagers were all in good cheer with smiles on their faces and laughter was heard all around as they stood apart from one another, and passed, and circled, and bowed or curtsied, and shuffled and jumped with the dance. Then the entire airship's crew was dancing with them, and the villagers dancing along with them all. Eilyth was beaming, a sheen of sweat on her brow from the quick steps that she had mastered now, dancing in the line with the other women toward the line of men where Joth and the others stood, waiting to do their circling and passing.

Although at first he had been nervous, Joth was enjoying himself too; even Elmund had a smile on his face, he noticed. After they had danced several rounds and different steps and rhythms to several different tunes the red-faced piper lowered his instrument and cried out, "I needs a rest now, my Gentles!" And though the audience called out for more, but the piper was adamant about needing a break.

Joth and Eilyth walked back to the bar between beams together. Out on the floor Galt and Kipren aped a dance and cavorted around each other to Elmund and the captain's amusement. As he looked at Eilyth, at the flushed cheeks, the happy expression in her eyes, he realized that this had been the good Oestern inn experience that he was hoping for back in Borsford. The joy was compounded when the serving girl brought a savory one to the bar and laid out trenchers for them all, complete with two cruets holding garlic sauce and a lemony parsley sauce as condiments. Joth had been famished and the smell of the pie set his mouth to watering. As the others landed back at the bar and the slices were cut and served by the young serving girl rather hurriedly and unceremoniously, Joth found himself smiling.

"I'm sorry that it took so long," he said to Eilyth.

"What do you mean?"

"This has been the most hurried, harried day of my life, lady. All I've wanted to show you since before dawn has been the friendly feeling of an Oestern inn, and it's taken until now to do so, with a lot of misadventure in between."

"I understand now, I do. Thank you for showing me, and this has been such fun, this dancing and the music!"

"I'm glad then."

"But I am not yet fully convinced we have seen the last of our troubles on this journey."

"Lady?"

Her face grew very serious. "Something is making me worry. Something I can not see clearly yet."

He looked at her and she met his eyes for a long beat and then turned her attention to her food. He did not know if it was the inn, the airship crew, the village, or Oesteria at large that was troubling Eilyth, but something inside told him it was all of those things and more—that it was part of Eilyth's mysterious knowledge whether that be magic or a heightened awareness or some sort of mystic perception that she was capable of. Perhaps she saw events that would come to pass? He could not know for certain, but he was certain that it troubled her.

"Eilyth, whatever it is, I will protect you." She smiled at him sadly. Why, he wondered? Had she seen something that was going to happen to him, to them all perhaps? "I'll protect you as best I can."

"Yes, I know you will."

They ate and drank on into the night for another hour and a half before the villagers began to shuffle off and they were the only patrons left in the Merry Haymaker's great room with its white walls and dying firelight. Another pie was brought before them, another savory pie full of mushrooms and smoked meat and root vegetables and peas. Elmund, Kipren, and Galt seemed to take that as a cue to throw caution to the wind and drink past their fill. Elmund seemed to be slightly less drunk than Galt, perhaps a bit more than Kipren, but altogether darker than both of the other men combined. His eyes were settling on Joth now more and more, and in the interest of keeping the peace Joth stood back from the bar and told Eilyth that he was turning in for the evening.

"I shall turn in as well," she said. They said their good nights and made to leave.

"That's a cute arrangement," Elmund said lowly. Joth did not take the bait, even though it burned him not to. "Perhaps we could help you save a bit of coin and you two could just—"

"Stand down, Elmund," the captain said tiredly.

"Just a bit of fun, my lady. Look at how cute they are, thick as thieves."

Elmund was stumbling back from the bar. Eilyth had a firm hand on Joth's shoulder, and if she had not been there he would have flown into the man already. Now Elmund had planted his feet to slow his swaying world slightly, and he had squared off with Joth and Eilyth.

"I said stand down!" Ryla was on her way around the bar to intercept Elmund.

"Black luck to have seen either of them! Dathe dead and here we are dancing and drinking. How do you like that?" He pulled his arm away from his captain and staggered out a few feet further toward Joth and Eilyth. "What did you do in that town? Eh? What did you steal to get them up in arms about? Everyone knows that the bloody Dawn Tribes are full of thiev—"

Eilyth moved like a bolt of lightning and struck out with her staff and hit the man twice on the head and then swept his legs out from under him and laid him out on his back in the middle of the floor. Kipren and Galt's eyes nearly shot out of their heads, and Ryla Dierns looked as though she had given up but was somehow impressed at the same time. Eilyth's face was calm, but her eyes burned with fire and passion. She held the moaning Elmund on the floor with the butt of her staff resting on his windpipe.

"Listen to me now," she said evenly. "We are no thieves, and my people most certainly are not thieves. It is the Oestermen who are consumed by greed, it is you and your vanity and your laziness and your disrespect of nature and your covetousness that poisons your world, not my people. We live with the earth, you seek to live off of it; can you not see your own folly?" She was looking at Elmund straight in the eyes and he had locked eyes with her and in that moment his eyes grew wide before they settled back.

He gasped once before he had his wind. "Please. Let me go. I'm sorry."

She released him and he rose to his knees, a hand on his throat and the unmistakable look of fear and confusion in his eyes. Kipren and Galt helped him to his feet. He was looking at them all as though he was disoriented, as though he did not remember having seen them all day and all night, and Joth was almost certain that Eilyth had used her power on Elmund in much the same way as she had used it on him those weeks ago when he and Wat had been captured in the pass. Of course, the man was drunk and had been hit with a staff on the crown and knocked to the floor.

"It's bunk time, lads. Fun is over for the night." The captain motioned for Joth and Eilyth to take to the stairs. Joth thought it a good idea and guided Eilyth in that direction as the airship crew sat Elmund in a chair and Galt fetched him some water. A serving girl showed them upstairs to their rooms, which were at the end of the hall and adjacent to each other. The serving girl wished them a pleasant sleep and trotted back downstairs. Joth stood across from Eilyth and bowed to her slightly.

"You are bloody quick with that staff."

"I could not let him keep talking."

"I suppose that was the last thing he expected to have happen to him." Joth could not help but smile. He had wanted to lay Elmund out from the beginning.

Eilyth smiled back at him. "Did you…wake him? Like what you did to me?"

She shook her head. "I only show the possibilities. The world as it is. It is up to the sleeper to wake."

Joth did not understand what that meant. Her powers were mysterious and subtle, and altogether foreign to him. He found himself staring at her without any words again, without any words to put together in any meaningful way that would grant him a window into her world or allow him for the slightest moment to have a clear understanding of how she understood things, how the world could be brought into such sharp focus and clarity as it seemed to be for her. He stood there searching for something to say, something that could encapsulate his ideas and his feelings, but he came to the realization that he was not able to speak of it now. It was larger than him, larger than his understanding would allow him to fathom.

"My lady, I wish you a good night and a good sleep."

She laughed at him. "Thank you, my lord."

"No, not lord. Perhaps Master, but even that's calling it close."

He shared a laugh with her then. She was very charming, gold and red and dazzling blue and green. It was easy to forget that he was essentially a prisoner trapped within the prospect of her safekeeping if he were ever to rescue his friend and commander Wat. Of course there was the issue of Lord Uhlmet, but to him that mattered little; Lord Uhlmet could rot for all he cared. No, for him the world had shrunk down to he and the Lady Eilyth and their adventures, even if he was being used he felt well used. Even if he had to pit his life against Elmund's or anyone else, he knew that he would do so willingly in order to protect her and preserve her, friends or no. They looked at each other there in the hall for a long while, and then Eilyth stepped inside the doorframe of her room.

"Well, goodnight, Joth, and thank you for your excellent guardianship today." She seemed a bit stiff as she addressed him.

"Please, lady, I am here across from you should you need anything at all."

"Yes, I see that." Her face was unreadable.

She stepped inside and closed the door as Joth stood in the hall and listened to the sounds of the inn and Eilyth shifting about in her room. After a moment he stepped into his own room and lay himself down on the bed. He pulled his boots off and unlaced his clothes. He slipped down to his shirt and braies and lie in the bed. It felt grand to be in a bed, a proper bed; he had not felt it in months. He thought of Eilyth across the hall from him and he wondered if he were in her thoughts at all. He fell asleep wondering as the airship crew filed up the stairs and into their rooms.

Captain Ryla paused outside Eilyth's door for a long beat before rolling up the writ Joth had given her then going to her own room and lying on the bed with her eyes on the ceiling for a long time before sleep took her.

Two seconds after the captain shut her eyes and faded off to sleep, Eilyth shut hers.

Seventeen

EILYTH WAS THERE ALREADY when he came down the stairs for breakfast. It was early morning he could tell by the soft light coming in through the leaded glass windows lining the lime-washed hall.

"How did you sleep?" she asked him.

"Not as well as I'd hoped." He had woken so many times in the night he felt as though he had hardly slept at all. After so many nights of sleeping out of doors and in the elements he would have thought that a roof and a soft warm bed could grant him a restful night, but they seemed to have had the opposite effect.

"Nor I," she said resignedly.

A serving girl came and put a pitcher of ale and some rolls still hot from the oven down at their table. She smiled and curtsied half-heartedly. "Can I get you both your breakfasts?"

"Yes, if you please," Joth said. "I'm still hungry from yesterday."

They sipped ale and put honey and butter on the rolls and talked of how much more distance they would have to cover to make it to Twinton and the High Mage. Joth did not know for certain where in Oesteria he was, and he had no idea how fast the airships could cover ground. He asked the serving girl how many days' ride it was from Grannock to Borsford.

"Perhaps four days, maybe five," she said.

Joth whistled lowly. They had made a week's journey in just one short day.

"It's not too far away to Torlucksford neither, closer by two days."

She laid out two platters laden with eggs and toast and marrow-bones, some grilled wild onions, sausages, and some roasted root vegetables and turnip mash. It looked to be a fantastic breakfast, at least to Joth's eyes. They were halfway through it when Ryla Dierns came down the stairs, and the rest of the crew shuffled down a few minutes later, Elmund last. All of them except Ryla looked the worse for wear, and Elmund looked worst of all. One side of his face was noticeably swollen and his eyes were bloodshot, and he was moving stiffly. To his credit, he approached the table where Joth and Eilyth sat and apologized for his words and his actions and insisted that he harbored no ill feelings and he hoped that they might forgive him his grief and drunkenness.

"Thank you, Elmund," Eilyth said to him, and inclined her head slightly in what Joth now recognized was a sort of gesture of dismissal, as though Eilyth were letting him know that he had said the right words and that he could now leave her presence. Elmund was not quite as well-versed in Eilyth's body language and he stood there for a long moment as though he were searching for more to say before he nodded a few times and walked over to sit with his crewmates.

"That was unexpected."

"It's the least he should do."

"Do not discount him, there is hope in everyone," she said absently.

"Hope, lady?"

"Yes. 'Hope in everyone, and for everyone a hope.' That is a saying among us."

They finished their breakfasts and the serving girl told them that their baths would be ready shortly and that the stews were out behind the inn at the back of the kitchens as she cleared away their platters.

"More ale?" she asked, but Elmund made a sour-looking face and waved her away. Ryla stood from the table.

"Ladies first. Pretty and I shall bathe first, then you lot can go and soil the water with your grimy trunks after."

Kipren and Galt laughed and gave her an "aye, lady" along with Elmund.

"Hurry yourselves along now, because we are in the skies again by mid-morning! And talk to the Innkeep about some provisions for our windsailing while I'm beautifying myself." She came over and took Eilyth by the arm and swept her off toward the kitchens at the back of the inn.

Joth was left with half a pitcher of ale at the now empty table. By the time he had finished the ale, Galt and Elmund had gotten up and walked to where the innkeeper stood behind the bar and they were in rapt conversation with him. Kipren was eating the rest of Elmund's unfinished breakfast. Joth decided that he might as well go and find the young groom and settle up with him while he waited for Eilyth and Ryla Dierns to finish in the stews.

He stood from the table and walked to the front of the inn and out the door. There was a crowd around the covered well, chatting and gathering water, and they all marked him as he came out and walked around the inn to where the stables lay.

The airship costume was anything but subtle, he noted. He missed the simplicity and practicality of his Dawn Tribe clothing. Two young girls pointed to him and snickered, and a third said something that sent them all chasing one another around the well in a tirade of screamed threats and screeching. He watched their antics until he rounded the corner and found the youth he had met the previous night mucking out stalls and filling a wagon with manure.

"Morning, Master," he said brightly.

"Good morning. I'll need the horses ready as soon as you can have them so."

"I've just about finished my chore here, and I'll start to tack them up for you."

Joth nodded. He turned and started away but then thought better of it and turned back. "When you say you've 'just about finished' what exactly does that mean?"

"Well, Master, that means I got about three more stalls to muck out and then I got to head out to the back paddock and—"

"Better to get to my horses now, and get back to your chores after. I'm a bit pressed for time this morning."

"As it please you, Master." The lad sounded put out. "It's just that I got a particular way of doing things round here, and I don't really like to get it all out of order because I tend to forget things then, you see, like the time I was supposed to have hitched up a team of cobbs and I was—"

Joth had held his hand up for a long beat before the lad stopped his blathering. "I understand. Please see to those three horses I handed you yesternight?"

"Yesternight, as you say, Master."

"What was your name again?"

"Bellan. Bell for short. That's what I'm usually called by most folks around here anyw—"

"Thanks, Bell. The horses," he reminded him.

Joth turned and continued on toward the back of the inn, leaving Bellan to stand looking back and forth from him to the stables and the manure cart. He rounded the corner and found himself staring at the naked form of Captain Ryla Dierns emerging from the bath and drying herself. She was stood on one of a pair of wooden runs that lined the short row of four wooden tubs that sat stewing in the cool fall morning, her lithe and sinuous form steaming in the pale sunlight. Joth looked away but felt as though he had stared at her far too long and not quite enough, an uncomfortable situation made worse by the fact that Eilyth sat submerged in the bath, her shoulders head and neck visible, having witnessed it all. He met her eyes and she only gave him one of her strange half smiles that he still could not decipher. The captain noticed him and did not seem to care that he had blundered upon them at all.

"Oh, it's Shiny come to see the ladies, is it?" She and Eilyth giggled like the village girls had at the covered well. "Well, feast your eyes, lad!" She opened her towel and revealed herself to him, shaking her breasts and hips at him before wrapping herself back up and laughing to Eilyth. "Look at him! I think I've given him a shock!"

Joth raised his eyebrows and tried to compose himself with a smile. "Captain, you are quite a beautiful woman but please understand that I wasn't sneaking around the bloody stews to catch a glimpse—"

"Oh, stop talking, Shiny." She was smiling when she said it. "I'll spare Pretty the indignity if you'll kindly go on your way. You can tell the lads it's bath time now."

She favored him with a wink and broomed him away with her hand. Joth saw Eilyth laughing again as he turned red-faced and walked back past the stables and the street with the covered well and back in through the entrance of the Merry Haymaker. Bloody fool, Joth, he thought. She was a fine-looking woman though, that truth was for certain. If he had let

Bellan talk for a few minutes more he might have avoided the sight entirely; or he would have rounded the corner and seen more of the Lady Eilyth than the airship costume revealed.

Joth went to the bar and asked for half a flagon of ale and tried to push those thoughts out of his head. He also paid for the stabling of the horses and for his and the Lady Eilyth's room and board. The prices were fair and he paid for it out of his and Wat's silver. He had to start paying attention to his spending, could not just hand out silvers to stable boys everywhere they went. He did not know how long the journey would take or even if they would be able to count on traveling back from Twinton by airship. Perhaps the High Mage would not think that the matter was of much importance, or perhaps he would want them to travel back slowly so that he would have more time to prepare should his answer be one of violence. Joth had thought little about what Eilyth's true message to the High Mage might be, but he was smart enough to know that he was not escorting her to Twinton for an audience where she would debate the High Mage and the Council of the Magistry and make them aware of an ancient treaty and an oath that they had broken and wag her finger at them before disappearing back over the mountains and into Dawn Tribe Territory. He was almost certain now that Eilyth meant to do to the High Mage what she had done to Elmund last night and what she had done to Joth himself in Rhael's Pass; she meant to shake the High Mage, to see if he would wake.

"It's up to the sleeper to wake," she had said, and Joth wondered what would happen if he would not wake. Would that mean war between the People and his people, war with Oesteria? If that were to come about he would be forced to fight the People alongside his fellows in the First Army. Joth thought of Eilyth and Traegern, of his time in the village by the mountain river, of fierce Eilorn, of the old hens who had teased and chastised him and wept when he left. His old life was gone, she had said, but what would happen when the Magistry mobilized its army and made for Rhael's Pass with its Goblincraft engines and magic-wielding Mage Imperators and the First Army and its thirty-five thousand fighting men? Would he stand with the People or with his own? He knew the answer. He told Kipren to tell the others that the stews were open for them and then he headed back there, his thoughts heavy on him.

There was no sign of Lady Eilyth or Captain Ryla Dierns at the row comprised of simmering wooden bathing tubs, and Joth was both relieved and disappointed in equal measure. He undressed and lowered himself into the hot water, paying attention not to step in the copper center of the barrel stave tub. There was a pail and a sponge. Sponges were said to be sea creatures, Joth knew, but why was it that they floated? He lowered himself under the hot water and held his breath for as long as he could.

He could hear the fire beneath his tub crackling through the water. He could hear the staves creaking and the water moving, constantly moving around him. When he lifted his head from the water and cleared his eyes, Lady Eilyth was standing above him on the wooden run. He was a bit startled and exposed. How long had she been standing there, he wondered? She handed him a small woolen bag.

"I thought you might wish to have some salts and oil for washing. I am sorry to have startled you."

"Oh, thank you, lady." He felt his face redden.

She regarded him with the half smile again then turned and left him to his bathing. The airship crew entered as she exited, and amidst crude jokes and boasting, and much talking and jocular behavior, they all finally settled into bathing themselves.

Joth used the salts and oils that he had been given. The scents themselves took him back to the village by the river, to evenings there in the cool mountain air, the moon, and the music by the table of the Roundhouse, laden with fresh bounty from the river and the fields, a simple dinner made rich with company and singing and fresh herbs. It made him long for the village, but it inspired curiosity in Elmund.

"What is that you're rubbing yourself with?" he asked gruffly. "If you don't mind my asking, that is."

"It's just salts and oils. You can try some if you like." He tossed the bag with the rest of his salts and oils that Eilyth had prepared for him to the swollen-headed man in the tub.

"Thanks," he said, catching it. It sounded like an apology. Good, thought Joth, still unconvinced of the man's dependability. Joth got out of the bath and toweled himself off as Elmund sniffed and tested at the salts and oils.

"You just rub it on your skin?"

"Yes, the salts you do. The oil's for after."

He nodded.

Joth got himself dressed and headed back around to the front of the inn, and as he passed through the stables he noticed at least a dozen horses all rigged out for light cavalry action, and Bellan the groom flagging him down.

"Hey, I've got your horses tacked and ready, Master! I'd be most pleased if you were to take them with you now. I'm a bit taxed for space, if you understand me rightly, Master. I think I should be mo—"

"You'll have to hold on for a moment, Bell. I've just to go inside and gather the others."

Bell looked flummoxed but just nodded as Joth went past him.

"What's all this?" he asked the boy.

"Magistry. Whole bloody division, look!"

Magistry? Not by their tack. Reddish brown traces of leather set with bronze medallions and slim upright saddles. Where did that fashion of saddle hail from? The horses were very handsome as well.

"There was a mage at the head of them too! Weren't much to look at, to be honest. But who am I to judge, I ask you?"

"A mage, you say? An Imperator or Alchemist?"

"What's the difference?"

He left the lad there with his question.

Joth was around the corner and on his way to the great room at the Merry Haymaker.

In front of the inn were several men, all wearing bastard swords at their hips and helmets on their heads—long, elegantly tailed sallets complete with visors. Some of the helms were polished to a sheen, some left blackened, some others bronzed and golden and burnished bright. Most of them had removed their helms by the time he had walked past them, but a few of the men had simply lifted their visors as they stood at their leisure. They all wore a dark coat cut from the same cloth embroidered with a livery badge of some device that Joth was not familiar with. A lion and a tree and some other device, like an eye or some such. He went through the door and saw a short, slight man in dark austere clothing talking to the innkeeper at the bar toward the back of the room, and several more of the cavalry men from outside standing behind him and the staff looking quite nervous and ill at ease, to Joth's eyes. Eilyth and Ryla Dierns were sat at a table in the center of the room. He made his way to them.

"Interesting development, Shiny. Wouldn't you say?" The captain grinned at him unabashedly. He could not stop picturing her as he had seen her outside of the stews. It made him embarrassed to think about it as he stood there before them both.

"May I sit?"

She motioned for him to do so. "Seems we have other Magistry business here in Grannock to attend to."

Joth did not like her tone. "You said you'd take us to Twinton. That's the pact we made."

"Relax, sweet boy, I only tease you." Her eyes never left his. How Eilyth felt about Ryla Dierns he did not know. She sat and watched the scene seemingly impassively, but Joth knew better. He knew she was taking in more than she was letting on. He met her eyes and stared for what he felt was too long, but somehow he could not look away, nor could she. She knew something that she was not saying.

Ryla Dierns was about to interrupt them when a high-pitched, rather jilting voice cracked out through the great room. "Ah! An airship's crew! What a fortunate coincidence." The short balding man in the austere clothing was pacing toward their table slowly, purposefully.

"I am Mage Alchemist Norden, and I shall have to requisition your airship for my own transport."

Captain Ryla Dierns did not miss a beat. She laughed and said, "I'm afraid we are already about Magistry business and we must respectfully decline service to you, my lord mage."

"Oh?" he said curiously, "I'm sure my authority supercedes your orders, whomever they come from." He said it somewhat haughtily as he challenged the captain with a look. "I'm on a special assignment for the High Mage, and I'll have you know that I have the highest authority in terms of allowance and requisitioning of materials for travel expediency, and I'll also have you know that I always get my way, no matter what else transpires. Do you understand me?"

His squealing register was somehow threatening and dark.

Ryla Dierns and Eilyth seemed to sense the darkness as well. They met his eyes with uneasy gazes. The short man, Mage Alchemist Norden, simply looked on before nodding his head and saying, "Very well, very well."

Joth looked from the captain to Eilyth and realized that all of them had been taken by surprise. Joth thought of his writ and Wat's assertion of Lord Uhlmet's power, but now he was faced with a mage who held a command that technically outranked Lord Uhlmet's, if what he was saying was true about being on assignment for the High Mage. "Officially speaking, I'm afraid none of you are to leave until we have resolved this issue. I'm terribly sorry." He smiled, and it seemed that in his smile Joth found complete disingenuousness. Mage Alchemist Norden turned away and went back to the innkeeper, obviously pleased with himself. It appeared that they had no choice in the matter; they would now wait upon the pleasure of the mage.

Eighteen

"THERE ISN'T A WAY of talking out of it." Ryla stood near the window and looked out onto the cobbled street where the short Mage Norden stood speaking to the foreign cavalry captain. "He means to have my ship and he 'always gets his way,'" she added mockingly.

"Yes, but he can't just take your ship! I have a writ."

She looked at Joth and then to Eilyth. The quarters were close and they were stood in Ryla Dierns' room so that they would not be overheard speaking by the mage or his cronies.

"I have been meaning to speak to you about that. Your writ."

"What about it?"

"Well, no offense, Shiny—but it's rather vague."

"Vague? Lady captain, my commander gave me those orders."

"Yes, your commander. Mage Imperator Rhael Lord Uhlmet?"

"Lord Uhlmet gave Wat the orders and he gave them to me."

"So you are bringing this girl back for him, then? You are his prize, Pretty?" She switched her attention to Eilyth.

"Lady Eilyth is no prize, and my orders aren't your concern—"

"They're my bloody concern if it involves my ship and my crew!" She had raised her voice and there was fire in her eyes.

"You'll tell me now what you're all about, the two of you; and you'll tell me how I can find Lord bloody Uhlmet."

"Uhlmet? What does he have to do with any of this?"

"Yes, that is an interesting question; it's one I'd like you to answer for me."

Joth looked from the captain to Eilyth. "I don't understand what you're after."

She looked at both of them for a long moment as if she was trying to decide whether or not they were lying to her. "I know you are trying to protect her, and I know that you are under orders to take her to Twinton. Why? What does Uhlmet stand to gain from this, and why has he ordered you to escort her? I want answers."

"Why should we make you privy to—"

Eilyth interrupted him. "It is fine to tell her what she wants to know, Joth."

"Lady, please."

"Go on then, she gave you her approval. I'm all ears, look at me," Ryla Dierns said.

Joth looked at the airship captain for a long beat. "You tell her then, lady."

Eilyth nodded and stood from the bed where she was sitting. "My father is the Elder of the People. He has sent me to seek an audience with the High Mage in hopes of preventing a war between your people and mine. Joth Andries is my guide and protector, but he is also my hostage. Our warriors defeated the mage and his soldiers in battle. My father is holding Lord Uhlmet and Commander Watron Kine as sureties for my safe conduct."

Even though he knew what he was, he felt strange hearing it aloud.

Ryla Dierns blinked once. "So you are seeking the High Mage, and this writ is just a straw horse to get you there. That explains its vague nature. Your warriors engaged Magistry troops?" She whistled and leaned against the window frame. "War then? The bloody tribes are going to unite and invade Oesteria? That seems a foolish idea. The Magistry will not blink their eyes at such a threat. What do you hope to gain?"

Eilyth just looked at her evenly as she continued.

"Threats and hostages, one real outcome. Someone will be paid and someone will be dead. How much does your father hope to get for Lord Uhlmet's ransom?"

Eilyth shook her head slightly. "You mistake my people for yours. We do not seek material gain."

"Then you're in the wrong business to be ransoming prisoners."

"Not when the ransom brings justice."

"Justice?" Ryla Dierns said it slowly, as though she were savoring the word and the very ideal it represented. "How does this ransom serve justice, Pretty?"

"It serves justice by allowing our voices to be heard by the High Mage of Oesteria."

Ryla smiled. "You're not going to give him back, are you?"

"Lord Uhlmet must answer for his crimes against my people—no amount of money will change that." Eilyth said it finally with great weight.

"I have a better plan." She examined her fingernails silently for a long moment. "I'll help you get to Twinton, as agreed. We shall throw this jackal Norden off of our trail, slip out in the night and make it to the Skyward and be up and away before any of them's the wiser. That shall be easy enough. Then you'll have cakes and ale with the High Mage and I'll fly you back to your father. Sounds like a dream, doesn't it?"

Joth could not figure where she was taking this, or what her stake in it might be.

She went on. "Here's the catch, if you can even call it that: you never mention Uhlmet. Not to the High Mage, not to Norden, not to anyone. You fail to mention that part. In fact, you don't even know if he's alive. He's lost for all you know, he is in charge of another Company, whatever; and when I take you back you give him to me."

"But my writ has his name on it. We'll need that to gain audience."

"We can have that amended." Ryla was looking at Joth like he was a fool. "It sometimes helps profits when one is good at adjusting trade duty invoices."

"You would have us give you Lord Uhlmet as payment?"

"Yes, I most certainly would."

Eilyth narrowed her eyes. "Why?"

She paused for a long time, and when she spoke it was careful and measured. "Because I will see him hanged for the crimes of rape and murder that I witnessed with my own eyes and body nearly twenty years ago."

"My father will hear you, you may ask him. Uhlmet is a prisoner of the People, it is not for me to decide." Eilyth was looking at the other woman and she spoke compassionately, saying "You are strong, to have endured such things. I am sorry for your pain and I will speak to my father on your behalf, but I can promise you no more. Uhlmet must answer for his crimes, and he shall answer for all of them. That I can promise you."

"I would be there on that day." Ryla held Eilyth's eyes for a long moment. "That is what I wish for with every fiber in my being."

Joth looked toward the door as he heard people passing outside in the hall. "Can we count on your help to Twinton and back then?" he asked in low tones.

"Yes. You can count on it." Ryla looked out the window once again. "We'll watch this lot bed down and keep everything light and friendly with them tonight and then slip out easy-like, two by two. I'll tell the crew later so the bloody fools won't give us away."

"What of the horses?" Eilyth asked.

"No horses, I'm afraid. Though it might be a good idea to turn theirs out."

Eilyth looked as though she might balk at the idea of leaving Aila there, but she simply nodded and looked down. Ryla Dierns walked past them both and paused before opening the door. "You'd best hope this works, because the idea of going anywhere with Mage Alchemist Norden appeals little to me." She went into the hall and closed the door behind her, leaving he and Eilyth there.

"You sensed this coming somehow, didn't you?"

"Yes, I did," Eilyth answered quietly.

"Then if you've seen something or know something say it!" He had not meant to raise his voice.

"It does not work that way." She remained quiet. "It only serves to warn, to be at attention. The future itself is too changeable to know."

He stalked over to the window and looked down to the street below. A girl carried water away from the well in a bucket. "Forgive me, lady, it's just that I don't know where we stand with that woman now. How can we be sure she isn't going to march downstairs and tell that mage that you are the princess of the Dawn Tribe and have us all carted off in chains?"

She laughed. "We do not have princesses."

"You know my meaning, though. We don't know if anything she's told us is true."

"It is true. I saw in her eyes that it was true."

He had, too. He knew that the airship captain was not lying. "I just worry, lady. I worry about trusting her, especially if vengeance is her guiding force. What if she tries to use you to lever Uhlmet away from your father's hold?"

"It is good to be careful, Joth. But one must also trust people at their word. Some things we cannot know or change. Some things are always hidden and always shapeless until the moments when they form." She smiled at him then. "Some things."

He smiled as best he could and tried not to worry. It seemed risky to become embroiled in some sort of escape plan with these unlikely allies, but he could not argue that the airship and its rapid transport was a golden asset to their cause. They had come one week's ride in a day! That was incredible, especially if Joth thought about being able to travel for four days and covering the same amount of ground one would cover in a month's time on horseback. That the airship captain and crew were onside with them was monumental in terms of achieving objectives in a timely manner, Joth reminded himself. The gruff old master bowyer, whose name was Joth as well, used to always tell him, "Tradesmen sometimes don't like the traders they trade with," and he would use the phrase to describe any situation that left a person feeling half satisfied as they were going into it. Turns out the old master had been correct.

"There's one thing she said that I can completely agree with without reservation."

"Yes?"

"The idea of going anywhere with Mage Alchemist Norden doesn't appeal to me either."

She nodded affirmatively. "Nor I, Joth Andries. Nor I."

Nineteen

RHAEL COULD SCARCELY BELIEVE how stupid people could be when they had hope in their hearts. It was the thirteenth trip he had made from the cells to the orb tower, and every time they had fallen for his ruse.

"Quickly!" he had said, barely containing his own mirth. "I've overpowered the guards! There is a portal, a magic portal that will take you to the surface! Follow me!" Some of the prisoners had not understood Oestersh. Their skin was a strange color that he had not seen before. They were not deeply browned like the Southeasterners that traded with the Oestermen in the eastern cities; they were fairer skinned but still darker than Rhael. They regarded him with some trepidation, but most were so weak and enthused by the thought of rescue that they simply followed him regardless of the words he spoke. His favorite moment had been corralling eight inside the tower as the door panels breathed and saying, "I've just forgotten my cat in the cell. I'll be right back." He watched their incredulous looks as the panels closed and then listened to their screams as the bolts arced out and captured their life energies inside the dark orb that he collected and used to burn their bodies to ash.

He had pieced together a raggedy outfit from his victims' wardrobe, and although the clothes were putrid and coarsely made he felt glad to have clothes on again. It also made it easier to get the others to follow him. His routine was getting tiresome now after two days had passed, but the prisons had been completely cleared and he was holding thirteen orbs brimming with power. He had repurposed a leather milk skin to hold the dense dark spheres that he had created out of the prisoners, and now he hefted it over his shoulder, held aloft the blue Goblincraft lantern, and made his way past the orb tower. The Kuilbolts working the prisons had been the first to go, and he had worked as quickly as he could to learn to operate the strange machinery that lowered and elevated the cell doors. Some of the cells had been empty, some of them full, but he had gathered groups of people and herded them with his lies to harvest their life energies and trap them inside the magic orbs. Then he could manipulate their energies with his own mind.

As he peered into the leather sack and saw all of the orbs shimmering there in the blue light. Most folk would see glass, but he saw kingdoms. He saw an empire. Nothing could stand against him. The Kuilbolts had tried and failed miserably. The warriors had provided some excitement, he had not expected the bronze-plate-clad creatures to storm into the prisons, but they had come leaping and thrusting, slashing. He realized somewhere in his mind that some Kuilbolt must have made it out alive and alerted others through their alien chain of command. One of them had been wielding an orb like his own, but he had sent a flurry of lightning bolts through the entire brigade and killed them all. They had been so tightly packed that it had been easy for the electricity to jump from one victim to the next. There had been one hundred and fifty of the warriors including their orb wielding commander, and he had laid them out dead in two heartbeats.

He felt the power in his orb diminish drastically, the feeling of energy becoming more faint, pulsating less as he held it in his grasp. He used it again against two more Kuilbolts on a scouting mission to check on the brigade's progress. When he pushed with the orb's power against the twelve who had attempted to flee from the orb tower as it was breathing open to accept them, it glowed brightly with a flash and then audibly cracked and split asunder. It fell from Rhael's hand in a smoky ruin. He had heard something before the split, a discomfiting sound that he could not quite place. But it was soon masked by the screams of the twelve people behind the panels as they were hit by the white energy bolts and their energies drawn into the orb.

It was the very orb he cradled now, as he took in a strange sight. The pathway was lined with twin rows of hooks hanging from the ceiling, and two deep channels were cut into the floor on either side of the path. There were channels above that the hooks were set into as well, as though the entire thing offered some conveyance. It seemed to Rhael that the hooks could be made to travel along the channels. There was a smell to the place as well, one that he did not like. He wrinkled his nose and pressed on, swirling blue orb and Goblincrafted lantern in hand. He passed the long corridor of hooks and entered into a larger chamber that housed low tubs, like those used in tannery. The same two-channeled path passed through the center of the floor. In fact, the smell of the place was precisely as repulsive as a tanner's pit to Rhael's mind. It smelled of rot and deterioration.

He saw hides half submerged in the pits and recognized immediately that they were human skins. His mind went to the gruel he was fed—namely the tiny pieces of meat strewn inside of it. Rhael involuntarily retched there on the floor and hurried out of the room through a passageway at the opposite end. He came upon a line of carts along the channeled path.

They were linked together and the smell of death and decomposition of flesh nearly forced him to retch again. Harvesting men and using them like chattel. The Kuilbolts had spoken of masters, but Rhael had not seen any. There was another question that had been gnawing on his vast mind: the question of logistics. How, for instance, had the Kuilbolts amassed these human prisoners here in the depths of the earth? Surely they were not trundling about in the dark reaches with their rat carts as Iztklish and Krilshk had done, waiting to stumble upon men whom had fallen down holes. No, thought Rhael, the Kuilbolts no doubt had to hibernate in the colder seasons, like the frogs and lizards and snakes. It stood to reason that the Kuilbolts chose their subterranean routes in the colder months, Rhael deduced.

They had been surprised to have found him, he remembered. They had been carting other things, not just him, but his mind was so clouded with pain and sleep milk for most of his trundling journey here that he couldn't remember what. He wondered how far their rat roads stretched. Time was disjointed as days passed and came again above the sunless catacombs without reckoning.

He felt that he had been under the earth for months, but he knew that he could not use that feeling as a guide for anything like a true reckoning. So be it, thought Rhael. I was cast into the belly of the earth and now I have gestated again in its womb to be birthed onto the surface once more in a wash of blood and fire; time is of no matter to me, especially the time that has passed. My life begins now, he mused. My life of power.

He walked past low tables with grooves worn into them. Upon examination the grooves were black with dried blood and old detritus. Chopping blocks, he knew. The channels in the floor diverged and Rhael ventured down the right fork and found the channel turned at a steep drop off and then looped back onto itself. When he peered cautiously over the edge, he spied many red glinting eyes made purplish with the glow of the blue light staring up at him through the darkness. It took him a moment to realize they were the eyes of rats, giant rats.

That was the Kuilbolt's kennel, no doubt, and in convenient proximity to its source of food, it seemed. Farther down he found a long hall with two great cauldrons of bronze filled with gruel sat in racks over dead coals. He must have either killed the cooks or sent them fleeing somewhere. A neat operation, he admitted, despite the thought of it making his skin crawl. Very efficient and leaving little waste. He had just burned the useless bodies of the harvested folk, but this was entirely more useful. Skins, meat, no doubt other useful resources, and all of them supporting the bodies of Kuilbolts as they toiled away. A self-sustaining operation of limitless power, this station or factory or outpost. A dark gold mine of epic proportions.

Unfortunately, he seemed to have destroyed all of the workers during his ascent to power, but it would be no problem finding more peasants to work the fields, so to speak. Rhael grinned again as he backtracked into the butcher's den and then followed the other fork as it climbed up and around through the underground Kuilbolts' lair. He heard no sound of any other being beside himself as he came to a junction where six other tunnels spoked from the central hub, where Rhael found himself standing and smiling to himself. Of all the events to have to endure, the humiliation and injury, the river drowning and captivity and torture, the presumed cannibalism, they had all been worth it for Rhael. Never again would he be tested to such limits, to be so near his breaking point as he was. But he was the Lord Uhlmet, one of the richest and most powerful lords in Oesteria, and well-rooted in the hierarchy of the Magistry besides. How could he be expected to do anything but succeed? He was a genius, a prime example of noble blood outranking that of a base commoner. The right to succeed flowed through his very veins.

He tried two passages before turning back to the hub and finding a third that led up instead of down. It was a long and low tunnel and Rhael had to lower his head and hunch over, something he did not like doing at all. At last it ended and Rhael was pleased to see sunlight for the first time in ages, though the sensation was brief as he shut his swollen eyes and grimaced in burning pain. The tunnel had opened into a broad cavern devoid of any activity. His eyes adjusted and he saw that he was perched slightly higher than a man's shoulder on the side of a steeply faced rock wall. His wounded leg screamed at him as he landed on it. It still had not healed, he thought maddeningly. He rolled to his feet and adjusted his bag of orbs on his shoulder.

Blinking and cursing, he limped through the wide-mouthed cavern and approached the lip of the cave mouth cautiously before peering over. Down below he saw what looked to be a mining operation enclosed by a high wooden palisade. Kuilbolt guardsmen clad in bronze-plated armor stood on the parapets and monitored a large group of humans carrying baskets and wheelbarrows, loading and unloading them at different stations, and then returning to the rounded mine entrance. Rhael watched as the workers were followed by whip-bearing Kuilbolts. A heavy bronze-banded wooden gate was closed over the entrance, barred from the outside by four of the bronze armored Kuilbolt warriors. He was studying the terrain trying to figure out possibilities of where he might have surfaced in the world. The sun was setting off to his left in the periphery of his vision, so he knew he was facing a northerly direction. Rolling hills, foothills he thought. He was at the base of a mountain range facing north. To the west in the shimmering distance he saw the sea and the sun reflected in it as it sank downward gloriously. He was so elated to see the sun after so long in the darkness. Now he thought again about the sun and the sea, and the mountains and the underground rivers that had brought him there to where he was at that moment looking down on the slave camp at the foot of a mountain. I must be somewhere in the Northern Reaches, somewhere in the disputed borderland between Oesteria and the Dawn Tribe Territory, he realized. If that were true, then he would be perhaps a fortnight's trek to Castle Immerdale, due east and south again once he hit the Magister's Road. That was amazingly and conveniently nearby to his station. Once he raised troops and they had seen their cowardly and poorly performing fellows dangling from the gibbet, perhaps they would be motivated to take up arms as the men they had advertised themselves to be. He would take this place for himself, and keep its secrets close to his own counsel and no one else's. If he were indeed in the Northern Reaches, this fortress would be an excellent base to supply his forces for his war against the Dawn Tribe.

Rhael realized a problem to his situation; not all men could stomach the sorts of tasks that he would order them to here at his new mining camp. Many would have sympathies, weakness brought on by the compassionate characteristics some men were prone to. He was certainly not taken by such notions, but the simple men that made up the soldiery of the

First Army would have among their number a fair few who were, especially if they were to escort prisoners to be executed in the orb tower.

He also could foresee a problem of keeping the operation quiet. Men would not work underground day and night without the need for them to work in shifts, and then the men would need some form of entertainment, drinks, and women. The men would cry into their drinks or talk to their whores and suddenly Rhael's secret operation would be known to anyone in the Magistry with eyes and ears.

The other issue was also insurmountable: unless they could be convinced of cannibalism, the entire operation would become a logistical horror of supply, supply, supply. Instead of killing the Kuilbolts, perhaps I should coerce them into forsaking their masters and working for me, he thought. That would solve the problem in one stroke. He thought gleefully of a long chain of Dawn Tribe savages disappearing into the mines, a bounty of orbs at his feet. He needed a lever that would lift the Kuilbolts to his bargain. Perhaps that lever was promising them the People of the Dawn Tribes? He merely needed to find something that they cared about more than the fury of their masters; and for that he needed to know who their masters were, and more importantly where their masters were.

Rhael let his gaze travel back to the mining camp and the palisade and its gatehouse, its three guard towers, the guardsmen who were eight to a tower, the eight additional guardsmen in the yard to mind the prisoners and operate the mineshaft gate. A score of other Kuilbolts clad in the pale humanskin jerkins sewn all over with bronze lozenges and carrying whips at their belts were breaking up the mined rocks that the prisoners had delivered them with bronze pickaxes and carting them off in handcarts to a roofed forge that billowed smoke from the hole in the center of its timber roof. They do not even give the prisoners tools as a precaution against armed rebellion, it seemed to Rhael, for he saw the Kuilbolts themselves doing the labor and reckoned in his own mind that he would have had the slaves break up the rocks. Apparently they only used them as beasts of burden, the men. Or else they were on alert because of his victory over their pathetic army and they were expecting a full-scale prisoner revolt.

He cast his eye over the structures that rested within the fortified edifice of the palisade and asked himself where he would lodge, were he one of these mysterious masters of Kuilbolts. It took him little time to find the squat-waisted tower with a ramp that accessed a door midway up its heights. It was built of stone and looked to be older than the double palisade and earthworks that had been constructed around it. It was the most elite-looking structure that he could see, perhaps there were caverns below that were opulent and well furnished, but he had only seen the orb tower room on its polished white dais, magnificent and deadly. He could only deduce that the masters would certainly be above overseeing an operation as macabre as this and would not have any desire at all to get their hands dirty. Therefore it would stand to reason that they might choose to surround themselves with luxury in order to compensate for the disgusting course their lives had taken. He could think of nothing lower, in actual fact. Peasants belonged to the land, and as such they were always and in eternity the property of their lord because he was their blooded lord, whose right to rule the land had been passed from father to son for a thousand years and more. In Rhael's mind it was an unarguable fact, and nothing would ever change that. That he had happened upon the operation and used another lord's stolen property for his own benefit was completely acceptable; that was a courtesy extended among peers.

Highborn men always looked for ways to profit. His family and many other noble houses had profited immensely from siding with the Magistry after the old king had died and a power struggle had ensued. Lord Illithane had raised his banner and those noble houses opposing Magistry rule had flocked to him, his generalship inspiring fierce loyalty in his men, fierce courage. They displayed it time and time again in the field, and Lord Illithane proved to be a genius at the art of war. The noble houses that had allied themselves with the Magistry had all been granted lofty ranks within the establishment, and although he had been on the cusp of manhood, he was granted his position of Mage Imperator through his father's position as Archmage Imperator, the right hand of the High Mage himself. It had been Rhael who suggested to the Magistry that they target Lord Illithane's family, it was the easiest and least costly way of stopping the man and it was staring them all in the face day after day. People often had to die, and he counted it fortunate that so few had to die in order to stop a drawn-out campaign, no matter if they were little more than children. His father had received the credit for the resolution of the conflict, the war being declared over even without Lord Illithane's official surrender—his armies had simply dispersed.

In fact, the man had eluded justice altogether after the event and disappeared those sixteen years before. The injustices of the world, thought Rhael. There were a few minor skirmishes after, but their leader had been defeated and stripped of all titles and property and he led them no longer; consequently they had to accept defeat. He would have liked to witness a grand execution of the man. It would have been a fine punctuation mark for the masterstroke of genius that he had delivered in his suggestion to the council, but it was not to be.

His father was credited with the order for the execution of Lady Illithane and her two teenage children instead of him. When he dared to ask why, his father called him a fool and told him that he was merely protecting him. Calling him a fool, there in the great hall! Rhael could scarcely contain his anger but he somehow managed to sit through a silent dinner with his father and the family's attendants. He had never seen his father again after that evening. He had told him that he was needed in Twinton on Magistry affairs and that he must leave at once, and he rode away on his fine steed and debauched his way across the countryside from town to town until he made it to the city of Twinton and took up his office in the Magistry council hall. His father died two months later. He traveled home for the burial and set his household affairs in order. He fired the staff and sent them all off and appointed new, more-attractive-looking peasants to run his house. He dismissed the ones that acted appalled at his advances and stayed long enough to make sure that the bloody commoners were not stealing from him, and then he was back in Twinton. The holdings that were bequeathed to him by his father were vast and profitable.

They had great interests in the shipping trade; they owned several ships and had part ownership in dozens besides. His family had been positioned for such a push for centuries, and the timing had fallen upon his father to be the head of the house when the opportunity arose. After much cajoling by Rhael, he seized it and brought it to bear in their family's favor. His father had lacked the ambition that drove great men to succeed, ambition that Rhael possessed in plentitude. As Rhael grew older, he had realized that his father would never be the cut of lord that he himself would make. His father followed the rules to a letter, whereas Rhael dictated the rules. I am a lord of the land, Rhael thought, I shall make my right where I see fit. His father had never forgiven him for putting forth the idea of capturing and executing Lady Illithane and her brats. He had said it was a great shame to the family, and a cowardly perversion of honorable war. Ludicrous, he had thought, that his father even held onto such an ancient and outdated concept. Rhael had seen victory and seized upon it like a hawk snatching its prey.

Of course, after his father's death, things changed at the Magistry. High Mage Albine had died a year later and Archmage Imperator Paifen, a bloody commoner, ascended to the seat of High Mage. Paifen had been a voice of opposition in the council and an ever-present thorn in his side and that of his father's. He currently sat in the High Mage's chair, and Rhael relished the day when the old man would let go his death rattle and allow him to take his rightful place as the head of government.

By rights he had outranked the man at the time of his ascension, and the position of Archmage was his due to the death of his father, but they had snubbed him for Paifen. Regardless of the man's uses and abilities, he was still a commoner, and commoners would never make the leaders that highborn men made. They would soon see the errors of their choice, Rhael thought darkly; not that he meant to kill them, on the contrary he meant to awe them with his power and his ferocity, his unwavering will. He would be the High Mage as the High Mage should ever have been, and woe to those who dared oppose him. His own destiny was laid out before him it seemed, and all he needed to do now was play his hand and reap the rewards. The Kuilbolts would either accept his offer to follow him as their new master or hc would destroy them all, he thought, a grim smile fixed to his battered face. Mage Imperator Rhael Lord Uhlmet had just extended his holdings and in the process worked out an even greater plan.

Twenty

I T WAS WELL PAST midnight before they slipped away from the Merry Haymaker, he and Eilyth. They darted from the inn and sprinted along the road until they were at the bottom of the hill and well out of town. Their breath threw great plumes of frost into the half-mooned sky as they slowed and caught their wind at a jog, carrying what provisions they had on their backs, wrapped up in their cloaks. Joth had his soldier's gear and the arming sword he had taken from the guard in Borsford, as well as a little food and water and the half-empty skin of mead left from their journey from the village by the river.

Lady Eilyth cried as she said farewell to her mare, her trusty Aila, whom she had raised from a foal. She threw her arms around the gray mare's neck and sobbed openly. Joth did not quite know what to do to comfort her but when they slowed at the bottom of the hill he stopped her and she stood wiping her eyes.

"This is what you saw. This is what made you so sad."

She nodded.

"I'm sorry, lady, but you needn't worry. Bell will look after them."

"Yes. So you have told me. Let us hurry, we are the last ones." She set out at an even pace. Joth matched her and together they quick marched down the wagon track that they had walked up the night before.

He knew that she felt wrong about leaving Aila and that Eilyth did not like feeling wrong about anything. They jogged on into the night, veering from the track when they could make out the two large steep slopes laying off to the west and venturing overland toward them, knowing that the airship rested in the valley between the track and the hills and making for it as quickly as they could over the broken ground.

After a long time, she spoke. "Thank you for your worry, Joth. I am sorry if I could not say it earlier."

He smiled at her and they pressed on through a small copse of trees and spied the airship resting on the ground just as they had left it the previous evening. Strange, thought Joth. He would have figured Ryla Dierns to have the ship hovering at its lines by now, as forward as the woman was with everything.

"Quiet," he stated.

"Yes. What do you think?" She looked at him intently.

"I don't like it. I can't see anyone moving on the deck. Have we beaten them here?"

"I know not. We ran a good measure of the way, but they left well before we did."

"So?"

She looked quickly from him to the motionless airship beyond the tree line and back again. "We could go back and finish the journey on horseback? I cannot think now. My mind is not right, my heart feels too much." She was nearly crying. "I cannot make sense of anything."

"You wait here," he said, trying to comfort her. "I'll walk out and spring their bloody trap, if that's what this is."

"No, do not be foolish. We will go together."

"I swore to protect you. Please let me honor the words I spoke to your father." He knew that would stop her.

She gave him one of her half smiles and inclined her head to him.

He started out. "Stay out of sight until I give you a signal."

"Be careful."

He strode out to the tree line and peered toward the ship. He saw nothing to worry about, but he could only see the near side of the airship. He drew the sword from his cloak and bore it before him as he walked. What was on the other side, he wondered? Was it Captain Ryla and dour Elmund, jug-eared Galt, and Kipren with his braided beard all huddled in the darkness waiting for he and Eilyth to show their faces? Why would they have waited to lift up the ship? He stepped out of the trees and walked toward the brightly painted hull. If it were a trap, then it would find him sword in hand at the springing. He crept through the grass until he could circle around so that the side of the airship that was blind to him could now be seen.

It was completely empty, he discovered. Everyone who was meant to have arrived already had not made it there it seemed. He liked it not in the least, and he had turned back and started toward Eilyth when a movement caught his eyes at the northernmost edge of the tree line. He saw the captain and crew emerging from the trees and he was about to start toward them, but he froze when he saw eight of the dark coated, sallet-helmed riders step out behind them on their elegant mounts with their lances dipped, herding the crew toward the airship.

Joth was caught in the middle of the field between the airship and the tree line and he knew he would be spotted if he tried to make for the trees. That would give Eilyth's position away for certain, he thought. He took one final look toward the trees where she was waiting and then made a quick decision, one that he hoped he would not regret. He moved back toward the airship and stood near the gangway of the ship and rested the sword on his shoulder, cradling the hilt in his hand. At the least he could give her a chance to get away and stay clear of these foreign lancers and that pompous alchemist. Perhaps he could pose as one of the ship's crew and take this bloody mage wherever he needed to be with Ryla Dierns. Then they could all double-back and meet Eilyth at the Merry Haymaker in Grannock once they were shed of the short, balding man and his vehement adherence to protocol. Bloody foolish, Joth thought.

There was no way to know whether or not the mage would try to bring them up on charges or attempt to detain them further just out of spite. They were drawing ever nearer to him from the tree line, but they had not seen him yet. No, he knew he would have to go against what he had said to the airship captain and show the mage his writ from Wat. It was riskier, if not more foolish, but it gave him an opportunity to reason with the man. Never as a peer, however, Joth reminded himself. He was a soldier and he would be a soldier speaking to his superior.

They spotted him then about fifty yards out from the airship and two of the riders spurred their mounts toward him with their lances dipped. He kept the sword on his shoulder but raised his hand to them and they slowed.

"What's the meaning of this?" he called to the riders.

They said something in a guttural tongue and poked their lances at him.

"There's no use in it, Shiny. They don't speak Oestersh at all." Ryla got a kick in the back by a pointy booted foot that sent her stumbling forward. These foreign lancers did not mess about with too many courtesies, or so it seemed to Joth.

He thought to keep them talking for a moment longer, to give Eilyth a chance to break away from the trees and get clear of this place.

"I am a soldier of the First Army of the Magistry and I demand to see your officer."

The two salleted heads swiveled and looked to each other then back to Joth. One jerked his head and lance in unison toward the crew, and Joth decided it was time that he simply nod his head and follow and so he did. Joth cast one last look toward the trees where he had left the lady Eilyth but he could not see her there. Good, he thought, she was smart and she would stay clear, that would give him something to bargain for once the mage began ordering him about. As long as the man did not have Eilyth, then Joth still had the upper hand— captive or not.

The man took the sword and flipped it around handily to rest across his fine saddlebow, all the while managing his horse precisely even as he transferred his reins to his lance hand to relieve Joth of his sword and then back again once the sword was secured.

These lads were good horsemen to be sure, he thought, as he turned and fell in with Ryla Dierns and Galt, though he had no idea where they hailed from. They were mostly young men and they were dark eyed and dark haired and their skin was dark as well, tanned a bronzy hue. Their bearing was that of soldiers, and they were no doubt some foreign mercenaries that the Magistry had brought over to provide escort and protection for their emissaries without pulling troops from garrisons to do the task. Joth did not know enough about the world and the lands outside of Oesteria, he did not know how to speak any other tongue than Oestersh, save a few words in the language of the People.

They paused at the airship for a long span, and six of the riders stayed with the captives while two others lit torches and rode out to search the trees from opposite directions. The leader of the group barked out orders in a guttural tongue and the others obeyed him unquestioningly. Joth looked to the west and found the bright star there that he wished upon, and he made a silent plea for Eilyth to remain hidden and undiscovered by the riders. He stared at the riders coursing through the trees until he worried that his concern might cause suspicion, so he took to looking at the ground or at the sky seemingly unconcernedly. They were speaking in their guttural tongue again, but he could not understand what was being said. He wished that he had been tutored, educated, shown more; he could tell you hundreds of facts about bowstaves and dressing them for a bowyer, how to stack them for drying so that they would not warp, how to mark out the good from the bad. Useless knowledge here. He realized that he knew nothing outside of Oesteria, and even his knowledge of that was lacking. Ryla was looking at him and he realized that some of his consternation must have been visible on his face, so he wiped it away as best he could and took a look around again. The torches were not visible within the tree line when he gave a cursory glance and swept his eyes out over the field.

The cold was settling in and he began to feel it in his feet. He envied the foreign cavalrymen and their fine tall boots and warm coats atop their elegant horses. The leader was looking out to the trees and speaking with one other rider as the rest of the horsemen looked on. They had rested there for a long time before the outriders returned, empty handedly to Joth's great relief. One of them was describing his journey to the leader, gesticulating and pointing to the landscape behind him, and Joth gathered that the men had ridden a great circle around the entire wood and met in the center and seen no sign of anyone.

The leader sat thinking for a long time before barking out an order and falling in formation with his men behind Joth. They moved them away from the airship and toward the break in the trees that led to the road and to Grannock. He hoped beyond everything that Eilyth would stay hidden and safe and that Mage Alchemist Norden would prove to be a reasonable man as he plodded on in the dim torchlight alongside the airship's crew with foreign lances at his back.

It began to rain as they left the field and he heard Elmund mutter a curse. In minutes their hair was soaked through and dripping, and by the time they made the track that led to the small hilltop town their silken garments were hanging from their shivering limbs like wet sheets. He thought about Eilyth and hoped she was faring better than they were out in the wet and cold. They trudged on toward the town and through the small hours of the night before making the inn.

When they were marched into the great room, dripping wet with teeth chattering, the small frame of Mage Alchemist Norden detached itself from a chair near the roaring fire and addressed them. "Well you do not disappoint," he said venomously. "I am a man who takes precautions against such antics. You should have seen that from the start. Where is the other one, the girl?"

It was unclear to Joth whether he was addressing the horsemen or their party or both. Norden said something in the guttural tongue and was quickly answered by one of the foreign soldiers.

"No matter. She'll not be able to pilot the airship alone. Especially not without this." He held up the elegant bronze wand that Ryla Dierns usually carried at her belt tantalizingly.

"Will she, now?" He gave a snide look to the airship captain, who stood fuming in her bedraggled state. "This little ruse of yours is a breach of the law and I plan on making you pay for that, captain. You have caused me delays."

Ryla stared daggers at the man.

Norden walked to the stairs and started up. "I've posted guards inside and out, so don't even think of trying my patience further, or I shall have to turn to more severe measures. You are to be confined to your quarters until further notice." He said something to the guards then in their tongue and Joth was being pulled and shoved toward the stairs with the others. Norden stood at the top of the stairs and watched with a smug expression as they were all escorted to their rooms at the inn and shoved inside. He turned in time to see the little man yawn and turn to his own door as the rough hands of the foreign guardsmen tossed Joth past the door frame and his door slammed shut behind him. Evidently their escape plan had not gone over well with their captors, and he could not blame them; he would have hated being roused in the middle of the night and sent out into the rain and the cold on round up duty.

Joth stripped his clothes off and wrung them out in the washbasin, then laid them over the chairback so that they might dry more quickly. He carried the basin to the window and opened it, the wind carrying the rain into his room as he emptied the dirty water out into the courtyard below. For a moment he thought he saw Eilyth step out of the shadows near the stable yard, but that must be his imagination as he stared for a long time to see if she would move again and nothing happened. After a long time of wondering about her, Joth climbed beneath the coverlet and fell asleep to the sound of rain against his window with a worry in his heart.

Twenty-One

JOTH WAS DRESSED IN his damp and wrinkled soldier's clothes but he was near the fire and its warmth was helping him to keep from shivering in the cold morning. He had woken an hour before and decided it would be best for him to present himself to the mage in his First Army kit in order to strengthen his claim. His helm was spotted with rust and his jack smelled slightly sour, but he put it on over his hosen and singlet. The People had washed his gear for him and it was clean, but being unworn and packed away for the last few weeks had creased his clothing in odd places and left him looking rather disheveled. He had combed his hair and shaved himself in the washbasin and used all of the water in the ewer to clean as best as he could. He took the last of the scented oil that Eilyth had given him and combed it through his hair and rubbed it into his skin to stop him from smelling sour.

Now he was stood in the great room of the Merry Haymaker in Grannock, near the fire, while Mage Alchemist Norden looked him up and down and read and reread the writ that Wat had drawn up for him—the writ that Ryla Dierns had been forcibly parted with at her capture, presumably. Norden mumbled to himself as he read the well-folded document.

Joth stood at attention and cradled his rusty helm under his arm. How many times was the man going to read the bloody paper before he said something? The mage folded the writ up again and placed it on a small table next to his chair and smiled at Joth for a long time before speaking.

"You have been keeping secrets it seems, Linesman Andries." He made a steeple of his hands in his lap.

"My lord, I was ordered to keep the mission absolutely quiet. I apologize."

"Yes, I understand. Of course you must recognize that as mage alchemist, I technically hold the same rank as Lord Uhlmet, therefore your reporting to me on the particulars does not truly break any protocol."

"As you say, my lord." Joth was not going to let the man squirm his way into more information than he needed to know. "Now that you understand the urgent nature of my mission, I was hoping that you would release the airship's crew and allow us to press on. Every moment we lose puts Lord Uhlmet's life in greater jeopardy."

Norden shook his head slowly back and forth, but a glimmer of his seedy smile remained. "What a shame. Truly." He accented the emphatic nature of the last word by holding Joth's eyes for a long beat before continuing. "Of course, this news will come as an absolute shock to the council—you understand, Linesman Andries? They would never wish for any detail of Lord Uhlmet's defeat at the hands of the savages to be spread publicly by word of mouth. It would have damaging effects upon the Magistry's rule, and it would start a public panic with talk of savages coming over the mountains." He leaned in toward Joth conspiratorially. "This charge of yours mentioned in the writ, it's that red-headed creature you're with, is it not?"

"I'd rather we left her out of it entirely, my lord."

"Yes, I'm sure. Unfortunately, as she is mentioned in the writ, I have no choice but to inquire as to her whereabouts, her role in all of this, and of course why the Lord Uhlmet is sending this girl to Twinton."

"My lord, with great respect, I politely refuse to tell you any more details—"

"Linesman Andries, I'm afraid that you will. I'm afraid that you will tell me everything." The little man rose from his chair and glowered at him. Joth stood for a moment, wondering which mage was worse, Uhlmet or Norden? Decidedly Uhlmet, but he admitted to himself that Norden was a close second. He had been cornered now. He knew that it was time to play his hand and he hoped that Norden bought his story.

"My lord, please. I ask you not to make me break my word with my superiors—"

"You will answer my questions or I shall have the Norandish guards beat the answers from you."

Joth did his best to look suitably frightened. The truth was that the fellows did not look like much off their horses. Where was bloody Norandia, he wondered? "My lord, please! The girl is a camp follower that our company commander took a fancy to, he included that in the writ so that I could send her home to his mother as the girl has gotten herself in the family way, my lord."

Norden stepped into him and jabbed a stubby digit at his chin. "You presume to use an airship and prevent my using it because your company commander can't control his lusty urges? I'll have you up on charges!"

"I am only following my orders, my lord."

"Yes, yes. Of course, you are not to blame." The man turned his back to him and paced back toward the fire and to where his chair stood. "What sort of company expedition was Lord Uhlmet running to allow such broad breaches of conduct? Obviously an ill-fated one, but of course if you start to allow protocol to slip then you've lost before it's even begun. I wouldn't think of Lord Uhlmet as the type of man to allow camp followers."

"They are everywhere in the Dawn Tribe lands, my lord, once you make the coastal territories. They were on us like a plague." Joth was counting on the fact that Norden's knowledge of the Dawn Tribe Territory was limited, and he could see by the slope shouldered man's expression that it was. He looked as though he may like to visit that place himself one day. There was something lecherous about the way the man had looked at Eilyth and Ryla Dierns, and Joth suspected that the man had "lusty urges" of his own. He resisted the urge to push the lie further. The mage seemed to have thought about the prospect enough. He sat back down and stared into the fire for a long beat. A rooster crowed. Joth could hear the kitchen staff bustling about behind the bar, preparing breakfast.

"So you expect me to believe that this girl has no bearing at all to Lord Uhlmet or his enterprise? That she is some tawdry whore that fell in with good fortune in the harlot's game of chance and landed herself with the company commander, and that is all?"

"It's the truth, my lord," Joth lied. He hated hearing the slimy mage speak about the lady Eilyth so.

Norden looked at Joth for a long while and studied him. "So you have said, Linesman. So you have said." Norden licked his lips and stared at the fire with his hands under his chin. "I understand the dire situation, the defeat of your company— Lord Uhlmet's company—at the hands of the savages, the need to bring urgent word. It would seem to me that expediency would have been better served had word first been sent to Immerdale?"

The man was right, but Joth was prepared for such a question. "My lord, my orders were to deliver my message to the High Mage in Twinton and at the insistence of Lord Uhlmet to avoid all delay in achieving that end."

Norden nodded. "He's a fool," he muttered. "The man is unfit for command. I knew this would happen. As soon as he got the appointment, I knew it would happen."

Joth stood there at attention.

"So no dispatch riders were sent out then?"

"Not that I know of, my lord."

"Not that you know of, or none at all?"

"None at all."

"Then according to your account, you saw Lord Uhlmet dragged from his horse as you were ambushed within the Dawn Tribe Territory and you, your commander, and company were pushed back to the camp by the savages and their warband?"

"Yes, my lord. Their army."

He looked at him a long time before nodding and continuing on. "So presumably before Lord Uhlmet was dragged from his mount and captured by the savages he gave orders to your company commander in the event of a catastrophe such as this, and by your account he wrote this writ out to you moments before your entire camp was overrun and you managed to slip out with the girl in tow and make your way to Borsford Sky Harbor, where you requisitioned the airship Skyward against the wishes of her captain in the name of the Magistry and flew here to Grannock in order to rest and bury a crewman killed due to some incident with an innkeeper raising the town guard?"

"Yes, my lord."

"And you swear you have spoken to no one, excepting myself, about your orders or adventures or the defeat of your company and Lord Uhlmet?"

"No, my lord."

The mage studied him.

"I mean to say yes, I swear that I have not," he clarified.

The mage studied him again and then nodded, satisfied. "Linesman Andries, I have prepared a document for you to sign. If you would be so kind, my clerk has a quill at the ready." He swept his arm back to a thin young man seated at a table behind him, who had been scratching out the deposition and recording it on parchment for the mage's files. The youth now stood and walked over with two sheets of parchment in a stack. He never looked Joth in the eye as he handed him the quill. Norden snatched the pages out of his hand and looked them over. "These fools they send me," he muttered to himself before shifting his focus back to Joth. "Right then, Linesman Andries, this is an affidavit claiming that the words you have spoken and the account you have given is truth. Should it be found to be untrue or contrary, then you shall be held accountable for your part in it. Do you understand?"

"Yes, my lord." It was the truth, more or less.

"Then make your mark here." He pointed to the bottom of the page. Joth signed his name. The mage flipped the page up so that the bottom of the page beneath it was exposed. "And here, Linesman."

Joth signed again. "Why sign the same thing twice?"

Norden smiled slightly. "Merely a legality, soldier. Do not concern yourself with things above your station." The mage walked back to the clerk's table. "We often keep copies of the same document. I'm preparing a new writ for you to speed you on your way." He sat down across from the clerk and put quill to parchment, adding, "and to get you some good accommodation in Torlucksford, courtesy of the Magistry."

"Torlucksford? My orders were for Twinton, my lord."

"Yes, but you will not be taking the airship there, Linesman. I shall be taking that." Joth seethed behind his tight-lipped expression. The mage regarded him evenly, enjoying his position of power. "I take priority, you understand. However, I understand that Lord Uhlmet's situation needs to be made known and that your orders must be carried out, so after I use the Skyward to my ends I shall send it to Torlucksford to skim you along on your way. Fear not, this should only delay you by a week or less, and to be honest, Linesman Andries, you look as though you could use some rest." The man was scratching out a writ as he spoke.

"Thank you, my lord, I appreciate your help." Bloody tyrant. He was doing this out of spite, Joth knew.

"Well after the merry little chase you led us on yesternight, you should appreciate everything that I am doing for you, and the fact that I am doing anything for you at all you should appreciate most." He glowered as he wrote. Norden finished his new writ and sprinkled powder over the freshly drawn ink, letting it rest on the table a moment before gathering some sealing wax and a candle. He blew the powder from the document and quickly folded and sealed it with his ring while Joth was made to stand there. "Linesman Andries, you shall present this writ to the gate guard at Torlucksford and he shall direct you to The Star in the Field, a fine inn where you may take your ease until Captain Dierns sends for you. I have stayed in this inn many times and let me tell you it ranks among the finest of inns. I have an account there, and I shall personally cover the cost of all your expenses during your stay.

In this way you can pass on to Lord Uhlmet how courteous I was to you once I discovered the true nature of your journey, should we ever have the chance to see him rescued from his plight." He smiled his oily smile again.

So was that it? Joth wondered. Mage Norden gets to exercise his high and mightiness and delay his and Eilyth's journey out of some personal rivalry with Lord Uhlmet? He did not have any education when it came to any kind of politicking or strategy, but he could not get his head around a man who was willing to lose his own silver to sate his ire. No, this mage was a calculating and methodical man, and there was no doubt in Joth's mind that the mage stood to gain at all ends of the bargain. Perhaps that was this man's art, thought Joth. The art of deceiving. He made one feel as though they were getting something of what they wanted when in actuality the mage had already found ways of winning at every point.

Perhaps Joth was right in everything he was thinking, but it changed nothing. The mage had trapped him, and now he was going to Torlucksford no matter what. At the least I kept lady Eilyth out of danger, he thought proudly. This mage would have snatched her up and held her like a prize, to elevate himself in the eyes of his peers; used her like a slave once she had run out of uses, like a whore through all of it. He would not let that happen, no matter what. Once the severity of the situation between the nations of the People and Oesteria became known, he knew that the Magistry would most likely attempt to hold Eilyth as a hostage in a strong-arming ploy to show their power and their willingness to sacrifice everything rather than negotiate with savages. He wondered if the Magistry would consider them savages if they had witnessed the wheeling cavalry, the stirrup-less lancers riding gracefully, the lines of javelineers throwing with precision timing so that the ranks did not run the risk of casting their darts into the backs of their compatriots; but these things would have been lost on the man.

"As you command, Lord Mage," he said simply, taking the document.

"You may set out when you like, but I suggest you eat something. You are free to go, Linesman. Good fortune in the search for your whore."

The man smiled again and Joth would have hit him in his smarmy mouth had he nothing to lose, but he knew that he would be hanging from a rope or rotting in a pillory box if he did, so he drew a deep breath and mustered a nod before turning to go. One last notion tugged at his mind and prompted a question. "Lord Mage?"

"Yes?"

"You didn't give me back the writ from my commander, my lord. I'll need that."

"No, Linesman, my new writ shall suffice. Is that all?"

"Yes, my lord," he said resignedly.

"Well then, I would say 'may the winds speed you,' but that no longer applies to your mode of travel. So, farewell, Linesman." He regarded him smugly and waited for him to leave.

Joth obliged him and went back upstairs to gather his things. When he returned to the great room Norden and his scribe were no longer there, and he was met by the half-hearted serving girl who asked him disinterestedly if he 'was wanting his breakfast,' or not.

"Yes, if it please you." He replied, "I'm just out to the stables for a moment." The girl gave no reaction, but he knew she must have heard him. Joth was out the door and around the corner and looking for Bellan the groom in the stable yard when he heard someone whistle from within the stalls.

He walked into the stable block and tried to discern where the noise had come from. He saw the gray mare Aila toss her head and then the lady Eilyth stepped into view from behind her. She smiled at him.

"Lady!" he whispered excitedly. Joth hurried toward her. "You are all right?"

"Yes, I am fine."

"Lady, forgive me. I tried to stop the mage, but he has taken the airship from us. I failed."

She nodded. "What now? We go by horseback?"

"He gave me a writ and accommodation in Torlucksford and said that if we wait there that he'll send Ryla Dierns to collect us. He said it'd be about a week or less. I'm sorry, lady, it's because of all the trouble with us trying to escape and getting ourselves caught."

"He must show his power. I understand."

"Yes, but he's a real bastard. I'm sorry but he is. He should have let us continue on." He studied her in the stall, her hand on her mare's neck watching him. She was beautiful, but it was a beauty that shone from inside and out. Being away from her for that brief amount of time after being side by side along the road for so long and seeing her now had reminded him of that.

"What is it?" she asked him.

"Did you have anything to eat? You must be starved." He covered, "I'll run to the kitchens and get food for us both and then I think we should best leave this place."

"Bell brought me food last night and this morning."

"You stayed here last night? In the stables?"

"Yes, with Aila. And Bell, too."

"Where is that lad?"

"He left to help the soldiers with their horses a short while ago."

"I'll get some food, and then I want to be shed of this place before I lay eyes on that mage again."

Eilyth smiled grimly and he left her with his belongings to add on to the packsaddle while he hurried back inside the inn. He breathed a sigh of relief knowing that she was fine and safe and right under the mage's nose. The halfhearted serving girl looked slightly disappointed to see him appear again, but she set a plate before him promptly and curtsied before leaving.

Joth ate his breakfast hurriedly and noted that none of the airship's crew had been allowed down from their rooms for breakfast. He had hoped to get a word in with Ryla Dierns before he and Eilyth set out. He had wanted to tell her that they would wait for her, that he had tried to save her from the mage's wrath by coming forward, that the man could be dealt with by no other means, but he knew it was most likely that Ryla Dierns would feel he had gone against his word by bringing Lord Uhlmet into Norden's full view. In Joth's favor was the fact that Norden had captured her and her crew and procured his writ from her, so she already knew that the mage had knowledge of Lord Uhlmet's involvement. He hoped that the captain would forgive him if she harbored him any ill will, for she was a hard woman and she seemed to hold on to slights and seek revenge for any wrongs done to her. She was good at keeping up the air that everything was as carefree to her as the day was long, but the truth was that there was a cold edge to her. Her desire for vengeance when she spoke to him and Eilyth in her room was so intense that Joth had second thoughts about continuing on the journey with the woman.

At the same time he had to admit that she was a thoughtful woman, and fair; as a captain she was very strong and good to her crew. Joth hoped that Ryla Dierns would meet them in Torlucksford. The airship was a frightening yet amazingly easy way to travel long distances over a very short period of time, even if Elmund gave him dirty looks and Galt and Kipren both did not trust him. He would rather sail the skies with those men than get dealt a new crew on a different airship once they hit the town. If Mage Norden's writ would even give him the opportunity to travel by airship, he thought ruefully; the man had sealed the writ so that he was unable to read it and he did not know if his fortunes were better or worse. Joth set his spoon down in the empty bowl of porridge, downed his ale, and made for the stable yard. He threw a last glance up the stairs and saw the two Norandish guardsmen at the top of the staircase chatting with one another.

He thought of the captain and her crew. The mage had fixed it so that he would have to leave without speaking to any of them, he realized. He was a petty man. The morning had turned blustery and the cool winds cut through him like razors as he walked around the corner into the stable block and found Eilyth with their mounts saddled and the packhorse laden and ready for travel. She was leaning on her staff and talking to the horses in playful tones when he arrived. He took the reins of the dish-faced bay from her hands and swung into the saddle. Eilyth mounted her horse.

"I don't even know where this place is, Torlucksford."

"Nor do I." She was sitting Aila with her staff across her lap and the lead to the packhorse in her hand.

"We'll ask someone at the well as we ride out."

She nodded.

"I want to be shed of this place." He wanted to be clear of that mage and his foreign lackeys. They asked a woman at the well the way to Torlucksford and she pointed north and east and told them to follow the road out of Grannock and stay on it, whatever crossroads begged direction of them they were simply to keep traveling on that road until they made their destination, always continuing straight. It sounded easy enough to Joth. They followed the road past the well and out down the gently sloping hill and startled some pheasants into the trees, then a single buck deer burst through and stood watching them for a long beat before turning back the way he had come. Eilyth seemed to be concerned with the portents.

"What does it mean?" he asked resignedly, for he could not get his head around reading into the "signs," as she called them.

"It is a sign of poor fortune to come, or perhaps the wrong path," she said thoughtfully.

He did not put his faith in such things. Joth could see that she was not pleased. "No offense, lady, but anything could have spooked that deer and those pheasants."

"Yes, but we saw the signs did we not? Was it not the two of us here who witnessed the birds and the deer?"

"Of course, but what does that have to do with anything?"

"It has everything to do with it. We see the signs as they happen; it is left to us whether or not we listen. Things are always happening, and the world is always speaking and telling us things, warning us."

Joth had never placed his faith in things that he could not touch or see, only things that bore substance and held weight; the idea of predestination or some sort of divination being possible and real seemed near impossible. Then again, he was still struggling with the new reality of being more aware of the life and energy flowing all around him everywhere he looked. Eilyth had woken him up to that in the pass that day when he had almost escaped with Wat, but he was still stumbling through the awareness in the way that someone who has not fully woken up falls out of bed and groggily ambles about, yawning and rubbing their eyes. He was not able to trust in the way that Eilyth could, he doubted and second-guessed himself every time he felt anything that he could not explain away to some rational, reasonable cause. To Eilyth it was as natural as breathing and her confidence in it was devoid of any doubt. There was no artifice, no ulterior mechanics or intentions to Eilyth's observations. Joth wished that he had her confidence. Joth placed his faith in his knowledge, his friends, and the familiar; her faith was in the workings of the natural world, and the great mysteries she seemed able to understand. She was grounded in it; it was a part of her.

"It's so easy for you. I cannot look at things the way that you do with such ease." He did not say it petulantly.

"I look at things with such ease because these are easy things." Again with the half smile Joth was beginning to interpret as an expression of triumph, some conversational victory she had won for herself.

"What am I meant to do with that knowledge anyhow?"

"Be wary."

"So if a deer bursts out of a forest because something somewhere startles it and I see it happen, then I have to look over my shoulder until something bad happens or almost happens? It just seems like fool's talk is all."

"Fool's talk? The signs are fool's talk? You speak, but your words are empty." She looked at him fiercely and she reminded him for a moment of her brother, something in her eyes. She looked away from him and whispered a word to Aila and rode a pace ahead of him, leaving Joth to stare at her back confusedly.

"Lady? Eilyth, I'm sorry."

She would not look at him again for the longest time. They rode out along the road over gently rolling hills as the sun stretched its way up from the horizon. They had paused near a stand of trees to relieve themselves and Eilyth had just returned to where Joth stood holding the horses when they both spied a cloud of dust over the hill ahead of them, and a smallish figure riding a tall horse came into view thundering down the dirt road toward them. Shortly after, he crested the hilltop and he spurred his mount toward them at lightning speed.

He was a good rider, Bellan, Joth noted, for he had recognized the youth almost immediately. The boy let his tall mount stretch himself out over the low rise and he brought him to a sit-down stop once he reached Joth and the Lady Eilyth. He was wearing his hat and a fine short blue coat with full sleeves, a modest array of pleats creasing the front. He also donned his finest hosen and some fine soft leathered knee boots with loose folds at the top, a sort of buff color. His spurs were harnessed on, as well, and at his belt there dangled a dagger, the military type that men-at-arms wore. It was a sandwich-hilted, round guarded affair, the blade a single-edged triangular spike designed to pierce plate armor or drive through the weak points in the harness. What this fool spruced-up groom was doing with that sort of a weapon, Joth had no idea, but once he put his mind to work, he had figured the lad had set out to join with the Norandish horsemen and belted on the dagger to make himself look a touch more imposing. His costume and bedroll and stuffed saddlebags told the story alone.

"What in blazes are you running from?" Joth asked the flush-faced boy.

"It's me, It's Bell from the stableyard!"

"I know who you bloody are, you dullard! What are you running your horse like that for?" He laughed and looked at Eilyth, but she was regarding the boy with interest.

Bellan hesitated and looked furtively over his shoulder back the way that he had come. His horse was blowing as he sat him.

"What is it? Tell us, boy!"

Eilyth looked to where he had looked and back to him when she saw nothing.

He regarded them both as he caught his breath. "You mustn't go that way. They're waiting for you. They mean to kill you."

"Who?"

"The Norandishmen. The mage has set a trap for you, you mustn't go that way."

Joth looked at Eilyth and back to the boy. It made no sense to him what the lad was saying, but the lady regarded him gravely.

"The signs do not speak falsely," she said softly.

Twenty-Two

RHAEL HAD CONSIDERED IT very fortunate that he had only to kill one of the Kuilbolts before they shrieked and surrendered themselves to him. It had been fairly simple to pick out the leader, who he simply set ablaze like a torch and listened to him shriek and crackle. He demanded the Kuilbots swear fealty to him, and it had only taken him lifting the swirling blue orb above his head and the strange fear stinking beings were prone on the ground calling him master and begging him not to bring the energies down upon them.

He bade them to unlock the gate of the tower and to leave him the key there on the stones. As the jerkin-clad Kuilbolt scampered away down the ramp, Rhael had bent to pick up the key and paused to look out over the assembly. He had a force of about fifty Kuilbolts, by his reckoning. Enough for a small raiding party, and more than enough to run his operation. My army, he thought. My soul harvesters.

"I am your master now." He let his voice carry over the yard and bounce back from the palisade. They regarded him with their strange unreadable eyes. "When the old masters arrive, send them to me."

He turned and strode to the gate. He shut it and locked it behind him. He would not leave anything to chance. The key was large and bronze and ancient-looking. Its teeth were intricate and complex in their form, the entire key an impressive object chased with silver along the many grooves in its surface. When he locked the gate, he heard a noise behind him and realized it was a lock mechanism being operated on the tower door just beyond the gate where he stood. He looked at the key again, realizing that there was some form of Goblincrafted magic at work here in the stronghold. Rhael was enjoying this more and more as he tried the tower door. It give way easily to the pressure of his hand, swinging on smooth, well-oiled hinges and opening before him.

Inside, the tower was far from utilitarian—much to his satisfaction. The floors were smooth and white, much like the floors in the orb tower beneath the mountain. A staircase spiraled up around the wall and disappeared through the vaulted ceiling. The stonework was elegant and intricate, the timbers beautifully carved and decorated. The furnishings were equally rich and tasteful. In the round room at the center of the tower stood a finely crafted desk with all of the paraphernalia for letter writing and document making: quills and inkpots and wax and candles, a stack of fine parchment, and several backed chairs scattered around it. It was stood on a woven rug of such intricate design that Rhael marveled at its beauty. He had never seen its like. A fireplace was set into the wall behind the desk and next to it a small narrow wooden door.

When he pushed against the door it swung on hinges that barely hinted at a whisper and revealed a small kitchen that utilized the same chimney as the fireplace. It housed a larder filled with sealed crockery jars and pots as well as a small trap door set into the floor that led to a fully stocked wine cellar, its racks brimming with dust-covered bottles of wine. Rhael forgot everything else for a moment and felt his mouth water at the thought of food and drink.

He tore into the waxed seals of the crocks and jars and tried to discern their contents. A gnawing dread in the pit of his gut compelled him to look as he remembered the cook pots and the slaughterhouse, where he had been in the caves below. He half expected to see a jar of ears but was pleased when he found a crock containing stacks of dense small loaves with dried fruits and nuts and honey baked into them as well as some sort of cooked beans in a savory sauce and another jar holding stewed pears. It was the best food he had tasted in months and he devoured it like the half-starved, half-crazed, ill-looking wretch that he was. After he had sated his hunger he searched the kitchen for a wine key and opened one of the bottles he had liberated from the cellar.

Swigging from it, he made his way back through the tower and started up the staircase. The wine was good, but unlike anything he had ever tasted. It was dense and rich and floral on his tongue and in his nose. Fine things, he thought, fine things. This was a seat of power, and the former masters could not be faulted for their tastes, Rhael acknowledged.

He made the first landing of the tower and saw a lavishly appointed room that seemed to be dedicated for entertaining company. A strange musical instrument, some sort of hurdy-gurdy or cased harp or portative organ, he guessed, but he had little taste or knowledge of music. Tables and couches and the fireplace at the rear of the rooms, several doors leading out from the central hub. Rhael peered inside them all and found comfortable but modest sleeping quarters: small beds with curtained canopies built into the walls and a small table, access to a garderobe through a small door near the window.

He continued up the stairs and found what he was looking for at the second landing. It was a large opulent chamber that had been sectioned off into three separate private areas. One was a sitting room or parlor of some sort with several elegantly upholstered silk couches arranged on another richly woven carpet, the other a sleeping chamber with a small writing desk and a small table and chairs set in one corner near the fireplace, the bed a luxuriously canopied affair taking up much of the room, and the last division of the chamber was the most interesting to Rhael because it was a private library and reading room with two full cases of literature. He stopped himself from going through them just then. He needed to explore the rest of the rooms and have a look at what the Kuilbolts were doing before he got lost in the treasures of his new tower. Not that he had anything to fear—he could at any moment unleash the power of a single orb on this fortress and kill every last living thing within the palisade if he should choose to—but he saw the usefulness of the Kuilbolts and realized within his dark heart that he needed them to help him farm the people of the Dawn Tribe. He could never fully trust them, but he would have them fear him. Out of that fear they would learn to respect him. In return he would let them live and continue their horrid practices of human tannery and gargantuan rat husbandry.

He still needed something better, something more threatening than pain. He needed to know what they feared most, for that was the only way he could solidly retain them.

And what of these Kuilbolt masters? What was immediately clear to Rhael was that they were no Oesterners. The furnishings, the textiles, the food, the kitchen, the bedrooms, the garderobes—they were all foreign in their execution. The food was spiced exotically, the furnishings and implements fashioned strangely, to Rhael's eyes. Opulent and luxurious, but assembled differently than an Oesterner would have done. The scale itself was grand and more lavish than any lord's estate that he had seen in Oesteria, but then again, comparing the two made one seem more alien than the other.

He made his way back toward the staircase and would have kept climbing up had a fluttering tapestry not caught his eye. Upon investigating he discovered a narrow passage that led into a private chamber set with a bronze bathing tub and dressing mirrors as well as a large cabinet filled with fine clothes cut in a strange fashion. Rhael regarded himself in the mirrors and wept. His once flawless skin was now littered with scrapes and scars, his nose a broken mess, his eyes still bruised and healing. His emaciated frame looked crooked as he stood on account of his game leg, and he looked like one stuck somewhere between life and death. He would have one of the Kuilbolts bring him some servants from among the human slaves and have the wretches draw a bath for him. Then he would dress himself in these strange garments he had found and emerge from his tower, the lord of the fortress. He left the mirrors and went back to the stairs and climbed up and out of the tower onto a battlement strewn wall that wrapped around the tower so that the land was visible in all directions and Rhael could see quite a long distance from this vantage point. He could also keep an eye on the entire mining operation within the palisade very easily. He followed it round until he came to another doorway, a staircase continuing to wind its way up inside, but the passage back the way he had come from was on the other side of the tower. He supposed it had something to do with defending against attackers should they manage to breach the tower's defenses and storm it.

He climbed the stairs, grimacing as his leg tightened and throbbed with pain. He was near the top now, and all the way round the arrow slits gave good vantage of the walk below, as well as the mining yard and the palisade. Yes, he thought, an entirely good and defensible position. At the top of the stairs was a trap door outfitted with a counter weight that could easily be removed in siege time, should one find themselves here at the last line of defense. Rhael pushed against the trap door and felt the counter weight assist him in lifting the heavy bronze-bound oaken door.

He emerged from the trap door and found himself on the top of the tower among the battlements and bracing against the cold wind. The top of the tower was planked with wide flooring and there were two large bronze rings set into the inside of the battlement stones on opposite sides of the tower. Perhaps the anchors for some siege engine, Rhael surmised. He could see for miles. It was a fine position to erect a tower upon. He had no doubts about that.

He was staring out to the south when something caught his eye to the west. A small speck in the sky growing larger in size as he charted its progress. It was an airship, and it looked to be heading for the tower and its palisade. Rhael sped down the stairs as quickly as his injured leg would allow and was putting the key into the gate when a Kuilbolt ambled up to him and bowed lowly.

"Master, my lord, the old Masters arrive. You asked us to tell you, so we have obeyed you. What would you have us do, Excellency?" He was a bronze-helmed warrior Kuilbolt, tall and powerfully built for his race, and he regarded Rhael with utmost caution and wariness.

Rhael thought about it for a long moment. "You shall welcome them, and bring them to my tower."

"As you command." The Kuilbolt crossed his arms across his chest and bowed in some fashion of salute and turned to leave.

"What are you called?" Rhael asked.

The creature stopped and turned again. "I am Trilk, Excellency."

"Fetch me some humans from among the slaves to serve me in the tower. Bring me two of the fairest and the best behaved. Do you understand me?"

"Yess. I beg your leave, my lord."

"I want them here in my tower quickly. I need a bath drawn and some proper food made up, and I want to have it done before that airship arrives, so be quick about it."

"As you command, Excellency."

"I shall look upon you with favor should you do this in a way that pleases me."

The Kuilbolt bobbed and nodded and ambled off.

For the first time in a very long while Lord Uhlmet prepared to receive guests. And he was practically giddy with anticipation.

Twenty-Three

JOTH RODE ALONGSIDE EILYTH while Bellan rode slightly ahead of them both, turned back in his saddle so that he could look at them while he spoke. They wound their way together down a narrow game trail and Joth felt for a moment that he was once more back in the Dawn Tribe Territories, riding away from the hill that Wat and he had sought shelter in after their flight from the battle. It all seemed so long ago now.

They had left the road at the boy's urging, but the logic was not clear to Joth. Why would Norden have let them go only to have them killed on the road? He made this point to the lad, but Bellan had dismissed it.

"Master, I am only saying what I gleaned off those Norandishmen."

"Those fellows don't speak Oestersh, in case you hadn't noticed," Joth said.

"Well, I know that, master! I speak a bit of Norandian. My own father was a Norandishman."

Even Eilyth looked surprised. Joth wondered if she knew where Norandia was.

The youth went on. "He come over to Oesteria to soldier in the wars, he did. Met my mother and the love grabbed them, like. He stayed here, a lot of the soldiers did. He made a trade out of horses. He knows a lot about horses, how to train them, raise them. He taught me everything I know." He said it as though he were a veritable tome of equine knowledge on legs, all fifteen or sixteen winters of him.

"So you understood them talking, then?" Joth steered the lad back to the point.

"What's that? Oh yes, master. I understood them clear enough." His face went from jovial to grave in the blink of an eye. "They were to kill you; and begging your pardon, lady, but they was to drag you back to the mage." Bellan said it in earnest, but Joth was scrambling in his mind trying to find a reason for Norden to want to kill him. As far as dragging Eilyth back to Grannock, Joth had a pretty fair assumption of what the lecherous mage had in mind with that order. This all assumed that the boy was not completely running off of some half-supposed threat he half understood in his second tongue, seeking to join a band of horsemen and follow in his father's footsteps. Joth was willing to bet all of their horses on the chance of that dagger at Bellan's belt belonging to his soldier father, and the same weapon being liberated without the lad's father knowing about it, and the son himself seeming to innocently set off for work of a morning as usual when in fact he was stealing away for his own taste of adventure.

Not that he blamed him. Joth remembered what it was like growing up in a middling town dreaming of different places and adventure; it was what had drawn him to military service once he realized that his situation would never be socially acceptable or forgiven. He had besmirched a girl's honor and shamed his family and hers in the process, and his father had told him time and again that it was a dire thing that he had taken part in, and then his father had passed away suddenly and Joth was left holding the reins.

What was Bellan running from? He did not doubt the boy's earnestness, and he recognized that he had not yet considered the bravery and the loyalty he had shown to them in seeking to warn him and the Lady Eilyth about this presumed plot. He was a young man seeking to do right and Joth felt his heart melt for a moment when he looked at the frail-looking youth astride his tall, rangy gelding.

"You were going to join up with those Norandish boys," Joth stated.

He took a moment. "Yes, Master. I surely was."

"But you didn't. You came back here to warn us. You were looking for us?"

The boy ducked a low hanging limb and said, "Sure I was! I didn't want nothing awful to happen to you. Either of you."

He covered it well, but it was obvious to Joth that the boy was enamored with Eilyth. That might have been his impetus for running away in the first place, once Joth thought about it. How could he blame him for that? Once he had thought about it, he knew that he could not blame the lad, nor could he disbelieve what he was telling them; he had to take it as fact and stop second-guessing Bellan.

"Thank you for your warning, and thank you for not just giving us up."

Bellan nodded. "You are most welcome." He looked fiercely proud for a moment. He inclined his head awkwardly.

Joth smiled and looked to Eilyth, who held his eyes a moment.

She shifted her attention to Bellan. "What then? How do we avoid these Norandishmen?"

Bellan looked at her, his jaw working slightly. "Lady, never you fear. I know the short way to Torlucksford through the wilderness. I'll have us there well ahead of them boys, and we'll never be on the road. Never you fear."

She let his words hang for a long while. "As you say then, Bell. We are in your hands."

She had said it lightly, but the lad still gulped. "As it please you."

They rode on together at a long trot in single file along the trails and switchbacks all the day, fording small brooks and leaping over streams one after the other, Bellan looking back with a grin as though he were offering them riding challenges whenever an obstacle or an adventure that required some skill on horseback to negotiate presented itself. They climbed their way through the rolling hills and valleys of the land, always within the trees and never truly being able to reckon how near or far the road lay.

Joth fell to wondering about what the mage could possibly stand to gain by telling him one thing and then laying a trap to have him done away with and Eilyth held as his captive. Besides the obvious, he thought grimly. He shook his head and spat onto the damp trail beside him, into the gathering leaves that lay scattered there.

The dish-faced bay was called Gwyrno, which meant something like "White Eye," and Joth had been reminded of what a fine horse he was upon taking to the trail and feeling him move along smoothly, ambling over the low rises stoically, stretching out and leaping the brooks at Joth's urging. The horse was happy to be doing something. Joth could sense that the horse was excited for the change from trudging along the roads, holding his head high with his ears perked forward, at his ease but full of life, his heart beating, blood coursing, his powerful legs picking their way through the rough terrain like a dancer steps across a floor.

Joth could feel himself stepping with the horse, moving with him and the strange sensation of stepping with four legs and the vast lungs breathing and heaving, so strong, so fast; he lost himself for a moment, and he was inside the horse's world. He labored easily under the weight of his rider. How strange it was to see through the horse's eyes, to have the flood of scents rush through you with every breath, the pounding strength of your chest…Joth shook himself in the saddle and came back to his senses.

Eilyth threw a look back to him.

What had just happened to him he wondered? Perhaps he had drifted off to sleep for a moment? Bloody fool, Joth, even you can't sleep at a long trot, he chided himself. Gwyrno had craned his neck around and was regarding him strangely out of his pale right eye. Joth blinked a few times and gently pulled the horse's head around with a slight touch of his left rein. Joth came to the realization that maybe Bellan was not the only person that he should stop second-guessing. What Eilyth had done to him in the pass had awoken more than just his awareness; it had awoken an ability in him that allowed him to sense others' feelings and perceptions as well. He had been lying to himself and denying every instinct he had, only to have it rear up and almost cause him to topple out of his saddle along the wild trails to Torlucksford. He knew he had to speak to Eilyth about it, she of all people would know what to say to him to help him get a grasp on how to handle this ability, this strange perception. She was looking at him again then, her eyes full of unreadable mystery. Her face was just a touch curious as she regarded him and Joth wondered if she sensed the fear in him, for that is what it was, he had decided; it was a fear of this new awareness, an inability to control or understand it fully. These were the things that drove the fear in his mind when he felt himself fully embracing it.

Joth was afraid of knowing things outside of his own head. It felt unwieldy and alien to him, as though he were somehow exposed and vulnerable or as if he were sitting too close to a stranger at mess without enough bench between them to allow for space. He felt naked and fearful in the face of it. There, he thought, I've admitted it to myself at least, at last. It did scare him, but it thrilled him as well. It thrilled him now to think of how he had felt as he experienced running like a horse runs just moments before. He could sense other space, other perception. It was vast and limitless, how he imagined the ocean to be. It was all hanging out there before him when he was least expecting it, dangling like a prize he was afraid of grasping. Then it would be gone as he was distracted or telling himself to stop daydreaming. Whenever he attempted to find it again, he would be left exasperated.

He wished that he had been blessed by a moment of keen insight and extra-sensory perception when Mage Alchemist Norden had been shaking his hand politely, a dagger hidden behind his back. Joth was at odds as to why the man would want him dead. Why not reassign him back to the garrison at Immerdale and be done with it bloodlessly? No, the man had been too curious as to whether other outriders were sent, too curious as to whether or not word of Uhlmet's capture had reached other ears. Lord Uhlmet was famously disliked and had a reputation for being a rather haughty and dislikable sort of a man, and a man like Norden may well stand to benefit from his staying gone for a long, perhaps indefinite, time. Joth and Eilyth were the only souls who knew of Uhlmet's capture, so perhaps Norden had dreamt up this plan to contain the knowledge of Uhlmet's dire predicament? It seemed far-fetched, especially going off of the word of an errant stable-boy and nothing else, but Joth could see the logic behind a plan such as that having some merit in the mind of a man like Norden.

It was obvious that the man held Uhlmet with contempt. He had said as much by saying nothing, let alone by telling Joth that Uhlmet had been unfit for command. The pity was that Joth agreed with the man. He thought Norden was right in his thinking and his observations on the character of Lord Uhlmet. He would be happy to say as much to a council should he be brought up on charges, but he wished now that he had kept his head up and his eyes ahead and gone about his business without any more excitement or intrigue than necessary.

Joth leaned out to avoid a limb and squeezed Gwyrno into a slow canter to catch up to the others. They had all been pacing well and the horses were lathered and blowing hard as they came over a low rise between two larger wood-covered slopes and a trio of hawks soared and cried out overhead. Joth regarded Eilyth as she noted it well.

She offered a half-smile before looking away.

Bellan pulled them up at the other side of the pass. "There's a stream here, Master, lady. Should we wish to bed down for the evening, this right here's most likely the best place we'll come across afore we make it to Torlucksford, if you take my meaning."

Joth looked at the sky. "It is barely late afternoon, Bell. Surely we have two, maybe three hours left to ride?"

The youth reddened. "Yes, master. I was just accounting for the lady, in case she were tired and whatnot, or having lady problems with the stream nearby and all."

"What?" Eilyth asked him.

Joth raised an eyebrow. "Lady problems? Bellan, I think perhaps—"

"Well what do I know?" Bellan kept talking. "I sometimes like to have a cool dip in a stream after I been riding a long ways, don't you? She ain't sitting no lady's saddle, how am I to know what that might do to a lady's, you know, a lady's—"

Eilyth spoke up. "My people are born to horse riding. We do not tire easily, I assure you. I have outridden everyone here, or soon shall."

Joth felt his cheeks flush.

"We shall water the horses here at the stream you speak of. Let us eat something, as well."

Bellan's ears were glowing. "Of course, lady."

She made a clicking noise with her tongue and Aila picked up into a trot down the hill toward a copse of willows growing on either side of the banks of a stream. "What did I say?" The youth seemed to be asking himself. Joth could only shake his head and squeeze his horse into a slow canter after Eilyth and her gray mare.

They watered the horses and decided to risk a small fire, as it was still somewhat overcast, and from what Bellan claimed the road lay somewhere between ten to twenty miles to the south of them as it circumnavigated the hilly lands entirely and led into the city from the south east, while his route brought them in from the south west. They managed to find some relatively dry wood and to get a fire going on the damp ground in short order. Eilyth gathered water into the small pot as she had done so many times before on their way into Oesteria from the lands of the People. She cut root vegetables with a small knife and added the strange dried leaves from the sea into a broth with her other ingredients and smiled at them as she went about her work, as though she were pleased to be able to be about it once again—as though it gave her great pride and pleasure.

Indeed, Joth thought that it did give her those things. Eilyth delighted in the simple things of life, the small moments and the tiny incremental things that made up a moment. He understood this about her now, after weeks of witnessing her greet each day with wonder and an expectant curiosity. Eilyth enjoyed adventure. She loved her horse, and she liked to cook her strange soup that seemed to be the staple of her diet and the cornerstone of good health and physical and mental fitness, at least according to her. She knelt there in the small clearing, her gray cloak wrapped about the garish airship costume she wore as she stirred her soup.

The witch and her cauldron, thought Joth. If she were a witch then he was enchanted with her and there was no need for a spell. He had put all of his meager faith in her, he had decided. His disenchantment with the First Army of the Magistry had run fairly deep with the tyranny of Mage Imperator Rhael Lord Uhlmet and his ill-conducted survey, a routine and ordinary outing, sometimes referred to as a "long march" due to most mage imperators' practice of avoiding contact with the tribesmen altogether and using it instead as an experience to understand the logistics of supply and campaigning should they ever be called to war in order to defend the Magistry.

Now, with Mage Alchemist Norden a potential enemy and threat to his and Eilyth's safety, his loyalty was even more aligned with her; he had given his word to see her safe and let no harm befall her, but had he not also given his word to serve the First Army of the Magistry and all his comrades in his now fallen company? He could not simply follow after the lad's word on the matter, that much he knew for certain. He had to be sure, and surely he knew of only one way of knowing. Knowing that may help decide many things, Joth mused.

Eilyth presented two bowls, but Joth gave her his bowl when he saw that she was about to eat from the still hot cooking pot and he picked it up instead with the edge of his cloak and sat down upon a large rock, one of many that littered the ground they had chosen to make a temporary camp upon. The pot was steaming hot, and the smell was distinctive. Immediately it brought him back to the first time he had smelled it on the road away from the village where he had learned so much about the People, about himself, the world, everything. He wondered at that and about how fast the change in everything he thought he had known had been wrought. A change that he still had not accepted, and he knew it was because he still had a foot in both worlds. Joth was straddling the fence between his old world and his new. He was decided in his heart but his mind was still waging a battle. After a long moment of thought, he reached inside his scrip bag and removed the folded writ with the mage's seal: the mortar and pestle and owl of the Mage Alchemists Order embossed on purple wax with a gray silk ribbon folded intricately beneath it and fixed with the seal. He studied it a long while before holding it over the top of his steaming pot of broth and subjecting it to a gentle flood of steam.

Bellan looked on alarmedly and quit his incessant flattery of Lady Eilyth's soup.

"You mustn't do that! That's a high crime to tamper with a seal!" he cried.

"Riddle me this. If a man tells you to deliver a letter for him, then you find out he's going to have you killed and the lady you're charged with protecting subjected to who bloody knows what, don't you think it's worth having a peek at what's written in that letter he gave you to begin with?"

The lad looked at him then down at the ground. "I'm just warning you is all. I deliver post all over these parts and the first thing they says to you is 'Tampering with a seal is a high crime.' So, just warning you."

"Thanks for your warning, Bell." Joth gave him a curt nod and went back to testing the seal. He had worked with beeswax a lot during his apprenticeship and he knew how much heat it could and could not take. He had made huge vats of melted beeswax for his master's special rosin used both in his treatment of the bows and more especially the strings. He tested the envelope and held it back to the steam.

"It's a high crime, which means they can kill you for it. Hang you, most likely. I mean to say, that's a Magistry seal there, master." He shrugged at Eilyth like he was speaking to a stupid person who could not understand him.

"You let me worry about the particulars, Bell. You can eat your soup."

Bellan nodded and did just that.

Joth felt Eilyth watching him intently as he used his belt knife to gently pry the softened wax seal from the dampened parchment and unfold the Mage Alchemist Norden's writ; the sealed writ given to Joth on explicit orders of delivering it to the captain of the town guard at Torlucksford. He opened it and turned to capture the best of the fading light to ease his reading. Once he began to read it his deepest misgivings were fully realized. The boy was to be trusted, Joth decided, for the mage had set Joth and Eilyth up so completely that Joth was shaking his head in disbelief.

"What does it say, Joth?" she asked him.

"It says in short to arrest us on sight as quietly and quickly as possible and hold us until Norden or one of his agents can take custody of us. He set us up from the start! Why?" Joth threw the writ down and stood up.

"Joth," she said, "this is not the way for us to solve the problem."

"I know, but it angers me! Here we are, speeding along on our way quite easily and all set for Twinton, and this bloody weasel of a mage heaps nothing but trouble on our plates. It's not our bloody fault that Uhlmet is a fool!"

Eilyth stepped over and picked the parchment up from the ground and read it.

"Who's Uhlmet?" Bellan asked tentatively.

"Never you mind, boy. You're better off not knowing anything about him, because it's all bad."

The lad gulped again.

"He has killed you twice today, if not more. Here he names you as a deserter, is that not a death sentence?" Eilyth said it as calmly as though she were discussing the price of figs at the market.

"Yes, indeed! The bloody man would have me hand over my own death warrant thinking he was true to his word! How dare he do something like that? I've done my duty is all, I followed my orders even if I didn't agree with them."

"When the three children were dragged away?"

"Lady?"

"Where were you when the children were dragged away?"

"I was in the ranks, lady. Believe me, none of us soldiers liked that. Wat, he even —"

"Yet you allowed it to happen." She looked at him evenly, unwavering.

"There were some children that got dragged somehow?" Bellan chimed in.

"We were just foll—. Yes, I allowed it to happen. I was afraid of disobeying orders. Lord Uhlmet was strict, and he punished even the slightest offenses harshly. I was afraid of him. I was afraid of disobeying him. He made Wat and me string a poor lad up because he made a joke! Seven bells, we had to murder somebody for him just because he told us to do it and we couldn't bloody break protocol! We liked the lad, even. His name was Tylner, and we had to bloody string him up. Mage was there watching us or we'd have let him go and told him to run for it. We were all of us scared of him, and that's no excuse, but none of us thought he was going to kill them kids, if that's what he done. That's not what any of the lads signed on for, lady. I assure you, it is not what I signed on for."

"That is most certainly what he did, Joth." Eilyth fixed him with her strange eyes. "And he made you a party to it. We are all of us responsible for their cruel demise now."

"I'm not. I don't even have a hair's-breadth of an idea what you're speaking of," Bellan muttered.

"Lady—" Joth began.

"No, it is true. We are all of us sharing a responsibility in their deaths because of this malformed creature and his wicked acts upon the People and their lands. We too shrank from his authority, this authority of men called the Magistry. We cowed and urged our folk to accommodate the Oestmen, to treat them with hospitality. We made excuses for him before we learned he was a monster, and I know that you were subject to his authority, but we must never let that happen again. I do not blame you for their deaths. You did not know, and I see that in your eyes. Now, I must know where your loyalties lie." She smiled softly at him a moment, and he felt as though a sack full of sand he had been burdened with had been lifted from his shoulders.

"My loyalty is with you, lady. It is with you and the People." Joth surprised himself when he said it.

Eilyth held his eyes.

Bellan looked between the two of them several times before the silence grew too untenable for him. "I'm not even sure what all of this talk is about, but I'm going to take a leap here and say I'd like to sign up as well. I am not sure if I can make an oath or anything quite yet until I get a clear view as to who and what and why, mind you."

"Now is not the time, Bell," Eilyth admonished him lightly. The boy reddened. "If you prove yourself to me in getting us to Torlucksford, then I shall consider your pledge."

Bellan's eyes went a bit far away for a split second before he nodded once determinedly and set back to his soup.

The boy hung on every bloody word she said and she knew it, Joth figured. As for himself, what else should he have said? Joth enjoyed the thought of never setting eyes on Oesteria again and grabbing Eilyth's hand and setting off west for the mountains; for the village by the river and its peaceful rhythms. He also realized that he could not simply retreat into his peaceful dreams, for lady Eilyth's life was at stake; all of their lives were in jeopardy, even Bellan now that he had conspired against the mage by warning them of his plot. Here they were now in a copse of trees far from any place he was familiar with. The people spoke with a funny lilt to their speech, especially country folk like Bellan. Joth looked at Eilyth and saw that she was looking at him, waiting for him to say something.

"I have an idea, and it's better than nothing." He stood up and took Norden's writ back from Eilyth. "Ryla Dierns gave me an idea." He fetched the parchment and quill and the ink vial from his scrip bag; all soldiers were given them all rolled up and tucked into a short thin leather tube. They were for reports, for letters home, for wills and testaments. "What's the closest town north of here? One large enough to have need of a skyharbor?" he asked Bellan.

"You mean north of Torlucksford?"

"Yes. What's the next larger-sized town that you would come to beyond that?"

Bellan thought for a moment. "Well, to the north it would be Kingsbridge, I reckon."

"Kingsbridge? I feel that I've heard of that before." Joth had met someone from Kingsbridge in Immerdale when he was garrisoned there. "Is it far?"

"Not too very far, master. A few days, most likely. I ain't never seen it to be honest with you. My father never let me range much past Torlucksford, even on a post run. I could have stood to make a lot of coin had he not obstructed me."

"Right. Well, either way, perhaps we can find a way to beat this mage at his own game."

They gathered closer as Joth explained his plan.

An hour later, as the sun was sinking low in the sky and they had covered the ashes of their fire with damp earth and cleared away the evidence of their having been there, they mounted their horses and set off once again at a long trot toward the northeast and Torlucksford. He was not the best scribe, any fool could see that, but he knew what writs looked like and he had seen his fair share of writs that had been scraped and rewritten with new orders, and his doctored version looked close enough to the genuine article to his eye. He had left the important bits, Mage Norden's name and seal and his introduction, but he had left the body of the writ wide open and full of vaguery. He had also written a letter to Ryla Dierns and entrusted it to Bellan with explicit instructions to get the missive to her without the mage or any of his cronies knowing about it.

It was a good plan, he thought, and if it worked out smoothly, he and Eilyth would disappear north to Kingsbridge before the mage or his foreign horsemen could catch their trail again. With any luck, Ryla Dierns would lose him as well and they would all meet in Kingsbridge to continue their journey to Twinton. They had agreed that the best course of action would be to ride through the night to Torlucksford. In that manner they would outdistance the Norandian guards and have at least a half-day on them by the time that they realized he and Eilyth had given them the slip.

Bellan assured them that he knew the trails well enough to navigate by moonlight, and although the lad talked too much, Joth trusted his horsemanship and his sense of direction. Joth had always been judgmental of people who spoke too much. He had always thought them full of deceit, but Bellan was not like that. The lad was honest.

The trail rose before them and the trees thinned out as the hill rose up to a towering height and they passed over the top of it and took a look out behind them and around them. Far in the distance ahead a glimmer caught his eye. Bellan caught it too.

"Torlucksford." He said by way of explanation.

"There!" Eilyth said sharply.

Joth followed her gaze and saw a rider far in the distance behind them atop a hill. It was far, and yet Joth could make out the distinctive helm and dark coat, as well as a spyglass in the horseman's hand.

"Yes. They've made us now."

"Are you sure? That could have been anybody out for a ride." Bellan looked a touch worried.

"I have sharp eyes, and that was one of those foreign boys. He's off now to tell the others."

"We are many miles ahead of them. We shall ride fast, but even so we shall beat them only by hours." Eilyth was gauging the distance as she spoke.

"The plan will still work. We shall simply have to speed it up a bit."

She nodded, and Bellan did as well once he saw Eilyth nodding.

The lad turned his tall buckskin gelding and set off again at a long trot. Eilyth took a last look behind her after the direction of the rider and then followed Bellan on her gray mare, leaving Joth to fall in behind the white packhorse. Urging his mount into a long trot he set off after his two traveling companions along the trail. They would make Torlucksford by midnight, and Joth hoped that he could pass his writ off to the guard once he got there. It had begun to rain again, but it was more of a heavy drizzle that slowly sought its way through their cloaks and coats as they road along through the fading light. The trail was slick, but the horses were used to this sort of footing and showed no signs of distress at the weather. Joth resisted the fool's temptation of running his horse full out over the trail in order to put a mile or two more between them. He would have to spend his mount more wisely if he were to outpace his pursuers and their sleek coursers. They looked as though they could set a quick pace, but it made no progress to dwell on it, he knew. He had the road before him and Eilyth's safety to worry about, and now he had the boy to worry over as well. It was risky if the boy went back to Grannock while the mage was still at the inn, now that he had been spotted traveling with them by the Norandian scout. Especially ponying three horses, Joth thought, as he pictured the talkative Bellan shouting out all his business to the world as he strolled past the covered well in the center of the small street.

No, he reflected, the lad had a touch more sense than that and he had a heart and an easy-going way about him, but he also had some mettle to him—enough mettle to stand up and intervene where he sensed a wrong turn about to take place. That took courage and Joth would hold him in esteem for that because he knew that had not been easy for the lad. He would also give the boy some credit for his skills on horseback and his ability to lead them down the trail in these conditions.

There were more hills to crest and more places where the trail was hemmed in and narrowed by a close growing wood and a small ravine that had to be leapt over to be passed and yet more woods and meandering game trails and switchbacks before they finally crested a last low hill and saw the silvery ribbon of the Peake river flowing down through the valley on the far side of the next hill to the east. A tumbling, wooden-walled palisade and a squat stone tower announced the town of Torlucksford atop the hill and looked down over its position on the river Peake, a bridge now spanning the town's namesake ford where the river channel was at its narrowest.

They could see the lights of the town glowing on the hilltop, the whole place silhouetted in moonlight. It was near midnight and they would be arriving at the gates within the hour. They rode on in matched pace, but here they paced out and rode abreast of each other and allowed their horses to have room after such a frantic ride through the trails and byways of the hilly country between Grannock and Torlucksford. Their horses were tired and well lathered by the time they had made it to the last stand of trees before the road led in to the palisade. It was there that Eilyth and Joth dismounted and handed their reins off to Bellan.

"Remember," he said looking up to the boy as he gave him the dish-faced bay, "be certain no one sees you in town ponying these horses."

"Master, you can rest assured. Never you fear."

"Get that letter to Captain Dierns as quick as you can."

"Master, as I said, never you fear." He patted his breast to show that the letter was safe and sound and tucked away inside his fine blue coat.

Eilyth reached up and put her hand to the boy's cheek. "Go with a care, Bellan. Those men will treat you poorly if you are discovered."

"Yes, lady. As it please you." He dipped his head awkwardly.

Eilyth favored him with a smile. "You'd better fly now. Every minute counts."

Joth shook the boy's hand. "Take care of yourself, Bellan. And thank you."

The youth smiled and nodded. "This has been a real adventure. I'll watch to see that you make it to the gates."

They all agreed, then Joth and Eilyth started out on foot up the slope toward the postern gate of the town. It was a short brisk walk and they were there. He and Eilyth looked back and caught sight of Bellan trotting back over the rise with their horses in tow. As he watched him leave, Joth realized that he and Eilyth were alone now, and should his plan fail they would be horseless. To be horseless would be the least of their discomfitures if he was accused of forging papers, assuming the authority of an officer, falsifying orders, and who knows what else. If that were not enough, perhaps he could find Mage Alchemist Norden to come shout out about him being a deserter and he could help knot the cord he was to be garrotted with.

The wooden walls of the palisade stretched a good twenty ells or higher, and the gatehouse was made of stone and timber, bound and cross-braced with riveted iron bands to reinforce and bring the timbers in to help bear up its stone bulk. Arrow slits and murder holes looking down on them, Joth and Eilyth approached the sally port set within the main ironbound wooden gate, and Joth raised his hand and knocked upon the door soundly. It was a long moment later when some shuffling could be heard and a lantern light showed behind the seams of a speaking window set within the sally port.

"Who goes? State your business?" a voice asked routinely as light flooded them and the speaking window was thrown open with a metallic clang.

"Commander Watron Kine, First Army of the Magistry." The man blinked a couple of times then shut the speaking window and threw open the sally port, holding out his lantern and ushering them in. The man was in his middling years and clad in a town guard livery watchcoat, a sword dangling at his hip. He wore a mail collar but a soft hat to guard against the chill in place of a helm. He brought them in to a small space between the walls, past the gate yet still behind the portcullis.

"I'll need to speak to your captain right away," Joth told the man urgently.

"Yes, Commander." The man bowed and turned smartly for a door on the other side of the gatehouse wall.

He was left to stand nervously with Eilyth. A few moments later, the man who had ushered them in returned leading a young foppish-looking man in a long formal robe who had obviously only recently been roused from his sleep. He blinked a few times and yawned before speaking. "Yes, I'm Captain Vell of the Townsguard of Torlucksford," he stated lazily. "How may I be of assistance to you, Commander Kine?"

It took him a second to remember that Wat's name was his own for the moment. "Oh, yes, Captain, I thank you and apologize for disturbing your sleep, but you must understand I need to transport this prisoner immediately and under the utmost secrecy to—" He cut his eyes dramatically toward the middling guard and then back to the foppish Captain Vell.

The captain raised his eyebrows for a moment before he nodded. "Andry, you may step back to your post."

"Yes, Captain," Andry said before bowing and turning smartly again and heading back to his post near the sally port.

"Commander? Please continue." Captain Vell eyed Eilyth up and down.

"It's all here in this writ." Joth forced himself to calmly say it as he pulled the letter from his scrip bag and presented it to the captain. He examined the unbroken seal perfunctorily and cracked it open crisply, much to Joth's satisfaction. He opened the letter, moving closer to the torchlight to see it better. Joth thanked the stars for arriving in Torlucksford at night.

"Hmm. That's interesting," the man muttered. "Tell me, how many scribes has this Norden got?"

What? thought Joth. What should I say? "He has two, my lord Captain. He has replaced his scribe of late."

"A pity that. His last letter was in a much neater hand."

Joth smiled uncomfortably and shrugged his shoulders. "You must understand I am not here by choice, Captain. I am merely following orders myself."

The man looked up from the writ and raised his eyebrows again. "Of course, Commander, my apologies. It's just that yesterday we were all on the alert after Mage Norden warned us of this red-haired fugitive and here you are now with a new writ and the fugitive in your custody. It's all just a bit overwhelming for us, Commander. We don't usually encounter this much activity."

So Norden had set yet another trap for them. The man was efficient. Joth would credit him with that, at least. "I understand, Captain. Of course, I'll have to insist that you help us now and send us on our way." Joth tried to say it with as much authority as he could muster. He stole a quick glance at Eilyth, whom he had been purposely ignoring as he stood there with her father's staff in his hand. She was looking appropriately browbeaten and demoralized. She looked like a prisoner, or at least like someone who was defeated. He had to force himself to look away before Captain Vell noticed.

"Yes, Commander, I am not aiming to impede you at all. Of course not. I apologize. I made arrangements for a prisoner's transport to be standing by when I had received word from Mage Norden of a possible fugitive. The driver and groom are staying at a nearby inn, and I'll have them roused and ready within the hour."

"See that you do, and see that your men fetch food for myself and the prisoner as I have lost my mount and all my provisions in taking her."

The man bobbed and backed away with a flourish. "I am making it my personal mission to see to it that you have the choicest delectable provisions, Commander. I cannot stand campaigning without proper nourishment. I take it upon myself to see to it by means of an apology to the mage for not being able to further aid in the capture of this dangerous creature." He once again ran his eyes up and down Eilyth's forlorn figure.

Joth felt his patience with the man wearing thin, but he held back and drew a deep breath and let it out slowly. "I am weary from my travels. Is there a place I can relax and have a flagon while the team is hitched?"

"Of course. Why don't you come with me to the inn? I shall rouse the driver and groom myself and see to it that you have a hot meal and a flagon."

That was more like it, Joth thought. "That's very kind of you indeed. Lead on, Captain." He took Eilyth by the elbow and followed Captain Vell through a door and out the other side of the gatehouse, past the portcullis and up a narrow, cobbled lane until they came to a small square with a fountain at its center and several stone and half-timbered buildings jumbled along its borders.

There were few people awake at this hour, and the weather was still damp and drizzling. Joth and Eilyth followed the captain to a building on the corner of the square with a large sign showing a boar beneath an oak tree, the name painted in golden letters across the top and bottom of the sign illuminated by torchlight and reading "The Duke of Acorns." Inside, the inn was quaint and quiet. An older woman worked at collecting earthenware mugs and bowls from the now empty tables as a fire burned in a central hearth and a barman swept at the floor behind the bar.

The captain sorted them out with two bowls of stew and a warm round loaf encrusted with seeds and nuts and fresh butter. The old woman brought a jug of ale and two cups, and Joth poured ale for himself and Eilyth as the captain took to the stairs and announced that he was off to wake the driver and the groom. He was so famished that he could not tell if the stew was as good as it tasted to him due to excellent preparation or his own hunger, but he ate it greedily and slathered his warm bread with the rich butter and ate his fill. Looking at Eilyth, he could tell that she too had been hungry, for she was closing her eyes as she chewed the bread as though it was the finest thing she had ever tasted.

As they were eating, the captain came back down the stairs followed by a sandy haired youth and a solid older man who was belting on a long knife and coiling up a coach whip as he yawned and nodded to the captain. "As it please you, Captain. Simma, run hitch up the team." The young man started off immediately, attempting to smooth his hair when he caught sight of Eilyth.

The captain walked over to the table where he and Eilyth were sitting, the older man trailing him. "Commander Kine,

I shall leave you in the hands of Master Durn. He'll be driving for you. I pray that you will give my kind regards to Mage Norden?"

"Thank you, Captain. I shall indeed."

"Good, good. May your journey be pleasant." The foppish captain bid them good evening with a sweeping bow.

The old woman put a basket on the table and nodded to Joth. Inside were a few loaves of bread and some other foods. A dried sausage, its casing white with mold, a wheel of cheese, a small clay jar of pickled onions, a large cask of ale— provisions to last he and Eilyth two, maybe three, days.

Durn, the driver, was staring at Eilyth's hair ornaments. "Bloody Dawn Tribe," he muttered astoundedly.

Joth stepped to immediately. "That isn't your concern, driver. This prisoner is my concern."

The man looked at Eilyth warily but nodded. "Yes, Commander, as it please you." Joth stood and pushed the basket of provisions at the driver. "Make sure there are blankets in the coach, and let's be off as quickly as we can be."

"Yes, Commander. Just one thing, I was wondering where we are off to? The captain, see, he never said where we was going."

Joth took a look around and saw no one to overhear him except for the old woman cleaning the tables, but she was halfway across the room. "You're to take us to Kingsbridge," Joth said lowly. "And we are not to make any stops along the way until we get there."

Durn came to get them a few minutes later and Joth led Eilyth outside, where a tall ironbound box sat perched atop a carriage. The sandy-haired youth Simma stood to one side of the open cell door holding a tatty-looking crossbow. A team of six horses plumed steam and stamped in the chill wee hours. Joth pushed Eilyth inside the cell and then climbed in behind her.

"I'll keep the prisoner in my sight at all times. No one must see me leave Torlucksford, so say nothing."

Durn handed him up the basket of provisions. "As it please you, Commander."

When they shut the cell door, Joth could see Eilyth smiling at him in the darkness. He smiled back and they both started to laugh while trying desperately not to, but the ironbound carriage cell was solid, and with the creaks and groans that the carriage was making as the team set out neither the driver nor the youth would ever be able to hear them.

"Well done," she said to him quietly.

"It isn't over yet, but at least we escaped Mage Norden for the time being. Now, if Ryla Dierns can have a stroke of luck and get clear of him, we'll be back on our way in no time."

"I saved something for us," she said, "from the packhorse. See?" She produced the wineskin with the last of the mead in it and held it aloft.

Joth grinned. "I forgot to include that in my plan."

"Lucky for you, I did not."

They shared the remainder of the mead as the rolling cell trundled over the cobbles and down toward the gatehouse, where they stopped briefly to pick up a basket of delectables hand chosen by Captain Vell, an assortment of crockery jars with waxed linen covers. It also included a sack of wine, much to Joth's pleasure. He picked through the jars using his nose to ascertain their contents, but it was too dark within the cell to be sure; everything smelled of vinegar. He put the basket back on the floor. He felt Eilyth looking at him through the darkness.

"What is it?" he asked.

"What if Ryla Dierns does not come?"

"We will give her a fortnight, then we will have to move on."

"Yes, but what then? How will we travel?"

She was worrying about her horse now, he realized. "We will find a way, lady. We can find another airship in Kingsbridge or book passage along the river, if need be."

She was silent.

"Don't worry about Aila, lady. Bellan will take good care of her."

"Thank you, Joth. You are right, and I am wrong to worry. Yet, I worry." He could hear her laughing softly to herself. The jailer's cart rolled on through the night as Joth and Eilyth at last fell off into sleep amidst the symphony of creaks and groans and rocking as it conveyed them along the road to Kingsbridge. They would ride through the next day and into the night in relative comfort until all hell broke loose in the small hours of the following morning.

Twenty-Four

THE INN WAS BUSTLING when the Norandian horsemen led her downstairs to the great room. Ryla was dressed as smartly as she could be, plumed hat cocked jauntily, hosen smooth and gartered smartly at her knees. She was a handsome woman, shapely in all the right places and aware of it, and she would use that to her advantage if she saw an opportunity— even if it were an opportunity that involved the smarmy mage and his bullying attitude.

Ryla knew how to out-clever the clever. She was a clever girl herself; a clever woman, now. Things had been hard for her, but she had persevered, and she had grown into something more than she had been. She had forged a life for herself out of the coals of her ruin. It was long ago that she had sworn the blood oath to avenge her family and her friends and her own honor, but before that she had wandered the way of the wind. In those old and lonely days, she had survived from hand to mouth, from day to day. Her grief was so deep and her sadness so profound that she nearly lost herself in them, but she had survived due in large part to the kindnesses of a short string of male benefactors, the last of whom had given her the Airship Skyward upon his death.

He had been good and kindly, and it was the closest thing to love she had known since the vicious Lord Uhlmet murdered her first true love, her friends, and family all those many years ago and denied her a life that she once held dear. Now, as she was led down the stairs of the little inn in Grannock, she reflected on her equally good and bad fortune and how luck had played such a role in the events of her life. It was not easy, but she had always survived, and she had always held on to the good and put the bad behind her as best she could. When she had seen the desperate face of the young soldier in the skyharbor at Borsford she had almost turned him away immediately, but she had been glad that she did not after reading the writ he bore and seeing the name "Uhlmet" scratched at the bottom of it. She had thought for certain that she may have intercepted someone of great importance to her most hated and detested former lord—someone she might be able to use as leverage to force a meeting. Then Ryla had planned on getting Lord Uhlmet alone on board her airship and dropping him from a great height onto the rocky outcrop where her small village once stood.

She would gladly go with the soldier if that was what it took to end Uhlmet's life. The skies love a volunteer, she thought ruefully, and better the satisfaction of ridding the world of Uhlmet the Monster and living on. She would retire to the Southwest Isle and buy a small holding there like she had wanted to do since she had first flown over the beautiful beaches with their coral sands and verdant mountain forests filled with colorful birds. She would keep the airship and continue running her shipping business, but she would captain it out—perhaps to Elmund, if he ever learned to control his brutish temper, the bloody fool. The man was a liability every time they left the decks but he was a fine hand in the sky. Not many could reef a sail or scramble up the rigging as nimbly or as fair as Elmund could, of that she was certain.

Losing Dathe had been a horrible thing for all of them. He was a sweet lad, quick with a laugh, even at his own expense, and the crew had liked him well. There was nothing to be done for it now, but she would see that this mage compensated her for her damages and delays, and she would see that whatever family lost Dathe would have his things and a bit of money as well. It was only right that she did so. It was a captain's duty, she knew, but she also had a strong sense of justice concerning such matters. She would not let that snake of a mage wriggle free of her demands, she was sure of that. And just as sure that she would watch Uhlmet die before her eyes.

She was a part of something larger, a secret, burgeoning society of tradesmen and intellectuals and workers alike who expressed dissatisfaction with the Magistry and their totalitarian rule, their usurpation of the Nobles, the upset of the ruling class and the unsettled peasantry whom were left with little option for change under the rule of the mages. Having arisen from the peasantry herself, Ryla felt a desire for justice. She had sought out men and women aligned against the Magistry and their rule, and she had conspired with them against the government in small ways over the years—transporting letters and smuggling cargo aboard the Skyward—but her ultimate goal had always been the death of Lord Uhlmet. But now that a clean end to the monster had presented itself, this slight and shrill-voiced Mage Norden had interposed himself between her and her goal.

The Norandians led her through the bustling great room aswarm with carters and drivers and drovers breakfasting at the tables as well as the foreign soldiers and the mage with his scrawny-looking clerk off at a table in the corner near the fire.

The slope-shouldered, balding man was gnawing on a strip of bacon like a rat. He looked up from his plate at her approach and wiped greasy hands on a napkin cloth. "Captain Dierns, what an honor," he said, rising and gesturing grandly at the table before them. "Please join us for breakfast. We have much to discuss."

Ryla looked to either side of her as the Norandian guards withdrew and then turned her eyes back to the mage. "I'm not interested in further delays, Lord Mage. I'd be most interested in resuming my journey. As you are well aware, the time I lose equates to a loss in profits on all my cargo." She said it with a smile.

"Yes, yes, of course, captain. You'll be happy to learn that our wagons have caught us up and it will be a simple exercise of loading my cargo aboard your airship and we will be underway. Have no fear, Captain Dierns. Your rough treatment at the hands of the Magistry is at an end. Smooth sailing from here on out." He smiled obsequiously and stared at her for far too long.

"I thank you, Lord Mage," she said, matching his lingering look and masking her revulsion. It was enough to do the trick she mused as she caught a spark of satisfaction in the oily mage's eyes. Now the fool thinks he has a chance with me, she told herself. Good enough for now; she did not want to push things too far too fast. "If you would favor me by releasing my crew, I can begin preparations to get underway."

"Yes, the Norandishmen will escort us all to your ship, along with my cargo. I'm assuming that during the loading you shall have ample time to prepare the ship?" He smiled innocently, but Ryla knew that behind it Norden was gloating. He was not going to give her an opportunity to escape like that.

She did not like the obligation of being pressed into service by the Magistry, especially when it left her at the whims of men like Norden and took her away from the prize of finally stopping Uhlmet, a prize that was actually in her grasp for the first time after so many years of waiting and hoping and plotting and failing. No, she thought, I won't let that opportunity escape me easily either, my dear lord mage, no matter what. She would have to wait until an opportunity presented itself and she could speak with her crew and Shiny and Pretty alone. She would gain the mage's trust, and at the first opportunity she would rid herself of the obligation of satisfying his whims. She masked her annoyance well, and instead looked a bit put out by the whole ordeal and held her palms up and shrugged.

"I'm only interested in speeding things along. Where's my breakfast?" She sauntered over to a chair and draped herself across it.

Norden licked his lips and chuckled nervously. "Serving girl! The captain has an appetite!" He called out with his shrill sounding voice. "Most pleasant, most pleasant," he muttered contentedly to himself as once again he ran his eyes all over her and for too long.

She pretended not to notice and instead reached for a flagon of ale and a cup and poured herself a long draught. She hoped that breakfast might afford her an opportunity to see her crew, the mage having kept them separated for the entirety of the previous day and night, imprisoned inside their rooms and served by nervous-looking tavern staff. Ryla had begun to feel as though she would start crawling up the walls before long, and then the guards had knocked on the door and told her in broken Oestersh that the mage wanted her to join him. She had been repulsed and relieved at the same time, but Ryla Dierns knew an opportunity when she saw one, even if it was only a window with a view to an opportunity. She had made more from less in the past.

"My dear lord mage," she said pleasantly, "my crew works much better on a full stomach, and the faster we get them fed and going the better."

Norden looked up from his breakfast. There was a bit of egg stuck to his chin. "Right, captain. See to it then." He said the last to his clerk and jerked his head toward the stairs. The thin man practically jumped off of the bench to accommodate his master's command. Ryla watched as the clerk said a few words to the Norandian captain and two guards started lazily up the stairs toward the rooms.

A plump serving girl set a plate before her and started away. The breakfast was the same as it had been the day before, but this time there was a small pie accompanying the eggs and marrow-bones and sausages. It was filled with parsley and mushrooms, and it smelled delicious. The food was quite good here at the inn in Grannock. Secretly, that was why she had liked to stop over here when her route made it convenient, that and the fact that she liked the little town on the hill. It was quiet and isolated and most of the time quite peaceful and pleasant. It reminded her of the small village where she had spent her early childhood, the way it had been before there were ever any troubles.

Though now it seemed to Ryla that trouble could find its way anywhere, especially now that she had found it in Grannock. It took her a moment to realize that Norden was staring at her again. She looked at him and met his eyes and looked away. Now he must be positively straining at the seams of his small clothes, she thought tersely. He was no fool, but he was one of those men who would always view women as ineffectual objects and conquests, beings incapable of matching a man's merit or worth—things to be coveted and prized and seen in public with, but without any kind of hope of ever realizing any equanimity or equality. For men like Norden, it was a man's world.

That was fine by Ryla, for those men were the easiest to fool as they were half fooled already. She caught him staring at her breasts and pretended that it did not make the bile rise in her throat.

"Is there something I can help you with, Mage Norden?"

"Hmm? Sorry, Captain. No, I am quite all right, I assure you." The man practically blushed. This would be easier than she had first thought, no doubt.

It was scarcely a few minutes later and Galt, Kipren, and Elmund were ushered down the stairs and seated at a table near Ryla and given their breakfasts. Elmund met her eyes and gave a slight nod. That was about as much as she would get out of the man, but it was all that she needed to know that he and the lads were ready to jump if she called out a command and bid them do so. Now was not the time, Ryla knew; it served no end to keep resisting the Magistry now that Norden had the upper hand. The most troubling thing to Ryla Dierns at the moment was that there was no sign of the soldier and his charge, the fiery haired girl with the face of a child and the eyes of an ancient.

"Where are the others?" She threw it away as best she could.

Norden was still smiling. "Others? I only kept your crew on."

I see, thought Ryla. I see how you work now. "Pity. They have far to go if they're to make it to Twinton."

Norden cocked his head slightly to the side. "Interesting. Linesman Andries made it sound as though he had to threaten and coerce a passage out of you. I see now the story may have a different cast to it." He raised an eyebrow in what must have seemed to him a threatening gesture, but to Ryla it just made him look ridiculous. In fact she laughed out loud.

"Come now, Mage Norden, surely you can see how a gallant young soldier would not have to exert himself too much to get my attentions?" She laced it with just enough suggestion in her eyes and almost broke when she saw her effectiveness in Norden's red face. At least Shiny had not sold her out—for that the lad had earned her respect. It was a fool's tale in any case. No airship captain allows themselves to be coerced and threatened into taking on cargo or passengers. Unless it's backed by a writ from the Magistry and a dozen foreign mercenaries, she thought ruefully. "How long will you keep those two under guard?"

"They are of no concern to you. I have sped them along their way." He spat it out satisfactorily. He flashed an obsequious smile and went back to his breakfast.

The spindly clerk cleared his throat in preparation to speak. "The drivers are ready to leave upon your command, my lord mage."

"Very good, very good," Norden squeaked. "Wait until you see our cargo, Captain. You will have never seen its like."

Cargo. The man was a fool. He seemed genuinely excited about being the High Mage's errand boy. "It's a rare sight, me getting worked up over cargo." She pushed back from the table. "I'll be outside, if you don't mind, Mage Norden. I can't abide with being indoors after being shut in all day yesterday."

Norden seemed to be weighing her chances for escape in his mind. "Of course, Captain." He crooked his finger at one of the guards.

Ryla gave a last look to her crew then turned and walked through the front door of the inn and out into the cold gray morning and stood on the side of the short stretch of cobbled road. It was later than she had thought, she saw by the dull glow of the shrouded sun that shone dimly through the overcast sky. The dark skies had made her think that the guards had roused her at dawn, and she had slept poorly the previous night besides. But now she reckoned it to be somewhere between mid-morning and noon. It would be a piss-poor day for flying, she noted, looking up into the swirling heavens and speculating whether or not she could get Skyward above the menacing cloud bank. A sky like that was difficult to gauge, and she would have to wait to see what the day brought as the sun's heat could burn some of those clouds away by the afternoon.

She frowned and squinted up and down the street. A murder of crows flew up from the alley between the stables and the building adjacent. She would have to snug up to Norden. It was not an appealing thought to Ryla Dierns as she watched a dark coated Norandian guard step back inside the door behind her and call out in his strange tongue across the din of the great room. He was leaning halfway with his head and shoulders inside the doorframe. Had she a fast horse and Skyward nearby and hovering, she would have made a break for it then and there, but alas she did not have any of those things and she did not fancy her chances sprinting at all. It was about that time that she heard a low whistle coming from the stables. She looked round to see if the guard still had his head through the door, which he did, and then she looked back to the low wall and saw the furtive-looking stable boy motioning her over to him. He was ragged and hollow-eyed, as though he had not slept in a number of days, but he was standing near the low wall and frantic as he waved her over.

Despite herself, she almost broke into laughter at the sight of him; hat askew and his fine blue coat, slim dagger hung at his hip, the lad looked as though he was off to go court some country damsel and though he was right at home behind the stableyard wall, he somehow looked incongruous and comical half-crouched as he was in all his meagre finery. She saw from the lather-sprayed riding boots he wore that the boy had ridden hard this morning, and by the look of his face she knew that he was not there for a lark. Quick as a cat, Ryla sprinted to the stableyard and pulled the boy down behind the wall with her.

"What have you got for me?" she whispered hurriedly.

"Joth bid me to give you this." He pulled a rumpled and creased letter from the breast of his coat and pushed it into her hands. It was warm and slightly damp from where he had carried it. "I've been riding for two days and two nights," he added, to no one in particular.

"Who do you think is more tired, you or your horse?"

He smiled and shook his head. "I don't know, lady."

"Where are they?"

"They're off to Kingsbridge by now. I've to get clear of this place afore anyone sees me."

She nodded. "Wait until they take me inside. Thanks for this." She put the letter into her sleeve.

He nodded and stammered.

"What's your name, anyway?"

"Bell. Bellan, if it please you, lady."

"Thanks, Bellan. Well done. Now wait here until they take me back in."

"Watch that mage—he's no good. He tried to have them two killed on the road after he sent them off." The words came tumbling out in a rush.

She saw his earnestness and knew he spoke the truth. Seven bells, they had escaped and were all right and headed for Kingsbridge at least! The thought was a relief to Ryla, but why Norden had sought their deaths defied logic.

Bellan was looking at her with his big earnest eyes. He would be handsome one day, she decided.

"I'll be careful. You be careful too." She gave him a quick peck on his smooth flushed cheek and was reminded of those faraway days of her youth and her young love and whispered dreams and promises that were no more; they were gone like her youth, like so much vapor. She smiled at him then and he returned it, innocently. She used his shoulder and pushed herself to her feet, then began strolling back toward the front of the Inn as easy as she pleased, leaving him crouched there in the stableyard behind the wall.

The guard who had been assigned to watch her was stood in the street, looking off in the opposite direction down the lane as she came around the corner. He began pointing his finger at her and rattling off words in his guttural sounding language as he hurriedly strode toward her. Ryla simply waved him away.

"If a lady wishes to have a piss, a lady wishes to have a piss."

She kept striding right for the door of the inn and never looked back. The guard shook his head and continued to harangue her as she pushed into the great room headed straight for the table where her crew sat at their breakfast. Galt, Kipren, and Elmund all subtly assessed her situation and smiled at her. She smiled back. This was turning out to be quite an exciting morning, she noted.

"When you're done with your breakfast, we'll be Skyward bound, boys."

They nodded, practically in unison.

"It's about bloody time," Elmund grumbled.

"You are not lying there, brother," Galt assented.

"Where's Joth and Eilyth?" Kipren asked lowly. "They get away?"

"The mage has sent them on. We are taking on some cargo and Mage Norden, who still hasn't told me where we're headed." Ryla was itching to open the note tucked away in her sleeve, but she did not dare—not while the smarmy mage could see her.

Elmund met her eyes and she could see the question forming there.

"Be ready, lads. I'll know more presently. Give me a word when I'm clear to fish a letter out and read it unnoticed."

They looked about them warily. Ryla sat between them at the table in a position where she was mostly shielded from Norden's view and poured herself a cup of ale.

"Don't look so nervous, boys." She downed it in one go.

Kipren went back to his breakfast.

"They're busy talking at the moment," Elmund said lowly.

Ryla raised her eyebrows at her empty cup and Elmund sighed and filled it as she caught the note blindly with two fingers and drew it out of her sleeve and unfolded it beneath the table.

"Still good," Galt said to her.

She brought the note out and read it on her lap. It read: "Captain Durns, Norden wants us dead, we are on the road to Kingsbridge and will wait for you there at the first inn we find. Get clear of the mage, he is not to be trusted. Please destroy this."

She passed the letter under the table to Kipren then cut her eyes to the fire. He gave a tight nod before pushing back and making his way to the hearth. Ryla did not watch him but she knew she could count on Kipren to quietly accomplish his task without drawing any attention to himself.

When he returned to the table he gave her a wink and went back to a half-finished round of bread, slathering some more butter on it with his eating knife.

"Well?" asked Elmund.

"As soon as we're clear of the mage."

He nodded but did not look very pleased about it. No matter, she thought. The less he knew, the better—particularly should Norden get wind of anything. She knew she could count on her boys to stand behind her if she gave the word, but she would wait and judge the best time to do so, and at the moment she still did not have the full view of the situation. Most especially she was curious as to what Norden was up to and, more importantly, why. "Let's talk to the innkeep about some provisions. We're going in style this time, and it's all on the Magistry's tab."

This elicited grins all around.

They outfitted themselves as well as the inn could provide and a few hours later they were being herded along by the Norandian cavalry and Mage Norden and his scrawny scribe as they rode ahead along the road out of Grannock, the two wagons making their trundling creaks and groans as they were driven along behind, canvas wrapped loads tied down securely behind the roughly hooded drivers. Amidst this strange company Ryla marched along beside her crew back to where they had drag-landed the Skyward days before, and all the while she bided her time and contemplated her next move. Hopefully the trip with Norden would not delay her too very long, and she would be off to Kingsbridge and back on the trail to her victory, her long-awaited vengeance.

She knew how to play Norden should he prove difficult, but she was not quite ready to sacrifice her self-respect without a quantifiable justification. Whatever the cost was destined to be, Ryla Dierns would pay it if it ensured a victory that would avenge her honor, her family's honor, the honor of her village. Javis had been just sixteen when Uhlmet came slaying dogs and causing a tumult. How horrible it had been for her to watch as he was strung up and hanged, his hands tied behind his back. Javis had stood proudly, defiantly as they put the noose about his neck. He had been shaking his head and staring at the little fawning lordling, saying over and over again, "He cannot do this, it is not just." Saying it time and time again, as if to reassure her, as if he might reassure everyone by his words that the lordling was having a grand jest with them and pushing it to the extreme for a lark, as if to see how much punishment they could all bear before denouncing him—a trial of their loyalties. Then he was dangling and kicking and spasming, and when she ran to help him, the others held her back and would not let her reach him so that she might try to lift him and save him from death, but they had held her and restrained her and protected her and she had almost been hanged as well, but she had survived and she had sworn vengeance, and now that vengeance was in sight. She would sooner die than see the opportunity flee before her. She was a woman who had learned patience and so she waited. She would be ready when the time came.

The Skyward rested in the field where they had left it, lines slack and swaying with the breeze, tubular mainsail sagging above the deck and billowing in the shifting wind. A resting airship always looked broken to the unfamiliar observer, Ryla knew. Once the mage returned her key, the thin and elegantly wrought bronze wand that she usually carried at her belt, and once it had been fitted to the mechanism at the helm post, she knew that the ship would hum with energy and that the sail would fill and become almost rigid, buoyant. It only took a few moments to accomplish, but she noted the look on the mage's face when he saw the ship resting there, and she realized straightaway that Norden was not familiar with airships. Perhaps she could use that to her advantage, should an opportunity present itself.

"Captain! Come forward." Norden sat atop a fine black horse. In fact, the only bad thing Ryla could see on the horse was its rider. She stepped forward and looked to the mage. "Prepare your craft and have your crew unload these wagons."

"Lord Mage," she stated by way of answer. "Make ready the ship, lads."

Kipren, Galt, and Elmund all muttered and started toward the deck. How it demoralized men to be forced to work, coerced into doing one man's bidding simply because he held some power and lorded it over them. Ryla despised the feeling, the very idea of it. Men were meant to be free, of that she was sure, and no one would ever convince her otherwise. She watched her crew as they took to the deck, moving slower than they would have normally, sullen looks on their faces. Norden had kept them locked up and hemmed in, and Ryla knew that was the one thing an airshipman hated more than anything else. If the mage was aware of it then he had deemed it a negligible issue. He could not have cared less about the attitudes of the men serving him, she realized; he simply sought after his own goal and used the people that interposed themselves between him and his goal as best he saw fit. For those he did not have a use for—like Pretty and Shiny, perhaps—he simply removed them from the arithmetic.

She approached Norden as he rattled off something to his bobbing and nodding clerk. "Mage Norden, I'll need my bronze ship's key."

"Of course, Captain." His eyes languished too long on her again as he swept his gaze down to her boots. "Oh, I should have found you a mount, Captain—your boots are a mess, I'm afraid."

"Where have all the gentlemen gone, eh? The sooner I get that key the better." She held out her hand in emphasis.

Norden let go a thin nervous chuckle as he fished it from his belt and passed it to her. "Thank you, Lord Mage," she said perfunctorily. She met his eyes and gave him a sly smile. That should confuse him, she thought. Judging by his flummoxed expression, she had achieved her goal, at least in part. She turned and strode toward the now lowered gangway and made her way up to the top.

"Captain on the deck!" Galt shouted as she stepped aboard. The others echoed him resignedly, but he was all smiles. Well, he should be, Ryla knew. The first to call out "Captain on the deck!" would have his meal and drink paid for by the other crewman at the next stopover, and Galt held the current record, having not paid for his own meals in close to a month. The short man would earn his pay today, though. There was much crane work to be done from the look of the wagons laden with their canvas bundles.

"Report, all hands!" she cried. The lads finished their tasks hurriedly and then made their way back to the helm as she was fitting the bronze wand into the helm post. The ship hummed with energy as the mainsail began to raise. "Kipren and Galt, assemble the ship's crane. Elmund, you go down and rig the loads."

"Aye, lady, aye."

Within the hour Galt and Kipren had pulled the disassembled crane from its place in the hold and rebuilt it on the deck. There was a small walking wheel beside the small crane. It was the type of crane that stonemasons used to lift items atop castle walls, only smaller, and Galt was just small enough to fit inside of the wheel and tread in it half-crouched. "The best wheelman alive," he claimed to be. "Born to it." It looked bloody uncomfortable to her, but she had to admit the man made quick work of loading and unloading cargo, especially with Kipren swinging the boom and Elmund directing. They were a good crew. Down a man as they were, they got the work done. She was proud of them. There was a definite precision to their work, and she had seen that same work done less skilfully at the hands of other crews. She had been given several candidates for crewmen when she had approached one of her fellows and asked if there were any members of their league who had experience sailing the skies, and of those candidates she had chosen Galt, Kipren, Dathe, and Elmund. She had brought them aboard the de-rigged vessel and asked them a series of questions and studied their ease with simple tasks like belaying a line or making something fast.

The four she had chosen had the most experience, but they also had good demeanors. Except for Elmund, she chided herself. Misjudged his temperament. Still, she knew how to control a man like Elmund, and stubborn and willfull as he was, he listened to her when she spoke, for she was his captain and for whatever other faults he had, Elmund was ever respectful of her rank and her person. He was boorish to be sure, but under it all Elmund was a gentleman, and she respected him for that. He looked to her from the bed of the wagon as the last load was hitched to the boom arm and Galt began his awkward-looking pace at the wheel and hoisted the load above the hold.

"That's the last of it, Captain," Kipren called out as he started for the hold. Dathe was usually there to pull and push the loads into ordered rows and stacks. Then all the loads would be made fast and secured, so they would not damage the ship or the other cargo should the airship get tossed about in the wind. Elmund and Dathe usually did that while Kipren and Galt broke the crane back down and stowed it away below.

"Elmund, you and Kipren secure the hold. I'll help Galt with the crane." That should get them in the air faster, Ryla thought, as she pushed her hat off of her head and let it hang there down her back by the woven strap about her neck.

She stood near the crane and waited until the small man emerged from within the walking wheel holding a steel pin about the length of his forearm. "Captain," he said. "Can you help me pull this wheel down, lady?"

She stepped forward as Galt removed another identical pin from the outside of the wheel. "Any news?" he asked her conspiratorily.

"As soon as I know, you'll hear about it."

He nodded and they lifted the wheel out of its carriage and laid it on its side on the deck. She stepped closer to the man and helped to hold the body of the crane as Galt went about the task of disassembling the gears.

"What do you think is in those bundles?" she asked quietly.

He did not look up from his work, but he also did not miss a beat. "Been wondering that myself, Captain. Heavy, I'll say that much."

She was about to speculate further when Galt's eye caught something, and he jerked his chin toward something behind her. "What's this?"

She turned and saw a rider approaching through the break in the woods, the same way they themselves had gone back and forth between the airship and Grannock in these last few harried days. He was one of the foreign horsemen. She could tell by the way he sat his horse and by his horse itself.

He was speeding along at a rapid pace, and the other horsemen had noticed and called to their commander, who looked at Norden and then sought to remount his horse and meet the rider halfway out. Norden was looking at the approaching rider with a face full of apprehension, but Ryla made sure not to let him catch her noticing that and shifted her attention to Galt again. "Get down there close to the mage and his clerk and find out what the messenger is about."

"Aye, lady." He set down his tools immediately and scrambled down the gangway and scoured the ground around the wagons as though looking for some bit of his rigging that had been lost. Galt was a gem of a man, she thought. She would finish taking down the crane. She knew every job on the airship and she could do every one on her own. Had she enough arms and legs, she would pilot the craft herself and sail anywhere in the world. She had often dreamt of doing just that, but she knew too well how hard it was for a woman alone in the world. She stole glances after Galt's progress as she took the crane down, removing the gears and the pegs that locked the body to the base. He had sidled up beside Norden and his clerk and hidden behind one of the wagons. Norden had been settling up with the drivers as they were off-loading the wagons and stowing cargo into the hold of the Skyward it seemed, and now the drivers were all quibbling with the master teamster about their individual wages in a knotted huddle off the bow of the ship.

She was removing the deck-irons from the base of the crane with a short pry bar as the messenger dismounted among his fellows and the Norandian captain pranced his horse up to the mage and his clerk. He bowed, and his horse bowed with him and she heard Norden's shrill chuckle and his voice floating thinly on the wind as he exclaimed, "I love it when they do that, these Norandishmen! What news? Translate for me."

The clerk's reply was spoken too softly for her to hear from this distance, but Ryla knew Galt would hear everything from his hiding place behind the wagon. The man's ears were good for more than just ridicule, she reminded herself. She took one final look as the Norandishman addressed the mage and she stepped to the hold and shouted down at her crew.

"There's a crane here on deck that needs stowing!"

"Aye, lady!" called Elmund.

Whatever it was that was being said, Galt would relay it to her. For now it was hers to bide her time, so she set about her tasks out of habit. She readied the ship as she had done countless times before, her movements and thoughts economical, measured, meticulous, fluid, and rehearsed. She knew this well, this captain's role. She executed it flawlessly.

Moments later she heard Norden's shrill voice let go a tirade of curses at the foreign cavalry officer. He swung his horse around and trotted him the short distance to the gangway and dismounted in a huff. He dropped his reins even though there was no one standing nearby ready to take them and started up the gangplanks. "Captain Dierns! How quickly can we get to Torlucksford? I have pressing business there."

She crossed the deck back toward the gangway. "Torlucksford? A few hours, if the winds are right. This weather is not favorable." She looked at the skies for a long beat before adding, "Lord Mage."

Norden just seemed to notice the weather for the first time and frowned. "How many of my horsemen can you take on with us to Torlucksford?"

She smiled. "I can take all of them, if they leave their mounts behind. But with the cargo in the hold, I can't take on any animals."

The man scowled incredulously. "Surely you can take a few on with their mounts?"

She kept her face as straight as could be, but inside Ryla was relishing the moment well. He was obviously bent out of shape with the news he had just received, but he also did not enjoy hearing anything contrary to his demands. She walked to the gangway and pointed to the hull. "She's barely hovering here as it is, my lord. We need enough buoyancy to float up and catch the winds. Unless you wish to draw us along and hitch us to a team, then we cannot take on any more unnecessary weight."

"Unnecessary? I shall decide what is necessary and what isn't, Captain. If I say I need my troops conveyed to Torlucksford, then I expect nothing but 'yes, my lord' and accomodation from you, am I clear?"

She smiled. "Make no mistake, Norden. I am the captain of this airship, and once you step onto the deck you must acknowledge that. I will do what I must to help you along your way, but don't think for a moment that I will forsake my crew and my ship's safety just to sate your whims."

The mage's face blanched then reddened with rage. "You will take on my men and their mounts and transport us to Torlucksford!"

She stood on the deck and regarded him calmly for a long beat. "Right. As you say, Lord Mage." She inclined her head slightly. "All hands!"

Norden was seething with rage, and he watched her warily as the crew fell in around her.

"We'll need the ship's crane back up and all this cargo off-loaded on the double boys."

They all wore incredulous looks on their faces as they said "aye lady" and started off.

"Belay that order, Captain!" Norden hissed at her.

"I am accomodating your request to transport your cavalry. I can't do both your cargo and your troops." She said it flatly, matter-of-factly. She had him now, she saw it; and she saw that he realized it now too.

"Wait, then. Surely you can take on one?"

She just stared at him.

"Very well then, Captain. Keep my cargo aboard and convey me to Torlucksford." He sighed, looking like a sullen child.

"Welcome aboard, Lord Mage." She inclined her head and walked back to the helm. "Belay that order, lads. Make ready!"

Norden called his clerk over to him with an impatient gesture and stood with his hands on his hips looking out over his assembled Norandishmen and the haggling teamsters and carters as the thin scribe dismounted hurriedly and trotted up to him. She was attempting to eavesdrop on the mage when Kipren approached.

"There's a problem in the hold, lady. You need to see it."

She kept the forestalled question to herself and followed him to the hold, leaving Norden on the gangway, his clerk scurrying off to do his bidding. Kipren stood to the side and let Ryla pass first down the narrow forecastle portal with its short stepladder and into the hold.

Elmund and Galt were stood on either side of a crate looking down at someone sat atop it. Ryla had to look twice before she realized who it was.

Elmund looked amused beneath his stern attitude. "We found him hiding in this crate. Galt saw the lid moving."

"Bellan? Seven bells, boy! What are you doing here?"

The boy went red and he looked as though he might tear up for a moment, but he took a quick breath and turned his earnest eyes to hers and pleaded, "I'm sorry for this, Captain. I truly am. But I been thinking a lot about a lot of different things really, and truly really thinking about them like, you see my meaning?"

"Bellan, what are you doing here?"

"Please, Captain, take me with you! I'm not an Ostler. I mean to say, I can do it mind you, I know all the ins and outs of it, the horse side of things well. I'm born to that, I can take care of horses all the livelong day should it be required of me to do so, but the truth is I've a taste for adventure, a calling like, if you take my meaning. And Grannock ain't a tall enough beaker to quench my thirst, if you—"

"If I take your meaning?"

"Yes."

"If I am to take your meaning then you wish to join the ship's crew, or are you looking for a free ride to Torlucksford? You shouldn't have come here. You've taken an awful risk. The mage may have learned of your involvement by now."

Bellan looked as though he had not thought of that until now.

"You'll stay aboard, and you'll stay hidden. No one says a word. At Torlucksford, when the mage is occupied, you will disembark. Understand?"

Bellan started to object but then thought better of it and just nodded his head. "Aye, lady," he said, and it looked to her that Galt, Kipren, and Elmund almost broke into laughter then, for he had intoned it like a perfect airshipman.

"By law, we throw stowaways over the sides," she said.

The lad gulped as Kipren stifled a grin.

"I'll make an exception in your case, but you will keep quiet down here and stay hidden until I send for you. Get him something to eat and drink before he faints away." She shook her head and turned away and climbed back on deck and made her way back to the helm. That fool boy had given her something else to worry about now, she thought. If Norden found out Bellan knew where Joth and Eilyth had gone, there was no telling what he would stop at to drag the information out of the boy. On one hand he was a liability, and on the other hand, they were a man short and she could put the boy to work learning the ropes once they were rid of this mage. Why not take the lad on for a few cargo hauls? He was earnest enough about his desire for adventure, and the airshipman's life was an adventurous one indeed. A lad that young should have his parents' blessing, she knew, and once this had blown over perhaps another few days in Grannock would not be so bad. But now the thought of inns and rooms made her skin crawl. She wanted to be up in the sky again.

She watched as the Norandian guards dismounted and handed their mounts off to the cavalryman whom had lately ridden in as a messenger. He gathered them and tied them together in a column and rode the lead horse off at a fast traveling pace as the men on foot took up their weapons and gear and strode up the gangway. The sky thundered and flashed ominously and a cool wind blew straight through her, making her wish she was already wearing her furs. It would be a poor day for flying, a rough one to be sure.

"Raise the gangplanks!" She called it after the last Norandishman had stepped aboard.

Elmund and Kipren hauled the boards up and stowed them.

"When can we be underway, Captain?" Norden whined.

"Immediately, Lord Mage."

He smiled, satisfied.

"All hands, make ready."

Ryla looked to the skies as the crew worked and she called out the orders by rote as the routine of taking to the skies unfolded and she felt the world fall away from her at last. She set heading for Torlucksford to the north, and the Skyward rose and plunged through the stormy skies above Grannock and away.

Twenty-Five

T HEY SENT HIM TWO women who cowered in fear every time he lifted his hands and who did not understand nor speak a word of Oestersh. Once he made them understand that he wanted food and a bath, one of them began sobbing, perhaps out of relief. Rhael did not know, nor did he care very much. After a few maddening moments they had set about their tasks and moved quickly. The bath had been most pleasant, and the slave had combed and washed his tangled hair expertly, almost painlessly—something of a near miracle in Rhael's mind, for he had thought to simply cut it off when he had seen his reflection in the mirror and the tangled matted mess of his once beautiful, lustrous hair.

Now as he stood in front of the mirrors, dressed in his newly acquired alien finery, the scars and bruises diminished with his cleanly appearance. Rhael felt pleased to see something of his old self looking back at him in his reflection. The clothes were strange and a touch on the small side, and the slaves were useless when it came to presenting him with choices, but he had finally settled upon an ensemble from the garments at hand that fit him fairly well and as he regarded himself, they made him look quite impressive and elegant.

Next to his skin he wore a fine silken shirt, the finest he had ever seen in fact. It was cut in a strange fashion that left it open like a coat, prompting the wearer to fold it closed and keep it in place by tucking it into their hosen. Over the pale colored silk shirt he wore a deep silvery gray silken sort of doublet or close fitting jacket that was slightly too small for him so that he had to leave it open a bit more than he would have liked, but the doublet was a beautiful cut and chased with silver thread in embroidered accents along its lines. Its execution and style were completely different than anything Rhael had ever worn before, but he liked the way the garment looked on him. The hosen had been the hardest article to fit, and he had in the end simply cut the feet out of a fine pair of silken hose and forced them up over his thighs. Masking the butchered feet of the hose were a fine pair of soft dark leather knee boots with elongated pointed toes, almost the sort that noblemen wore for hunting or falconing. Over the doublet Rhael had donned a knee-length, open-sleeved velvet coat trimmed in fur in a rich dark color that complimented the silken doublet beneath it. It made him look regal, he thought. A broad silver belt held the coat in place, and from it dangled a jewel hilted sword, its strange hilt complex and ornate, encircling one's hand almost when grasped. On his shoulders a fine cloak of wine-colored wool was draped, its borders woven in intricate patterns, pinned with a golden brooch set with amber and jet and coral.

The slaves bowed when they had finished dressing him, and he hefted the leather sack of orbs onto his shoulder and pushed past them. He left the bedchamber and made his way to the balcony so that he might check the progress of the airship. He turned to them as he left, clapping his hands and miming someone eating.

"Food! Bring me food to eat!" he said to them.

They bobbed and scurried. Rhael did not know from what sort of race these strange women had emerged. They had strange complexions, strange features. They spoke a strange language. Ultimately, it mattered not to Rhael, he decided. These were simply tools to further his goals, these slaves, these Kuilbolts, these "old masters" he was about to meet. He would use them accordingly, however he saw fit. He caught sight of his reflection once more as he passed out of the tower and onto the balcony and into the cold swirling winds that buffeted him as he surveyed the progress of his new guests. He would remedy problems of logistics such as tailors and other specialized peasants once he had secured his powerbase. For now, he was most concerned with the ornate green and golden airship that had just set down within the walls of the palisade and the figures he saw on its deck. They were too far away to make out in any clear detail, but Rhael could make out a dozen figures, at least, and all of them seemed to be helmed in gleaming bronze and wearing swords at their hips. Rhael narrowed his eyes and judged the distance between the tower and the airship. It was within a bowshot, and it would take them no time at all to close the gap between the wall and the tower.

Did they have a key to the tower gate, some means of circumventing his security within his tower keep? He reached down into the leather sack and removed one of the cool glass spheres and saw it swirling with a reddish blue light in his hand. Such power he felt within it, and all of it at his command. He looked back to the deck of the airship as one of the figures raised his hand and the others formed up in front of him in two neat ordered rows, then drew their swords as one and placed the blades on their shoulders.

The figure with the raised hand walked down the gangway, the soldiers following behind in formation. Rhael would enlighten them to the art of wielding power. The audacity of them to refuse his generous invitation to treat with him, the new lord of this fortified mine, this elegant tower. Soulspire, he had named it. Now they had come seeking to kill him or capture him; this was an assault on his person and his right to call himself Lord of Soulspire, Lord Uhlmet.

They were not Kuilbolts. He recognized that immediately by their stature and their bearing. No, they looked man-like, yet they moved weirdly. Gracefully and fluidly. It was unsettling, Rhael decided, and potentially deadly, given their numbers. Now, much to his dismay, the leader of the newly arrived soldiers was shouting orders to Rhael's Kuilbolt soldiers and they seemed to be heeding the commands. Duplicitous wretches, he should have known not to count on the fear stinking monsters so soon after his coming to power.

Rhael felt himself begin to panic at the onset of a gnawing fear in his gut, a fear of the unknown in the form of these strangely clad and alien man-like beings marching up the hill toward his tower. They wore rich crimson-colored silken surcoats that shimmered as they moved, and beneath the coats shone their burnished bronze armor, ornate and gleaming like their crested helms. Their leader wore a helm chased with silver. His crest was variegated and transverse, and he carried a long bronze rod with a stone finial in his hand and a sword at his hip. He saw now as they marched that the soldiers carried bronze wands with mounted crystals in their other hands and they were already halfway up the hill. Rhael drew a deep breath. He stood at the battlements, where he could be seen and drew himself up to his full height and flung his cloak back to reveal his garments and the sword at his hip, the ancient signifier of nobility and martial power. They could not argue his right to have added this fortress to his holdings through force—after all, it was he who had been captured and he who had turned the tables on his captors and taken his share as he had seen fit. They would not doubt that to look upon him now in his new finery standing atop the battlements of the tower, holding out his hand toward the advancing knot of bronze and crimson soldiers below. They have no idea whom they are dealing with, he thought.

"Come no farther!" he yelled down to them. "I see you have refused my invitation to treat!"

They stopped and looked startled when appeared, but as he spoke, Rhael saw that the knot of soldiers was rippling with movement and jostling and he heard sounds drifting up from them. Soft sounds—a sort of laughter, perhaps? Rhael was not sure, but then he made out words on the wind.

"An ape-monkey?!"

"That's a ladies garment, is it not?" a strange voice growled.

They were ridiculing him, belittling him, calling him names, guffawing in their ranks at his expense, doubting his birthright to rise and be a leader of men and lord of all creatures. Doubting his power. Rhael experienced a brief moment of shock as he realized that these beings were looking at him in the way that he viewed peasants, but it fled as soon as it arrived with rage taking its place. Rhael's bony pale hand raised the orb with its swirling auras and brought it into view. For a long moment it grew deathly quiet and the laughter ceased as the leader straightened and leapt backward an amazingly great distance and raised the rod he carried up before him.

"Stagger lines and let fly!" The leader sang out in the wind, and the formation of soldiers began to fan out into two lines, one slightly forward from the other, both of them bearing at Rhael's position on the battlements. He saw one of the soldiers on the far end who had already formed into his position level his bronze wand at him, and then he heard a low splitting sound and dodged a fist-sized chunk of stone as it cracked off of the battlement in front of him. Rhael dove behind the battlement as several more of the low *whump whumping* sounds cracked out and shook through his very bones. All around him lay broken rubble, but the battlements were holding and providing shelter for him. The loud cracking continued for another earth-shaking, bone-jarring, agonizingly long moment, and Rhael felt something trickling from his nose and realized it was blood. No matter he thought, this will be over very shortly. He peered out through the crenelated wall and saw that most of the soldiers were now kneeling and removing the stones from their bronze wands, replacing them with others from somewhere within their costume.

Summoning his will and his courage, Rhael rose from behind the stone wall and brought the energies of the orb down to bear on the soldiers below, oblivious to the wall erupting into sprays of potentially lethal gravel around him. The power passed through him from within the orb, and it fell in an arc like sheet lightning over the soldiers, forking out and striking them multiple times and tossing them into the air like rags in the wind, one after another. Three stood behind their leader, who still stood with the rod he bore before him, and now Rhael could just make out a silvery nimbus emanating from the rod and extending out in a dome around them that crackled and spat like a hot skillet when the energy from the orb tried to penetrate it. Rhael watched as the three soldiers knelt and saw to the crystals atop their bronze wands, their leader looking to them, marking their progress behind his shield of crackling energy.

They were about to redouble their attack, Rhael realized. Perhaps the shield rod worked off of a finite source of energy as well. He poured more energy from the orb out at the shield in a torrential storm of electrical lashes, thinking all the while how he wanted to grind his enemies into powder, fry them into dust. He saw the leader struggle beneath the onslaught, pushing the rod out from him with both arms against the tide of energy thrown at him relentlessly. Rhael let go the energy for a moment and gazed down at them. The leader looked back to the others one more time and Rhael knew his moment was coming and that he would have to act fast. A low, thin laugh began to form in the pit of his stomach and he struggled to keep it in as the leader let the shield go and leapt backward again as the soldiers raised their wands and began to crack the energy out at Rhael where he stood on the wall, kicking up dust and debris all around him. But Rhael stood and faced the flurry of stones and stinging splinters and let go another wave of lightning so powerful that the orb he bore before him split with a sickening crack and a jet of hot vapor. He looked down and saw the leader of the soldiers writhing on the ground, his armor smoking and his once glorious crimson surcoat a blackened mess. All of them gone now. Dead. He was the victor. He was always the victor.

Rhael reached down into the leather sack and removed another orb, tossing the ruined orb at the slowly crawling leader on the ground below. It thudded into the ground an ell shy of its mark. "You were fools to refuse my overtures. Do you see where it has left you now?" He screamed it out so that all could hear. "Trilk! Assemble my warriors!" Rhael turned from the wall and sped down the stairs of the tower, past the cowering slaves huddled in his bedchamber sobbing to each other, past the ornate parlor, and out the gate to the scorched killing ground before the tower. Rhael drew the sword from the scabbard he wore at his belt and held it lazily at his side as the gate closed on its whispering hinges and he heard the mechanism slide and lock behind him as he started forward. He could see down the hill that the Kuilbolts were creeping forward now, warily watching the outcome of the battle. Perhaps Trilk had assembled them, he knew not.

Or perhaps he would have to kill all of them for their lack of passion. Not one of them had come to his aid, and he would punish them. He would inspire loyalty in them after this day, of that he was certain. The soldiers had been farther from the walls than they had seemed as he encountered the body of the first one lying face down before him. He stabbed the lifeless body with his sword just to be certain and heard the satisfying sound of the bronze-bladed sword making contact with the back of the breastplate that the dead soldier was wearing as he drove his thrust through. He continued along his path, going from soldier to soldier, making certain any remaining life was expunged from their fraternity. As he plunged his sword into the neck of the third one he felt the body jerk and spasm and he was forced to place a booted foot on the body to remove his sword. And when he did so, he dislodged the soldier's helmet and gazed at the face of his enemy for the first time.

What a strange face it was that stared back with its fixed grimace. The features were sharp and fine and vaguely feline in their shape, the hair long and glossy black, a pale greenish tint to its skin and a bluish color to its lips and eyelids, and its blood was dark, almost purple in its deep shade of red, and its ears ended in points. They were approximately the size of men, but more slight and willowy it seemed. Rhael's eyes rested on the bronze wand and its crystal mount that lay near the fallen soldier's hand. He picked it up and shoved it into his belt before continuing on down the row of dead or dying and plunging his sword into every one of the bodies to make certain none had survived, all the while calling out to the desperately crawling wounded creature that was fleeing back toward the resting airship as Rhael made his grim and patient progress toward him.

"Who are you? What land do you hail from?"

The leader continued crawling hurriedly, but he could never hope to outpace Rhael, who was collecting the bronze wands as he picked his way leisurely between the last of the bodies. "There is no point in dying without relaying your message to me. Who was it that sent you here?"

He wiped the blade of his sword on the last soldier's smoldering crimson coat and paused to regard the retreating commander as he scurried toward the hovering airship. Rhael seemed to be weighing the odds of him making it to the gangway, adjusting his gait slightly so that he timed it to intercept him perfectly.

He hailed the wounded Commander again as he closed upon him. "Pity that you underestimated my power. You were sorely outmatched, and I had the upper hand from the start. Had you been imaginative and taken me unawares, perhaps you would have had more success. At least it may have seemed more hopeful to you in the beginning."

The creature continued to crawl, but now he turned his head and snarled back at Rhael as he fled. "Ape-monkey!" he spat. "You will die soon enough, wielding energy from a raw orb!" He laughed thinly, coughing and grimacing in pain. Rhael narrowed his eyes.

"What lands do you hail from?" he repeated as he drew closer with every stride.

"We are the Guatha Avlin, fool!" he hissed, still crawling frantically.

"Gowapflyn? Goblin? You are Goblinkind?" Rhael was confused. He had been to Kuilgarthen as a boy and he had seen the Goblinkind, but they had looked nothing like this. They had looked strange, but they had looked akin to men. "I was in Kuilgarthen as a boy and I saw none of your green-skinned kind there."

He was panting, or was he laughing? "Kuilgarthen. A market place of degenerative products for your degenerate race. Why would any of the highborn serve slaves at a common shop, you wretch?"

He was trying to goad Rhael into finishing him, more than likely seeking an end to his suffering through this false bravado and insulting language. The Goblin had almost made it up the gangway, but Rhael could catch him in two strides whenever he wished. He fished one of the wands from his belt and tried to use it but could not make it function. Perhaps it needed a new crystal.

"I cannot say that I admire your attitude toward me in the least, Goblin. I am the new lord of this place."

"Ape-monkey!" he spat as he crawled his way up the gangway, trailing blood in a long smear. "You have sealed your own tomb today." He was getting weak and slowing as he climbed and as he neared the top his rod slipped from his grasp and clattered down the gangplanks to bounce against Rhael's feet.

Rhael picked it up and hefted it. It was slim and elegant, but it had a weight and balance to it that felt somehow dangerous. The stone at the top of the rod was a flanged chunk of quartz that slotted into the mount and locked into place with a half-turn and a push to engage the mechanism, he could recognize the function of the mechanics by looking at its construction. He sheathed his sword and held the rod out before him as he remembered the Goblin commander doing, but he could not make it function in the same way he made the orbs function. "How does this work, your bronzen rod?" he asked as he started up the gangway.

"Fool!" the Goblin commander hissed. He had almost pulled himself over onto the ship when Rhael interposed himself between the Goblin and the deck and stared down at him.

"The fool is you. You will tell me everything I want to know one way or another. You understand, do you not?"

The Goblin stared up at him, seething.

"You nearly made it." Rhael swung the bronze rod as hard as he could and brought it down and around into an upstroke that smashed into the helm of the Goblin commander and lifted him up off of the gangplanks and sent him crashing to the ground over the side. Rhael laughed and peered over the side. He was breathing but unconscious. Excellent, thought Rhael. He shall make a fine source of information while he survives.

"Trilk!" he screamed again, standing on the deck of the airship. It was the finest airship he had ever seen, and the most immense. Its decks were wide and it looked as though it would hold plenty below within the walls of its hull. Its striped tubular mainsail was streamlined and elegant and rose like a dorsal fin above the ship. He wondered if the captain's quarters and the lord's quarters were as finely appointed as his newly acquired tower? All in due time, he knew, he would have a chance to explore, but for now Mage Imperator Rhael Lord Uhlmet, Lord of Soulspire, had to bring the Kuilbolts' loyalty to bear. Without them his goals could not be met as easily nor as subtly.

Trilk had assembled the Kuilbolts near the gangway and they had formed up in two loose squares, five ranks deep and five to a file. He approached the gangway bowing and gesticulating grandly.

"Excellency, your servants have assembled."

"My servants? Where were you when I was being attacked?"

"Excellency, your—"

"Select one warrior from every two ranks and have them brought forth."

Trilk bowed and turned to the ranks and did as he was ordered. He returned with five bronze armored Kuilbolts trailing warily behind him.

"Very good," said Rhael. "For your cowardice and disloyalty, I destroy a tenth of you." He then lifted the orb he held and sent a chain of lightning energy coursing through the five blue skinned warriors that left them writhing on the ground in smoking agony. Trilk leapt between Rhael and the warriors and prostrated himself on the ground.

"Excellency, mercy! I beg of you, mercy! We serve you and we forsake the old masters!"

"I could burn you all to ash now if I wished it. Worse shall befall you if you ever fail me again. I will have your unwavering loyalty or I shall feed the rats with your useless husks!"

The Kuilbolts hissed and prostrated themselves before him, a moaning sound emanating from their huddled mass. "Mercy! Mercy!" they moaned.

He called Trilk forward. "You are the commander of these others now. I shall hold you responsible for any short-comings. You are to report to me on all matters and to me alone. Am I clearly understood?"

"Yesss, Excellency. I am honored to serve."

"Quit calling me that. I am a lord and you shall address me as such. I want all these bodies stripped and thrown to the rats."

"Yes, my lord."

He pointed to the body of the Goblin commander. "Confine this one in the cells and see to his wounds. I want him kept alive for questioning."

"As you command, my lord." Trilk saluted and started away.

"Trilk? Assemble the female human slaves before my tower. I wish to have a woman tonight."

"My lord, it shall be done." The Kuilbolt ambled away with its strange gait. He watched as they stripped the Goblin commander of his armor and weapons and dragged him away. As the crowd of Kuilbolts dispersed Rhael wandered down the gangway and retrieved the commander's gleaming helm with its transverse crest and studied it in his hands. There was a small dent in the side where he had struck the helm with the rod, but otherwise it was pristine. He walked back onto the deck of the airship and eased the helm down over his head, testing the fit. Surprisingly the helm was comfortable and rested on his head almost perfectly. He was reminded of his youth, of training at the lance on horseback, of his first tournament, of his first jousting harness. His vision was unobstructed, perhaps only a touch of his peripheral vision was gone, but he was impressed by the style of the helm, and besides that, it was his war trophy. Things were falling into place quite well, and now he had a prisoner to interrogate for valuable information, a prize airship, and a plan to consolidate his power.

Twenty-Six

RYLA HANDED THE MERCHANT the trade invoice once Elmund had counted his coin and given her a nod. The man thanked her and went to fetch his carters to haul his goods away. She had been fortunate to have off-loaded all of her surplus cargo in Torlucksford, but these sprawling river towns were always dependable for buying up goods brought in from the east. She still did not know where Mage Norden planned on having her deliver his precious cargo. She scowled up at the sky. It had been a harrowing flight here from Grannock, and the skies showed no signs of letting up. Though there was no rain at the moment, thunder pealed and the clouds had drawn in together so tightly that they had blocked out the sun and loomed gray and menacing overhead.

Torlucksford was too small to have need of a skyharbor, so Ryla did what she had customarily done in smaller towns in the past and set the Skyward down in the market square. Most towns had a broad green square that they used for market days, and most market squares were adequately sized to set an airship down in. Keeping her steady enough in these winds had proven difficult, and they had made several passes before the inexperienced townspeople below were bold enough to grab hold of the draglines and walk her down to anchor. Norden had proven progressively more impatient at every setback they had encountered. When they had finally landed the little mage had demanded the ship's key from her and then stormed off of the deck with his clerk, leaving his foreign soldiers to guard the airship and keep an eye on Ryla and her crew. He was too thorough to make such a mistake, but she had harbored a hope that he might.

They could have slipped away in a heartbeat had he not taken the key, but now Ryla Dierns was confined to waiting. She knew he was going to the head magistrate's office, the head of government for such places, generally appointed by the Magistry to officiate over towns and regions, and she knew he was looking for answers as to the whereabouts of Joth and Eilyth. She still did not understand why the mage was so preoccupied with obstructing them, however. All that she had gathered from what Galt had overheard was that they had escaped detection along the road and slipped around the Norandishmen in the night and then disappeared without a trace at Torlucksford, and that had maddened the mage beyond all reckoning. She also gleaned that Norden had plans for the girl; of course he had, the lecherous wretch, but Joth was to be done away with. "It's imperative that the three of them are silenced, do you understand me? Tell your men to find them and see to the soldier and the boy, and bring the girl to me. Scout every road." That is exactly how Galt had quoted Norden as he passed an order to the Norandian captain through his rail thin clerk. Galt had been in a fine position to overhear Norden clearly, there were no doubts. So now the mage had extended his death sentence to include poor Bellan, the Ostler of Grannock.

Obviously, he was not beyond murder if it helped him get what he desired. The one thing she still did not fully comprehend was the reasoning behind it. Why, she asked herself over and over again? Why did the mage insist on their capture and their deaths? Perhaps she would never know. I'll never find out if the weather doesn't let up, that's for certain, she thought. She had been on deck the entire time, stuck behind the helm post, and the opportunity never arose for her to spring the trap behind her measured looks and for her to see if she might dig a bit more information out of Norden. He had gone green in the gills at the first lurch the Skyward took and had gone below decks and only reemerged moments before they touched down in the market square, and his ire had not dissipated in the scant few hours that it had taken them to get from Grannock to Torlucksford. In fact, he had seemed even more incensed as he had stepped down from the gangway, as though the rage had built in him somehow along his journey. It was valuable information, the news of this cargo, this mission of Mage Norden's.

She would still be able to meet the mage's demands and achieve her goal, it was just that deep inside of her heart she hated having Norden lord his authority over her; she hated giving up the control over her own life that she had fought so hard for so many years to establish. Had she the opportunity to do so now, she would simply clear these Norandian soldiers from her decks and make away for Kingsbridge, but Norden had the key and the soldiers had been very vigilant in their guard duty and had not even allowed them the slightest of respites from their vigilance, nothing near enough to allow them to smuggle the young Bellan out from below decks and get him clear of danger. That worried her most of all. If Bellan were to be discovered, she would have to act, she would have to intervene. He was an innocent and she would not allow him to be killed simply because this man of power wished to keep his hands clean and his hair tidy. She had seen the dirt beneath his nails and the oil in his thinning hair, enough to know how unclean he was; and she had recognized it from the very beginning. She would stop him if she could, she certainly would not allow him to kill the youth and take advantage of the Dawn Tribe girl. Shiny wasn't too bad either, she reminded herself.

She watched as the carters finished loading up the goods she had sold the merchant and roll away with it through the busy square. There were many people here today, thought Ryla, and not a one of them appears to have ever laid eyes upon an airship nor a female airship captain. They gawked and craned their necks as they passed her, but she was used to that.

"Elmund?" she called.

"Aye, lady?"

"Fetch us a few fresh pies and a bit of ale, would you?"

She saw Galt perk up, the man had a good set of ears.

"Any preference?" Elmund asked as he began to stride away.

"Whatever is fresh, and get enough for our friends." She meant Bellan—the Norandishmen could all be hanged.

Elmund nodded and a slight altercation erupted between the Norandian guard and the airship crew, but it was finally resolved when it was understood that Elmund was simply traversing the square to visit a street vendor selling fresh pies and then purchasing some ale before bringing it back to the resting airship. At last they agreed to let him go with an armed escort of two guardsmen. Elmund was angry, Ryla knew, but to his credit he laughed it off and went to get the victuals as he had been asked to do.

Somewhat later, as they sat finishing their pies, sipping ale, and critiquing the skills of a rather poor juggler performing in the market, Mage Norden and his clerk arrived back. Far from looking pleased about the outcome of his interview, Norden seemed absolutely livid with rage as he addressed his soldiers through his clerk.

"Half of you shall come with me. The rest of you shall divide to scout the eastern road and the northern road to Kingsbridge. How long until the horses arrive from Grannock?" he asked the Norandian captain through his clerk. Ryla could not hear the thin man's reply.

"Very well then. Those of you without them shall go and hire mounts." He seemed less than pleased with the Norandish captain's answer and he snapped at the man exasperatedly. "Set off at once. Give them the silver, you dullard!" he spat at his clerk. As the clerk moved off with the Norandian captain, Norden turned to Ryla and her crew. "Captain Dierns," he began, "We shall need to get into the air at once." He produced a leather pouch from beneath his coat and placed it onto the bar of the market stall they had been using to eat their pies and drink their ale. It jingled with the sound of silver coins. "I appreciate your hardships, and I am giving you this as an installment for your services thus far."

He said it as though it was meant to amaze her, but as she hefted it Ryla gave him a wry look. "It's a bit light, to be honest. And I am still owed for the loss of my crewman."

He smiled, but the corners of his mouth were twitching nervously. She could tell that Norden was nearing the end of what he was able to bear. The man had to be pushed little before he broke, she noted.

"Give Captain Dierns her silver," Norden barked at his clerk. "Get us in the air below the cloud banks," he said to her through his clenched jaw. He shoved the ship's key at her and strode up the gangway, leaving the clerk fumbling with his coffer.

"What a pleasant man," muttered Kipren as he cleaned pie debris from his beard. Norden had not won any favoritism among her men.

"Well, I don't like it, boys, but let's get her underway." Ryla pushed back from the stall and turned toward the ship, passing the clerk counting out coins into his hand. "You can pay me on deck."

He looked up distractedly before muttering agreement and gathering his things together.

"Fine pies," Galt said, licking his fingers.

After all of the necessary preparations had been made they lifted off into the sky above Torlucksford, a crowd that had gathered to see them take flight cheering and waving as their ship was pushed and pulled by the currents of the wind in the stormy skies. Airships were still relatively uncommon in most places, generally reserved for use by the wealthy and the elite. They were also a relatively new form of transportation, the first airships appearing in Oesteria in the lifetimes of her grandparents. They inspired feelings of adventure and awe wherever they were seen. Elmund would always say that if he had a silver for every lad who asked to take him with them outside of every skyharbor he had seen in Oesteria, then he would never have to fly another run in his life. Skies like these could change the minds of those adventure seekers and make them cry like babies for firm ground beneath their feet. They had seen that before also.

It had been two hours of being told to circle here and look there, and Ryla was fed up with it and genuinely concerned at the weather she saw growing more and more severe all around them.

Norden had remained on deck, much to her surprise. Although he still looked a bit sick every time the ship took a sudden shallow dive, he was half kneeling and bracing himself near the side and peering intently down and out at the landscape below. He was looking for signs of his riders and for any horse drawn carts with teams of six, Ryla had heard him tell his clerk to relay to the Norandians, all of them pressed up against the rails around the ship and trying to fulfill their master's wishes. The crew had all donned their furs, as had Ryla, but the mage and his men had only their stout woolens and she knew it was not enough to allow them to bear the cold winds for long.

The weather was bad, worse than it had been flying up from Grannock, but Ryla had found a comfortable current in the air that the Skyward seemed to be flowing along with, and she felt a distinct sense of relief. But the relief was short lived when she looked ahead of them and to the north and saw ominous-looking dark clouds heavy with rain and the bright flashes of lightning sparking in the distance.

Now she decided to put the pressure back on Norden. "Lord Mage, what is our heading?" she shouted into the wind.

"What?" he said, turning from the rail and looking annoyed.

"I shall need a heading if I am to convey you and your cargo anywhere!"

"We are looking for something along the roads, Captain!"

She fixed him with a steely glare. "Lord Mage, you are looking for something along the road, and I am looking for a heading to deliver your cargo! I can't simply fly about in this weather—it's dangerous!"

"Ha!" he laughed, "Dangerous? Surely this is just another market day for you!"

"Lord Mage, I am advising you as an experienced—"

She was interrupted by the clerk and two of the Norandishmen screaming and waving their hands excitedly and pointing at something in the distance. Norden broke away from her at once and went to investigate what they were on about. She tried to listen in, but she could hear nothing over the howling winds. Looking over the side and following their eyelines, she could make out something along the road. It was nothing more than a speck, but it may have been a carriage far in the distance on the northern road, the road to Kingsbridge.

"Captain! Your heading is north." Norden was quite pleased with himself. North would take them right for the heaviest darkest cloudbank, but the mage did not seem to think that weather was anything to be concerned about.

"Can you not see that?" she asked him incredulously.

"North, Captain. North to Kingsbridge." He flashed a smile and then stalked off as confidently as he could on the pitching deck. She almost shouted for them all to get below decks, but after she had thought about it, losing Norden and his lackeys over the side would have eased all of her troubles. She raised her voice and called out so that her boys could hear her.

"It's going to get a lot colder, lads. Let's see if we can't fly over this storm." Ryla made an adjustment to the bronze wand on the helm post and the Skyward began to climb slowly and steadily higher toward the mounting wall of storm clouds. They climbed and headed northward for the better part of three hours, battered by the winds and tossed about like rags, rising and falling on volatile currents through freezing cloudbanks and hair-raising lightning storms. Finally, Ryla made for the forecastle, where the mage stood huddled and she told him that she had to get out of the skies and make for land, and for once the man simply nodded and went back to looking ill.

It had grown so dark that it may as well have been night, Ryla thought, as she and her crew brought the airship down through the cloud bank and tried to lay eyes upon some sort of landmark to get their bearings. It felt almost pleasant in the skies for a moment, but Ryla was not sure if it truly was calmer or if she had simply grown accustomed to the turbulence. The land was settling in under them, and Ryla could see firelight and its twinkling amber glow pouring from open barn doors and glazed farmhouse windows scattered across the hillsides below them. It was too dark to make out anything else, and her eyes failed to land on anything familiar. She was beginning to despair when Elmund called out. "Ho! There's Kingsbridge off the starboard bow, lady!"

They had been blown off course, but not too very far. There was a concentration of lights and the unmistakable feature of the trio of bridges that spanned the river that bisected the city's two wards. It was one of the most recognizable cities from the air. The winds were buffeting the airship now, and the sense of calm that had presided for a brief moment vanished in a blink as the wind slammed them into a gut-wrenching descent that had all of them hugging the deck until the ship rose and fell again before finally evening out.

Norden was crawling on the deck, inching out from the forecastle and trying to get her attention. She strode over to him. She was confident on the deck in a storm—she was the captain, and she had to be.

"Captain! Don't put this ship down in the town." He was shouting to be heard.

"Don't worry, I can't in these winds. We will have to drag-land outside the walls."

"Very good then, on the hills along the northern road! We shall await our quarry there." He inched back toward the forecastle in a ridiculous fashion, half-crouched and using his hands to hold him steady as he crawled his way back. Ryla watched his progress for a moment and sighed inwardly. Getting shed of this mage was proving more difficult than she had hoped. She yelled out to Galt, who was belaying a line on the starboard side.

"Tell Elmund to cast his eyes down to those hills there and bring us around for a drag-landing."

"Aye, lady, aye." He sounded relieved. This was the worst storm they had found themselves under in quite some time, and the boys all knew that if she had any say in the matter that they would never have been in the skies in the first place. The mage was too inexperienced in sky travel to fully understand the danger he had placed them in.

It was rough and rainy and the wind caused the ship to bottom out and bounce on the turf as they pulled her in, the force with which it hit causing everyone to go sprawling across the wet deck. Ryla swore under her breath. If the ship was damaged, it would be one more black mark against the Magistry and the irascible Mage Norden. Elmund went down and wrenched his knee, now he was stalking about the deck grim-faced and limping.

"All right, Elmund?"

"Aye, lady, it's nothing."

She watched him for a long beat before calling to Kipren. "Get below and make sure we didn't smash open the hold."

He gave her an "aye" and headed for the forecastle, making way as the Norandian guard came tottering out onto the deck followed by the queasy-looking mage and his equally uneasy-looking scribe. They ambled about on the deck peering out into their new surroundings as the rain pelted them with its heavy drops. The rain made a tinny sound as it peened noisily off of their helms. The wind tearing at the billowing mainsail was causing the ship to list dangerously.

Ryla called out to Elmund at once. "Storm lines on the double, Elmund!"

"Aye, lady, aye!" He moved at once, barking out orders to Galt and Kipren as he pushed through the meandering Norandians and made for the gangway. Ryla eyed the sky warily as the crew staked the lines down with a mallet and cross-tied the ship where it rested atop the last low hill along the northern road from Torlucksford to Kingsbridge.

After she saw the first stake driven in and the lines secured she felt safe enough to leave the deck. Ryla removed the ship's key from the helm post and attached it to the hook she wore on her belt, smiling as she felt its familiar weight on her hip. She would not surrender it to the mage again, not without a fight. This ship was hers, and until she left the deck and put her feet on the ground, her word as captain trumped all comers. She left the helm and stepped down to the door that marked her quarters, the captain's cabin, and pulled the key she wore round her neck from inside of her shirt. She gave a quick look round, but the mage and his lackeys were all looking off toward Kingsbridge sprawling over a convergence of rivers behind its stone walls. They were pointing at the road and the hill that lay across from them on the other side of it, arguing through the bony clerk who served as interpreter. She worked the lock open and went into the cabin, shutting the door behind her and bolting it quickly and silently. The cabin was not cramped, but one could hardly call it opulent. Most airship captain's cabins were reputed to be grand, but in actual fact captain's quarters were unusually uniform from vessel to vessel—the reason being that not all captains were owners, and not all owners were captains. The rich lord's airship would have a lavish suite for its lord, but for its captain, who may share that duty with several other captains, the accomodations were typically a familiar, utilitarian cabin that could easily be evacuated and made ready for the next occupant. There was a bed and a chair and a stool and a small stove, and the bronze furniture in the room was crafted in swirling patterns and shapes that resembled those found in ship's keys. She moved past the small writing desk that doubled as a dining table and sat down upon her bed. She let out a deep breath and put her head in her hands. That had been a harrowing day's flight, and she had held all day without breaking her calm; but she had been sure they were going to fall several times, and had the crew not been there depending on her she would have broken into hysterics. Ryla had instead focused her anxiety into anger, which she directed at Mage Norden, and indirectly at his scribe and the foreign horsemen as well. His ignorance of air travel and desire to capture this girl had impaired his judgment so severely that they had all almost been killed.

She rolled back over the bed and went to the desk and pulled the drawer out, a bottle resting inside atop some trade invoices and writs and other random parchment scraps. She pulled the cork stopper and had a long pull from the bottle. It was sharp and smoky tasting, and it warmed her throat to a point of burning, but she had a taste for Malvane Lightning and kept a bottle of it in her desk for occasions like these. That bloody fool of a mage, she thought, how am I going to ever shed him? Now she was expected to sit idly by while Norden and his soldiers planned an ambush. The blood of that young man would not be on her hands, she promised herself, nor the ill treatment of that girl. Courage now, she told herself, and find a way to get Norden alone and separated from his guard. Once she did that she could find out what she needed to know and then detain him until Joth and Eilyth had escaped his clutches. Elmund, Kipren, and Galt could hold off those soldiers if they tried to board the Skyward, and now that she had the ship's key all she would need do is let go the storm lines and raise her up above the tree line. It would be a hell of a chance she would be taking in doing so, she knew; both in long-term problems with the Magistry and the weather at that given time there on the hill outside of Kingsbridge. Ryla thought for a moment and then removed the ship's key from her belt and placed it in the drawer where the Malvane Lightning had been and closed it.

When she emerged from her cabin a few moments later, the mage and his scribe were still in argument with the Norandian captain and paid her no heed. To her surprise, the rain had let up slightly and a break in the clouds let the moon shine through for a moment as it rose to its place in the heavens. As she was gazing skyward she heard the mage laugh derisively and launch into the Norandian captain.

"Ha!" He spat and turned to his clerk. "I have a better idea, since our Norandian friend has shown me nothing but ineptitude thus far in this simple task that I've given him!" He turned and swept his gaze across the deck until his eyes came to rest on her. "Captain Dierns, have your men unload my cargo immediately!"

"What, here?" she could not help but ask.

"Immediately, Captain Dierns," he said flatly. "I promised to show you what we carried, and I always make good on my word."

"I thought it was that you 'always get your way'?"

His jaw worked for a moment, but he resisted the jab. "Let us just do as I bloody say, Captain, and everything will be fine. Get my men some light to work by."

"As you command, Lord Mage."

He turned and tottered down the gangway. She could see in his eyes when he spoke to her that he was afraid, genuinely afraid, and she wondered whether it was the fear of failure or if there were a justifiable reason that Norden would wish to "silence" them as he had said? She still did not know, but perhaps she did not have to know. Perhaps she could simply choose an opportune moment and lift away into the moonlight. She could if the weather let up, she thought ruefully, but as it stood the weather had her in a tighter prison than Norden could ever have devised for her with all of his clever scheming. He had her, and he knew it, but he had been pushed past his ability to find satisfaction in that. He was exhausted and worried of failure that his quarry would escape him. Ryla had noted it well, and by her reckoning, Mage Norden was about to crack.

She had the crew bring the crane out from below decks and after building it they unloaded the long, heavy, canvas-wrapped bundles that they had taken on in Grannock at the mage's orders. The rain was spitting down at them as Galt lowered the last bundle and Elmund guided it onto the spongy turf of the hillside.

"That's the last of them, lady," Kipren called from the hold.

Galt clambered out of the wheel and stood next to her on the deck. "Shall I break her down now, Captain?"

"No, stand down Galt. This bastard will probably want it loaded up again the next time the wind shifts." It was not very ladylike, but she spat over the side of the airship.

"Aye, lady. Looks like we'll get to see what's in those bundles now."

She nodded absently. Norden's scribe was directing the Norandians at the task of untying and opening the bundles and removing their contents. Elmund had passed around the ship's lanterns, and now the light pooled out around where the soldiers gathered. There were four stacks of canvas-wrapped materials that the men were working at, and when the covers were pulled back Ryla saw beams of a dark, slick wood bound with bronze hardware throughout.

"Seen anything like that before?" Galt asked her under his breath.

"No. What is it?"

"Can't really say, lady."

They watched as the other canvas bundles were opened and their contents revealed. They all seemed to hold an assortment of beams of varying lengths, all of them alike in their bronze and wood construction, and beneath the beams a bronze carriage of some sort rested amid several gears and levers. The only exception was the largest and squarest of the bundles, which had ridden in the belly of the Skyward on her journey north and was comprised entirely of small barrels of a peculiar construction. That had been the heaviest, Ryla knew. The small crane had strained to lift it, and it was no wonder, now that she saw what lay beneath the canvas tarp. The mage had refused to split the loads any further.

A less confident crane operator would have refused, but Galt knew the crane well and adjusted some of the gears and tried it again, testing it before giving her the nod. She had a good crew, she was thankful for that. They had all gathered near her now and all of them stood together in the swirling drizzle looking down at the Norandians being bossed about by Norden as he fussed and pointed here and there at his strange cargo. The clerk was interpreting rapidly, checking in with the mage often, verifying and reverifying his orders. Norden was wound fairly tightly at this point, and Ryla noted that his scribe was taking extra precautions not to set him off. One of the Norandians then held up a bronze rod and called to the clerk. Norden picked up the exchange at once.

"Aha! Bring that to me!" He kept looking out at the road and back to the bronze and wood heaps that lay beside the ship. He trotted over and snatched the rod from his man and held it in the lantern light to examine it, as if to be certain that he had found the correct one. "Find the other one as well. There were two rods!"

It was about three ells long and crested by a strange spherical crystal or glass orb. Norden looked it up and down in the lantern light and nodded, pleased.

"Very good, very good." he muttered by way of dismissal. The guardsman went back to his task. Norden continued to look at the rod as he paced back and forth, waiting for the guards to pull away all the ropes and tarpaulins. He walked back up the gangplank and called to her.

"Captain?" He stood there unimpressively, his hood covering his thinning hair and the ornate bronze rod resting on his shoulder, posed like some bedraggled monarch.

"Yes, Lord Mage, how can we assist you further?" she asked from where she stood.

"Further? You shall be loading these machines back aboard your vessel when we are finished here. Kingsbridge is not my final destination." He was barely containing his rage. It was time to play her hand, she knew. Ryla thought about it for a moment, and then slowly and carefully she spoke.

"Shall I? I believe I have provided more than enough in terms of what was required of me. I shall be leaving you here to collect your company and move on. I have pressing business to attend to. Best of luck to you, Norden."

The mage's jaw worked for a moment before he was able to speak. "What? Oh no, you aren't going anywhere, Captain."

"The hell I'm not, and if you want to try to stop me, the skies love a volunteer. That means go take a flying leap."

"You were paid!" he cried.

"I was paid for services rendered, now get off my ship."

He just stared at her incredulously, but he realized he had slipped; he had drawn all of his guards off the decks and set them to work, and in his haste to accomplish everything in the most rapid way possible he had trusted in the storm too much, and now as the skies were less threatening there was nothing keeping her from flying away and he saw his mistake, and she saw him see it. She walked past the mage and toward the helm without looking back and cried out. "All hands, make ready!"

She had barely said it when pain exploded into the back of her head and she was laid out on the mid-ship deck. There was blood in her mouth and a ringing in her ears. She thought she heard shouting and felt the deck pounding, but was it just the throbbing pain in her head? Blurrily, she looked up and tried to rise and felt a booted foot push her down and saw the rage-filled face of Norden looking down at her, pointing the bronze rod at her menacingly. He had hit her with that. She felt at the back of her head and her hand came away bloody. That bastard hit me with that rod, Ryla affirmed to herself stupidly, cursing his name and wishing she had never seen him. Her bloody head was on fire, or at least it felt that way. She pushed his foot off of her and rolled back and onto her feet unsteadily.

"You filthy bitch!" he hissed at her.

Elmund had drawn his sword and held his knife in the other hand, Galt had his sword as well, and Kipren had the long-handled ship's axe in both hands, and all of them surrounded her then and faced the mage down. She blinked and tried to clear her vision. Everything was blurred and moving. Her head throbbed.

"Give me the ship's key, now!" Norden raged.

"You heard the captain, get off the ship!" Elmund roared at the little man.

The Norandian guards had left their tasks and now all stood back on deck and were advancing with drawn swords and shouting to each other in their foreign tongue. She had to do something, this would get out of hand quickly. Someone would die, one of her boys. One more of my boys, she reminded herself. She felt at her belt and worked free the length of bronze she had hung there. Her vision was still swimming.

"Here, take it then. No more bloodshed." She stumbled forward on shaky legs and held out the bronze wand with a bloodied hand. The mage snatched it from her and then hurriedly passed it to his clerk.

"Give that key to the Norandian captain and tell him to guard it with his life!" Norden was puffing with rage. "Put them in the ship's hold and let them be confined there until I see fit!"

"Surrender your arms!" The clerk cried.

"Do it. Stand down, boys," Ryla said.

The crew reluctantly placed their weapons on the deck and stood there before the Norandians grabbed them all roughly and shoved them around the deck.

"Hey!" Galt cried as a stout guard shoved him hard.

"We know the way to the bloody hold," Kipren muttered.

They were pushed down the ladder and confined to the now nearly empty hold. The guards closed the hatch behind them as they left, and Ryla and her crew were sat huddled in a pool of moonlight coming in through a porthole on the starboard side. The skies had cleared for a moment, but more clouds were threatening. She could see them off to the north, or perhaps it was north east.

Her mind was in a fog, and her head was throbbing with pain.

"Captain? Are you all right?" It was Kipren.

"She's bleeding. Wait until I get my hands on the bastard!" Elmund said. They gave her a handkerchief one of them had doused with water.

"I'm all right. I think." She rose and leaned against the hull.

"We failed you, Captain. I failed you, I'm sorry." Galt's jug ears were fiery red.

"No. It was my mistake. I turned my back on him and thought that he might not hit me because I'm so pretty. I didn't think he'd hit me, that wasn't planned."

"We're sorry, Captain," Kipren said. "We think you're pretty."

They laughed, a little. Not a one of them liked any piece of this business they had been handed by Norden and his cronies.

"What was the plan, then?" Galt asked.

"The plan was to make Norden demand the ship's key from me."

The crew looked at her confusedly.

"Good one, Captain. It worked," Kipren said dolefully.

Just then, a muffled voice called out to them from within one of the crates. She had almost forgotten about Bellan.

"Help him out, lads." She wiped the blood away with the dampened handkerchief. Her head was still throbbing, but the pain seemed to be subsiding in its intensity. Her vision had cleared to a near normal state, but things were still moving too fast for her eyes to keep up with.

Bellan was whispering excitedly to them as he was pulled out of the crate, and he stood there stretching his cramped limbs as he jabbered. "I was sleeping when we hit the ground like that. A 'whallop' like. That's what it made, a 'whalloping' sound when she hit, didn't she? Woke me right up, I'll tell you." His face grew worried when he caught sight of Ryla with the bloody handkerchief. "Seven bells! Are you hurt badly?"

"Be quiet now, lad," Elmund said sharply.

Bellan paled and looked as though he were about to protest before nodding resignedly.

"No use in staying crated up now, Bellan. We're getting out of here."

He looked as if he were waiting for more, but then he just nodded again.

The crew looked to each other confusedly.

"Begging your pardon lady," Elmund started, "but you surrendered the ship's key to Norden less than an hour ago. Maybe you need to lie down, Captain?"

"Stand down, Elmund. He didn't hit me that hard," she snapped. What a fool that man was, she thought, looking at her like she was mad. "I gave him a fake. I swapped it out with the real key earlier. It's in my cabin."

They all looked at her incredulously, and immediately everyone began to ask questions at once until she quieted them.

"What did you give him then?" Elmund asked.

"A bracket from beneath the table in my cabin. I shall have to take my meals at my desk for a time, but it will be worth it to be shed of that miserable man."

Kipren shook his head and laughed.

Galt and Elmund were smiling too.

Bellan nodded and then tentatively opened his mouth. "How are we going to get out of the hold and get to your cabin?"

"You can get to a lot of places if you know the way," she said conspiratorially. "They think they have us trapped? This is my ship. Our ship! We shall see who has who." She winced and put a hand to her throbbing head. "Double pay to the man who hits Norden in the head at the next opportunity."

They would wait for the mage to calm down and for things to grow quiet before they would sneak away, and so they peered out of the portholes to mark the progress of the Norandians and counted the different rhythms in footsteps on the deck above to discern that there were only two guards posted on the airship, eight more on the ground building the machines that Norden had transported from who knows where. As the machines took shape, a dire feeling of dread that had been welling up inside the pit of Ryla Dierns' stomach had risen to her throat.

Siege engines of some sort, she realized. That is what those machines were. There was some sort of arm mounted with a harnessing point and a counterweight. Norden was talking excitedly to his clerk and pointing toward the queer small barrels and a curved bronzen basket that extended out above and behind the base of the apparatus. They looked to be siege engines without carriages. Ryla assumed the engines to be a form of catapult, and the barrels were the ammunition. He had three of the bloody things assembled now, and she supposed that was all of them. What was the mage planning, she wondered? He was going to blow a coach from the road, horses and all, by the look of it. He had cracked for certain now, Ryla realized. They could easily slip away, that was not a problem. Ryla knew that there was a trap door that led to her cabin here hidden behind some loose boards in the ceiling. She and all her crew could be up in her cabin in moments and they could easily overpower the two guards and scurry up the rigging, cut the lines, and be away before Norden could even blink.

The problem was that Ryla could not bring herself to run away knowing that at least two innocent people were riding to their deaths and there was a chance that she could prevent it. She turned back to the others.

"We aren't going to let Norden win tonight. We are going to foil all his plans before we leave and rescue Shiny and Pretty in the process." She had a steely glint in her eye. "I'm going to get some sleep. My head hurts. Wake me up when things get quiet."

"Aye, lady, aye."

She went to the forecastle and climbed into a hammock and pulled a fur blanket over her and shut her eyes as the ship creaked and groaned in the wind. She drifted off into sleep almost immediately.

She was gently woken what felt like moments later. It had grown colder, and Elmund's breath was frosting as he whispered to her. "There's some activity out there, Captain."

"How long have I been asleep?" she asked.

"A few hours, lady. Hurry up and have a look."

A few hours? Her head hurt still, but the throbbing was gone and her vision was back to normal after she had blinked the sleep out of her eyes. She rose to her feet and swayed slightly.

Elmund reached out and put a hand on her back to steady her. "How's your head?"

"Better. I can stand steady now, I think."

"Sure?"

"Yes, I'm steady now. You can let go." She had not meant it to sound harsh.

"Aye, lady."

He stood away and went to the porthole, waiting for her. She steadied herself and stepped carefully to him.

"What is it then?" she asked as she looked out.

"They sent scouts out down the road earlier and they came back not twenty minutes ago, and now the whole group's aflutter."

She saw that Norden had swiveled one of his engines toward the road but the other two were left pointing northward. He means to release his engines upon them as they come into view, she realized, and he had staged the engines so that he would have several opportunities should his first attempt fail.

"Why did you not wake me earlier?"

"You needed your rest. That was a nasty blow to the head he struck you."

"Were you boys worried about me? I'm touched."

He smirked and shook his head at her. She heard a snippet of Norden's shrill voice cut through the air and turned her attention back to the porthole in time to see the Norandians dividing forces. It seemed that Norden had ordered them to send half of their number over the road to wait on the slopes of the hill opposite the one they now occupied. That must be his last line of defense, she thought. He means to run his engines at them first, then failing the absolute success of that his Norandians would sweep in and take care of any survivors. A neat and well-ordered plan, she had to admit. But it was one that was easily ruined.

"Well I'll say this for him, he's predictable."

"How's that? He screams a lot?" Elmund was watching the soldiers' progress as they trotted down the hill together. "I reckon they're the ones sent in to do the fine work after these engines spew their loads."

She nodded grimly. "I was thinking the same. So we have to make sure those engines miss their marks."

"Aye, lady. I'll wake Galt. He might know best how to deal with them."

"Wake everyone. We need to be ready to move quickly."

Elmund did as she said and soon a tired-looking Kipren stood next to Elmund as bleary-eyed Galt stood with his hands tucked into his armpits looking out the porthole.

"There ain't no wheels on them carriages. How'd they set them like they are now?"

"I was sleeping, don't ask me," Kipren said wryly.

"I saw him do it, Norden. He walked to each one with that rod and the bloody things floated off the ground like airships."

They regarded him incredulously. How could that be possible without some sort of mainsail, Ryla wondered?

"Then he angled them and brought one to bear down on the road, easy as you please." He made a motion with his hands to demonstrate the ease with which Norden was able to shift the bulk of the engines and angle them, as though it took no effort at all.

"That's problematic. We'll need that rod then."

"Why did he make us load and unload the bloody things so many times if all he needed to do was use that rod and make them float?" Galt looked angry. "That was a lot of wheel work."

"It will be hard to get from the mage, he's fond of that." Kipren was watching the activity through the porthole. "Better if a sneaky man were to sneak down there and switch them around once they was afloat."

He cut his eyes at Galt. "Is that you volunteering me to do something?"

"You are good at that sort of thing," Elmund put in.

Galt scowled at him. "What is the plan then? There's six soldiers to one side of the road, and four here. Two on the deck and two on the ground. Two more if you count the mage and his clerk."

Ryla nodded. "We stay hidden until the action starts, then we move once they are distracted."

They listened to their captain as she laid out the plan. It was easy to reference the position of the guards by looking out the porthole, and Ryla knew it was a gamble, but she also felt that they had the upper hand. Norden had been lured into a false sense of confidence. That had been her plan from the start with the ship's key, and it had worked.

Now he had divided his troops and he was shorthanded on the ground. Everything had fallen into place so far, but that was no reason for everything else to work out in her favor, she knew. The tricky part would be subduing the deck guards quickly and silently enough to avoid detection by the troops manning the engines, for if that went wrong they may have to abandon the idea of leaving the ship and take to the skies. She could fly back along the road and try to warn them of what lay ahead, she supposed, but there was a large chance that she would not be able to spot them in this weather at night, and she could not be sure that way. No, she thought, we rush Norden and overwhelm him and leave nothing to chance. By the time word reached the authorities, she would have her revenge and she could lay low in the southwestern isles for a few seasons, repaint the Skyward and rename her, and with Elmund at the helm no one would ever be the wiser. Then what, she asked herself? What will I do once Uhlmet is dead and my people have been avenged? Will I know peace in my heart then, or will it be empty as I stand there and gaze down remorselessly at my fallen enemy? She hoped that it would leave her with some degree of peace, but she did not truly know how she would feel once a reckoning came. It was all she could do and so she had strived for justice. It was all that she would do, let the pieces fall where they may.

She would stop Norden if it meant getting the prize of Uhlmet, the Magistry be damned. And as loathe as she was to admit it, the girl was special, and she liked the young soldier, and the idea of Norden having his way with either of them was something she could not stand idly by and allow to happen.

"What about me? What shall I do?" The stableboy was standing there bleary eyed. It must be well past midnight and closer to dawn by now, Ryla thought.

"You'll stay below decks."

"Captain, if it please you I can—"

"Do you aim to be a part of this crew?" ahe asked pointedly.

"Lady? Yes, I mean to say, that's what I'm driving at—"

"Then learn to follow your captain's orders and stay below." She did not need this boy getting himself killed on her account.

He looked down dejectedly. Hopefully he would not sulk about like a sullen child. Not that it would sway her; she had other nets to bring in. Still, she could give the lad a task and lift his heart a bit.

"Here, lad. You are to watch and listen out the porthole for any action and to let me know on the double, are you clear with that?"

"Aye, lady, aye?" he asked tentatively.

She smiled and left him there. It would not do to have him spitted on the sword of one of those Norandishmen. She would not have it. All those dead boys in her village, all the dead friends and family, gone now. Places gone, forgotten, but not forgotten by her. Nor were their deaths forgiven. She walked to the place where her crew stood huddled beneath the trap door that led into her cabin, or more precisely the smuggler's hold that lay beneath the bed in her quarters. They eyed her expectantly.

"I'm asking each of you to risk your lives with me. If anyone has any complaints or reservations, then voice them now." She was met with silence. Her boys were with her, she had known it anyway. "Good. Ready, lads?"

"Aye lady, aye." They answered softly, and then Galt and Kipren let down the door. Elmund pulled himself aloft and then offered his arm down for her and helped her into the small space, and together they pushed the bed over enough to give them access to the room above. Galt and Kipren followed and soon they were grouped on either side of the door, peering out of the twin portholes that looked out on the deck toward the bow. The guards were huddled near the forecastle, wrapped in their cloaks against the chill, lanterns in their hands, looking down absently at the engines and their fellows on the ground.

"Good," said Ryla. She opened her closet and reached into the back where her sword was hanging and she passed it to Elmund. He drew it and tested the edge before nodding. She gave a knife to Galt, and Kipren was wielding a heavy wooden mallet they had found in the hold. She carefully opened the drawer at her desk and removed the true ship's key and hung it from her belt again. She uncorked the bottle of Malvane Lightning and took another long draught before passing it in turn to each of her crew.

"Courage, boys," she said. "Everyone remember your roles. There's no turning back from this point on."

They nodded.

Ryla fished the key from inside her shirt and worked the lock on the cabin door and silently opened it a hair's breadth. Then, mimicking the wind rattling a door left ajar, she banged the door shut and let it open again slightly wider, and then banged it shut a few times in succession.

"One's coming. Get ready."

Elmund moved behind the desk. Galt was in the corner, and she and Kipren were waiting behind the door. Her heart was pounding in her chest. Everything seemed too loud, even the sound of their own breath. She could hear Kipren's breathing speeding up and his hands grip the mallet tighter. She saw the lantern's glow growing brighter and brighter as the guard drew near, and then the room exploded with light as he pushed the door wide and pushed his way into the room. Time stood still for a moment, what felt like an eternity for Ryla, and then she quickly shut the door and heard a clamoring sound and a dull thud and when she looked the Norandian was being tied up by Galt while Elmund was removing the man's cloak and helm. Kipren was stood over the man with the mallet at the ready.

She righted the lantern and looked back out at the deck again. The other guard was looking toward the cabin. "Ready, Elmund?"

"Aye, one moment." He finished belting on the man's sword and wrapped the cloak around him. "Ready."

He handed her sword to Galt and he took the ship's lantern from her. He waited until they were hidden from view and then threw open the door and leaned out, motioning the other guard toward him before turning and walking back into the room. The other guard on the deck called out something to him, but Elmund pretended as though he did not hear the man and just impatiently waved him over. The man was talking as he entered the room, and his tone was getting more and more insistent, but he stopped talking when he looked down and saw the body on the floor bound and gagged. His eyes had just enough time to register shock and surprise before Kipren took him in the head with three strong mallet blows that landed the soldier in a heap next to his comrade.

"Well done! Quickly now, get out there," she whispered hurriedly. Kipren tucked his long beard into his shirt as Galt handed him the fallen guard's cloak and helm. Elmund was unbelting the man's sword.

"I'll do that, Elmund, you get on the deck!" She traded places with him. He took the lantern and strode out on to the deck, trying to mimic the man's walk as they had watched him draw close. Elmund was a gem of a man, she thought. There he was, sauntering out on the deck, just like the Norandishman.

Kipren belted on the man's sword and donned his cloak and helm and took up the lantern. "How do I look?"

"Hold your lantern low or your bloody beard will give you away!"

"Aye, lady," he said, and he hurried after Elmund.

She helped Galt bind the fallen guardsman's hands and gag him and then on a three count they lifted and carried the men to the smuggler's hold.

"Here, Captain." He handed her sword to her. "You'll need this if things get hot."

Galt went below and Ryla pulled the bed back in place after he passed. He would get the boy and together they would haul the Norandishmen to the stern and lock them in the ship's larder. She would sneak back to the helm post when the time was right. For now, she would wait and watch. Galt still had more work to do once he had stowed the prisoners. He would have to sneak out and scurry up the rigging and see to those storm lines. Their getaway depended upon it. She picked up the bottle of Malvane Lightning and drained the last of the amber liquid from the bottle and made a whistling sound through her teeth as she swallowed it down.

She peered out of the porthole and watched as the figure of Galt slid out of the hold and crawled out behind the forecastle and into the rigging as stealthily as a thief in the night. Galt had no doubt been a thief before he had entered into her service. The man was quiet and quick, and he had a sound mind. He had disappeared behind the mainsail and ascended out of Ryla's view now. He would rig the storm lines so that the knots would slip but leave them in place so that Norden and his men would be unaware.

Elmund and Kipren were standing near the forecastle and trying to look relaxed. They were doing a piss poor job of it, too, by her estimation, but thankfully the guards on the ground seemed to be preoccupied with pleasing the excitable Mage

Norden. She could hear him shrieking incoherently from time to time, though she could not make out the exact words.

Something was amiss, though. It was apparent from her men on the deck and their body language. The mage had cried something out that got their attention and now Elmund was walking casually toward her cabin, seemingly unhurried. Had Joth and Eilyth come into view so soon, she wondered? She hooked the scabbarded sword onto its hanger on her belt and adjusted its position until it pleased her. She went to the door and cracked it open surreptitiously as Elmund drew near.

"What's happening?" she whispered.

"They've spotted a carriage down the road, but he can't figure out how to make the engines function. The men can't make the things throw! It's really pissing him off."

Maybe this would be easier than she had ever dreamed. "Now's our chance, while he's distracted. Tell Kipren and Galt. We'll move once we are all in place."

"Aye, lady."

She left the door open and stole a look down over the side of the ship at Norden and his men. Norden was berating his clerk by the sound of it, but he broke off in midstream and looked down toward the road. She tried to follow his gaze but could see nothing from where she stood. That would have to wait, she thought, for now it was her turn to get to the helm post and ready the airship for liftoff.

With Norden's attention drawn to the road, Ryla crept out of her cabin door and made her way quickly to the stern. She did not even need to bother with creeping about however, for Norden's attention was locked on something now and his rod bearing arm was being raised aloft over his bent frame. Ryla hurried to the helm post and put the key into position. They had moments to act before they lost any element of surprise.

They had to be swift and sure now. She left the helm post and slunk back down to join her lads near the forecastle. She saw that Galt was there huddled near the ladder, sword in hand and waiting for her command. Elmund and Kipren were watching something on the road.

"Captain, there!" Elmund whispered.

She saw a team of six horses come into view along the road down in the distance bearing a carriage with a prisoner box atop it. Was this the quarry that the mage had been waiting for? Were her comrades inside? Ryla did not know, but she knew that the time was ripe for them to act and that a better opportunity would not present itself. She was about to call the signal when a voice hailed her from just below on the ladder.

"Captain, there's some activity out there just like you told me to come tell you when I saw!" Bellan whispered in a rush.

"Thanks, Bell," she said, "Let's go, boys. Now's the time!"

The men looked at her and nodded. Then they all stood as one and rushed down the gangplank, drawing their swords. The Norandian guards had time to turn and draw their weapons just a moment before her boys laid into them. She saw one of the Norandians go down and Kipren stumbled back as Elmund and Galt tore the other man down to the ground and were on him in an instant. The clerk let out a blood-curdling scream and ran for the road toward the other soldiers, but Norden was white with shock and incomprehension for only a moment before he swung his rod at her head with all his might. She set the blow aside with her sword and thrust at the other side of him, piercing his cheek and causing him to scream.

"Surrender! We have your men!" she urged him.

"Whore!" he screamed at her, wiping blood away from his mouth and spitting. He hit her then and knocked her down, surprising her with his ferocity. He was near the back of one of the engines and he suddenly thrust the rod out and the engine lifted and moved rapidly toward where she lay on the ground struggling to find her feet as the world swam in her vision. Be quick, Ryla! She told herself, roll! Find your feet and get that rod from him.

Elmund was yelling for her. Could they not see her there? She leapt up as she felt a strange weight of energy begin to push her, crush her down, and she rolled to her feet and grabbed the rod between Norden's hands where he held it. He was stronger than she was, but not by very much. Still, Ryla was in the contest for only a moment before she realized that she would never be able to beat him. It was a losing struggle, but hopefully she could hold him long enough for her boys to get there and subdue him.

She heard the clash of steel and briefly between the engines she saw Elmund locked in a struggle with one of the Norandians, but she had no time to gawk. Norden was raising his arms and trying to twist the rod from her grasp, his face bloody and set in a cruel malevolent grin. She felt herself failing, but she reached deep inside of her last reserves and gave a twist of her own to the rod and it sprang free of Norden's grasp for a second, proscribing a wide arc, and as it did so a thunderously loud sound erupted from around her and the siege engines all flung their arms forward and sent the queerly fashioned barrels spinning in spirals like bullets from a sling with astonishing speed and power, whistling with a strange low sound. She stood there dumbly for a moment struggling with Norden as she realized they had whistled through the sky toward Kingsbridge and she heard and saw the first reports against the wall as the barrels exploded in fire that spread up and over the other side into the town. The engines were still firing, repeating at an astounding speed, launching the barrels randomly out at the road and into the countryside as they struggled for control of the rod.

Ryla was losing strength, she was failing. Norden ripped the rod from her hands and hit her hard atop her shoulder and neck, driving her down painfully to the ground.

"You stupid, stupid bitch! You've made a real mess of everything! Guards!" He kicked her over onto her back and looked at her there for a moment. She struggled to rise, but her shoulder was on fire and her vision was swimming. "Pity. I wanted to see you like this from the beginning." He raised the rod over his head to bring a finishing blow down onto hers, and Ryla saw her death coming for her. And suddenly he was on the ground next to her gasping in pain, a dagger sticking out of his ribs. A figure detached itself from him and rushed to her side.

"Captain!"

It was Bellan. Bellan the stableboy in his fine blue coat had slammed into the mage and saved her. He pulled his dagger free and Norden screamed. "Serves you right!" he said to the mage. "Lady, quickly, let's help you away!" He pulled her to her feet and supported her with his surprisingly strong hands, and she felt as though she was in a daze and she could not get clear of it. The engines had stopped launching the barrels and thrumming. How long since they had ceased? She had no idea, but when she looked out to the road she could see scattered fires that stretched all the way to Kingsbridge. There were bells ringing there, she could hear them now.

"Elmund and the lads?"

"All good, Captain. All wounded a little but, we are all right. Four more of them boys showed up out of the blue, as it were, if you take my mean—"

"Don't talk anymore now." She picked up the bronze rod from the ground where Norden had dropped it and let Bellan guide her away.

"I told you to stay below, did I not?"

"Aye, lady, but Elmund was calling for you and I couldn't—"

"Thank you, Bell. You'll never hear me say this again, but you did right not to listen to me." He smiled at her but she saw in his eyes the fear and the innocence of his youth. He so wanted to be praised, so desired to be held in esteem, but he was stricken with the fact that he had just slain a man, no matter how it had been justified, and she realized as she watched his face that he was just a scared little boy, and her heart went out to him. "I owe you my life, and I thank you Bellan."

"I couldn't just let him kill you, lady."

"You did well, sweet boy."

He blushed when she kissed his cheek.

And then she was up the gangplank and standing there swaying slightly on the deck with her sword in hand. "All hands, report!"

"Aye, lady!" Kipren ambled up with Galt. They were both binding wounds, Galt pressing a cloth to his left arm and Kipren holding his side and grimacing.

Elmund limped forward.

"Are you hurt badly?" she asked.

"We're all right, Captain," Elmund answered. "Some of those Norandishmen came back when we weren't expecting them. The others that stayed over the road got hit by those engines!"

"Did they? That was a stroke of luck!" She looked out at the fires over the road as they raged in the wind. "Did the carriage make it through?"

"There, Captain!" Galt pointed toward Kingsbridge and she could make out the team disappearing over a low hill, pulling the prison cart out of view as their driver cracked his whip.

"Make ready, boys. Good work. We fly now. Elmund!"

"Aye, lady?"

"Let's take one of those engines with us."

"Aye lady! Galt!"

Bellan followed Elmund down the gangway as Ryla made her way to the helm post, using the ship's rail to steady her as she walked. She watched as her crew rigged up one of the engines as it stood there floating. She wished that she could haul them all aboard, but one would do. It was hardly conceivable that any engine could reach the walls of a town from this great distance, and as she looked around at the destruction she could scarcely imagine what horror a score of the machines might be able to unleash upon a beleaguered city.

Galt tread the wheel of the crane and Kipren moved the arm over and they placed the engine down mid-ship on the deck and watched it hover strangely there.

"Much easier like that!" Galt exclaimed as he climbed from the wheel. Elmund and Bell carried up a dozen of the strange barrels and Galt and Kipren were heading to haul up more when Elmund called out to her from the gangway.

"Captain! Riders on the road!"

He dropped the helms and swordbelts he was carrying and pointed to where the stand of trees near the road stood ablaze. She raised her spyglass and followed the direction of his gaze. It was the half-dozen riders that Norden had sent out from Torlucksford, she saw by their helms and coats. The bastards had ridden hard to have made it this far so quickly, she thought. They had slowed their advance along the road and were taking in the scene of flaming destruction all around them, and Ryla knew it was time for her to get her crew in the air. Those riders could be on them quickly if they decided to charge up the hill. They would spot the airship momentarily if they had not done so already, and with their fallen comrades all around them she doubted that she and her crew would be given any kind of quarter.

"Raise the gangplanks! We're lifting away!"

Her crew made ready as she stood and manipulated the bronze wand at the helm post. The airship hummed with life and began to slowly rise and strain against the tethers of the storm lines. She saw the first line go taut and then slacken and fall and she knew Galt's knots had been tied adroitly. She swept her gaze over the hill side and saw the cavalry forming up along the road below, their leader directing them with his sword.

"Seven bloody bells!" she swore to herself. "Get those Norandishmen out of my larder and on the ground, boys!" She had almost forgotten about the prisoners. Kipren, Bellan, and Galt ran below as Elmund limped from one side of the ship to the other preparing to unfurl the sails when the elevation allowed. Ryla looked down and saw the figure of Norden struggling on the ground. So the worm is still breathing, she thought. That may ease Bellan's conscience, but it presented her with a problem, an inevitable life as a fugitive once word got back to Magistry officials of her involvement. She had committed piracy among other crimes—including attacking a Magistry official, conspiracy, treason, and the list went on.

She did not care enough to risk running down there now and ending him, and the truth was that she did not particularly wish death upon him, even though she had seen his willingness to deal it out to those who opposed him. He would have killed her, no question about it, she knew. But Ryla wished death only upon one man.

The crew was coming out of the forecastle frog marching the Norandians onto the deck. Elmund looked at her questioningly.

"Over the bloody sides with them quick, their lancers have formed up!"

Not that charging the airship would avail them much, but it would be easy for six mounted men to overwhelm the vessel before it rose aloft, and all of her boys were wounded except for Bellan. Better to escape now and live to laugh about it.

The Norandishmen screamed through their gags as they were tossed over the sides, and it occurred to her that they most likely had thought themselves at a much higher altitude than head height to a man. The unforgiving ground might have been welcome to them as it punctuated their short descent, but Ryla gave it no more thought as she saw the last of the storm lines fall away and felt the ship rise on the wind. The Norandishmen were riding up the hill as they rose into the sky, and Ryla watched as a rider dismounted and went to the fallen figure of Norden. Others dismounted and saw to their bound and wounded comrades.

She and her crew went to the ship's rails on the starboard side and let out a victory cry as they flew away, all of them there with Bellan too, cheering exuberantly. They had won. Her plan had worked and they had made it away and thwarted Norden's scheme, but all of them were hurt now, and Joth and Eilyth were still in peril. Those horsemen could overtake that carriage easily, even with a head start and a coach whip. You did what you could, Ryla told herself, and considering the odds against them she was satisfied. There was only one thing left for them to do.

"Bring her round lads! We'll keep circling low and jeering at them as long as they'll have us!" Whatever time they could buy the prisoner's cart gave Joth and Eilyth a greater chance of slipping behind the walls of Kingsbridge and disappearing. She adjusted the bronze wand at the helm post and sent Skyward into a slight shallow dive as Elmund and the lads hauled on the lines and sent her banking in around the low hill, as high as a town wall might reach if one had stood there, and they circled. Against the rails they jeered at the Norandians, who were in turn yelling back curses in their foreign tongue, but Ryla was watching the clerk on the torchlit ground as he helped his master out of his coat.

Norden was struggling and she saw a glint of metal as the clerk lifted the garment from the mage, searching for his wound. A ring shirt, Ryla knew. Of course he was wearing a bloody ring shirt—he was well prepared, she reminded herself. Bellan's dagger had still managed to pierce him, as evidenced by the blood she could see, but it was less than fatal, or so it seemed to her. Norden was saying something weakly to his clerk and then the clerk was yelling something out to the horsemen and they broke away from jeering.

"That's it," she said to herself first, "That's it, boys, they'll not tarry here any longer, let's make for the town, and keep an eye out for that prisoner's cart!"

"Aye, lady, aye!" they called back.

She moved the wand and the airship began to climb higher as it circled and gathered speed. Norden and his ring shirt and the lantern light and the Norandian horsemen disappeared below in the distance, and Ryla turned north toward Kingsbridge and the gathering storm beyond. It was almost dawn, and the sun would rise to find the town in flames. They rode the winds northward, and she hoped to find Joth and Eilyth before the storm forced her out of the sky.

Twenty-Seven

I DON'T MEAN YOU any harm. I'm merely opening this door so that you may escape. Your attackers have all been subdued for the moment, but you must hurry." The voice spoke to them through the blind door of the jailer's cart. Joth could hear a key working the lock. He stole a quick look at Eilyth. She stood ready with her staff at her side, calm despite their harrowing last few hours. Joth still had no idea what was happening, only that there had been some kind of an attack on the road, and they had ridden through flames, and there was a flight to the town that jarred their bones and then just moments before they had stopped moving. He had heard fighting, and horses, and then all had been quiet until the man spoke to them through the door. Eilyth peered out cautiously as the door slowly opened and the soft light of the early morning let them see the cloaked man stepping back from the door. He was watching them cautiously, intently; but he was not a Norandishman, and Joth did not get the feeling that he was in league with Norden. The Norandishmen had been screaming at them as they kicked at the door, then the sound of a short fight and they had been silenced.

"Who are you?" Joth asked as he leapt down from the cart. The Norandians were all on the ground, and there was a fire raging in the town. He looked and saw the driver from the inn at Torlucksford laying dead on the stones, his face slack and gray.

"The town's been attacked, you'd better find shelter."

Eilyth stepped down and stood beside him. The man took her in, but he did not seem shocked or surprised to see a Dawn Tribe girl before him. Instead, he inclined his head to her and then to Joth.

"Bloody mage tried to kill us again," Joth muttered to Eilyth. He turned back to the cloaked man. "You did this alone?" Joth was looking around for others but no one was stirring.

"Your driver and his boy, I came to their aid. I was too late."

Joth saw a dead man with a quarrel sticking through his guts and took the swordbelt that lay next to him. "Do you know the way out of this place?" He asked as he belted the sword around his waist.

The man nodded. "I was going that way when I happened upon your cart."

Eilyth had studied the man for a long time and he had regarded her quizzically as she watched him, but he did not shrink from her scrutiny. Finally, she spoke. "Let us gather three of their horses and ride together away from this place."

He looked as though he wanted to say no and refuse her, but as she fixed him with her eyes he seemed to reluctantly decide against it. He simply inclined his head again and turned to gather the reins of a horse that wandered nearby the dead driver. Durn was his name, Joth remembered.

"Fortune wears many guises," Eilyth said, flashing one of her half smiles. Had she bewitched the man, Joth wondered? Is that what Eilyth did, go around bewitching people to make them do her bidding, you great bloody fool? He knew better. The past day and night had gained him more insight into

Eilyth and her power, and compelling people against their wills was not in the nature of what she had shown him. His own perception of other beings, their emotions and energies, these were new and mysterious to him, and somewhat frightening since he lacked any kind of control over it, but it was never about compulsion.

Eilyth called it a "window and a mirror." She showed things to people through a distant window, and she could redirect energies the way a mirror redirects sunlight, she said. She had shown him how to do something on the journey here from Torlucksford—a simple exercise to focus his mind, focus his thoughts. He felt as though he was getting the gist of it, as though he could clear his mind of peripheral thoughts and concentrate on focusing, but it felt somehow forced and he grew impatient often as he lost the ability to concentrate and became distracted by a bump in the road or a creak in the cart.

He needed time to understand things, she had told him. being able to focus was the first step. He would love to have an opportunity to sit and close his eyes now, but the town was up in smoke all around him. Most of the Norandian's mounts were standing near their fallen riders. Joth had caught two horses and he saw two of the Norandishmen stirring, one of them struggling to find his feet.

"Help me," Joth called out.

The man who had opened the door handed his horse off to Eilyth, and Joth saw her regard the stirrups queerly. He made his way to Joth and together they dragged the Norandishmen to the jailer's cart and loaded them inside. The man took the key and locked the door. They'll have plenty of fine food in there when they come to, Joth thought. The man gathered a swordbelt from those they had collected and belted it on next to his long knife with a quizzical expression on his face.

"You all right?" Joth asked the man.

"Yes," he said as he broke from his reverie, then he fixed Joth with a steady eye. "We must be swift now." The man moved to the horse and mounted up smoothly. He frowned. "These horses are nearly spent."

Eilyth had mounted and was sitting and standing in her stirrups testingly, regarding them as though they may break at any moment. She held her staff across her lap. Her stirrups looked a bit long, but there was no time for him to fix them. She had never ridden in stirrups before, Joth would wager all his silver on it. Joth mounted the tall bay horse. "There are more of those Norandishmen out there, remember."

"Right. Follow me and stay close. If there's trouble, follow my lead." The man set his horse off at a slow canter down the street. Eilyth looked at him for a moment, as though she were weighing the choice, and then turned her horse and followed after the cloaked man who had rescued them. He would ride between them, should this be some sort of ploy and this man prove false. But Eilyth seemed to trust him enough, and truth be told, so did he somehow. He could not quite explain it, but the man had a trustworthiness about him. He hoped that he did not prove him wrong as they rode out along the street amidst a seemingly abandoned, smoldering town. It was dangerous being here, a fire was raging and there was no one there to put it out, or even curtail it to any degree.

Joth looked to Eilyth as she rode, staff clutched across her chest with one hand and her reins in the other.

She glanced down at her stirrups a few times before she caught him looking at her. "Everything is good now, Joth. You need not worry."

"If it please you, lady, I'll decide when I can stop worrying."

She smiled and continued to keep watch all about her as they rode. He did not bother to ask any further. The mounts were spent. Joth's horse stumbled often as they clattered down the cobbled street and the low wall and gatehouse came into view ahead. The walls looked abandoned, but Joth could not quite tell—there could be soldiers within the stone gatehouse or its two squat towers.

"Is this the only way out?" Joth asked.

"Yes. I don't like it either." The man looked at them both. "But unless you fancy a swim, this is the way out."

"We can make it. The horses will carry us," Eilyth decided.

"Let's ride for all these mounts are worth," the man said gravely.

Joth nodded. "No harm must befall the Lady Eilyth."

"None shall, if we are swift." The man galloped away.

Joth urged his mount up into as near a run as he could summon from the beleaguered animal and made for the gate with Eilyth and the man, the three of them matched for speed and riding abreast down the road. As they thundered through the arched gateway that stood below the gatehouse, Joth half expected to be shot through by a quarrel, but the gatehouse must have been abandoned by the town guard when the fire spread through the buildings here. When they had made it through the gate and were outside the walls, the sun was shining palely and Joth looked back and saw that the gatehouse itself had been set ablaze. The entire outer face was a smoldering, blackened mess. The man urged them on, even though their mounts were spent they kept up pace with him and only slowed once they had come to a copse of trees on a low hill east of the road. They were moving at a walk now, letting the horses rest, when Eilyth called out to them and pointed over the road to the top of the hill.

Joth looked and muttered a curse. He could make out the sallets of the Norandian guards, and he saw that Mage Norden and his clerk were there amidst them standing around two strange-looking machines.

"We can't risk being spotted by them!" he said, "We shall have to double back and skirt the walls around the other way."

The man was studying the machines at the hilltop intently. "There's no way around Kingsbridge for miles. The rivers. One has to go through the town to cross the river." He said it distractedly as he watched the Norandians and the mage shuffle around the hilltop. He was shaking his head. "I can't fathom it," he muttered.

"Well, it's no good here, and we can't make a run for it on these mounts. Let's at the least get away from where they might see us."

"I have an idea," Eilyth said lowly from behind them.

They turned and followed her eyes as she looked off into the sky. It took him a moment, but there in the distance was an airship. Even at this distance he could make out Skyward's brightly painted hull and striped mainsail, and he knew Ryla Dierns had gotten his message, that Bellan had followed through and made it safely back to Grannock. At this, he could not keep himself from smiling. "We'll have to get her attention," Joth said.

The man looked confused. "An airship?"

"A friend. She will get us aboard and away." Eilyth was looking at the man. "You want to run? Where will you run to?"

"You know me?" The man asked it sternly.

"I do not need to know who you are to see you." Eilyth's gaze was unwavering.

"Eilyth what are you—?" Joth started to ask, but she pressed on.

"I can see you running and running. When will you stop?"

The man looked at her for a very long uncomfortable moment. He looked away and out over the road where Norden and his henchmen stood atop the hill for a moment and then he fixed her with his piercing eyes. "We strike out over the plain there." He pointed. "That's the best place to land an airship, and it will be hard for them to be on us before we are away."

Eilyth nodded, and then she smiled at the man. He looked surprised at himself, but he covered it quickly. "Let's ride," he said.

The Norandians spotted them almost immediately, but they were all of them afoot, and they could not hope to catch up to them even if their mounts were spent. Eilyth rode out ahead across the plain and Joth followed her, the three of them riding abreast again. When Joth chanced to look back he saw all the Norandians running for them with their swords drawn, but they were so far away that their chances of catching them seemed nigh impossible to him. Ryla Dierns had seen them and had brought the airship down low, dragging it to a stop in the distance.

The Skyward was resting on the plain, hovering a few ells above the green turf, and Joth could see Elmund and Galt hurriedly throwing out the gangplanks and the captain shouting out orders as he rode toward them. His horse was stumbling but he urged it on over the last low hill and across the broad sweeping plain. Eilyth dismounted first.

They removed the saddles and bridles from the horses and cut the girth straps so that they could not be used. Horses could not catch them, but they could be used to help speed word, and any help to their foe was a hindrance to them. Better to ruin a few girth straps, Joth thought. The horses began grazing on the turf between them and the Norandishmen.

"Let's away before those boys get here!" Ryla cried from the helm. Eilyth was already up the gangway. Joth nodded to the man wrapped in the cloak and they turned away from the advancing soldiers and boarded the airship together. Once they were aboard, Elmund and Galt drew in the gangplanks and set about their tasks as the captain ordered them, and Joth saw that they were all wounded and moving stiffly. As he turned around, he was surprised to find Bellan.

"Bellan?"

"Master." He inclined his head awkwardly. "You're wondering why I'm here?"

"I'm sure you'll have a good story for me. I'm glad you made it safely, lad."

The boy smiled at him, then turned as Ryla Dierns shouted something out and he cried, "Aye lady, aye! I've to get below, now." And he sprinted off.

Joth could feel the airship rising and he looked out and saw that the advancing soldiers had halted and given up, seeing the futility in trying to reach them. They stood there in the distance cursing and catching their breath. Joth watched as they grew smaller and smaller and Kingsbridge fell off behind them smoldering beneath the clouds as they climbed higher and banked eastward and flew toward the pale sun. To the north, storm clouds rolled in a steep dark bank, but to the east the weather looked fine. Joth felt exhaustion wash over him in a wave. It was growing cold.

"You all should get below!" the captain called out.

He looked to Eilyth and she followed him to the forecastle and came below with him and the cloaked man. Kipren was there with Bellan and they had laid out a table with cheese and apples and some smoked meats and crusty bread. They had a cask of ale opened and were filling some mugs when Joth came down.

"Hungry for breakfast? I ain't slept in so long sun-up feels like sundown and everything the other way round, if you take my meaning."

"It's a strange breakfast, but I've had stranger," Kipren chimed in. They sat and ate and drank. It was warmer in the hold than it was on deck, but it was still cold. The ale tasted good and the food even better. He was halfway through a small round loaf when Galt and Elmund came down the ladder followed by Ryla Dierns.

They were moving stiffly, all of them. Joth could see now a purplish bruise on the captain's neck that stretched from her jaw to her shoulder. Eilyth stood and embraced the woman immediately. "Thank you, Captain."

She flinched but she smiled warmly. "Shiny and Pretty, back underway at last." The captain looked at her crew and then back at them for a beat. "Looks as though we got the rough end of the stick."

They all came forward and took up cups of ale and began to eat. Ryla drained her cup and held it out to be refilled. "I've not yet met your traveling companion," she said, turning to the man in the cloak and began. "I'm Ryla Dierns, Captain of the—"

When she saw his face her eyes went wide and the words stuck in her throat. She blinked at him disbelievingly and stammered a few times before her eyes grew wide again and she sank down to her knees. "My lord!" she said astonishedly. "My Lord Illithane, my noble lord. You'll not remember me, but you took in my family and others from my village after cruelties were visited upon us by the young Lord Uhlmet. You saved us, my lord, and I am forever grateful to you." The words tumbled out of her. Her hard exterior was gone now, and Joth was looking not at an airship captain but a young woman just past the flower of her youth with her heart in her hands expressing her genuine gratitude to this stranger who stood before her.

Lord Illithane? Joth looked at the man who had rescued them as he stood there bearing all of their scrutiny. Galt and Kipren were whispering excitedly to each other. Elmund was on his knees next to his captain, staring up at the man in wonder.

The leader of the rebel armies who had opposed the Magistry? They had killed him, Joth thought. Killed his entire family. Could it be true, he wondered? Could this legendary general and warrior be the somewhat plain and normal-looking man who stood before them now? Everyone was on their knees, except for he and Eilyth. He looked to Eilyth but she was staring at the man, studying his face. The ship's crew and young Bellan were all looking up at the man, their faces full of adoration. The man himself seemed overcome with emotion. What at first seemed a reluctance to admit his identity had fallen away and was replaced with something else, something that was hard to define. It was not shyness. Was it embarrassment, or shame?

At last Joth realized it to be the admission that he had failed. There was a guilt involved. Guilt over the lives lost, the battles fought in vain. Joth could see it in his face, but he could also feel it coming from the man, could sense it in his energy. He had been broken by failure, by loss, by heartache, and misery so debilitating that it had marked him. It was not so much that the man was ashamed of his identity, he was ashamed that he had failed, that he had given up, that he had lost. And all of it was wrapped inside the raw wound of a broken heart. It was easy to see now that Joth knew where to look.

"Please, get up. You needn't do this." The man took a step toward them, but they stayed kneeling. Joth felt Eilyth's eyes on him for a moment but when he looked back at her she was looking to the man in the cloak. The Lord Illithane. He met her eyes.

"When will you stop running?" she asked him quietly.

He looked at all of them for a long time. The wind whistled coldly through the hold. They were all watching him expectantly.

Finally, he spoke. "I already have."

Acknowledgments

I'D LIKE TO THANK Marianne Moloney for her early edits and infectious enthusiasm about the story. I would also like to thank everyone at Rare Bird Books for their hard work and wonderful support.

One

Oesteria.

THE CHILL WIND BLEW across the deck of the airship, distorting the tubular mainsail as it passed. Joth watched the sail ripple and rubbed his hands vigorously against the cold. The weather had taken a turn for the worse a few weeks before and forced the wounded crew to bring the Skyward down and ground her in a small wooded valley. They were days away from anywhere and their pursuers were far behind them, but a watch was still necessary. Joth was striding across the deck in the blustery dawn with his eyes on the horizon when Elmund emerged from below, wincing as he climbed the steps.

"All clear?" Joth asked by way of greeting.

"All clear." Elmund frowned. "Bloody cold enough…" He muttered as he shambled lamely to check the drag lines at the stern. That would be the end of the conversation, Joth knew. He and Elmund would never be fast friends, but at least their interactions were no longer dripping with ire.

Elmund and the rest of the ship's crew had all taken wounds escaping Mage Alchemist Norden and his band of Norandian mercenaries. Elmund was the least impaired from the fight, but that did not mean that he bore his wounds lightly. Joth watched him wince as he pulled at a line and made it fast, the exertion causing him to pause and take his breath slowly. In the first days after the fight, when their battle vigor had died and pain stood in its stead, the stalwart crew could not raise themselves from their hammocks. Kipren seemed to have fared the worst in the fray, with Galt close behind him. The captain herself had been bed ridden for much of the time, her poor head aching from her treatment at the hands of the horrid Mage Alchemist. She had sauntered out of her cabin with a bottle of Mulvane Lightning in her hand and passed it around to them all.

"Get below decks and tend to your wounds, I'll train this batch of fledglings to get us clear while you stitch yourselves back together."

The men were too wounded to put up much of an argument, so it fell upon Joth, Bellan, Eilyth, and the Lord Illithane to man the sails and follow the captain's orders and keep the Skyward on course as she sped through the cold clear skies far above Oesteria—and far away from the burning walls of Kingsbridge. Eilyth worked to help the wounded by dressing their wounds and treating them with her medicines, under which they showed remarkable improvements. All of them might have perished from their wounds without her care.

As the days passed Elmund and Galt began to make appearances above decks, their faces pale and gaunt. After one too many times of interjecting their opinions on how badly the "fledglings" were performing even the simplest of airman tasks, the captain ordered them below to rest their wounds, their pride, and their mouths. Joth had watched them hobble over to the forecastle and good-naturedly acquiesce to their captain's order. They had saved his and Eilyth's lives and brought a ghost back from the dead in the process: Lord Illithane.

Joth had managed little in the way of getting to know the mysterious exiled Lord, the famed general and rebel leader who, with a cavalry charge, had defeated the full might of the Magistry in the field at Valianador. He said very little and betrayed even less in his silence. He wandered about the woods most days, then would set about arranging stones on a patch of ground at the edge of the clearing in some sort of pattern. He had laid out some pathways it seemed. No one really understood what it was all about. No one dared ask him. He mostly only spoke to Bellan, whom he sent on errands, presumably fetching the stones and boughs the strange man was using in constructing what the crew had come to mysteriously refer to as the "Lord's Garden." The strangest thing about him was the way he "felt" to Joth in his "awakened" mind, what Eilyth referred to as his "window." It felt impossible to fix his gaze upon the Lord Illithane. Looking, as it were, at Lord Illithane through his window mind, Joth could pick up even less than with his two eyes. It felt odd though, almost as if Lord Illithane were hiding from him there as well.

It also was hard to ignore Eilyth's attitude toward the man. Joth could not know what it meant, nor could he understand what the tension had stemmed from, but he knew it was there and he had watched it wax and wane in these days spent traveling North and Eastward away from the walls of Kingsbridge and their pursuers. He had asked the lady Eilyth if there was something she saw about the Lord Illithane that had some evil bearing, but she merely shook her head and told him no. He had not pressed her. It was a mystery, but Joth did not have time to dwell on it too much, as they were short-handed above and below decks and there were wounded men to feed and tend to, and the airship always needed looking after.

The time they had spent traveling to their wilderness retreat was a rush of activity, and now they had been landbound for a few weeks and Kipren was finally able to be on his feet and ready to get back to some light duty.

Joth gave a final nod toward Elmund and started below.

He was not surprised when the nod went unacknowledged.

When he reached the galley he found himself alone except for the chorus of snores coming from the forecastle, where Kipren, Galt, and Bellan were slung in their hammocks sleeping. He gathered a few scraps of kindling and pushed them into the iron stove and set about coaxing some life back into the dying coals. It was getting noticeably colder day by day, and the pre-dawn watches left his hands and feet stiff and numb.

He stifled a curse as he banged his knuckles on the open door of the furnace, the cold delaying the pain from registering. Eilyth would be waking soon, he knew. She would need a fire for her daily ritual; tea and soup started her every day.

Joth was watching a curious stag eye him from the edge of the clearing through the porthole when he felt her enter the room. She smiled at him by way of greeting and he smiled back. Eilyth was wrapped in her silvery gray cloak with its intricately patterned weave, her red curls undressed in the cold morning.

"You are a good man to start a fire for me." She gave one of her unreadable half smiles.

Joth muttered a lame dismissal, which only seemed to amuse Eilyth further. He went back to the porthole and saw that the stag had emerged from the wood, his breath frosting in plumes as he stood watching the airship. Joth stared at the animal as it regarded him.

"You had the early watch this morning, did you see anything?" She was slicing the vegetables with her knife, despite the galley knives being in their leather sheath alongside the butcher's block. She had told him that she liked to use her knife because she missed her home and her father had gifted it to her when she was no longer a girl but a woman. He had nodded lamely and she had smiled unreadably then, too. "Joth?"

She snapped him from his reverie. "Lady?" He looked at her as she made her way starboard and peered out the porthole to see what had his attention.

"No, nothing of interest. Sorry, I was watching this—"

"Yes, I see him now."

They spoke lowly, as if the sounds of their voices carrying might spook the animal.

"He is bold. He's stood there for a time as still as can be." Eilyth regarded him placidly.

"This is a good sign for you, Joth Andries." She nodded once more, satisfied.

The stag seemed to sense movement at that very moment and bounded back into the safety of the dense wood.

Joth had learned not to question Eilyth about the validity of signs and their portents, but his own doubts were always gnawing at him. Perhaps I just don't believe in anything outside of what I can see, he thought. Perhaps I cannot believe in these things for that? It still seemed ludicrous to him that a flock of geese changing direction mid-flight could have any bearing on his fate, no matter the other palpable changes that his awakening had wrought upon his mind, his very soul. The changes she has brought forth in me, he thought. Then he remembered Eilyth telling him that she had only asked him, that it was for the sleeper to decide to wake or not.

It did not sit well with him either way.

He felt as though half the time he was failing to grasp the full experience and the rest of the time he was simply failing. It had grown even more confusing in the past weeks as Eilyth began to instruct him in the ways of her subtle arts. So far they had done naught but stare at a spring they had found on top of a hill in the wood near the airship. The "thinking," she had called it.

"One must master thinking; from thinking comes everything."

Then they would stare at the water gushing forth in small pulses as it ran over the rocks and down to form a blue pool in a recess below.

"You must try to think of nothing."

"How can I?"

"Breathe," she instructed him.

"Think only of the spring."

They had stood there staring for longer than Joth knew, but it felt like an age had passed. When it was done, whether it was the end of an appointed time or a change in the wind, Eilyth would nod once satisfactorily and turn away from the spring and they would walk together silently back to the grounded airship. Joth had suffered through over a week of this ritual without a complaint, but he had been working up the courage all morning to ask Lady Eilyth if she might consider a foraging expedition into the outlying woods they had spied from their hilltop vantage instead of thinking. They were running low on food, after all.

Eilyth sat the bowl of soup in front of him and poured the fragrant tea into his cup. He had grown fond of this part of the ritual at least. The soup tasted of the sea, or what he thought the sea must taste like.

He had never seen the sea; he hoped to one day.

When they had finished their breakfasts, Eilyth took the wooden bowls and cups and rinsed them out in the galley buckets. He could hear Bellan, Galt, and Kipren stirring from their hammocks. Kipren had been the slowest healing, his wound the direst. It was the first day since Kingsbridge that he wouldn't be back in his hammock after breakfast.

"Are you ready, Joth?" She was wiping her elegant hands clean with a cloth.

"Yes, Lady."

Her luminous blue eyes regarded him intensely.

Perhaps he would suggest foraging tomorrow, he thought.

⊙

THEY LEFT THE GANGPLANK and walked north across the clearing following a newly worn trail that they had tramped into the landscape themselves. Moments later they were weaving through a stand of birch as the ground began to rise around them and they wound their way up the hill that dominated the landscape above the clearing where Skyward had come to rest. The trail split amidst the birches, a better worn path leading eastward toward a silver brook that splashed down a cleft in the rocky hillside. Bellan had found it the first morning after they had drag-landed here and it was where they drew their water. It was cold and clear, and it tasted sweet. The other path was less well-worn and narrower. It continued north and west as it wound its way up through the jutting outcroppings to the top of the hill. Joth and Eilyth walked together in the cold morning under a steel gray sky and climbed their way up along the trail that led to the summit. As they made their way up, the golden light of early morning bathed the valley and Joth and Eilyth paused amidst the thinning trees as the sun pierced through the heavy gray curtain overhead and they felt the warmth of sunlight on their faces through the cold.

How long had it been since the last glimpse of the sun? he wondered.

It was a welcome warmth, that feeling. He was standing there with his eyes half closed when Eilyth's hands fished out his. He started.

"I know you don't like coming here every day, Joth Andries."

Her half-smile again, and she held his hands in hers. Her hands were so fine, yet she held him fast. He was not trying to escape, he decided. He started to say that he did not understand, but thought better of it.

"Lady…"

"You can tell me when something does not interest you."

"No, I would. To be sure, I would."

She held his gaze for a long beat, as though weighing his words. "Good." She smiled and let go of his hands then. She started ahead apace and turned back to find him staring. She stopped and adjusted her cloak until he caught up to her.

"Good."

They climbed over the rocks and up the trail past the sparse pines and brush that grew in the hardscrabble. As they made their way eastward the ground sloped down and formed a shallow ravine, and amidst the rocks on the eastern end of this lay the spring, the source of the brook and the source of their water.

Joth hoped that it was not a source of frustration for him today.

It was a beautiful morning at least, and the spring rocks gave a beautiful view of the surrounding vale if the spring-gazing grew too tedious.

He tugged his cloak free from a bush that he had snagged it on as he scrambled over a rock. He saw Eilyth check her pace a moment ahead of him, and when he scanned the path in front of her he saw what had given her pause.

Lord Illithane stood wrapped in his cloak next to the spring rock. "I hope you don't mind," he began. "I thought I would join you today."

They could only stand and stare for a moment before Eilyth simply nodded curtly and continued toward the rocky outcrop.

Two

JOTH HAD BEEN STARING at the spring for what felt like ages, but his mind and his attention kept drifting toward the man adjacent to him near the rippling waters, the mysterious Lord Illithane. He was not short but not extremely tall and of middling age, his face handsome if rather plain. His hair was well kept and mostly gray, but Joth could see that it had been blonde and no doubt curly in his youth. His eyes were a crisp blue green and they danced with intelligence. He moved with the grace of a lord and he held himself well. He looked strong and sure and able to lead. He also carried with him a wound. Joth could feel it there on him, he could feel the intensity of it, the depth to which it hurt him. It was more than just the wound, there was a sort of a shield like energy over it as well, as though Joth's thoughts could not find purchase there. As if his thoughts were sliding off of something every time he turned his mind to the man. His other cloak, Joth reminded himself. The Lord Illithane looked directly at him just at that moment and Joth felt a shiver go through him until the man at last gave him a slight smile and looked back to the spring. Eilyth was watching as well. Her eyes were unreadable as she took Joth in. The spring gushed on and the water splashed rhythmically down the rock face and into the crystal pool that had formed in the basin below. It was such a deep clear blue. Like her eyes, he thought, the eyes that now held him in such sharp focus. She could feel like a knife sometimes, and seem as soft as lambswool when she spoke. At times her voice could be a balm, at others she could make you shiver. She was a creature of nature and a wild thing and he loved her, he knew it. He tried in vain to hide it, but he was sure she knew too. He could see it in the way she regarded him. Not unkindly, yet Joth could not help but feel like a fly in the spider's web. She was the equivalent of Oestern nobility to her people, and he was just a simple soldier. She was regarded more highly than any Oestern lady ever to live in terms of the people's adoration, Joth would wager. It was hopeless for him to dream of her but he did it all the same.

As much as he knew the futility of his heart's longing his mind seemed to always rest on thoughts of her, especially since they had escaped Kingsbridge and been at rest here in this wilderness. He had grown fearful of her in the beginning, her mysterious powers and her alien ways had frightened him, confused him; but her kindness had changed him. Her compassion had led to his survival, he realized. She had saved him when she had brought about his strange awakening. In a way, Joth had died in the pass that day with Wat alongside him for those two men were no more. Those soldiers of the First Army of the Magistry did not survive their survey under the brutal tyranny of Lord Uhlmet. In their place were two very different men. One whom could feel his mind and body attuning to a subtle flow of energy he had never known existed before, and another whom no doubt was brewing mead in a roundhouse by a peaceful river somewhere now.

Joth wondered how Wat was faring in his captivity. Hopefully his wound had healed well and he was flourishing. Wat had looked well when Joth had left him on that brisk night many long weeks before, but he had not spoken to or heard word of his friend and captain in months now. Thinking of Wat reminded Joth that he was still a captive; he was a prisoner of war and his friend's life depended upon his success in bringing the Lady Eilyth back to her homeland after her mission had been seen to. She sought an audience with the High Mage himself and he had sworn to protect her on the journey and see to her safe return. He remembered the night in the village when her brother Eilorn had pressed that into him, especially his neck.

Eilyth at last stepped back and looked to him briefly before smiling and nodding. "That is all for today."

She gathered the hem of her cloak and tucked it out of the way, leaning with her cupped hands to drink the cool spring water.

Joth felt thirsty as he watched her drink, so he joined her and caught some water in his hands and drank as well. The water was clean and cold and it tasted faintly mineral and sweet. Lord Illithane seemed compelled to join them, perhaps thinking that this was part of the daily ritual of spring gazing, and he cupped his hand under the running water and took a perfunctory sip.

Joth shook the water from his hands and ran them through his ash blond hair. "Thirsty work, this staring at springs."

Eilyth cut her eyes at him as a smile played at the corners of her mouth.

He considered it a victory when he could illicit a reaction like this from her, for it usually meant he had said something that she found humorous.

"Joth Andries, we are not staring at springs."

She was shaking her head slightly, but her smile grew.

"If you are looking for the spring you should have no trouble finding it here."

With that she turned away and started back toward the clearing where the Skyward rested, and Joth could hear her laughing to herself.

Laughing at me, he thought, at my ignorance.

It's true, he thought, I am ignorant. He was trying to understand, trying to search and divine something other than what he plainly saw before him but it felt nigh impossible to discern anything other than the physical world outside of himself. Eilyth turned back, almost as if she had sensed his thoughts.

"There is a world below us and a realm beyond us. They meet in many places. This is one of those places."

They walked on in silence.

"A world below and a world beyond…" Joth mused.

"Yes, a realm beyond and all of them close here near the spring."

Lord Illithane was shaking out the hem of his cloak where it had snagged on a bramble.

"Can you harness power from such places more abundantly than others?" he asked.

Eilyth regarded him for a moment. "Power is not associated with places in that way. Easier to find yes, but there is neither more nor less here." Eilyth paused as three small rabbits burst from a small stand of Hawthorne and scattered westwardly away from them. Her eyes danced with delight as Joth's met them.

Those rabbits must be a good sign, Joth thought. How beautiful she looked there in the morning light, as radiant and pleased to be alive as he had ever seen her. His heart leapt in his chest when she smiled.

Lord Illithane was examining the hem of his cloak with concern.

"Surely it must have some significance that the power is easier to find in a place such as this?"

"There is significance in the finding of such a place, but that is in the seeking..."

He heard her voice trail off and she had stopped moving.

When he looked around he realized that she had not stopped because of any perceived danger but instead she was leveling her gaze at Lord Illithane and narrowing her eyes slightly.

Lord Illithane for his part smiled almost imperceptibly. "What?"

"Do you toy with us my Lord? For I have no wish to be toyed with."

"You may speak your mind, girl. I think you will anyway." He winked at Joth.

"You know the ways of the thinking and the window and the mirror, they were taught to you by my father."

Joth was almost certain he made an audible gasp, but Lord Illithane just seemed at his ease and slightly distracted. Eilyth did not like it one bit.

"I remember you well, Lord Illithane, though I was but a small child when we met."

If the news startled him he hid it well.

Joth's head was reeling. Eilyth had met Illithane before?

"My father had newly been named speaker of the people, and you came several times to seek audience with him, and you met his children. Do you recall it now, my Lord?" Eilyth had turned to face him and leaned on her staff as she spoke.

"I recall it, yes."

"My father and all of the people held you in high esteem."

Lord Illithane held her gaze and nodded slowly. "But you take issue with my having left off with my promises to your people for my part in the war with the Magistry, no doubt?" He seemed to be finished fussing with his cloak now, the pretense was gone. "The war had been lost for me. It seemed folly to drag the people into the fight at that point." A strange sort of resigned half smile appeared on his face. "You'll have to forgive me this, but there's a long list of disappointed and dissatisfied folk waiting for their own retribution and they're well ahead of you in waiting."

Eilyth paused then shook her head. "That's rubbish my lord. You had victory in your grasp and you squandered it because of your pride."

Joth's eyes nearly popped clear of his skull.

Illithane raised his chin ever so slightly. "The Magistry only half wants to find you or your head would have adorned a pike years ago. You are a fireside tale, a monster they can use to keep the people in fear or perhaps in hope, but they know you pose no threat or you would be dead my lord. Your great captains are all dead or subdued, you have no support amongst the people. In your grief you allowed the Mages to take hold of everything and now the Oestern people are like lambs who go and do as they are told."

Joth could not believe Eilyth's candor. For his part Lord Illithane seemed as though he took it in stride, but Joth could see that the words stung. He cleared his throat and shrugged.

"Perhaps you are correct. Regardless of the Magistry, there are many who would see me dead or held to account for my part in the war, and perhaps you number among them? I don't truly know, but the past is gone and I cannot change it. I cannot erase the horrors I endured." His look seemed to challenge Eilyth, to dare her to answer.

After what felt to Joth like an eon of tense uncomfortable silence, she did say something.

"Is that your idea of a parry my lord?"

Illithane blinked. "What?"

"You mean to deflect me with this childish 'poor woeful me' strategy?"

"My concern for self-preservation is quite valid…"

"Rubbish!"

Eilyth had raised her voice in intensity, but the volume had remained even. "What would you have me do? Shine my bloody light like a beacon and shout my battle cry?"

He raised his eyebrows emphatically and shot Joth a look that seemed to infer his desire to hear Joth's opinion on the matter as well. Joth was not so big a fool as to rise to Lord Illithane's bait. He kept his mouth shut and met the Lord's gaze as evenly as he could. He was sorely out of his depth on the subject of worldly politics and the War. He certainly felt that it was completely above his station to interject his opinion. This was the type of situation that could land you in dire trouble in the military. Joth had learned it was generally a bad idea to open one's mouth and start spouting off ideas, especially if you held no rank. Thankfully he was only holding Illithane's eyes for a moment before Eilyth spoke again.

"I ask you again if you toy with us, my lord?"

"I haven't any idea what you mean, girl…"

"You know exactly what I mean. You came here to speak to us for a reason today, and then you stand here pretending. We all see it. Take it off."

"What?" Lord Illithane looked genuinely confused this time.

"The cloak you wear. Take it off."

He smirked. "You wish for me to remove my cloak?"

He shrugged amusedly and moved his hands toward the golden brooch at his shoulder.

"Not that cloak, Lord Illithane. That one you may keep. I speak of the other cloak you wear."

This time Joth's jaw did actually drop. He had never told Eilyth about what he had seen or felt concerning Lord Illithane, but she obviously knew the same feeling when she looked at him.

She could see the same thing I could, Joth realized.

Which also meant that there was something to be seen and he had seen it! How could he not see it? It was one of the most striking things about the man: He wore two cloaks, one inside and one without.

Lord Illithane stared at them both for a long time, considering Eilyth for the majority of that span. His hands moved away from his brooch and he clasped them behind his back, his gray green traveling cloak sweeping back and revealing the hilt of a long knife at his waist. It was a commoner's weapon, the type of all-purpose tool a farmer or a huntsman might have on hand to dispatch an animal or defend his home from unwanted guests. It looked oddly out of place on the hip of the straight-backed and noble figure Joth regarded now. He had thought Lord Illithane rather plain and less than what his legend portended him to be, but Joth realized he had expected a legend and was met with only a man.

Lord Illithane? The dreaded enemy of the Magistry? The Rebel Lord? Surely that man was as tall as an ash tree and rippling with muscles, resplendent in his finery? Surely his face was fixed in a grim battle hardened rictus smile and his unblinking eye would inspire terror in the hearts of all it alighted upon? The stories and legends and tall tales Joth had heard over the course of his life concerning the rebel lord had all conspired against the image of the somewhat weary and aging man whom had rescued him and Eilyth from the jailer's cart. Now he could see the man a bit more clearly and separate from his legend. He could imagine him in the flower of his youth. He could see that his first assessment of the man as appearing average or less than impressive was wrong.

Lord Illithane seemed to stand a bit taller now. "Very well, but I have long kept it in place…for scrying eyes." He cut a quick look to Joth. "There are however some conditions that must be met first. So indeed I did come here to talk to you for a reason today."

Eilyth nodded in approval at his admission. "Good."

"I take it you are the Gwyngrwnach?"

Eilyth closed her eyes and bowed her head in acknowledgement. Gwyngrwnach? What did that mean, Joth wondered. It sounded like the language of the People.

Lord Illithane seemed to sense his confusion. "The White Witch. The High Priestess. I thought you might be."

Eilyth nodded. "Yes. I am the Gwyngrwnach, but it must not be known."

Joth's mind was racing. He was learning so many new things it struck him as being odd that he felt he knew less and less with each new fact he gleaned.

Illithane looked at him pointedly. "You guard an important lady. You only live because of her. You understand that, don't you? They would have killed you if not for the word of the White Witch." Lord Illithane said it matter-of-factly, as if he were ordering all the details of their identities and Joth could only nod. He had known Eilyth had a hand in his survival, but he never realized just how much until now. "You truly intend to seek audience with High Mage Paifen? In Twinton?

What terms will you offer? What will you do if he refuses your terms?"

"I shall present those details to the High Mage in front of the Mage's Council in Twinton. There is a path for peace and a path for war. Whatever the outcome, I shall bring word of it to my father."

Illithane looked thoughtful for a long moment. "I have to know this little company can survive and defend itself better if it comes down to fighting, and it will inevitably. Judging by the state of the crewmen they fared poorly in their last engagement, and that won't do if we are to make it very far together. Those Norandishmen weren't even mounted during the fight, and I will not venture into the den of my enemy if I can't be sure of my escape."

"Bellan and the staves…"

Eilyth smiled slightly. Illithane had been sending Bellan to the woods to cut staves since shortly after their landing. At first he thought Lord Illithane meant to use them in the Lord's Garden, or perhaps have crutches made for the wounded, but now Joth understood Illithane meant to train the crew and order them into some sort of fighting unit.

Lord Illithane nodded absently. "Yes, and we have this Goblincraft engine to master as well. I feel confident that with that in place on the airship and the crew trained to fight properly that we may stand a chance of keeping our heads on our necks long enough to make the journey at least." He looked out over the clearing where the Skyward sat, its deck empty but for a limping Elmund near the prow. "I also need to see the extent of the Gwyngrwnach's power. Is it true you have mastery over the elements or is that a tale for children?"

Joth saw Eilyth straighten ever so slightly.

"There is truth in everything, even children's stories."

"Spoken like a Witch! I'll not dangle myself like a prize in front of my mortal foe just so I can be dismembered and put on display if I'm caught without knowing who you are and what you are capable of. I need to know if your power can stand up to the Mage's."

Eilyth regarded him evenly. She scanned the skies and looked back to Lord Illithane for a moment. "Do you see in the tree line there? The ash that has been broken?" She pointed with her staff to the tree she spoke of.

"Yes. What of it?"

Eilyth drew a deep breath. "Mark it well."

Joth could see her plant her feet squarely, almost the same stance she adopted when she took up her staff to fight. He could see her steady herself for a moment with her staff held at her side and then Eilyth drew a deep breath and raised up taller than she seemed and held the staff aloft. The sky seemed to grow darker, and Joth could feel a strange pressure rising in his head. It felt the way it sometimes felt right before the first raindrops of a coming storm. He glanced at Lord Illithane as the wind began to pick up swiftly around them. The man was staring at Eilyth, his expression unreadable. Suddenly the pressure came to a head and was almost unbearable. The hairs on his arms and the back of his neck were standing on end.

At that moment Joth felt something in the air and a flash occurred in his window awareness at the same time his eyes perceived a light flash in the sky.

For a moment he was almost blinded, then he registered a jagged streak that hit the broken ash's trunk and split it in a thunderous crack as the sound finally reached them.

Joth thought for a moment he had imagined it all.

The smoking stump sat in stark contrast to his doubt, its splintered top dancing with flames.

He looked to Eilyth in awe as she turned to regard Lord Illithane. He saw Illithane regarding her with wonder as well. How had she made that happen in an instant? In an instant she had called the lightning down and split a mighty tree asunder.

"The wood of the Ash makes strong staves, Lord Illithane. You should send Bellan to collect the splinters, perhaps some will serve." She turned to continue toward the airship in the clearing.

"I shall Gwyngrwnach. I shall. And then,"

Lord Illithane took her in for a moment, his expression a mix of surprise and reverence.

"When we are ready I shall see you through to Twinton and this meeting, and carry news of it with you to your father."

Eilyth raised an eyebrow. "What of this cloak you wear?"

Lord Illithane nodded. "I shall cast it aside."

Eilyth held his eyes for a moment before nodding satisfactorily. She began to walk away when he called out to her again.

"Should the High Mage refuse to see your terms I shall fulfill my promise to your father and lead the hosts against the Magistry and bring to them death and destruction until they know nothing but defeat and all of their cries are empty…" He looked to them then with a fire in his blue green eyes. "This I promise you both now."